Some are dedicated, some are opportunists—
and maybe one will be a genius. They are the
doctors of the future, the ones who will end up
on Park Avenue or Main Street: the eminent
specialist, the tired pill-pusher, the quack, the
Nobel Prize-winner. Some will marry the
daughters of rich men, some the nurses they
work with. But whatever happens to them,
whatever they become, they will never forget
the year they were

THE INTERNS

"Shocking, sharply revealing."
—*The New York Times*

"Pulses with realism. Best fiction of the year."
—*Louisville Times*

THE INTERNS

by

Richard Frede

BANTAM BOOKS · TORONTO · NEW YORK · LONDON

THE INTERNS

*A Bantam Book / published by arrangement with
the author*

PRINTING HISTORY

Random House edition / April 1960

Bantam edition / August 1961

2nd printing ...... August 1961	11th printing ...... October 1962
3rd printing ...... August 1961	12th printing ...... October 1962
4th printing . September 1961	13th printing .. November 1962
5th printing . November 1961	14th printing .. December 1962
6th printing .. February 1962	15th printing .. November 1964
7th printing ...... August 1962	16th printing .... June 1966
8th printing ...... August 1962	17th printing .... May 1970
9th printing ...... August 1962	18th printing .... June 1971
10th printing . September 1962	19th printing .. December 1979

*Bantam Books are published by Bantam Books, Inc. Its trade-
mark, consisting of the words "Bantam Books" and the por-
trayal of a bantam, is Registered in U.S. Patent and Trademark
Office and in other countries. Marca Registrada. Bantam
Books, Inc., 666 Fifth Avenue, New York, New York 10019.*

To Helene, Henry, and Karen

in·tern[1] *v.t.* 1. to oblige to reside within prescribed limits under prohibition to leave them, as prisoners of war or enemy aliens, or as combatant troops who take refuge in a neutral country. 2. to hold within a country until the termination of a war, as a vessel of a belligerent which has put into a neutral port and remained beyond a limited period allowed. —*n.* 3. someone interned.

in·tern[2] *n.* Also, **interne.** 1. a resident member of the medical staff of a hospital, commonly a recent medical graduate acting as assistant. 2. an inmate. —*v.i.* 3. to be or perform the duties of an intern.

THE AMERICAN COLLEGE DICTIONARY

intern 1. A graduate of a medical school serving and residing in a hospital preparatory to being licensed to practice medicine. 2. To confine within certain geographical or physical boundaries.

DORLAND'S ILLUSTRATED MEDICAL
DICTIONARY
23rd Edition

CONTENTS

For the convenience of the reader, a listing of the full names and offices of the staff of the hospital will be found in the back of the book.

The outside door was marked *Dr. Wohl;* and beneath the name, entirely in capitals, *MEDICAL SUPERINTENDENT*.

This door usually stood open. You entered a pleasantly bright-hued room which contained a couple of wooden contour chairs (with no tables or ashtrays to accompany them), several filing cabinets, and a desk.

Mrs. Lawrence sat behind the desk. Depending upon whether you had been *summoned* or had dropped by of your own accord, Mrs. Lawrence either barely looked up and peremptorily stated *Sit down* or, when it was *not* a case of your being summoned, smiled and called you by name and disregarded her work for a few minutes to ask how you liked the service you were on and wasn't the head nurse there a riot and did you hear about the patient in Medicine who said to Dr. Farrell . . . ? and could she help you or was it *absolutely* absolutely necessary to see Dr. Wohl? You rarely concluded by seeing Dr. Wohl, but whatever the problem had been, it was usually nonexistent by the time Mrs. Lawrence smiled you back into the hall.

She was equally sympathetic to the numerous pharmaceutical salesmen who never got to see Dr. Wohl but whose samples eventually and systematically got investigated by her and then by the doctor himself once she had insured that they were worth his time and attention. Mrs. Lawrence also attended to complaints from patients and families when such complaints were not dramatically and uncompromisingly insistent. Thus, if the office of medical superintendent ideally required the full-time services of six trained men, Mrs. Lawrence made it possible for Dr. Wohl to carry the burden of only four full-time men.

Passing Mrs. Lawrence's desk, you went through a door and into Dr. Wohl's own office. A number of diplomas, citations, and company photographs from the First World War and class photographs from college and medical school had been carefully framed and less carefully stacked in a corner. They had been left that way since the doctor had taken office four years before. Hung, they would have, for reasons unaccountable even to himself, depressed Dr. Wohl. But he kept them about on the theory that he ought to have them available in case anyone should ever challenge his credentials or background.

Some worn leather chairs which Dr. Wohl had had for years in many different offices were scattered in front of his ultra-contemporary, clean-lined, paper-deluged desk. The desk was so littered that he usually did most of his work on a battered old table set behind the desk in a dark corner of the room. The light was without a doubt bad there, but at least there was working space. He'd been planning for possibly three and a half years to have a light put in above the table. But he always forgot the plan the instant after he remembered it, having, in the instant, become too involved with the work that had brought him there.

Lew Worship (M.D., practicing provisionally) received a smile from Mrs. Lawrence and felt somewhat easier about having been summoned to Dr. Wohl's office. Mrs. Lawrence buzzed and was told to have Worship come in.

Lew entered, and waited to be asked to sit down.

Dr. Wohl, in a swivel chair, swung away from the window where he'd been looking at the river three blocks away. It looked cold and black even in the sunlight, Lew thought.

The roofs of the tenements surrounding the hospital were equally bleak.

"Sit down, Dr. Worship . . ." Wohl leaned back in his chair and folded his arms. "I want to talk to you about something that's not really my province."

Lew nodded without letting his face commit him.

Wohl abruptly leaned forward and folded his arms on the clutter on his desk and sighed. Then he said, "Dr. Worship, it has come to my attention that you have not yet made application for a residency."

Lew nodded, his face still carefully blank.

"Dr. Worship, I'm sure you're aware of it, but it is already December. Most hospitals require applications for residencies to be in a good deal earlier than this. I think it's safe to say that *all* of the hospitals with the better staffs and training facilities require a somewhat earlier application."

Lew only nodded.

"My God, Worship, most places have already sorted through their applications. They're now arranging for personal interviews."

Wohl waited. Finally Worship said, "Yes, sir, I know."

"Well, Worship?"

"I don't know, Dr. Wohl."

"Worship, please don't speak in riddles. *What* is it you don't know?"

"Well, I . . . I, uh . . . Well, Dr. Wohl . . . I guess I don't really know yet what I want to do. I mean, I'm not *sure* yet."

This time Wohl waited long enough so that Worship was the one who was forced to go on.

"I don't want to do anything till I'm sure. I *think* I'm almost sure . . . but, uh . . . not entirely. I mean, since I have to pick a specialty before I apply for a residency, I have to be sure of what I want . . . since it'll be for the rest of my life unless I waste a lot of time switching and starting over again."

"Dr. Worship, this is almost incomprehensible. This is your sixth month of internship. You've had four years of medical school preceding that. And in all that time, exposed to every facet of medicine, *nothing* interested you enough to . . . ?"

"It's not that. A lot of things have. That's part of the

trouble. When I pick one I want to be sure it's *the* one."

"Of course. But Dr. Worship, you want to do it damn fast if you want a residency commensurate with your ability." Wohl regarded Worship. "Do you understand?"

"Yes, sir," he said, and moved to stand up.

Wohl looked at him, but did not dismiss him. "Worship, occasionally we get a man who just doesn't want to go on or go any further with his medical career. He wants to stay where he is, remain an intern. For one reason or another— fear of additional responsibility, or he's discovered he really doesn't like medicine . . . Any number of reasons. He just wants to stay an intern. The way some people go to school for years just to avoid the outside world. They become professional students . . . I hope you don't fall into this category. But if you do, Worship . . . perhaps you've begun to suspect or question the extent of your commitment to medicine as a career? If you have, then I suggest you face up to it and come to an appropriate decision. Not applying for a residency is a very good way of not having to face up to that realization directly."

"No, sir, it's not anything like . . ."

"Very well, Dr. Worship. Bear in mind what I've said. You'd best return to your duties now."

ONE
THE INTERNS

1

Dr. Parelli—he was at any rate an *M.D.*, though only provisionally a *practicing* one—had just finished a thirty-six-hour shift on Obstetrics. During this time, the shift being Obstetrics, he had not even had a chance to doze, much less sleep. And after his official on-duty hours were up at six P.M., it had taken him another hour to bring his charts up to date and to pass along—for his own satisfaction and not because it was required—some additional prognostic comment to one of the OB-GYN (Obstetrics and Gynecology) residents.

Then he had changed from his scrub suit—baby-blue in Obstetrics, though in Surgery the scrub suits were gray-green, each color chosen because, as opposed to white, it reflected a minimum of light and presented less contrast with blood, the baby-blue of Obstetrics having the additional value of aesthetic appropriateness as well—into the routine whites of general hospital life and gone down to the staff dining hall in the basement to catch some dinner.

The six-o'clock rush had been long since over, the nurses and nurse's aides had all gone home or on duty, and there

5

were only a few interns and residents sitting around over
coffee and, in one corner, a group of attendings finishing up
dinner before making some final rounds or operating or just
going home.

Parelli, not seeing anyone who interested him, had sat by
himself and had tried to eat. Though he was hungry, he
was hungry in a rather intellectual way instead of in a physical way, and his stomach was too contracted and numb to
take any encouragement or coaxing from his mind. And too
—though he liked the dining hall's food—every time he
raised his fork to his mouth he had received from his hand
the saccharine odor that accompanies most obstetrical practice. Even rubber gloves could not check its permeance for
long, and familiarity could not check Parelli's dismay when
he had found that he was too tired to overcome this rather
childish sensitivity his very tiredness had made him vulnerable to.

After a while he had just given up and concentrated on
some coffee and a cigarette. Then he had gotten up, gone out
to the elevator, taken it to the first floor, walked through the
long hallway-arcade past a flower shop, a tobacco shop, a
magazine stand, a gift shop, an information booth for the
west entrance, the Records Office, a row of bank-teller-like
windows (now closed) which were the public side of the
pharmacological dispensary, and thus, without having to
go outside (since the two buildings were connected by a
heated corridor), had gotten himself from what was New
North Hospital to what had once been North Hospital but
was now only the sixty-year-old building that housed residents, interns, some game and TV rooms, two lecture rooms,
and a number of file-storage rooms.

Parelli went up to his room and was pleased to find that
his roommate, Otis, was out. Not that he disliked Otis, but
the room was hardly a room at all, merely a cubicle which
was not big enough to house comfortably both parts of a split
personality, much less two individuals. And Parelli needed
some sort of privacy for a while.

He had been on duty for thirty-six hours and the next
thirty-six-hour stint would begin in less than ten hours.
But he didn't get undressed. He sat on the side of his bed and
refused even to allow himself to lie down. He had a decision to make, and he had to have it made before he went

back on duty. He had to have it ready for his chief resident when he came around for morning rounds at eight.

Not that it was—by itself—so important a decision, but a number of alien factors and potential results had to be considered. The question was merely whether he would prefer Christmas Day or New Year's Eve off. He could take Christmas Day or leave it. Home would be too far to get to and back from in twenty-four hours. Nor was he likely to be invited anywhere—he didn't know anyone that well. So, obviously, he concluded, if he took Christmas Day he'd be spending it in a private gray ghetto of his own that would be turning darkly indigo as the day went on and as he moved from one street and restaurant or bar to another street and restaurant or bar.

But the question of New Year's Eve was more problematic.

He had, in his own terminology, been banging Cynthia James for some time—since, to be exact, his service assignment had been changed to OB some five or six weeks back. She was one of the regular night nurses and, a few times, they had been on duty alone. Obstetrical tables, being of half length and equipped with appropriate leg braces and stirrups, were, he had discovered, with both humor and passion, very efficient for other, though associated, purposes than child delivery. He and Cynthia had found each other quite satisfactory and had continued and supplemented their relationship in his room on nights when Otis had been going out or when Joe had been able to convince Otis to go out; and, he recalled with both satisfaction and amusement, had once continued, and supplemented, their relationship in, among, and beneath coats piled on a bed in an apartment where some of the interns and nurses had gathered for a party.

They were a good pair, Joe had to admit. They even *liked* each other—which was not necessarily a norm among other such relationships of his knowledge. And Cynthia would be expecting him to take her out New Year's Eve—as was her due, and a due he would enjoy rendering. She had, in fact, told him that she had arranged to have New Year's Eve off.

There was, however, another consideration, and not one of which Joe Parelli was by nature proud. He had had to frame the question of which time he wanted off not in terms of which he'd prefer, but in terms of which he ought to work. *All right,* he said to himself, *in terms of which one would be more advantageous*—Parelli had never been able to misrepresent anything to himself, particularly himself. It was a good quality for a physician to possess, but a difficult one for a human being to accustom himself to, especially if he had human aspirations.

Dr.—practicing provisionally—Parelli was not *dedicated* to his profession in the sense of total commitment of self. He loved it, but his love stopped clear of negation of self. However, the self that was *Dr.* Parelli was at least ninety percent of the self that was *Joe* Parelli. And the self that was *Dr.* Parelli knew it could do itself a lot of good by being in the right place at the right time. The self that was the doctor knew that it could, at this point, make the difference between a doctor who *did* and a doctor who merely *wanted* to do. And what he wanted to *do* was to *be* a physician to more than colds.

That could come only from training. And training was harder to come by than compatible females or the marks you could get in med school from hard study and from even harder cramming.

That is, you needed to train with the best physician in your chosen specialty—by getting a residency under him. Parelli had decided upon psychiatry, and the man who could at least *teach* him the most about psychiatry was Dr. Harvey Bonny at Century Veterans General.

Century was only a few blocks away. But if things weren't worked right, it could be forever away. And even if things *were* worked right, Parelli was not the only potential psychiatrist in the country; and among those who would be looking right now for psychiatric residencies for the following year, perhaps three out of five of them would be trying to place themselves with Harvey Bonny. Only those who figured they had no chance at all, not one single one, would fail to apply. Bonny would have, at the *outside,* four residencies open.

Parelli had to work things right just to be in the running. Getting angles, pulling strings, promoting letters of recommendation—all these were at the least *unwritten* requirements of application for any of the better residencies.

Bonny's decision would be based on the applicant's record

in college and in medical school and in his internship—and upon the impression he made upon the hospital's examiners in a personal interview. But to be successful, he needed more than that. He needed an angle—out of self-defense, just to remain in the competition. And this, Joe Parelli thought he could construct through a relationship with a nurse named Flynn. She was not just a nurse, but a head nurse: head nurse, with two others (each on an eight-hour shift), of OB's *post partum* floor. And not just one of the head nurses of the service Joe would be working on until January, when his assignment changed to Medicine, but a nurse who was a friend of one Dr. Harvey Bonny.

Parelli did not know Dr. Bonny personally; but Head Nurse Flynn *did*. The two were old friends; had, at one time, supposedly been more than that and, as far as rumor knew, might still be.

While wandering around the *post partum* floor and passing time with Flynn when things were slow on the labor floor, Parelli would be in a position to talk to her at length, perhaps impress her. Eventually, he would, after they had become friends, *discover* from her that she was a friend of Harvey Bonny's. He would then tell her about his interest in getting with Bonny and leave it at that. He would make no direct requests of her.

Dr. Parelli had done some research—the amount of successful research he had done in terms of this proposed residency very nearly convincing him that he had been intended by nature to be a *pathologist* rather than a psychiatrist—and discovered that Head Nurse Flynn had scheduled herself to work the twilight shift on December thirty-first.

Thus, Parelli had reached the decision he knew he would have to reach, Cynthia or no Cynthia, if he were to protect himself against self-blame should Bonny refuse him a residency—he would at least have the comfort of knowing he had tried every single conceivable angle, possibility, and approach. Along with Flynn, he would work the New Year's Eve stint too.

He allowed himself to lie down. He'd have a lot of explaining to do to Cynthia. And it would be explaining that she deserved and that he wanted to give her—which would not make it easier, in fact, would make it almost impossible.

Yet still, it amused him—for if it weren't possible for it to amuse him, it would have sickened him—that in former years (in high school, college, and even med school) he would have, at this season, been concerned with *who* his New Year's Eve date was going to be. The idea of taking Christmas and missing New Year's would never have occurred to him. But Parelli wanted to be one of Harvey Bonny's residents.

When he closed his eyes, there was no darkness, nothing to sleep in. Instead, there was a brightly lit delivery room. He could feel his own perspiration—under the scrub suit and gown, and above his lip beneath the mask, and in the outside corners of his eyes . . .

He opened them again. Of course, he wasn't perspiring at all. It had been a sense memory . . . by association . . . or would you call it a physiological memory? None of the terms sounded right to him. But when he closed his eyes, there was the brightness of the delivery room again, and the sensation that he had sweat in the corners of his eyes . . . No rest for the bleary, he thought . . .

And this time, when he closed his eyes, he could hear Granchard, his chief resident, talking . . . "Tell me, Parelli, is there any reason why I should assume you've had the benefit of a medical education?" . . . or Sato, also a resident, "Gently now, gently, gently . . ." Or Otis, "Joe, look, I've *got* to get off for a few hours . . ."

Parelli laughed. He could see Otis working up a patient—intent, cool, efficient, managing his procedures as if in slow motion . . . Yet finishing faster than most of the residents were able to, and going on to whatever was next, Granchard watching him, Granchard's face hard with, perhaps, respect, but also with disapproval. He could hear Granchard's voice, that morning, saying to Otis, the voice a little *too* heavy with disdain, "You're good, Otis, sure you are, but you're not interested." "No, I'm *not* interested," Otis said directly back. "I'm not an OB man and I don't intend to be." And Granchard saying, "What makes you so arrogant, Otis?" And Otis, "Just don't ride me, Granchard. I like medicine, *Dr.* Granchard, but if I let you ride me the way you do the others, by the time I got off your service I wouldn't even like myself."

Overhearing that little conversation had put quite a strain on Joe. It did now, just remembering it. It had had absolutely no relationship to the normal resident-intern relationship. And Worship blundering into it and getting beautifully chewed out and Otis just standing there smiling slightly. Joe had taken that opportunity to get the hell out of the dressing room.

He closed his eyes again, and there was Worship, his voice saying, "What the hell was *that* all about?" And Otis saying to Lew, "He's made easy game out of us just too damn long." And Lew saying, "So what? I'm not here to be part of a vendetta."

Worship was all hell-fire and chivalric eagerness—the knight fashioning a grail out of his own need and aspirations even if such a thing didn't exist. There was too much passion, too little practicality. Worship was heading for all kinds of trouble. The kind of trouble that when it arrived it would be much too late to do anything about. Dr. Worship would just find himself no longer an intern and without a residency— at the very best, an intern without a residency that he could respect or learn anything from, a residency quite beneath his ability. Worship, Joe thought, might as well retire right now. But, Joe knew, Worship wouldn't retire now, he'd just keep on badgering people with his enthusiasms and passions . . .

The brightness had let up a little. The images were gone. Only Worship's voice remained. Badgering Joe with enthusiasms and passions . . . Sure as hell, *Lew* wouldn't have any trouble deciding whether to work Christmas or New Year's. He was such a kook, he'd probably consider it a favor if they let him work *both* nights . . .

Then even Worship's voice had gone away, and all there was was a long dark corridor, black at the end he was trying to walk toward, trying to see into, wondering whether in that blackness there was somebody to hand him the residency he wanted, wondering if the residency was way down off there so far away in February or March . . .

2

When Joe Parelli had gone off duty, Lew Worship had come on—had, in fact, not been off. He had just finished a thirty-six-hour tour, during which time, by taking advantage of the slow hours whenever one came up, he had managed four and a half hours' sleep.

Now he was on again till six A.M. At six A.M. his own next

thirty-six-hour tour would begin (again). At the end of *that* tour, he'd have been continuously on duty for seventy-two hours of his own plus twelve hours that were not really his own that he should have spent sleeping. He'd have been on duty continuously for eighty-four hours. Three and a half days.

His tour should have ended at six P.M. But two hours before that, after finding no one else to suit his purpose, he had finally figured *Well, why not?* and rung up John Paul Otis (M.D., practicing provisionally).

"You sleeping?" Lew said.

"Hell no. I just got back from clinic."

"Yeah, but you were out last night."

"So?"

"So I figured you might want some sleep now. How was it outside?"

"It was *Outside,*" John had said. "With a capital *O* followed by no *B.*"

"Crazy," Lew had said.

"Yeah, isn't it."

"They still got real air out there?"

"Listen, Lew, I thought I'd catch what sleep I can before rounds, so . . ."

"That's what I called about, John."

"You're carrying this doctor stuff too far, kiddo. I'm not a patient."

"Yeah, I know. John?"

"I'm here. Standing right here in my stocking feet. Thinking how nice that bed looks."

"Boy, I bet it does," Lew said eagerly.

"*Lew . . .*"

"John?"

"I haven't moved a muscle. Neither has the bed."

"I want to ask a favor."

"Ask."

"It doesn't really *sound* like a favor, but it would be, I mean, it would be for me."

"*Worship!*" Then, gently, mildly, "How many patients have died on you while you were talking to them?"

"Okay. I get the point."

There was a silence. "Well? Lew, *please.* I plead with you. I beg of you. Just, please, tell me what it is, okay? You know—as a professional courtesy?"

"Sure. Sure, John. What I wanted to ask you—as a favor, even though it doesn't sound like one . . . What I wanted to ask you is, could I cover for you tonight? I mean till six A.M.? Then I go back on anyway."

"Could you . . . ? Lew?"

"Here."

"Lew . . . Has anyone questioned your sanity lately?"

"For chrisake!"

"Okay, okay . . . *Sure* you can cover for me. What about Granchard?"

"He okayed it. He said just put my name up for whoever I'm covering for."

There was a silence. Then Otis said, "Thanks, Lew. I appreciate it. Fact is, I could use a few hours more off." Then, "You sure you really wanta go on an extra twelve?"

"Positive."

"Okay. Fine. Listen, Lew, anytime I'm third call tomorrow, I'll take your duty. It'll give you a *little* time to sleep, anyway."

"Fine. Thanks, John."

"Thanks *John*. Jesus Christ," Otis said, and hung up.

"*Nuts*," Lew heard behind him. "Nuts nuts nuts!" He turned around. Amos Sprague (M.D., practicing provisionally) was standing behind him, leaning against a wall. "*Certifiable*," he said with disgust. "Did I hear right? Did I hear you request the privilege of *covering* for someone?"

"You heard."

"*You heard, you heard*. You sound like you're tryin' to make somethin' outa it."

Lew couldn't help himself. He licked his lips. "I am God damn well fed up with people criticizing the way I go about my business. You understand?"

"Who else?" Sprague asked, surprised.

"Don't be clinical. I'm not kidding you, I'm fed to my teeth."

"This is a little known side you're showing me," Sprague said. "Who else?"

Worship said, "Fuck you."

"Unh, unh, unh. Nasty talk picked up in Surgery. Who else? I'm interested."

"Confine yourself." But he'd lost the power to be vicious. He was weary and sat down.

"Who?"

"You, you sonofabitch, for one. And every other bastard around, and believe me, this profession sure breeds some of the pretty ones."

Sprague was silent. "This happens on OB sometimes," he finally said.

Worship looked up. Slowly, he said, "I wish I had a magic ray that would evaporate you."

"It's like skin-diving, I guess. In skin-diving they call it 'rapture of the deep.' "

"How're things over on GYN?" Lew said wearily.

"How're they ever? Dilatation and currettage . . . D and C, D and C. You could forget there're any other letters in the alphabet . . . You *asked* to cover for someone?"

"Otis."

"So I heard. What're you, a glutton for punishment?"

"Maybe just a glutton. Experience," Lew said wearily.

"That's the last thing you'll get around here, Doctor. Don't forget yourself. You're just an intern."

Lew felt too weary to reply. "Yeah," Sprague said, weary himself now from Lew's condition and his own day, patting Lew on the shoulder. He moved tiredly away from the wall he'd been leaning against. "Yeah . . . Well," and he nodded, "it's admirable, Lew. I mean, putting in more time than you have to." He stopped. "What're you, *dedicated* or something?"

Lew thought. "No. Excitable, I guess."

"Is this good for the patients?"

"Who knows?"

"Yeah. Right. Who ever knows? Man, anyway, if *I* ever skipped a relief—except when I *have* to—I'd be lousy for the patients. You ever thought of that?"

Lew nodded.

"Well?"

"I can't help it."

Again Sprague studied him. "You mean that? You really mean that?"

"I told you. Not now."

"Crazy," Sprague said, wandering away and shaking his head. "*Absolutely crazy.*"

Maybe, Lew thought. Maybe I am. It always comes out in

unusual ways. You can't recognize it yourself. Like being drunk.

I'll just sit here and *be,* he thought. That way nothing will happen. To me or from me. I'll just sit here and be.

What will I be? he thought. No, he thought. No. I'll just be. But I can't, he thought. Even the grammar won't allow it. You can't just *be.* You have to be *something.*

But what? he thought. That's what I'm trying to find out. Then, *sic,* that's why I can't just sit here and be.

Maybe I want to, maybe I have to . . . Why is joy so like fear? No, he thought. Why does joy make you fearful? Am I so weak I can't sustain joy? Are other people like this? Was everyone always like this?

Get up, he thought. Get up. Go get some sleep while you can.

But Otis, he thought with disgust. The other extreme. Anyone who spends that much time off duty ought to be known as an out-tern. In this morning at six A.M. after twelve hours off. Obviously hadn't had any sleep. Or very little. *That* sure wasn't very good for the patients. Going without sleep like that. How could you be efficient?

Well, Lew had to admit without taste for the admission, *Otis* managed it. It never seemed to interfere. No matter how little sleep Otis had had, he was still a damn good intern. Still a damn good doctor, Lew thought, begrudgingly. Almost as if it were a point of strict honor with him not to crump out after he'd spent a night without sleep screwing around with his girl, or whatever he did.

And, Lew considered, after all, Otis didn't even often skip duty by getting someone to cover for him. He just used his own hours off for something other than sleeping. Maybe once every ten days or so he got someone to cover for him so he could have an extra twelve hours off, but back on duty, Otis always carried twice the load he had to: his own plus, whenever it was practicable, the duty load of whoever had covered for him. And, somehow, Otis made it *very* practicable.

And that's why it bothers me, Lew thought. Because it comes from ability. Just plain ability. Maybe that was it. Otis managed things well, exceptionally well, too easily. He didn't seem to go through all the complex hell your mind could give you before it let you do things the best you could. Otis didn't strain, so, thus, he was able to work in his own top form.

Which, in part (though not the greater part), was why, Lew reflected, he had begun pushing himself beyond anything he'd ever expected himself capable of. The major part, of course, was just this new experience of being on OB. OB itself was his major stimulus—or rather, the way in which it had been affecting him. But that discovery a while back that Otis could carry both his own load and Worship's and manage them as well as Worship could his own alone, had been at least a small part of why he had gotten the way he was and was pushing so hard.

So. All right, Lew thought. I'm unfair to Otis. Maybe, Lew considered, I just *begrudge* him his ability. Well, that I sure do. Just because he could do so much more with it than just be efficient. He could do a helluva lot better than I can. And that's why I begrudge him that ability. Because I want to be doing as much as I can, and it never amounts to so very damn much. And he *can* do it, and doesn't care. I work every bit of myself, Lew thought, and felt embarrassed by his immodesty; and don't get very far. But with *his* ability, Otis just coasts.

For Otis had come in at six A.M. after his regular official twelve hours off, and had not had any sleep, and had gone through the regular OB duty day, from rounds through afternoon clinic, and then had gone up to catch what sleep he could before dinner while things were light, and then, when Lew had offered, had accepted a second night out immediately. That was what Lew couldn't, in a way, forgive, though he himself had offered John Paul the opportunity. And that was why Lew had tried everyone else before John Paul. Because he knew John Paul would accept immediately. With no professional qualification, no professional questioning of himself whether he ought to or not. Which, to Lew, amounted almost to irresponsibility. Professional irresponsibility.

And, knowing that it was really his own responsibility that Otis had the opportunity to have the night off, Lew remembered Otis explaining once before, "Hell, man, why shouldn't I? For godsake, we're only interns. All we get is scut, anyway. Clean-up work. Procedures that're simple and automatic. Why *should* I stay in when I have a chance to get off? The kind of work *we* do, I can do in my sleep. There's no reason for sticking around when I don't have to. Because there's no challenge. Give me a challenge and maybe things'd be different."

"There's nothing stopping you from setting up your own challenge," Lew had said.

Otis had grinned sourly. "Who said I haven't?"

Well, Otis was right. There *was* nothing much you could do that gave you that warm feeling of respect for yourself, a feeling of accomplishment. So why not? Like Otis? But still, Otis' attitude irked Lew. It wasn't professional. Oh hell, Lew thought. *Professional* doesn't describe what it is or isn't. It wasn't a *something* about Otis. It was just Otis. And me, Lew thought. Everyone else gets along with him.

So, after having had last night off, he's taking tonight off too. Why should I censure him? Hell, it's my responsibility. *I* was the one who gave him the opportunity. Still. Still, he shouldn't have accepted it.

And why not? Lew asked himself . . . He didn't know. Because Otis was right. All you got was scut work, no chance, or very little, to use years of training. The God damn training was *atrophying*. His knowledge, Lew thought, wasn't expanding during this year of internship, it was contracting from lack of use. And there wasn't anything available to make up for it by giving you that feeling of having *done* something. Of *doing* something. . . . Except, Lew thought. Except maybe. This thing OB was doing to him. Which was why he'd wanted the extra twelve hours on. *Yes,* he thought disgustedly. *Yes,* but human emotions just aren't built that way. They break down or go numb . . .

. . . *It can't happen again, it can't, it can't* . . . Lew thought, now himself unsure. Human emotions just aren't built that way.

The girl had begun to scream. The screams came irregularly, but they were no longer voluntary. This one wasn't his, though. He was just watching till his was ready. His was somewhere out on the chalk board, a name only, with a fetal heartbeat of x and a blood pressure of y, contractions now *R*egular or *I*rregular or maybe marked in terms of minutes and with membranes *I*ntact or *R*uptured.

Delivery might be half an hour away. Or five hours or ten hours or more. He hoped it would be four hours or more—so that it would be after ten o'clock. Yukio Sato would be charge resident then, and even if things were light, Sato might let him handle the entire delivery. Sato wasn't the hog kind of resident who left the intern only the scut work, the clean-up work, when things were light.

The girl had fallen into semi-unconsciousness between contractions. She must be very close, Lew thought. Then he left her room to study the board and see if he could deduce from rates of contractions and dilations of cervixes, and pluses and minuses of stations which one might be his. He hoped the girl in the room he'd just left would have an easy time and have a beautiful baby. The words in the thought didn't embarrass him. They were the words to fit what he was thinking. He studied the board, studied the names to see if any name had a special rapport for him, and thought, *Christ God, it can't happen again, it can't* . . .

3

Dr. Constantine Mercouris, on his way to the Park North Lounge and Grill, was considering much the same problem as Parelli, with much the same hoped-for results in mind. His intentions were to place himself, the following year, as a resident under the tutelage of Harvey Bonny. How he was going to effect this, he didn't know. He had filled out the necessary application, he had written for an interview. But he suspected it wasn't enough; had, in fact, a surety that it wasn't enough. He had to find an edge somewhere.

Mercouris had always been without a place of his own that he could respect—first as the son of refugees from the Greco-Turkish War, second as the resident of a poor neighborhood in which he didn't fit into any of the major national stocks, and third as a student at schools which he did not consider to be first rate and which he therefore automatically considered to be second rate, himself along with them.

Harvey Bonny represented Mercouris' first reach for something which, in his considered evaluation of himself, he felt to be quite beyond himself. He had to find the edge *now*—if he got the residency, he'd find the means of living up to it *later*. Somehow. There were means, of course, other than Harvey Bonny, by which you could establish yourself in psychiatry. But since Mercouris doubted his own motives for choosing psychiatry as his specialty, he had, as a sop to his conscience, forced himself to accept the challenge of the most difficult entree to the field. His mind had fixed upon Bonny. He recognized that the fix was almost obsessive. He recognized it and tried not to think about it. He thought only of how, out of the number of applicants Bonny screened, he might be chosen. Mercouris' problem seemed always to be how to separate himself from the crowd, from mediocrity, from the place he himself felt he deserved.

His service that day—as it had been for the past five weeks and would continue to be for the next three—was Surgery. The first four weeks were spent in Female Surgery, the second four spent in Male Surgery (or vice versa, depending upon in which section one started). Surgery was bad enough, but *Male* Surgery was, to him, hopelessly depressing. Women, at least, kept themselves relatively clean; but the men who came through the clinics at New North, and especially the men who ended up in Surgery, were atrocious.

Morning rounds had been made that day, unusually, with one of the attendings, Dr. Riccio. Riccio was a tough, admirably competent surgeon who had no put-in with phoniness of any sort, whether it be unfelt humility and modesty or a concern for a patient which was, to Dr. Riccio, uncalled for by the individual case.

Thus, rounds had been swift—an almost cursory stop by each of the six beds in each of the six rooms that comprised, along with three semiprivate rooms, Ward B of Male Surgery. A brief summary by Duane, the chief resident, at each stop. Usually only a grunt from Riccio. A few times, a comment like, "Discharge this man" or "Who the hell ordered high protein for this patient?" Twice, bandages were removed and Dr. Riccio looked—and grunted and moved on to the next bed.

Nothing important. Nothing you could even learn anything from. But Riccio was followed from bed to bed by the chief resident, two other residents, six interns, four juniors who were observing, a head nurse and two other nurses, five student nurses and the head nurse who was their teacher, and a nurse's aide whose delivery of tea coincided with Riccio's rounds. All this attendance, as if upon a religious progress, in order to hear Riccio grunt and swear.

Mercouris had been shuffling along in the troupe, unable to see, unable to hear, and more shuffled than shuffling, when he became terribly weary.

He had just stood there, weary, disgusted, and frightened, and had let them move on without him. He would not by Christ degrade himself by taking part in a farce.

Another intern hadn't moved on either. Two beds away, van Wyck was talking to a patient Riccio hadn't bothered with. Van Wyck had had the man pull up his hospital-issue nightshirt and turn over on his stomach, and was examining the lesions on the man's back.

"No soreness today, Mr. Nola?" van Wyck was saying.

"Not so bad, Doctor."

"You can feel me touch you there?"

"Sure, Doc."

"Doesn't hurt?"

"Hurts a little up above. But not like before."

"Fine, Mr. Nola, that's good progress. Fine. How does this feel when I touch you?" and he began palpating the un-affected tissue immediately around the lesions.

Mercouris had become aware of a patient staring at him, a rheumy-eyed fat man, sitting up leaning on one arm and just staring at him. Mercouris had left the room immediately, feigning by his look that he had just remembered something terribly important. That *bastard,* Mercouris had thought, not knowing whether he meant the fat man or van Wyck.

After rounds he'd overheard Riccio and Duane talking. "Some group," Riccio had been saying. "They don't know their ass from their elbow; and they're not interested in find-ing out. Not one of 'em so much as asked a question. Forty-two patients, and not one intern asked a question."

"One of 'em in this group I like," Duane had said. "In fact, he's about as good as any intern I've worked with so far."

"Which one is that?"

"Peter van Wyck."

"Duane, for chrisake, I don't know them by their goddam *names."*

"The one who stuck with some of the patients after we got through."

"What's his specialty going to be? Surgery?"

"I'm not sure. Medicine, I think," Duane said.

"Screw him," Riccio said. "See if you can get hold of his records for me anyway."

Mercouris didn't know whether they'd known he could hear them or hadn't known or just didn't care or had even intended for him to hear them. He had continued to sit there in the nurses' station at the long, wide, glass-covered shelf that served as everyone's desk and writing table. He had continued to fill out an incomplete admitting form he was late in getting finished. But he had been thinking, That bastard van Wyck, I've got to get out of the crowd.

4

Mercouris walked along in the cold, punching the soles of his shoes against the snow-encrusted sidewalk.

"Hey, man," a voice behind him called cheerfully, "wait up."

Mercouris turned. Big and ambling, Jim Aptshult came grinning up to him.

"Walking *alone* in this neighborhood," Aptshult said. "Man, unless you're wearing your whites, you're nuts to walk alone around here. That's goddam near the first thing I was told when I got to North. I delivered a baby before they told me how to do *that,* but they sure as hell told me right off not to go walking alone at night around here."

"I grew up in a neighborhood like this."

"Fine. Without your whites maybe you'll die in a neighborhood like this."

"Whites or no whites, they'll come after you if they feel like it."

"Only," Aptshult said benignly, "if you've got your bag with you and they're looking for a fix."

"Bag or no bag, whites or no whites. You're a helluva one to talk, *you* were coming along alone."

"I'm a big *stupid* bastard. No one'd bother me. Man, *man,*" he said, leaning down and hardly breaking stride and scooping up some snow, "snow before Christmas. Man, man, I'll have to write my folks. They used to live here," he said equably, "till they had me and decided to move to a drier climate. Going to the Park North?"

"Yeah. I thought I might. You?"

"Like yes, man."

Mercouris suddenly laughed and nodded understandingly. "Hey! I bet *Alicia's* there."

"Whoo-*ee*. Where'd y'all get that cotton-pickin' idea?"

"Har. And double har, Doctor. That's the simplest diagnosis I've made all day. Whither goest the fair Lee Liu, there findest thou also the ugly Aptshult."

"So? There's a law?"

"Some cases it's best to give up on."

"Like I ain't never yet seen one."

"Yes, you have. And the case's name is Alicia Liu."

5

Along the park the neighborhood had changed during the past few years. A number of tenements had been torn down and a number of luxury apartment buildings had been put up. Sensing a change in the atmosphere and a potential change in his clientele, the proprietor of the nearby Safe Harbor Bar and Grill had changed his establishment's name to the Park North Lounge and Grill. He had then redecorated suitably, raised his prices accordingly, and thrown out the rowdier hangers-on who had not been disestablished by the new prices or disenchanted by the new décor. The Park North had then become a regular hangout for New North's interns (and occasionally even other members' of the staff) when they were off duty and too tired to go further afield but felt the need just to go afield, just to get out of the hospital.

The Park North had several major inducements with which to recommend itself to the members of New North's staff and particularly to its interns. It was convenient—only a few blocks away. Though more expensive than other places in the neighborhood, it was not *that* much more expensive, and it was certainly far less expensive than the bars downtown. It was also a lot safer than the other neighborhood bars: the tougher elements in the neighborhood (out of respect and appreciation for the work done by the free, or nearly free, clinics at the hospital) usually left doctors alone; but sometimes they didn't know you were a doctor, and sometimes they didn't care, and sometimes they cared in particular because they had a gripe against New North doctors—an uncle who had complained about unsympathetic treatment at the hospital, a friend whose condition had failed to improve satisfactorily (in his friends' opinion) after medical treatment at the hospital, a wife who had been told (to someone's indignation) that she mustn't get pregnant again if she wanted to keep living, a brother whose malingering had been spotted by some doctor at the hospital with the result that the brother had been taken off relief. At any rate, you couldn't, with tranquillity of mind, take a girl to any of the other bars in the area.

There were other factors too. The owner of the Park North, George Bucca, had not only tolerance and respect for interns, but also a genuine affection for them. They were doing *important* things. Thus, unlike other of George's customers and unlike any of the customers of George's local competitors, the interns could sit talking indefinitely over one beer or even over one cup of coffee without ever a single complaint from the management, even on weekend nights when the place often got crowded (with the luxury trade that lived along the park).

And when the interns got fed up with the food at New North (which was often before they'd even eaten it), they could get a plate of spaghetti and meatballs for fifty-five cents at the Park North. True, the size and consistency of the meatballs was such that a humorous intern might occasionally, given the proper light, confuse them with kidney stones—but there was plenty of sauce and plenty of free Italian bread.

Thus, the Park North was almost nightly filled with voices loudly and sometimes conspicuously discussing vesicating properties, biliary fistulas, hyperestrinism, narcoma, penis palmatus, Gartner's phenomenon, cranial aneurysms and other equally unlikely cocktail-lounge conversational fare.

6

They had pushed three tables for two together in a line in the back of the room and there were enough of them sitting around so that there seemed to be hardly enough room for the drinks and ashtrays on the tables, much less comfortable room for all the chairs to be within good reaching and con-versation distance. The chairs were variously angled to allow more approach to the tables than seemed actually to be there.

Only Alicia Liu was accorded an amount of respect which allowed her to sit directly at the table. This was not because she was the only girl there, though she was. It was because she was the only beautiful girl there and it was based even more upon the fact that she was the only beautiful girl there who was willing to take advantage of the rights her fellow interns would allow her to assert. She asserted these rights because, as a woman, she felt that nature had provided her with certain natural disadvantages and certain natural advantages. A person, she felt, who didn't take advantage of the advantages, but merely accepted the *dis*advantages, was bound to be *dis*-happy. So that when a young man forgot that he was an intern and remembered that he was a young man, Alicia was perfectly willing to sit directly and comfort-ably at the table and forgo all disclaimers.

"You've got a *lot* of opportunities, kid. The almost most I've ever seen," she heard Jim Aptshult, across the table and two chairs away, say to a sullen-looking Conny Mercouris. "Hell, man, you could run for medical superintendent and every nurse in the hospital'd vote for you." She saw him clap Conny on the back, and smiled.

When Jim and Conny had come in, Alicia had been pleased to see Jim look around the table and, his eyes finding her as if he'd been looking for her, seat himself near her—not too near, of course; he hadn't pushed in directly opposite her, but he'd sat nearby and she'd wondered whether her hair had kept its last combing.

Most everybody was on a second beer—the one that had to *la-ast*. The first was therapeutic and could therefore be drunk in good conscience as fast as desired. For the second there was no excuse and it therefore had to be nursed as if a patient in Private. So they sat there, talking, killing time, slowing themselves down so that they could go back and get to sleep and be ready in about ten hours to go on duty again for thirty-six hours. But mostly, they were just being *away* from the hospital. Not out of dislike for the hospital, but out of need.

The only person other than Alicia who wasn't on a second beer was John Paul Otis (M.D., practicing provisionally); he was on his third Scotch mist. Alicia, having delivered or assisted in the delivery of eleven babies in the last thirty-six hours (two of which deliveries were sets of twins, one set which she had delivered, and one set which she had assisted Joe Parelli with), was happily at work on a piece of pie and a cup of coffee into which she had dumped two containers of cream on the fallacious—as she knew—theory that the more cream in a cup of coffee, the less it would keep her awake.

She was pleased by Jim's attentiveness, but she hoped that her pleasure would not be confused with acceptance or reciprocation of what she felt his attention meant. She was happier making rounds and delivering babies and eating pie than, she was certain, she would be having an affair with a married man—especially a doctor, *any* doctor.

Jim always described his marriage as, "Just one of those things that cooled down but failed to peter out." The failure to peter out, he maintained, "is due to the person I'm married to's insistence that I give her a monthly check for life just because I slept with her a few times. That *person* even contested when I went out and sued her for divorce in Las Vegas. *And* offered her a *settlement* to boot. A settlement I was *borrowing* from the bank on my father's countersignature. Christ, you'd think that anyone with the opportunity to get rid of me would take it like anesthesia." He'd stop, while telling the story, and consider this enigma for a while, still confused by it a year and a half after last seeing his wife. Then he'd say, "That person has slept with so many people since we got married I could take her into court for just being worn out. I've got people who've *offered* right to my face to go to court and testify as corespondents. Offered right to my face."

"Well why don't you take them up, Jim?" Parelli had asked.

"I'm *stupid*," he'd said. "I've got to do things the hard way. She's got to agree to it, not have it forced on her. No one forced me to marry her."

Aptshult was saying to her, "When you get ready to go, I'm big and strong and I'll walk you back if you want."

She smiled at him and shook her head.

But he seemed not to have seen the *no*. "I'm too stupid to even make a pass," he said. "Ask my chief resident. He'll vouch for my stupidity."

"Mine will vouch for mine, too," she said, carefully, through the din. "Anyway, I've been asked already."

"Who is he!" Aptshult thundered. "I'll beat the fink's head!" He rose to his feet. "I'll trepanize! I'll euthanasia-ize!" He sat down. "I'll offer him my congratulations."

"Mon cher docteur," John Paul Otis said, getting up and bowing to Aptshult from over his Scotch mist, "I have the honor of accompanying *mademoiselle le docteur* to her place of internment, but"—and he burped and sat down—"but, with *la permission de mademoiselle le docteur,* I will excuse myself due to the cotton-pickin' fact that needs be I must get myself downtown by nine o'clock and *la jolie fille le docteur* has been sittin' over her cotton-pickin' pie too long."

"Yeah," said Aptshult.

"And I . . . *I* have been sittin' ovah the mist of Scotland too long to . . . too long to be able to . . . *see through it!"*

"Yeah," said Aptshult.

"And besides . . . I gotta get downtown to muh shack job. I mean, my *mistress.* Who isn't as delightful as the fair Alicia, but who nevertheless makes the difference between me and beer. Also me and sexual mal-*noo*trition . . ."

"Go screw," said Aptshult.

". . . I haven't eaten tonight. Which explains my present inebriate condition. Also me and Alicia. The difference, I mean, is made up by this girl who makes up the difference between my tastes and forty dollars a month." In the silence that had developed during his speech, Otis thought things over. "She loves doctors," he said, standing up. Then he sat down again. "Does *she* ever love doctors. Can do no wrong, you know. Hippocratic oath and all that, you know." He stood up again and yelled at George behind the bar, "Check, *mon cher!"* He turned back to the table. "He understood the *check* part." Then back to George: *"Everybody's* check."

There were no's and, "Hey, Otis, give it up!" and "Jesus, let him, he's got the dough" . . . Only van Wyck, sitting slightly removed from the focus of conversation, remained, as he had been, silent, relaxed, and observant.

Otis turned back to the bar. *"Everybody's* check, now mind me, George."

George brought the total check. The tables were silent. Otis flicked down a twenty-dollar bill on the small pastic tray. "Keepa change, George, old man," Otis said. He started away. Then he turned around again. "Ah. *Man.* Like you say, Jim: *man.* And woman too, of course. But *man.* Like you say, Jim. *Man,* my loss is your gain and I bow to a fellow

southerner, and my apologies to you, ma'am, but it's gettin'
on toward nine o'clock and I gotta go-*O*." And he took his
coat with a wide sweep of the arm and left.

7

"What a fink," de Traunant said quietly.

"I think he's just drunk," Alicia said.

"*Oi vey!*" Mercouris said, looking to the heavens for understanding. Then, to Alicia, "Such huh vonduhful doctuh. Such
huh-cute diagnosis."

"Only a fink gets drunk the way Otis was," de Traunant
said.

"Hell, Otis is that way when he's *sober*," Aptshult said.

"He's huh vonduhful doctuh," Mercouris said. "I heard he
almost got thrown out of med school for cheating on an
exam, only they couldn't prove anything."

"Conny, for chrisake," Rosconovitch said, turning from a
conversation further down the line of tables, "you're *drinking* his *beer*, the least you could do is wait till you finish before you slander him."

"Okay, okay," Mercouris said. "You're right."

"Anyway," Rosconovitch went on, "he *wasn't* thrown out.
I lived down the hall from him and I know how it happened.
He wasn't doing so hot with his grades and it looked like
he was going to flunk pathology for certain. So, he took the
path exam and got a mark five points higher than anyone
else in the class." He stopped and drank some beer and then
turned back at Mercouris. "A ninety-eight, buddy, a *ninety-
eight*."

Mercouris wasn't impressed. "But he was *flunking* path up
till then, right?" he said. "Explain me then the sudden change
to being a genius."

"Because maybe he is. Anyway, he's smart as hell when he
wants to be."

"Yeah, but a *ninety-eight*, Art," de Traunant said, "when
he'd been flunking. If he got a seventy or seventy-five, I
could understand *that*, but . . ."

"He crammed," Rosconovitch said.

"He just simply crammed, huh?" Aptshult said.

"For two days before. He's just got the kind of mind that

can do it when he wants it to. Only, he doesn't usually bother."

"I see," Mercouris said. "That's why they almost threw him out. Too brilliant."

"Conny, look, for godsake the guy worked his ass off for that mark . . . Look, what happened was, the dean and the chief of path called him in and when they asked him to explain, all Otis said was that he'd crammed. He convinced *them*."

Mercouris considered this. Then he said, "Lew Worship was at school with you two, wasn't he?"

"Yeah . . . ?"

"Worship says that another guy got thrown out right after the exam because they learned he'd swiped a copy of the thing beforehand. Worship says the guy told the dean, or whoever it was, that he'd looked at it and then burnt it up. But he told *Worship* he'd sold it to someone."

"Circumstantial," Rosconovitch said. "Anyway, Worship couldn't diagnose a hangnail."

"*That*," said Alicia, "is hardly the impression I've gotten."

"Nor me," Rosconovitch said, embarrassed and apologetic.

"There's a *real* nut," Donnecker said. "He's been going around like he's just short of complete stupor. What's he *on*, for godsake?"

"Hashish, by the look of him," Aptshult said.

"OB," Alicia said. "I thought he'd be over here tonight. It's his night off too."

"He's covering for Otis," Sprague said. "I heard Lew call *him* and ask *him* if he could cover for him."

"A nut," Aptshult said.

"Where's Worship applying for residencies?" Donnecker said.

With horror, Rosconovitch said, "Jesus. You know he hasn't even *written* anywhere yet?"

"He hasn't applied *anywhere* yet?" Sprague said, equally horror-stricken.

"The jerk," Mercouris said.

"Maybe he wants to be an intern forever. Maybe he's making *internship* his specialty," Rosconovitch said.

"He doesn't know yet what he wants to specialize in," Alicia said. "*That's* why he hasn't applied anywhere."

"He better damn quick," Donnecker said. "Otherwise he's going to be just in time to apply for absolutely nothing."

"Hey," Sprague said, "there's *Elwood* sitting at the bar."

"Another nut," Aptshult said. "They're coming in the god-dam windows tonight."

"Someone go get him," Alicia said. "He looks lonely."

"Oh God," Mercouris said, "the *mother* instinct yet!" He looked at Alicia. *"Okay,"* he said. "Okay, *okay!"* And he went over to the bar and led Elwood back by the sleeve.

Elwood didn't sit down. He stood there, his boyish face flushed with embarrassment. "I want to thank you all," he said, "for inviting me over to sit with you . . ." Then he stopped and stood there without a word more to say.

"Well then, for chrisake, *sit down,"* Sprague said.

"No, actually, I think I'd better . . ."

"Oh, siddown," Aptshult said. "Get a chair and we'll make room."

Elwood, as if too embarrassed to do otherwise, brought a chair over and pulled it up to the tables.

"I'm going to make a real night of it," Aptshult said. "I'm going to have a second beer. Alicia?"

"No, I think I'd better get back. I have to write a letter."

"There goes my beer," Aptshult said, shrugged, and smiled. "I'll walk you back."

"Have your beer. I'll wait."

"Hot damn," Aptshult said. "Cake and eat it too."

"So," Donnecker said to Aptshult after various orders had been placed, "you're still going to be a surgeon, hunh?"

"You know me," Aptshult said, knowing by instinct and experience what was coming, "I'd rather cut than cure any day."

"Man," Rosconovitch said, "you guys scare me. Hand the surgeon mentality a knife and he's in another world. Way, way out."

"Is it true," de Traunant said, awakening from some private reveries, "is it true that the ideal of every surgeon is to be able to take out *everything* and still have the patient alive enough to write a check for the fee?"

"Certainly it's not true," Donnecker said heatedly. "That's a real erroneous and fallacious conception and it's time it was wholly rebutted and destroyed. The ideal of every surgeon is merely to take out everything."

8

Van Wyck sat near the end of the line of tables, his chair tilted a little and placed a little further back and away from the others, who were now all crowded in.

Van Wyck's feelings were almost sexual, as if immediately after coitus: he was drowsy and removed; incapable of any more, satisfied, and even incapable of *asking* any more of himself; enjoying the company, but too relaxed to take part in its conversation, yet pleased to be listening to it. In a while he'd walk back and go to bed—he'd have to be up even earlier than usual, six, the next morning, for it was his turn to draw bloods and carry out the other pre-rounds assignments in the order book. Then there'd be the rest of the day—rounds, admissions, Clinical Pathological Conference, rounds, clinic, a scrub if he was called, more rounds, and then he'd be on call all the next night for Emergency. But as long as he had this—these things to *do*—there was nothing beyond to desire or ask for or even hope for. He had achieved the very rare state of satisfaction without hunger.

9

Tom Elwood had forgotten to bring his bourbon and water over from the bar. But with these people he felt somehow embarrassed to get up and go get it. He couldn't explain it to himself—why he felt this way—but he'd felt it for a long time, ever since he'd gotten to the city, how long ago?— months; months; five or six months. He'd never leave it— this, this hospital, this city. He could see no end to it. He could see no going on of it either—maybe a month, maybe another month. But he could see no future. He had forgotten why he was here—in this city, at this hospital, sitting here now with these people . . . these people with whom he didn't know what to do with himself, how to talk to them . . .

These people with whom he could not bring himself to call attention to himself by even ordering another drink.

Was this where he was supposed to be . . .?

This was not where he was supposed to be . . . He was supposed to be somewhere else . . .

10

Donnecker knew he oughtn't to stay. He had finished a long time ago the one beer he had planned to allow himself. He wasn't planning on having another. He didn't want another. He hadn't wanted the first.

He hated living with himself this way. He hated living by compromise, doing things he didn't want to do (stop off for a beer) to avoid doing other things he didn't want to do (go home).

Going home . . . It was just what Mildred made him feel. Guilty somehow. Responsible for something gone wrong somehow, responsible for some injustice she was suffering somehow. He loved her, but he couldn't account for or face the onus she somehow placed on him and made him feel just by her presence and manner.

And now he'd have to explain being late. But why should he have to explain? He loved her and she loved him. Why must he be on guard against her all the time? Why must he defend himself to her all the time? Why must he defend himself?

He didn't want to sit here with these boobs. He wanted to go home to his loving wife, whom he loved, whom he'd married seven months ago. But he wondered if he had a loving wife. Had he a marriage? Marriage was supposed to be something to cherish. He had. When had he stopped— what had done it? Had he?

He waited for an answer from himself. There was none.

He had expected so much more; though maybe it wasn't *so much*, maybe it was just what he should have expected, and gotten. He would try again. Harder. But there was this damn business of having to leave her alone by herself so much of the time; and with not being able to be with her often, how could he try harder? But he would try harder anyway. If you tried hard enough . . . wasn't that all you had to do?

He didn't want to sit here with these boobs . . . But he

wanted to—he just couldn't face that feeling of being at fault just yet. Because he didn't want to go yet, he looked at his watch. He made an appointment with himself to leave in five minutes. He had never failed to keep an appointment with himself in his life.

But it was almost fifteen minutes before he got himself to leave.

11

"About Otis," de Traunant said, "what you think of his story about this girl keeping him?"

"Vell," Mercouris said, "he's soitenly huh vonduhful doctuh . . ."

"Jesus," Aptshult said, "get the accent right or give it up."

Rosconovitch sighed with a sigh that he felt could only be equaled for tragic and passionate depth by a sigh from another suffering soul of Russian descent. "Stunning," he said. "Absolutely, clinically positively, laboritorially infallibly stunning."

"You met her?" de Traunant said.

"I met her. I should live so long I should meet another like her, I'd be a geriatrics case . . . A figure and face, Alicia should pardon me, you'd want to bang till you had a coronary . . ."

The tables were silent, awed by Rosconovitch's obvious awe, and, since it was so rare a feeling for any of them, awed by their own awe.

"A skin," Rosconovitch continued, ". . . a skin . . ." There were obviously no words for it. "You would cut your own throat before you'd put a knife to that skin, such a sin against God it would be . . ."

Aptshult, raising his eyes to heaven, muttered, "All poets think they're Jewish." Then he added, "Except Ezra Pound, of course."

Rosconovitch was not to be deterred. "Eyes . . . eyes you wouldn't put glasses on . . ."

"It would be a sin against God," Aptshult said.

"It would," Rosconovitch said. "Hair no dermatologist will ever touch . . ."

"This is good?" Peterson—a new arrival and embryo dermatologist—said.

"Everybody's Jewish tonight," Aptshult said. "Everybody wants to get into the act."

De Traunant leaned forward. "And this paragon of femininity belongs to our friend and benefactor Dr. Otis?"

"She does," Rosconovitch said.

"Truly," de Traunant said, "he's huh vonduhful doctuh."

Rosconovitch nodded agreement. "Twelve hours out of every forty-eight he spends shacked up with her. Every other weekend he spends late Saturday and all day Sunday shacked up with her. I wouldn't want this to get around, but sometimes, when things are light, he gets fools like me or Worship to cover for him and he . . ."

"I know," Alicia said. "He shacks up with her."

"Right."

"No wonder he's so thin and nervous and drunk," Aptshult said. "The boy's under a terrible strain."

"Such strains I could learn to adjust to," Mercouris said.

"And also," Rosconovitch said, "as John himself is the first to tell you . . ."

"I know," Peterson said. "Also she's rich and provides him with liberal pocket money with which to squire her and bring her vintage champagne."

"Yes," said Rosconovitch, himself awed by the facts, "that's the history. And the diagnosis is . . ."

"He's lucky as hell," Peterson said.

"Him and that attaché case he's always lugging around," Aptshult said.

"It's probably full of pajamas," de Traunant said. "He's a real fink."

12

Worship could see them all together over at the Park North, wearing their dark suits for a night out, all black-blues and black-grays, the lot of them together giving the impression that some much-loved, mutual relative had died.

He had no immediate desire to be over at the Park North, certainly no envy of being over there drinking just so you could pretend to yourself you'd cut free from the hospital. Not that he hadn't pulled this ruse on himself often enough, but that had been before he'd gone on OB.

So, in a *way*, he wanted to be over there with them, all right. But only in a way. He'd love a beer right now—cold, slightly bitter . . . And he'd like to be raising conversational hell with van Wyck or some of the others; it would be fun, even, to get Conny started on what was wrong with patients . . . But he knew that if he *were* there, he'd be restless, even depressed, waiting to get back, to be doing, to see what was happening to him.

13

Parelli was having the old dream. He'd been having it irregularly for as long as he could remember, at the very least since junior high.

He was in a classroom. All the other kids were looking at him. The teacher was asking him a question. If he didn't answer the question he'd fail out of the class and be put back with the little kids. It was a question about something he'd never heard of before. He was sure he'd done all the homework, all the assignments and preparation he was supposed to, but he didn't know this answer. He didn't even know what the teacher was talking about. The others were beginning to laugh at him and the teacher was coming terrifyingly close to him, angry, furious at him, and he felt he was going to get up and run . . . and . . .

And he came awake. As always at this point. The dream no longer frightened him. He was too used to it. But it annoyed him because it always succeeded in waking him up, and that was time lost from sleep he needed.

He understood the significance of the dream—in a *general* way, he realized. It was something, of course, about feeling inadequate or inferior. But bridge-table knowledge like that didn't get rid of the damn thing. So every so often he lost sleep, and that annoyed him so much he had trouble getting himself back to sleep.

Well, he'd have to find the origin of the dream and deal with *that*. At least it might change the dream. He could dream about the origin then . . .

This started him thinking about Harvey Bonny and he cursed himself for an idiot for letting another block (Harvey Bonny) get between him and sleep. Now there were two things to get out of the way instead of one.

If I stay awake, he warned something or somebody somewhere, *it's the* patients *that suffer.*

And having stated his warning, he unthinkingly turned over and went back to sleep.

14

Donnecker was the first, after Otis and Sprague, to leave the Park North. Once, *just one time,* since he'd begun his internship, he'd stopped off for a beer with his friends. His goddam *colleagues,* for godsake. Why did he have to feel guilty, defensive about it?

15

A while after Donnecker left, Jim Aptshult walked Alicia Liu back to the hospital. He wanted to ask her who she was going to write the letter to. But his pride wouldn't let him. It was either his pride or his stupidity; and he couldn't decide which.

But there was something he *did* have to ask her. He felt weak, he felt boyish and adolescent about this simple question, this simple, innocent question that held in his throat like a carcinoma he could feel every time he swallowed.

They were only a block away from the hospital and he had to ask her before they got inside. They'd go up in the same elevator (Alicia lived on the floor above him in the women's separate rooms with two other female—Aptshult questioned it—interns and three—Aptshult questioned it—female residents; they even had a kitchen up there and his impression was that all they did all day was brew tea and talk about what bastards the male interns were) and there might, probably *would,* be others in the same elevator, so that he certainly couldn't ask her then.

He said, looking straight ahead, tough old Jim Aptshult,

the Greatest and Toughest Surgeon in the World, "Is this your every other weekend off, Alicia?"

She said, *"What?"*

"Are you off this Saturday night?"

"Yes," she said, "I am," and looked away.

"Well, would you like to go out with me?" He managed to get himself to look at her.

She had turned back to him. "Jim, thank you. But I have a date."

"Who?" Aptshult said violently. He cut his voice down level. "I'm sorry. It's none of my business."

They walked on. He said suddenly, "Yes it is, God damn it. Yes it is my business."

Alicia said, "I'm going to see a French movie with Art Rosconovitch." Then, after a few seconds' pause, she added unexpectedly, "He asked me last week."

Aptshult said nothing.

There was no one else in the elevator when they pushed their respective buttons and went up.

Alicia said, "There's no reason for you to have a look like that on your face. After all, you're married."

"I know," he said, as the door slid open at his floor. "I know. I've been told I'm married . . . by my wife. Good night," he said, and went furiously out of the elevator.

16

He had never had an outright hatred for his wife before. It just hadn't been necessary. Married, single—no sweat either way, as long as he didn't have to be with her. But now he hated her, that beautiful, dumb, bitchy, promiscuous coed he'd married for no reason at all except that she was beautiful and a good lay, and maybe to prove something.

What he'd proven, he still didn't know, except that he could be as tough as the next guy, as big a bastard as the next guy, with a wife as beautiful as the next guy's. More beautiful.

He'd also proven that something by joining a telephone line crew the summer after his freshman year. He'd run into a little too much anti-Semitism that he couldn't take care of at the Southern university he was attending. So, malice in him like a malignancy, he'd joined the line crew to toughen himself up. He'd done it. He'd been tall before the summer. After the summer he was slightly scarred, but he wasn't just tall, he was big. And after the summer, whenever anyone made a remark that Jim felt was gratuitous, he invited the someone—challenged him as a "gentleman"—down to the gym for a few friendly rounds. After a few such invitations —offered as publicly as possible so that the someone could not very well back down and still remain a "gentleman"— Jim found that either his hearing was going or else remarks weren't being made any more. At least not in his presence.

He felt so tough he even made the third-string football team as a guard. It was a team of national repute. But it wasn't enough, he told himself, back in his room, lying on his bed. It wasn't enough just to be big and respected—because I was big, *I* had to have glory too. *I*, big Jim Aptshult, had to *prove* something. So I found a girl so impressed with my sexual prowess that she married me. So dumb and rebellious that—with *her* background—she'd even marry a Jew. Of course, the fact that she was Campus Queen that year had nothing to do with my choice.

And now, he told himself, you're the biggest, toughest surgeon of them all. You've got brilliant fingers. Even Riccio told you. And next year, if you don't screw up this year, you'll have your choice of choice residencies. And in the meantime and forever after, Alicia Liu will be just a nice, understanding, warm, humorous girl who might as well be living in China for all the proximity you're going to manage with her . . .

Well anyway, he thought, and picked up the receiver of the phone, and when the operator came on said, "Dr. Liu, please. No page, she's in her room."

Then he said, "Alicia, I just wanted to tell you I'm sorry about stomping out of the elevator. I wasn't mad at *you*."

"I know," she said.

And the way she said it, he realized he'd been mad, and was mad, not at his wife, but at himself.

17

Soon after Jim and Alicia left, Peter van Wyck left. He'd just as soon have left when they had, but he'd felt they might have wanted to walk alone.

Van Wyck was worried about himself. This satisfaction and no hunger. He was complacent. *Complacent* was *just* the word for it, he suspected. Maybe it was worse. Maybe this was what people meant by "smug" complacency.

He laughed. He was walking himself around in a circle. He was accusing himself of being satisfied with no hunger and being, thus, complacent—and then he was worrying about his complacency, and worrying certainly didn't indicate a great sufficiency of either complacency or satisfaction.

But just the same, Why the hell was tomorrow enough? And why, tomorrow, would the next tomorrow be enough?

He had better, he decided, get himself a pretty nurse—maybe Joan Feldman—and cash his last check from home and take her somewhere they could both have fun and enjoy being with each other and see what would happen . . . Aside from whatever else might happen, he might stop trying to be dissatisfied with his own satisfaction.

18

By ten o'clock every intern except Elwood had left the Park North. By ten twenty a lot of them were in bed. At ten thirty, sure of not running into anyone he'd have to be something to, Elwood left. When someone had suggested they all head back, Elwood had stayed on just to avoid having to be part of something he had found himself disquietingly unable to be part of. What it was, he didn't know. He couldn't ask himself about it, except to ask, *Am I part of it?* and hear his answer, as if fevered, *No. No. No. No* . . .

He walked slowly, hearing it over, *No*, and over, no longer in answer or even reference to something, but just *No*. Just *No*. Until the *No* went on by itself against or behind or with or in front of something . . .

There were two of them. One on either side of him. The

one on the right side said, "You shunt be out walking in this place, alone and all, at night."

The one on his left said, "A nice-dressed boy like you."

"Pretty-dressed."

"Look at them shoes."

"Nice coat," said the one on the right, rubbing the sleeve of Elwood's overcoat between thumb and forefinger and then holding the loose material of the sleeve tightly in his fist.

"Look at that hat. Nice."

"You get yourself the right things, man."

"We'll walk with you."

"It's dangerous around here at night."

"You need us."

"Here's a short cut over to the avenue."

"You'll be safe there."

"C'mon. We'll show you the way."

"I don't think he wants us to proteck him. I don't think he wants us to show him the way."

"Sure he does. Don't you wanus to show you the short cut back to the avenue? Sure he does."

They maneuvered him toward the opening of an alley.

They would have switchblades. Knives of some sort, anyway. But. But still. They were both smaller than he was. Wirier, but smaller. Maybe weaker. But it made no difference. He was resigned to it. He had been resigned for a long time to a lot of things. He had been resigned to this and to anything else this city might offer him from the first day when he had first smelled the city's exhaust, its bad hot breath and unwashed summer body odor.

They had him in the alley and they were leading him further into it, into its blackness. They each held an arm, tighter, blatantly now.

He saw light. A block, a half block away? At the other end of the alley. Light. An opening. Not a dead-end alley. They had stopped him, stopped him walking any further. Not a dead-end alley—even his resignation was not strong enough to resist the other, far, *open* end of the alley. He pulled his arms free angrily, almost disparagingly, and ran— Ran and ran and ran, free of the darkness of the alley, across a street without looking for cars, on, somehow toward the hospital, running, his lungs burning with too much unexhaled carbon dioxide, running still, and hearing in his head at every contact of his feet with the pavement, *No, No, No, No . . .*

But he didn't know what the *No* was being said to, shouted to.

Not even when, toward dawn, he was halfway to sleep, did he know.

19

Ted Eckland—who had been at a bar further downtown with some med-school friends who were interning at another hospital, De Witt General—hadn't untensed himself enough with two beers to be able to get himself easily to sleep. Well, on two beers, what could you expect?

The problem, though, wasn't so much the tension he had built and failed to get rid of from this day as it was the tension he was already building up about the next day. OB was just not a service he was built for.

. . . Sure, Kalik, the chief resident of B Ward (OB), was a terrific guy. And sure, it was wonderful the way he gave his interns so much responsibility and opportunity to be practicing the specialty they were attached to under him—not like that martinet Granchard in A—but if OB just wasn't your cup of tea, it sure was your cup of depressant.

The *mystery of birth* it was called. He'd forgotten there was supposed to be a mystery to it. It was just something phantasmagoric he had to live through for three more weeks. Somehow, nothing about it was akin to life, and somehow the adjustment he'd made to it was not even akin to himself . . .

He wished his roommate, Elwood, hadn't come in yet, or anyway, hadn't sacked out yet. He felt like getting up and turning on the light and studying for a couple of hours to relax himself. But that would probably wake Elwood.

20

Through the early part of the evening, Lew Worship had gone back repeatedly to the big, lined and sectioned, green chalk board in the OB lounge to study the condition of each patient and to determine which (if Granchard would just go home and Sato come on) might be his.

The board was chalked with the name of the patient, her room number, the time of the last examination, the name of the examiner and whether he was regular clinic or attending, remarks and medications, contractions (whether mild, moderate or strong; regular or irregular; and the frequency by minutes), the position of the fetal head (*vtx, vx*), the cephalic presentation (vertex, brow, face), the estimated fetal weight in grams (2300 to 3600 this night), the condition of the perineum, the membranes (whether *I*ntact or *R*uptured), the extent of cervical dilation (so far only 2-to-3 up to 4-to-5), the *b*lood *p*ressure of the patient, the station (numbers preceded by a plus or a minus to indicate the position above or below the ischial spines), and the position of the fetal heart (illustrated on the board by a cross representing the patient's abdomen with an *x* placed in the appropriate quadrant).

But nothing gave him any special expectancy. If the rate of contraction looked like it might pay off for him later, dilatation was too far advanced to make it seem likely that the patient would wait that long. And it was a mild evening for the labor floor—only about seven patients in various stages of labor. As long as Granchard was around, even the routine work would go to the residents on duty, and Worship, along with the other interns on call, could expect nothing but scut work.

OB—at least in Ward A—was a service at New North in which the chief resident gave the interns credit for absolutely nothing—not training, not ability (except the ability to do the most menial jobs, the jobs that any high-school graduate could do, and do well, with just two weeks of technical training . . . scut work), not even common sense.

With any, just the slightest, luck at all, Worship thought, staring at the board, I would have been assigned to B, under Kalik. Everybody worked like hell with Kalik as chief in B, but everybody got to do *everything*.

If things would just stay mild . . . If Granchard would just go home . . . If Sato would just come on . . . If a normal delivery would just develop . . . Then maybe he could find out if the damn thing could happen again . . . But Christ it couldn't keep happening . . .

Granchard, from only a pace away, yelled in his ear, "You *memorizing* that board, Worship?"

"No, no, I'm not," Worship said apologetically.

"You the fair-haired intern who's been writing up the Davis woman?"

"Yes," Worship said. "I just put her up on the board."

"And *I* just went into her room and looked at her chart. No fetal soundings."

"I just put them up on the board," Worship said.

"What am I supposed to do—walk in here every time I want to know how a patient's doing? Do me and the patient a big favor, Worship, and scribble at least *some* of your scribblings in the book. *Okay,* Worship?" he said kindly. "Now get your ass down to her room and wait for me. You might also take your pen with you and see if it still works while you're waiting. See if it works on the paper in the *chart,* Worship."

What a sense of humor, Worship thought. At the very beginning, in another service, he'd learned he had to think this way—make this kind of gratuitously degrading onslaught something to be amused by. If you didn't, your internship would likely be cut short by your sudden suicide. Even so—even getting yourself to be amused didn't quite do. Something of yourself got lost or destroyed every time; something microscopic, but something that didn't get replaced easily. Worship hoped that whatever that something was, he had enough of it to last him through his internship.

21

Granchard came in and handed Lew a prep pack—a tray of instruments wrapped in a cloth of the faded OB blue. It was marked *RM Prep* for Rupture of Membranes Prepared Package. Prepared and packed under sterile conditions and wrapped to remain sterile indefinitely, it contained the instruments and accessories necessary for the artificial rupture of membranes during prolonged labor. Prep trays of various sizes and for various procedures were to be found in almost every ward in the hospital—certain specialists even having prep trays with their own names as well as operative designations on them, these specialists demanding (and needing for their own peace of mind) a set of instruments ready at all times that varied subtly from the set normally used in the same procedures. In OB-A alone there were possibly two hundred and fifty prep trays available within a minute.

Lew held the cloth-bound prep tray and waited.

Granchard sighed. "*Open* it, Doctor. Please." Then he turned to the girl lying on the bed, her legs partially raised under the covers, her stomach making a hump even higher than the partially raised and spread legs.

"Ellen," Granchard said, "how does it feel getting ready to be a mother?"

"It's all right, Doctor."

"This is Dr. Worship."

The girl said, "Hello, Doctor," and Worship nodded to her.

"All right, now," Granchard said, drawing the covers back and down to the foot of the bed. "I'm going to help you along now so you can be a mother a little sooner than you would be if I didn't help you. Sound all right?"

"*Sounds* all right," she said, and smiled.

Granchard drew the knee-length cotton nightgown up and back until it rested above and behind the girl's distention. "Come on, Worship, the *gloves.*"

Worship had laid the open pack carefully on the other— empty—bed. He took out the paper-wrapped gloves.

"Open them, Worship, c'mon. And hold them for me."

Lew looked directly at him, as furious as he'd ever allowed himself to get at Granchard. "Dr. Granchard," he said, "perhaps you'd like the assistance of a nurse, she'd be better trained in this aspect of *operative* procedure."

"No, no, Doctor," Granchard said with surprising gentleness and mildness. "Nobody with a brain needs a nurse."

The girl giggled and Worship held a glove for Granchard, and then the second glove.

"Now, Ellen," Granchard said, turning to her, "what I'm going to do is rupture the membranes—that's the sac that has fluid in it. Then you'll be that much closer to holding your baby *outside.* I'm going to insert a long instrument, and when I tell you to, I want you to bear down to help me. The instrument is nothing to be afraid of, it's just a long knitting needle with a hook on the end to catch the sac and open it. There won't be any pain at all; you haven't got a single nerve in the membranes anywhere. All right?"

"The way you *say* it, it's all right."

"The way I say it is the way it is, Ellen. Unless you've been hiding something, you're put together the same as every other woman is and always has been."

She smiled at him, but made no further commitment.

"Okay, Dr. Worship. A little PhisoHex for our doubting patient."

Worship unscrewed the cap of a small plastic container and placed the cap on the bedside table.

"And some time *today,* please, Doctor," Granchard said.

Worship didn't even look up. He carefully poured the thickish, white-green liquid—an antiseptic disinfectant—along and around the vaginal line.

Granchard slowly inserted his right hand until it had made an opening a little larger than itself.

The girl whimpered slowly and seemed to be beginning a contraction.

"Fast, c'mon, buster, the rupturer."

Worship held it over to the resident's free left hand.

"Jesus, hand it to me by the right end!"

Worship refaced the instrument.

Granchard inserted it with his left hand, the instrument guided from within by the right hand until it was finally held and governed entirely by his right hand. "Now, Ellen, *now* bear down . . ."

The girl doubled her legs tighter, and raising herself slightly, pushed down.

"A little more, dear," Granchard said. Then the white napkins under her buttocks suddenly showed the vaguely yellowish stain of the amniotic waters. Granchard stood up. "Nothing to worry about, dear—no danger of drowning."

Worship poured some more PhisoHex, recapped the bottle, and drew the girl's nightgown down and re-covered her again.

A nurse appeared at the door. To Granchard she said, "There's a very active patient that just came in, Doctor. Two minute pains."

"Be right there," Granchard said, pulling his gloves off, throwing them into a metal receptacle in the corner, and going over to the basin to scrub. Then he said, signaling Worship out into the corridor, "Stick with her for a while, and after her next contraction, get the position of the fetal heartbeat. Get me the station, too. And time the interval between contractions."

Worship nodded.

Granchard said, "Call her by her first name, she's not married."

"What about the kid?"

"Oh she wants it, all right. She's putting it in some adoption home through some social service. Then she'll adopt it back through her parents so it'll have a legitimate name. Her parents'll sign all the papers for her."

"Yeah. I'd like to meet them . . ."

From down the corridor, the nurse called, *"The head is crowning!"*

Granchard was standing there talking to him; then Granchard was running and already paces away.

Worship lit a cigarette and then went back into the room.

22

Unless you were a patient (and therefore *desirous* of respecting him beyond the suggestion of his physical person), Lew Worship appeared to be only a somewhat gangly, medium-built young man whose cheeks were naturally a little too rosy and whose face was naturally a little too smooth. But in his eyes and in his expression, there was enough muted worry to convince anyone—even a non-patient—of a substantial amount of maturity.

The worry was a little more pronounced now as he put the contents of the prep tray back together for a nurse to have resterilized and repacked. He was going to be alone with this patient for a while, perhaps twenty minutes, and he was going to have to talk to her and comfort her and discover the things she wanted to hear and tell them to her the way she wanted to hear them.

Some of his fellow interns had gotten to be pretty fair bull artists. Actually *artists* at it. But he wasn't quite up to their level of accomplishment. At least not since he'd gotten on OB. He'd been pretty good at it in Pediatrics and in Surgery, but he had a hard time saying the right, light things to a woman in labor. He always wanted to explain the world, the whole universe to her.

And it worried him. Because it was particularly important in OB. He remembered bulling with Kalik one day and Kalik saying, "The big thing is the uncertainty of the mother. She's *always* apprehensive—no matter what the act is she puts on, and no matter how many times she's been through it before. But you've really got to watch the first-timers, the primips. The woman next to the flowerpot across the way has started talking, you know? Told her everything that can go wrong and then told her, 'But don't worry, dear. I'm sure you'll be perfectly all right, they do such marvelous things nowadays.' So, *like she isn't apprehensive?* Boy, I'll tell you she is. And you know, the best sedation you can give her—or any other patient, no matter what the service or specialty—is just plain *confidence.*" Kalik had shaken his head *Yes* several times. Then he'd said, "Like *dig?*"

He turned around and sat down on the empty bed. The girl had turned her head toward him and had been looking at him while he'd been cleaning up. She smiled at him. It was the smile of a benevolent fellow conspirator. She had already recognized, and accepted, and was pleased by their sharing an intimacy—not a physical or sexual intimacy, but an intimacy far more personal.

Yet the intimacy was as nonspecific as its physical aspects were specific. She seemed to know this too—by her look, better than he. It was as if he were the patient and she the doctor. And for a while now, until the contractions got regular and strong, every doctor would be her patient.

Worship knew it was beginning to happen again.

He hadn't looked at her before. Her face was calm and beautiful, faintly smiling, almost as if she were asleep dreaming a pleasant dream. But the lights in the room were on fully and her eyes were open and looking at him. She was a tall girl he saw, too—five five or six, her bones big, her body full enough to be handsome, as if she had been made for bearing children and smiling on them; and any man would enjoy her smiling on him too, for she'd been made for that as well . . . Christ, Worship thought, remembering what Granchard had told him of her history, she must be brave as hell.

It *was* happening again.

He started to take out his pack of cigarettes, then remembered he shouldn't smoke in front of a patient, and let the pack slip back into his pocket.

"I thought doctors had *given up* smoking," she said. "Especially cigarettes."

Lew grinned. "I know better . . . but, well . . . Anyway, I don't *prescribe* them."

"Will it be . . . soon?"

"Before Christmas, I guarantee." Christ, he thought, if you have to talk to her on that level, don't talk to her at all. She deserves more than clichés . . . and so do they all, he thought . . .

She had giggled. But now she said, with more concern than she was able to hide even under her smile, "Does it take very long? Usually? The whole thing?"

"Long enough to be interesting . . . I promise you, you won't be bored. And short enough to just cover the subject." *Christ!* he thought, furious at himself.

She giggled again, and then, still smiling, said, "I bet that's the same question all the time. And the same answer, too."

"Not all the time. Sometimes we don't like our patients. Then we don't talk to them at all. Just holler at them." *Christ!!!!* he thought desperately.

"I'm going to *try* to be good."

"You will be." And he relaxed because he had said something that was real and not just glib words, not just bull artistry.

After a pause, she said, "How do you know?"

He thought about it. *How do I know?* he asked himself. I *don't* know. But I do. But I do know. He said to her, "Because I'm a doctor." But that wasn't it. It wasn't his medical training that knew.

"*Oh,*" she cried, and then pushed herself up so that she was sitting. "Oh. It feels better this way," she told him.

"I know," Lew said. "But you ought to try to lie down and relax."

"If you want me to," she said; and eased herself down and sighed. "I'm sorry I sat up."

"Just shows how healthy your reflexes are. Sitting up's a characteristic position to avoid pain in labor." *Christ!*

"Oh," she said, beginning to breathe heavily. "*Oh,* I think I'm starting to get one. *Ohhhh!*"

Then she was quiet again and Lew uncovered her and felt her abdomen and listened to the heartbeat in it with a fetuscope and looked at his watch to find the fetal heart rate. He made his entries in the chart and said, "Ellen, I've got to go down the hall a minute to put you up on the board. I'll be right back, so don't go away."

"I'm not going anywhere," she said. She seemed pleased by this thought, and giggled.

"No, I wouldn't," Lew said. "It's a cold night outside."

"I'm sorry about being so loud complaining."

"You go right ahead, you don't become a mother every day." He stopped at the door. "If you want anything, just push that bulb."

"I know. The nurse showed me."

23

He erased some of the last notes and chalked up the new ones. Under the heading *F.W.* (for fetal weight), Granchard had chalked 3450. Just to give Granchard something to *really* annoy him (since it would be something done on purpose), Worship, in the space allotted for *Remarks,* chalked up *F.W.*: 3600—*L.W.*

Going back out to the corridor through the nurses' station, Lew said *Hi* to the night head nurse. She looked up from a furious battle with her lighter and said, "My God, I've got a patient here who can outtalk *me.*"

"I don't believe it," Lew said, and took out a book of matches from the pocket of his scrub suit and lit her cigarette for her.

"Swear to God," she said, stabbing smoke at him.

She was a pleasant-looking, plain-faced girl in her late twenties. Worship had had an instant affection for her the first time he'd met her. It was an impish look in her face, a look that suggested that if you told her to go to hell, she might just do that thing and enjoy the trip to boot.

"Slow evening," Lew said.

"I've been on OB four years," she said. "And I haven't seen a *slow* night yet. All it takes is for one good placenta praevia to walk in off the street."

"You'd scare her into place, Bobbie," Sid Glick said. Glick, another resident, leaned against the shelf desk and lit a cigarette. He was in a scrub suit and had retained his cap from the delivery room. His mask hung down on his chest, the top two strings loose and the bottom two strings holding it around his neck.

"You're not supposed to be on," Bobbie said, almost indignantly.

"We had a long one." He looked at his watch. "Three hours, plus minutes. It started ten minutes before I was supposed to go home." He sat down wearily. "Transverse lie, mother and baby are doing fine, thank you . . . The particular mother *I'm* married to, however, is probably *not* doing so fine. We're having company for dinner." He looked at his watch again. "They arrived two and a half hours ago."

"I'll call her and tell her you're a hero, you made medical history tonight, or something," Bobbie said.

"She won't believe you. She's married to me."

In the corridor again, Lew heard a woman's voice crying, "Mother, *Mother!!!!*" It wasn't Ellen's voice, but the fact didn't console him. At this stage, whoever she was, why wasn't somebody in there with her?

He followed the voice, which had now become a series of short, desperate screams. A nurse, an intern, and a resident stood by the woman's bed, the resident talking to her in an even, comforting voice, all but one small light out in the room.

The intern, Jay Fishbein, came hurrying out. "Christ," he said to Lew without stopping, *"why* are we always short of anesthetists?"

Lew went back to Ellen.

"I had another pain," she said. "Just now."

"What did it feel like? A boy or a girl?"

She giggled and sat up, but Lew eased her down again.

"A girl. A sweet little girl. I'm going to give her the starchiest, frilliest little dresses in the world."

"I hope it's a little girl, then," Lew said. "Of course, after you've been in obstetrics long enough, you discover it couldn't *possibly* be a *big* girl."

"I wouldn't mind if it's a boy. But if it's a girl, I think I could take care of her better than I could a boy. I could do things with her and dress her prettily, and I could talk to her, too . . ."

"You'll be a good mother either way, a girl *or* a boy."

"You know that because you're a doctor, I'll bet you're going to tell me." She got up on one elbow and giggled so that he had to laugh too.

"Because I'm male," he said.

"I bet you'd be a good father."

"You know, I'm beginning to think I'd like to be—a father. But right now I haven't got the time or the money. *Or* the energy." He didn't mention that he didn't have the girl either. It might hurt his status as physician with this girl. He was in love with her, of course, but it was because it was beginning to happen again, *was* happening. It seemed like she would be a girl he would enjoy talking to and having as a friend—she had such an honest, outright warmth—but . . . but his feelings showed no potential of including areas that would draw him to her as someone more than a friend.

She said, "Oh. Oh! *Ohhh!!!*" She drew her knees back tensely and put her hands over her eyes. "*Oh!* . . . Oh boy. So painful."

Lew looked at his watch.

When she was nearly calm again, she said, "I can't help it —I'm sorry—why doesn't someone start the anesthesia?"

Lew said, "It would be better if you could wait. I'd rather not give you anything till later because, you see, your contractions will be stronger this way and you'll have the baby sooner. And too, it helps the baby not to be too sedated. That way he'll—*she'll* be yelling almost before she's out."

"I'd like that," Ellen said.

"So, do you think you can be brave and take it for a while?"

She nodded *yes.*

He uncovered her, poured the antiseptic, opened a new pack of gloves and put them on.

"What's the dust on the gloves?" the girl said, watching him closely.

"That's just on the inside. See? When I put them on, that part rolls under. The dust is just talcum powder to make them slide on easily." He held up his gloved hands for her to see. "What this is, is, I'm going to reach inside you and see how wide your cervix is now and see where your baby is—roughly speaking, above the cervix or starting to come through, or even beyond it."

"You're not going to *see*," she said, moving her legs apart for him. "You're not really going to *see?*"

"Touch. The master's hands." In a moment he said, "You are, in medical jargon, *minus one.* That means your baby has moved just short of the cervix."

She sat up again. "Will it be long?"

"Anything I told you would be just a guess. Now why don't you try to lie down and rest? Maybe you can even sleep a little."

"It feels so much better sitting up . . ."

"Good," Lew said as she lay down again.

"I'm a giggler," she said.

"I've noticed."

She got up on her elbows again and couldn't keep herself from giggling, though her face, in a funny, little-girl way, showed she was trying to manage the proper decorum for a prospective mother. "But tonight I'm giggling more than I ever do."

"I wish we could inspire the humorous approach in more women." He put the chart down.

"Are you going away again?"

"I want you to rest if you can."

24

In OB-A's physicians' lounge, cap on and mask hanging down, Granchard sat on a couch, smoking and reading a magazine. The stubble of a beard was beginning to show on his face. He looked up. "Damn near all I had to do was catch it," he said. He looked back down at his magazine.

"She's having ten-minute pains," Lew said. "Moderate. She's three to four and minus one."

"Fine," Granchard said, without interest and without looking up. "Chalk it up."

Worship chalked it up and couldn't resist saying, "I put it in the chart, too."

Granchard looked up grinning. "Worship, you are, without a doubt, the orneriest goddam intern it has ever been my displeasure to come in contact with. What makes you think you've got any right to be treated different from any other intern?"

"I don't think an intern is necessarily scum," Worship said, sitting down and poking a cigarette in his mouth and talking with the unlit cigarette poking up and down in the air. "I don't think *any* intern is scum just because he's an intern."

"He *is* till he proves different, buddy, and don't you forget it. Even then, if he needs straightening out. You guys come out of med school and think you're all gods. Well nobody's a god in this racket, and it's our job, residents and attendings, to teach that to you jerks early. So you'll never forget it."

"That's a fine excuse to make little tin gods of yourselves," Worship said, the unlit cigarette still jumping up and down belligerently.

"Worship, you better learn the facts of life. On that score is there any difference between this and any other service in this hospital?"

"So what?"

"So there's also no difference between the intern's lot in this hospital and any other hospital. So *that's* what. That's the way it is," he said mildly.

"It's a crock."

"Live with it or take up a profession that puts less of a strain on your tender ego, Worship." Granchard looked down at his magazine again; then, slowly, grinning unexpectedly, looked up. "By the way, Doctor, I see you disagree with me about the probable fetal weight of a certain imminent delivery. Is that correct?"

"It is."

"Would you mind telling me how you reached this learned conclusion?"

"I looked at the mother—her size and health. I looked at the distention of her abdomen and felt it. I approximated the occipitofrontal diameter—okay, just by eye—and put all the factors together and decided it was going to be a good-sized baby even for a girl of her size."

"I see. A *truly* impressive diagnostic procedure, Doctor. In other words, you just guessed . . . I assume you considered her bone structure as well? The size and weight of the pelvic section and the spread of the hips before distention—such minor considerations as that?"

Worship hadn't really given these aspects much thought except in a cursory sort of way, but he said, "Of course."

"Of course," Granchard said mildly. "Now take my wife. She has rather narrow hips. But every so often she likes to clothe them in a new skirt. This just happens to be one of those times. I just happen as usual not to have the money. Perhaps you'd like to make a small *wager* about this fetal-weight business? Say—ten dollars, even money?"

"I only *get* forty."

"I only get a hundred and ten. And *I* have a wife and children."

"Ten bucks out of forty . . ."

"I'd considered that, Doctor . . . But for a doctor of your eminent qualifications, surely ten dollars is a *piddling* sum to wager on your own diagnosis. After all. It's a sure thing, isn't it?"

Worship eyed Granchard furiously. He said, "Okay. Ten even."

Granchard smiled malignantly at him, but in a pleasant sort of way said, "Don't fuck around with a resident, son. You'll get fucked yourself much more than you'll do any fucking."

"I'll bear it in mind."

"This sort of language is very upsetting to the Oriental affection for moderation in life," a new voice said.

"Hello, Yuky," Granchard said, his tone of voice suddenly that of a human being—as it always was when he wasn't addressing an intern.

Yukio Sato relaxed efficiently in a chair across the room. He was fresh-shaven and clean-looking in immaculate whites, his Oriental features absorbed and dissolved in his perpetual look of bemusement and intense intelligence. His eyes looked as if the intelligence behind them might burn through at any moment, destroying anything in the path of its focus. Yet clearly, Sato was among the most benign and understanding of men. Life, for him, was undoubtedly the most refreshing and interesting aspect of the universe.

He said, "What have you for me tonight?"

Granchard said, "Well, except for one case, I figure everything else is going to hold off till three or four in the morning. I can't foresee any complications with any of them. Balakian's in delivery now, and . . . uh . . . Stevens is on second call, and Bentley third, if you need them. Interns . . . Worship is here, as you can see, and Fishbein's on the floor too. The others I'm not sure about. Bobbie has the call list. Just let her know if you need more."

He looked at the clock on the wall. It said *nine.* "There's this one patient. I figure by midnight. Twenty-three years old, white, primip, overdue. She's on the board there. Ellen Davis."

Sato studied the board, then turned back to Granchard.

Granchard said, "Dr. Worship and I have a slight disagreement about the fetal weight. Otherwise I believe we're in general accord about the case. Is that correct, Doctor?"

Worship said, "That's correct, Doctor."

"Good. Then I can proceed? Thank you. A little problem with this girl. She's between a week and two weeks overdue —we can't be certain, she can't remember when she had her last period. Anyway, she started labor about seven last night. Nothing strong or regular. She wasn't sure whether it was true labor or not. But just to be safe she followed instructions and skipped breakfast except for tea."

Granchard lit a cigarette and went on. "But she's a big girl and she was famished at lunch. So she ate half a broiled chicken. That was at noon. Around three she had a peanut-butter sandwich and a glass of milk. She arrived here at seven with twenty-minute pains. But just before she left for here she managed to grab herself a little snack. Cucumbers and oil."

"A remarkable young woman," Sato commented.

"Exactly. So we have to assume a full stomach. That rules out general anesthesia. Do you know *why* that rules out general anesthesia, Dr. Worship?"

It was such a simple, basic question that Worship had no choice but to accept it as the insult it was meant to be. Therefore he attempted to treat it with humor. For himself as well as for Granchard. He replied, "Because anesthesia might make her toss her cookies, the cookies might choke her, and our statistics would suffer."

"Levity," Granchard said to Sato. "Always from Worship, levity. There might also," he said to Lew, "there might also be abdominal complications which would affect *both* mother and child. I suggest you familiarize yourself with them—unless, of course, you have already and you're just keeping it a secret." Then, back to Sato, "The only thing that saves the medical profession from anarchy is the fact that interns are only interns."

"Until they become residents and see the light," Sato said.

"Granted, granted," Granchard said unhappily. "Anyway. Full stomach, no general anesthesia. I consulted with our eminent superior, Dr. Tyssen, and he forbids a spinal."

"Dr. Tyssen trained at a time when and in a hospital where, I believe, spinals were considered highly dangerous," Sato said. "With a good deal of validity, at *that* time."

"That must have been 1860," Granchard said with disgust. "Where I trained we used nothing *but* spinals—for *every* delivery. You know, we *never*, in all the time I was there, lost a patient for any cause attributable in any way to the use of a saddle block? And we had about six hundred deliveries a month."

Worship said, "What about that girl last week? The one who went home a human vegetable."

Someone sat down next to him. He looked around. Dr. Gower Bloomberg, capped and in the green scrub suit of Surgery, his mask hanging down on his chest, was looking at him wearily, though not unpleasantly. He said, "I presume you gentlemen are discussing the Davis case?"

Bloomberg was one of New North's attending anesthesiologists. At New North's teaching affiliate, De Witt General, he was chief staff anesthesiologist for all services and an associate professor of anesthesiology at its medical school. He was also an associate staff member of at least five other major hospitals throughout the country. If Bloomberg wasn't in a hospital, he was either in a lecture room or on a plane.

Granchard said, "Yes. Dr. Tyssen has ruled against a spinal."

Bloomberg said, his southern accent soft and unexpectedly deep and melodious, "I know, I know. Someone got a cigarette? Thanks. Nasty junk, but I can't stay off them . . . Tyssen called me. Asked me to look in . . . Thanks," he said, taking a light from Worship. And to Worship, "I know something about that case you're interested in. I've been talking to most of the men involved. Saddle block anesthesia for any long OB procedure is ideal—for this Davis case, too, from what I know of it—but with this woman last week, well, there were other complications, and during delivery her heart just stopped beating. The man in charge elected to save the baby since he couldn't be sure about saving the mother. Then he went for the mother. But it was too late to salvage much of her . . .

"It was, as far as we can tell, a simple matter of not enough blood getting to the brain because she seemed spontaneously to have developed a series of emboli. The secondary result was that the action of her entire cardiovascular system was slowed and then stopped. Every indication is that the spinal could not even have contributed to the development of the emboli. Faulty administration of a spinal just doesn't take its

effect that way. And physically the mother was entirely
eligible for a spinal course.

"So, as you say, the baby was saved, but the mother left
here a human vegetable. Well, ideally, what you want is
enough men around the table so that one man can go for the
heart while the other delivers the baby. As I say, in this
case the man in charge elected to go for the baby. Under the
conditions, I believe he was right—there was no assurance
that the mother could be saved anyway. If you're interested,
come see me and I'll get the chart and we'll discuss it."

"Thanks," Worship said.

"I took a look at the Davis woman's chart, and, of course,
Tyssen briefed me," Bloomberg went on, turning back to
Granchard and Sato. "As I said, I think a spinal course
would be ideal—complete anesthesia and no danger of
abdominal upset. But this is Jack Tyssen's service and what he
says goes. I'd suggest a straight local course of anesthesia.
Pudendal block. That'll take care of the most severe pain in
the second stage of labor while delivery is actually in progress. Scopolamine and Demerol as usual during the first
stage. Much more than that I can't suggest. There just isn't
anything more that'll help her much . . . You might try Demerol intravenously once she's on the table. But I can't see
that she'll have an easy time no matter what you do working
this way. Demerol makes you feel like you're drunk and
what the hell and all that, but getting hit in the stomach
when you're drunk hurts just as bad as when you're sober."

Worship said, "What about nitrous oxide? I know it's
general, but it's awfully light stuff, isn't it?"

"No general would be light enough to be safe." Bloomberg shook his head. "Between her getting herself a full
stomach and Jack Tyssen ruling out a spinal, I'm afraid she's
just going to have a pretty rough time."

Granchard said to Sato, "Well. It's your baby."

"So to speak," Sato said. Then to Bloomberg. "A spinal
would be, as you say, ideal."

"Don't dream," Bloomberg said.

Granchard stretched and said, "I'm going home, have myself an icy cold martini, and try and make my wife pregnant again."

"How many have you got?" Bloomberg said.

Smiling like a little boy, Granchard said, "Two. A boy and
a girl."

"Well," Bloomberg said, raising an imaginary glass, "*luck*. Keep up the good work."

"My wife's beginning to think she'd have been happier with an anesthesiologist than an obstetrician."

"Undoubtedly," Bloomberg said. "I have four. Children, that is, not wives."

As he moved to the door of the locker room, with its showers, beds, lockers and toilets, Granchard said to Worship, "You see, if she's pregnant, she doesn't need any new skirts. She has a fine wardrobe of maternity outfits."

Worship thought—and didn't know what to think. Granchard disappeared through the door marked *Male Physicians*. Then he stuck his head out and said belligerently. "Ten bucks, Worship. I hope I don't have to wait till the fifteenth of the month."

Smocked, capped, and a little flushed, Bobbie came to the door of the lounge. "You know that patient I told you about who could outtalk *me* . . . ?"

"Impossible," Bloomberg said.

"Hello, Doctor," she said, smiling. "And my favorite resident, Dr. Sato," she said, going over to him and putting her hands on his head. "I just love to run my fingers through his bald scalp."

Sato slapped her behind for her.

"Be careful," she said, moving away, "My husband's decided that's valuable property."

"No one ever doubted it," Sato said.

"This patient who can outtalk *you* . . . ?" Bloomberg said.

"She just delivered. So, as usual, while we were congratulating her in the recovery room, I said to her, 'Well, *how* did it *feel* having a baby?' And you know what she said? She looked me straight in the eye and said, 'Did you ever try to shit a watermelon?' "

Sato said, "Is she married?"

Bobbie said, "I think she is."

Sato said, "Every woman I fall in love with is married already."

Bobbie said, "By the way, Suzie-Jane's been in with Ellen Davis. She says it's still ten-minute pains. That is," she said, looking menacingly into Sato and Worship, "*if* anyone's *interested*."

"I'll go look in at her right now," Sato said.

Bobbie said, "The others are covered already, Davis came in late."

"Good," Sato said. And to Worship, "Did you get dinner yet?"

"At five thirty."

"I mean have you been down to the late dinner yet?"

"No."

"Maybe now would be a good time to go," Sato said.

"All right," Lew said, getting up and stretching. "But, Yuky? I was sort of hoping she might be mine."

"Let me look at her and her chart, I'll see what I can arrange."

"Page me, hunh? If she starts soon and there's time?"

Sato looked at him closely. With a distance in his voice, he said, "We'll see." Then he nodded his head, "Yes," he said, "we'll *see*," still examining Worship with his eyes.

Bloomberg got up. "New North's food is so medically interesting, I can't resist. Besides, I haven't eaten since lunch. If I may join you, Doctor?"

Lew said, "Sure, of course," never certain when he was called *Doctor* whether it was a joke or meant seriously as a means of address.

At the elevator, Lew said, "Is she really going to have a tough time?"

Bloomberg said, "It'll be almost natural childbirth. And she hasn't done any training for it. I'm not even sure she'd be physically eligible for it if she'd *wanted* it that way."

25

John Paul Otis looked across his bourbon-and-water to another table and a girl dressed in extreme décolletage. Her skin was tanned—a tan retained or newly acquired long after the season—and she had accented it by wearing a white dress. The décolletage was so deep that it displayed her breasts below the line of the tan, the skin there whiter even than the dress and an even more startling contrast with the rest of her body than the dress was. Her breasts were so intensely white and so fully revealed that they possessed both innocence and voluptuousness at the same time, and John decided that the effect must have been studied, not accidental.

The man sitting with the girl became aware of John's stare and stopped talking and looked directly at him and waited. John smiled slightly and continued to look at the girl's breasts. The man put his cigarette down. John continued to look. The girl smiled at him slightly. The man continued to look at John and then failed to make any decision and then uncomfortably turned away, angling his chair so that he could not easily see John watching.

The girl sitting next to John said, "She's exquisite." John nodded without changing the direction of his look. It was an observation. The girl sitting next to him was saying nothing about his looking at the other girl.

She was exquisite, exactly; but he was interested only theoretically—as he might be by a girl in a painting. The girl sitting next to him inured him to the other girl, inured him to any stimulation which did not find *her* as its object. So, he felt only impatience to leave this place and get where he could undress the girl that sat beside him. Yet he didn't feel that he was aroused at all, merely impatient, as the heart is to beat, or the mind to occupy itself, or the eyes to see.

He had, earlier, been drinking Scotch. Scotch was his drink. But when he was with this girl, he drank her drink; had habituated himself to it. That is, bourbon. Because he wanted to be like her? Because he wanted to have things in common with her? Because he wanted to appear to her to share the same tastes? Because it was simpler not to admit of any dissimilarity between them?

He didn't know, and he didn't care, and he felt only that it was strange that he didn't care about not caring.

He did not need to look at her to see her. She hardly displayed herself like the girl at the other table. But he saw the nervous, self-aware glances men gave her—looked at her, looked back at their own women, made conversation, laughed, looked serious, ordered drinks, and always, always looked back again.

It gave him no thrill, provided no nourishment for his pride. He knew these men and their looks as he knew himself. He was the man across the room who *got* to sit with this girl; who fondled her and made love to her. He felt it was sufferance on her part that had done it.

"I'd like another drink," she said. Yes, of course, he told her and signaled the waiter, and then she said, "No, the check, I forgot." Forgot what? he asked her. "The money situation," she said. Oh we've got that all fixed up, he told her. "Still?" He told her they'd been pretty careful. "That's true," she said. When the waiter came, he made a circular motion over their glasses. Again, she said, "That *is* a beautiful girl you're looking at." Again, the interesting thing was, she meant it entirely without censure. The remark had no further significance than that the girl he was looking at was, in another woman's opinion, beautiful. He was looking at the other girl, the white décolletage, the lushness of the breasts rising from it, and still without interest; it was the girl next to him who was exciting him; was, in fact, stimulating him to look at this other girl in order to keep his desire under control, the desire he knew would mount in its own desire to express itself if he gave it the opportunity. Mount uncomfortably. And he did not want it to be so for the time being. He did not want to call the evening off too early by taking the girl next to him home to bed now. That would leave too much time unaccounted for—time when, later, they would only sleep, and, thus, time that would disappear with no value received that he could retain consciously, and, therefore, time that had not existed that could have.

He had met her at a party. That was when he had learned about the choking sensation, and seen it work in other men at the party. They had each stayed late, along with the hard drinkers and the serious talkers and the men doing business and the women admiring their lipstick marks on their glasses and the singer from the show who had stopped singing and begun playing the piano *quietly,* and along with the host's shirt-sleeved gin game in the corner and the writer who had gone noisily asleep on the stairs to the second floor of the duplex, and among the empty glasses and half-filled glasses the maid wasn't bothering to take away any more because she had gone to bed, and among the smelly smoldering cigarette butts the maid wasn't bothering to empty from the ashtray any more because she had gone to bed, and with the lights mostly turned off except where they'd been pulled up and turned on high and brilliant around the gin game so that the cigar and cigarette smoke could be seen billowing around the light fixtures, making it seem like the whole apartment was in the first stages of devastation by fire. The host and his partners were playing gin at a dollar a point, he had heard. Among and along with all that, they had stayed. And had each gotten very drunk. And he had noticed that though the rest of him had become almost numb from the drinking, the choking sensation had not been dulled at all, had remained constant at what he had first thought must have been a peak of some sort.

Sitting on the floor in the dark in a corner next to a hi-fi speaker that was carrying a record in competition (though equally quietly) with the singer who was playing the piano, she had said to him, getting even tighter from laughing so much, "Are you really a doctor?" and he had assured her that really he was and she had said, "That's very funny. Because, you know what? I'm pregnant and I'm not married, and maybe you could do something about it." He had laughed and said, yes, there was something he could do about it, he could marry her. "Something more practical, darling." He had asked her if she'd tried falling down stairs or anything like that. She said, "You wouldn't like me to, would you?" She had been serious. Everything had been serious, really, he realized, the realization not at all new. He'd said, no, he wouldn't like her to. "What then?" He didn't know.

26

Because New North was a city hospital, all meals there were free. On the theory, perhaps, that since interns and residents got no sleep, but had to live on *something* (if only nutriment energy), there were as many helpings available as were desired.

Lew picked up a tray and silver and slid the tray along to the steam table. They were serving the leftovers from lunch and dinner. The sight of the meat loaf almost ruined his appetite, and the look of the stew from lunch was equally ghastly. So he had his plate piled with two kinds of potatoes and four kinds of vegetables, picked up a salad and two half pints of milk, and sat down with Bloomberg.

Bloomberg said in disbelief, "You intending to *eat* all that?"

"No. I just take a little of everything. It lends variety to an increasingly vegetarian diet."

"I see."

"You know the morgue's right next door to the kitchen?"

"I didn't know," Bloomberg said warily.

"I've always felt there was a causal relationship."

"Doctor, if you don't mind, I've had a difficult day."

They began to eat.

A resident, Chuck Stein, whom Lew knew from Surgery, came over carrying a tray and sat down with them. On the tray were two cups of black coffee and nothing else. He was still, like Bloomberg, in his green scrub suit.

He looked belligerently at both of them and announced, as if he disbelieved it himself, "You know I just assisted at an emergency abdominal section? You know the guy I assisted—who shall remain nameless—cut a few too many bleeders? You know he started calling me *kike* and *yid?*"

"So?" said Bloomberg.

"SO? So *nothing*! The shit."

"Exactly," Bloomberg said pleasantly. "There are people, and there are people who aren't such people."

Stein slammed his cup down, sloshing coffee into the saucer and onto the tray. Lew felt embarrassed, as if he were an unwilling eavesdropper. Stein said, "You mean that kind of thing doesn't make you mad?"

"What'd you do about it?" Bloomberg said pleasantly, continuing to eat.

"DO? *Do?* What could I do? I was assisting the bastard. So I assisted him."

"All right. Drink your coffee."

Stein, who had been raising the scalding black liquid to his lips again, slammed the cup down again, spattering himself and half the table around him. "Drink my coffee, he says," he said to Lew. "Drink my coffee!"

"Or go slug the man," Bloomberg said equably.

"Oh boy," Stein said. "I thought you were a Jew. Now I find out you're a psychiatric case, you've been breathing too much of your own dream stuff."

Bloomberg had finished eating. He turned full face to Stein. "You didn't do anything, right?"

"Yeah?"

"Is this the first time you've run into this sort of thing?"

"Hell no! Listen, I had some of the highest marks in my

class in college. And you know what? Three med schools in
the East refused to even grant me an interview. I wrote to
find out if they'd gotten my application, and they said yes,
they had. Period. That was all. I never even got invited for
an interview!"

"You know, med schools try to diversify themselves nowadays. Okay, they take in a certain percentage of Jews. They
take in a certain percent of Presbyterians and Episcopalians
and . . ."

"A goddam *larger* percentage!"

"Granted. But you're from New York. They have hun-
dreds of applicants from New York. That's two percentages
they try to limit in order to diversify themselves. And you
fell into both of them."

"That's a pretty cruddy excuse. I'll lay you odds there were
very few *applicants*"—and he made the word sound like
something nasty—"very few *applicants,* as you say, who had
better marks than I did. Sure as hell not enough of them to
make up a whole class!"

Bloomberg said equably, "Chuck, assuming these were
sound institutions, they have a number of pressures on them.
From legislatures or horny old trustees or whatever. Those're
the facts of life. Now, assuming they are also possessed of a
conscience, they might have turned you down just *because*
your record was so good. If they had to turn anyone down
due to these outside pressures, they'd automatically turn
down the man they *knew* could place himself."

"That logic can lead to the ghettos."

"It's not that logic, it's the pressures that induce it. And I
have every confidence that these pressures are gradually being reduced."

Somewhat mollified, Stein said, "I still say a man ought
to be judged on his record."

"And so he should."

"Well, something oughta be done," Chuck said, mollified
but still trying to express anger that had been unexpectedly
undermined.

"There's only one thing to do," Bloomberg said. "It's the
same way that's always been open—since as far back as
there was history of this sort of thing. The only way. You've
just got to be a little bit better than the next man."

Going out to the elevator and back up to the labor floor,

Lew felt that what he took from Granchard and most of the others wasn't so bad after all. Not compared to that. *The only way open is to be a little bit better than the next man.* But being a little bit better hadn't helped Chuck to get into some med schools. And there were hospitals—some good ones, Lew knew—that never allowed a Jewish physician on their staffs. Jay Fishbein had probably run into that. And he knew for a fact (he had seen the indirect, but plainly worded letters Jim had gotten as replies to applications) that Jim Aptshult had already been turned down for two residencies even before the deadline for application for those residencies had come up.

Well, he thought, getting out of the elevator, at least I don't have to buck being Jewish. He smiled. And Chuck and Jim and Jay probably figure, at least I don't have to buck being Negro.

That's one helluva consolation all around, he thought.

27

"Just in time," Suzie-Jane said. "New admission and everybody's busy. Thirty-minute pains." She led him down the corridor.

"Ellen Davis?" Lew said.

"She's being faithful to you. Wouldn't have her baby even for Dr. Sato till you got back. He says look at this new one and wait for him in the lounge. A thirty-two-year-old P.R. multip."

Outside the door to the new admission's room, she turned to him partly and said, "She hasn't been shaved yet."

"Oh God. Another independent type."

"Till it gets time to go to the delivery room," Suzie-Jane said.

"Well, let's look at her, then get someone in here . . . I suppose the someone is me?"

"Right."

"Wonderful."

"That's what you get for being an intern."

She led him into the patient's room. The patient was standing uncertainly by her bed. Suzie-Jane said, "Get into bed, dear." The patient, a passive but uncertain-looking woman, climbed into the bed and pulled the covers up over herself to her neck. Suzie-Jane said, "This is Dr. Worship, Mrs. Ramonez, he's been waiting for you."

The woman nodded at Lew.

"How do you feel, Mrs. Ramonez?" Lew said, picking up her chart. "Feel like having a baby?" he said, looking back up at her.

"No hablo inglés muy bien," the woman said.

Lew felt a certain amount of new, or *extra,* confidence with the patient. It was regrettable that he didn't speak her language. But the deficiency had its compensations. He wouldn't have to be maintaining two statuses at once—the status of doctor and the status of person, of friend—as he had to with Ellen. He wouldn't have to offer her the bull and clichés that misrepresented him both as a doctor and as a person.

For him, that necessity of always maintaining the two statuses simultaneously was the most difficult aspect of being a doctor: being a person as well as a doctor without overcommitting himself as a person. The fear of overcommitment of the person at the expense of the physician often made it difficult for him to establish any tenable rapport with the patient. In this case, because of the language barrier, the problem would not exist—he could just be a doctor. With Ellen, the problem existed severalfold because the warmth of her personality made it dangerously difficult first not to overcommit himself as a person to her and second not to (out of fear of overcommitment) *under*commit himself to her.

He sent Suzie-Jane off for the necessary instruments.

When he went through the nurses' station to return to the lounge, Bobbie said, "Dr. Sato said you're going to have a baby and wait for him in the lounge."

"If you want to make a note of it, I started the work-up on Mrs. Ramonez and she voided."

"On behalf of the nursing staff, Doctor, I thank you."

In his locker he had a couple of books he ought to be reading during spare moments like these in order to prepare himself for the oral examination by the National Medical Board he would be having at the end of his internship. But it was too comfortable just to sit and not move . . .

. . . open doorway to the nurses' station, open doorway to the delivery rooms, closed door marked *Male Physicians* to lockers, cubicles with beds, showers and all (a shower would feel pretty good, wouldn't it? need a shave, too—rubbing his hand over his face), tables, chairs in blond battered wood (a new school of furniture design, no doubt, *battered*), a radio its plastic case cracked, telephone books city and hospital, telephones two on a table, model of torso in delivery—a removable pelvic section lying irreverently in a chair, soundproof ceilings as throughout the hospital, pale green ceramic-brick walls as throughout the hospital (sanitary as hell and much easier to clean), fluorescent lights, clock on wall, one window looking down a dismal alley to sootstained dark house fronts . . . his eyes beginning to close, his mind thinking about a shower and a steak and maybe twenty hours' sleep . . .

"Good dinner?" Sato said.

"Lousy. I ate vegetables."

Sato sat down. "I gave your patient one minim of pitocin intramuscularly, the shoulder, at nine fifteen. That should encourage some contractions, don't you think? We'll take a look at her, and if she's coming along, we'll try two minims I.M. again," Sato said, explaining everything very basically, but somehow not offensively, not gratuitously.

"Maybe we ought to give her scopolamine soon. I mean, she's going to have such a rough time, it'd be nice if she couldn't remember any of it . . ." remembering the woman who had said, *It's so strange and wonderful, Doctor. You're divorced from your own agony, as if you were standing on the other side of the room watching yourself. And you can't remember anything but that sensation afterwards. No details, no pain, nothing but that sensation* . . .

Scopolamine being standard procedure, it was only a question of when it was to be administered, a question of when its occasionally depressant effect on the uterine contractions would be least damaging to the strength of the contractions. Lew was quite aware of this, but he wanted the drug for Ellen because of its analgesic qualities and its ability to induce amnesia. So that Ellen wouldn't remember when she thought about a second time. Because he thought she ought to have a second time . . .

Sato had been looking at him, the fierce quality of his eyes focused on Lew intently. As if Lew had been thinking out loud, Sato said, "But remember how scopolamine would excite her. She'd be sitting up all the time. We'd probably have to hold her down long before she's ready to deliver."

"I'd still like her to have it now."

And in that strangely distant voice he'd used before, Sato said, "We'll see. We'll look at her. If pitting her is work, we'll give her the scopolamine and try to balance it with Demerol."

Lew nodded. That would be fine. The Demerol would help check the excitement provoked by the scopolamine; and its analgesic qualities would help, just a little, to relieve some of Ellen's pain; and, of course, it would sedate . . . But he knew, also, that nothing was going to help Ellen very much. Nothing that was available to her.

"Come along," Sato said.

The lights in her room had been turned out except for one small lamp. Lew remembered his own room looking that way when he was a child and sick. Bobbie was standing by the bed.

Ellen was crying when they came in—crying, struggling to hold her own voice, and then unable to struggle, "OHHHH! Help me! Get him out!" her voice both accusing and involuntary.

Then she relaxed and Sato drew back the covers and Lew disinfected her and Sato began another examination. He said, "I think there's a baby in there. I think he wants to come out soon."

When she had relaxed, she said to Lew, "I remember you. You're my doctor. One of my doctors. I have so many doctors now." Then she turned her head to Sato. "I'm sorry I'm being so much trouble."

"What we can deal with is not trouble," Sato said, smiling. "And we are only *assisting* you."

She said, her voice changing suddenly, her voice quieter but sharper, "Oh God Oh—Go away!" and tried to sit up.

Sato held her gently back down to the pillow. "Lie down now. You'll help assist yourself."

"All right," she said. "I'm so much trouble."

Sato said to Bobbie, "Stay with her please, Nurse," and took Lew by the arm and out of the room. "Soon," he said. "Come."

They went to the nurses' station and Sato filled two hypodermic syringes. "You may have the pleasure of administering the scopolamine and Demerol," he said, smiling, and presenting the single syringe containing both to Lew.

"Thank you," Lew said.

"Don't thank me. Thank your patient. She's the one who manages the condition that makes it possible."

Half an hour after the injections had been given, they returned to her, the room still black except for the one small light, Bobbie sitting on a chair at the foot of the bed. Bobbie said, "She stands on her head with every contraction."

The girl began to thrash. "Take deep breaths," Sato said, leaning close to her.

"*Ohhhh!*" she screamed. "Help me! Please help me! Get him *OUT!!!*" the last word more a scream than a word.

Bobbie had put the sides of the bed up.

"Deep breaths," Sato said.

The girl said, quieter now, "Oh but it hurts so."

"Deep breaths."

After a moment she sat up, dull-eyed and woozy from sedation—a little girl suddenly awakened by adults during the night, not understanding why, sitting up on her bed with the covers thrown off, her legs tucked apart and to the side, her nightgown all over her at funny angles. All make-up had disappeared from her face, and her face had become more that of a child than of a woman, a wet forelock hanging down and her eyes not understanding but wanting so hard to understand, through the wooziness, through the sedation—helpless, a child like the child inside her. Lew thought, She'll see her child like this so many times, and never know it's her . . .

They gave her the injections of pitocin, and of Demerol and scopolamine. Then she lay down, Lew guiding her shoulders.

Sato left. Lew said to Bobbie, in a whisper, "Call us."

Bobbie looked disgusted. "No. I'm going to keep it a secret."

"I'll go check Mrs. Ramonez," Lew said to Sato in the corridor.

"I have Fishbein watching her. He's reporting to Mason."

"Oh."

"I think I'll make a call."

"Well, I'll stay inside awhile."

She had just finished a contraction again. "How often?" Lew said.

"About three minutes now."

The girl was asleep. At least, her eyes were closed and her

face was relaxed, composed, as if with some strange far-distant thought.

Bobbie signaled him to bend down to her. "Don't look so solemn," she whispered. "It's a baby, it's got to come out. Right?"

He laughed and straightened up. "It's a baby, it's got to come out," he agreed.

"Go call your girl friend, like Dr. Sato. Obviously we need the business."

Sato was saying into the telephone, a great pleasant knowing grin on his face and a uniquely modest tone to his voice, ". . . patients screaming, nurses screaming, interns running all over—like a warfield . . . Yes, but I have excellent colleagues to assist me. They mask my blunders . . . Oh yes, you're right . . ." There was a long pause. "Well, one of these Saturdays. But things are so difficult. Other people tell me when to get up, when to go to bed . . . Yes, one of these Saturdays. I'll call you soon without fail."

Sato hung up. He said to Lew, almost reverently, "I wish I had time for every woman in the world." Then, in an unexpectedly sharp voice, he said, "*Woman*, I said. Not girls."

"Right," Lew said. He began to light a cigarette.

Bobbie ran in. *"We're going to have a baby!"*

Lew dropped the unlit cigarette and the unopened book of matches on the floor and ran.

28

Another nurse—Phyllis—had already come in to help move the rolling bed. Lew helped them get it through the door and started down toward the delivery rooms. Then, hearing the girl crying, sobbing, "Help me, help me *please* . . ." pleading through her pain, he hurried ahead to the scrub room. Sato was already at work on himself.

From the boxed shelf over the scrub sink, Lew took a mask and tied the two sets of strings until the mask was drawn tight across the bridge of his nose and below his chin. Then a cap, pulled down almost to the last of the hair on the back of his head, and tied behind . . . Methodically, he poured some antiseptic sudsing detergent on his hands. Then, count-

ing *one one thousand, two one thousand* he began scrubbing
with a brush, every so often letting a few drops of water fall
on his skin, thinking, half a minute here, scrubbing, half a
minute, thirty seconds, *thirty one thousand* just as the clock
indicated it . . . Then he rinsed, wet his arms almost their
full length, poured more of the detergent, and worked up a
lather even above his elbows, watching the clock, two minutes
here, two minutes for this part, two minutes, getting the brush
down to his closely trimmed nails again and in the spaces
between his fingers, his eye on the clock, two, minutes, two,
minutes . . . then rinsing and grabbing a sterile towel and
quickly, but methodically and efficiently, drying himself.

He hurriedly went through the glass door into the delivery
room. Sato was already inside, saying to the girl as she lay on
the roller bed beside the delivery table, "Move one leg over
. . . That's it . . . Now the other . . . Now slide yourself
over. . ." Bobbie already beginning to secure the girl's arms
with leather straps while Phyllis raised first one leg and then
the other and buckled the girl's calves into the raised metal
braces that kept the legs high and apart . . .

Lew felt again reassured—with her weight on them the
girl's buttocks were still quite full and developed enough to
show a line an inch above the table before the now weightless
legs began. Every woman ought to have buttocks like that, he
unthinkingly thought as he offered a glove to Sato . . .

Sato, already gloved and gowned, shook his head and nodded down. He was holding a glove for Lew. Bobbie came
around and held a gown for him and tied it. Then he
stretched into one glove and then the other and then rolled the
cuff of each up over the cuff of each sleeve of the gown . . .

The anesthetist, another young resident—masked and
capped, but not gowned—sat at the head of the table, his
equipment, a standing box with lights and dials, next to him,
a mask in his hand, several tubes and wires from the box now
attached to the patient. He looked up questioningly from behind his own mask. His presence was so usual that no one
had seen him, nor did they notice him now.

The girl screamed.

Bobbie said, "It ought to be a *big* bouncing baby."

Sato said, "We'll see soon, I guarantee."

Phyllis said, "If it's a baby, it's got to come out." She,
Bobbie, the anesthetist, and even Sato laughed.

The girl screamed again. "Help me. Please! PLEEEEASE!!!!"

"It's all right, dear," the anesthetist said. "We're going to help you."

"Oh, thank you, THAAAAANK *you*," she said, her voice becoming involuntarily loud from the pain of a contraction.

"Now breathe deeply whenever I put the mask on your face."

"Oh thank you," she said in a gasp.

The anesthetist moved around to where he could touch and feel whenever a contraction was beginning, before the girl herself would even know, and from where he could put the mask on too.

Sato said, "Breathe deep and push, Ellen." Then, "Take deep breaths."

Her screams became partly muffled as the mask was put on. When it was taken off she was quiet.

Sterile towels were laid on her abdomen. Bobbie had wheeled the instrument table up next to the high stool placed at the end of the table between the girl's uptilted legs. Lew unwrapped the prep tray and laid the various instruments out in order while Sato flung out and open a pale blue sheet with a large hole in the center. The hole exposed the obstetrician's working area.

The girl's legs stretched out rigidly at short intervals, her feet shaking frantically. But there were no sounds. The anesthetist had the mask on her before she could feel the pain that ultimately expressed itself, for an instant, through her legs—and then withdrew, allowing the legs to relax as she passed out.

The door to the delivery room opened and Bloomberg came in. "Dick. Take the mask off her."

The anesthetist looked up bewildered, but complied.

"That nitrous oxide?"

"Yes sir."

Sato and Worship looked up from their end of the table, surprised by the presence of another voice, surprised to see the anesthetist with a mask in his hand.

"Just keep a watch on the B.P. if you will," Sato said.

The girl screamed sharply twice. "Please somebody help me I'm in terrible PAAAAAin."

Bloomberg, tonelessly loud and deliberate, said, "This

could have been avoided with a spinal." He looked angrily at the table and the girl on it and then withdrew.

Sato handed Lew a syringe with a three-inch, twenty-gauge needle. It contained a local anesthetic for the pudendal area, a pudendal block. Lew presented the needle just below the labia, narrowly aside from an imaginary line from the anus to the vagina.

Sato said, "Aspirate."

The syringe had three circles of metal with which to hold it—one on each side and one on the head of the plunger. Lew, with an upward motion of his thumb, withdrew the plunger slightly while leaving the needle in its position. No blood showed in the contents of the syringe. He therefore hadn't entered a vein.

"Good," Sato said.

Lew introduced a quarter of the syringe's contents, withdrew the needle slightly, redirected and reintroduced it slightly, aspirated again, introduced a quarter of the syringe's contents again, and repeated the procedure twice more. Then he introduced a catheter and voided the girl.

"Again good," Sato said. He had clipped a number of instruments to a second series of white sterile towels laid across the girl's abdomen on the sheet that covered it.

"HELP!" the girl cried. "Oh God, *G-OD!!!!*"

"You're doing very well," Bobbie said to her.

Phyllis said, "Mrs., it'll be over in just a few minutes and you'll have your baby."

"I'm not married," the girl said, as if she were sitting across a table in Schrafft's discussing the weather.

Phyllis said, "That don't make *no* difference, it don't take no longer."

The girl screamed. The anesthetist looked up from his dials, hurt, as if he were going to be sick. But he remained silent and turned back to the dials.

Lew said, "I just gave you something that'll take care of a lot of the pain, dear."

"Oh, tha-*ANK YOU* . . . You've been so good and I've been so BAAAAAD!"

Lew hoped the pain would pass her out. He stood back behind Sato, his arms raised up and out from himself, his hands loose and away from his body in an almost effeminate gesture of watchfulness and waiting. She screamed again.

Sato completed his examination and looked up. "Straighta-way. Very good, very good." His voice seemed to have come from a smile.

The girl's legs went rigid and then her feet shook violently as she cried out, the voice much more desperate now that the nitrous oxide had been taken away from her.

Sato said to Phyllis, "Demerol, fifty mgm., I.V."

Phyllis went to a shelf and took down a bottle while Bobbie readied an arm for the intravenous drip.

"Ohhhhh*hhhhhhh!!!!* Oh God, oh God . . ." And then, in a quiet, as if quietly crying, voice, *"I knew I'd never live . . . Ohhhhhhhh!"*

They had been in the delivery room for twelve minutes.

29

Everything the girl said came out as if between parentheses. She—the part of her that spoke—had ceased to be reality. Reality was the structure around her—the self of her that was delivering a child and those who were attending upon that self that was delivering. The great, round, slightly tilted light over the end of the table, with its glareless green frosted lens that somehow produced only white light, had more reality than that part of her which cried out or spoke.

Earlier, Lew had had the thought that a woman in labor be-lieves only in the future, and the future is something which she feels does not necessarily include herself. He had had the thought many times, seen representations of its validity many times, and it had always moved and impressed him. Yet, in spite of this, he had long since ceased contact with that part of the woman which minutes before had been a tired and be-wildered little girl—that part of her which cried out and spoke and pleaded for help. The tired, bewildered little girl had been all of reality only fifteen minutes before. Now she no longer existed at all.

New North believed in prophylactic forceps—that is, the assistance of the actual delivery of the child by means often quicker and more comfortable and less dangerous than those which the mother could provide for herself under the most optimum of conditions, the forceps also preventing the child's head from being jammed against the perineal area and thereby suffering.

Lew held the forceps—gleaming steel and fabricated handles which themselves seemed alive and possessed of life. He wasn't a worshiper of knives or of anything of a surgical nature just because it was surgical or of a surgical nature. Such instruments held no mystical significance for him. But these—the forceps—were different for him. Perfectly made and balanced, a strong, supple feel to them, they seemed perfect instruments, embodiment of perfection, perfectly shaped in two directions at once in the blade ends, shaped up and down to fit the vaginal wall and shaped lengthwise in an angled curve to fit the head of the child . . . These, unlike knives, could be respected for what they were and for what they could do rather than for some implicit danger they contained—even though that danger was benign and usually dormant in a knife, any knife, surgical or not. But these were *only* benign, *only* capable of beauty—unless they were used stupidly or bludgeonly; and then, of course, anything could become a danger.

The girl had quieted, had perhaps fallen into seminarcosis from the Demerol and scopolamine.

Lew inserted his right hand with its back against the vaginal wall. With his left hand he took one of the blades from Sato and inserted it, running it along and against the palm of his right hand, letting his hand guide and cup it away from both mother and child.

"Light, very light," Sato said gently. "Don't force it, no forcing . . ."

Lew removed his hand, repeated the procedure, slowly, carefully, almost motionlessly, by feel and not by eye, with his *left* hand this time inserted. Then he joined and locked the two stems to form the forceps.

Next he took a scissors from Sato and cut down in a straight line from the vagina through the perineum. At New North episiotomies were also a regular procedure, on the theory that renting of the perineum was almost unavoidable in delivery and that it was of advantage to both patient and doctor that the line be a straight one, and therefore easier to suture than a jagged one. This also avoided the likelihood, after healing, of potentially dangerous perineal weakness. So, concentrating on the episiotomy, Lew had divorced himself from even the *memory* that the tired, bewildered little girl had ever existed. Without ever even having to will it consciously, the little girl had not only ceased to exist, but had ceased *ever* to have existed. Reality—immediate reality—denied by its immediacy even the possibility that the little girl had ever existed, much less could be existent simultaneously with either immediacy or the nature of this reality.

He noticed, but did not register, the first blood he had seen so far. It was no more than a not yet entirely congealed run along the perineum and a streak on the white cloth coming out from under the girl's buttocks and hanging down from the edge of the table. He didn't even register that it was blood because it betokened no danger. It was not blood, but an expected by-product of the episiotomy and therefore of no significance. Thus, his eye noticed it, but his brain did not.

She seemed to have lost all her strength, even the strength to cry out, even the strength to articulate at all, even the *will* to do either. Instead, she mumbled, her tongue no longer bothering to move enough to help shape her words—as if she had drunk much too much and was slowly passing out while talking. Occasionally she managed a barely audible, barely articulated phrase. She was saying, ". . . knew I'd be lost . . . *oh please*"—quietly, and begging without the strength even to sob—*"please* help me because I can't . . . take . . . much more . . ."

The voice went away, went some far distance away, and no one noticed its silence. Then, as if it were trying to get back from way far away, it said, "Please, somebody wipe my lips . . . ?"

Bobbie took a sterile cloth and touched it to the girl's lips. "There, dear, there. You're doing beautifully."

"Very good," Sato said to Lew. "Beautiful."

Lew began moving, barely moving, manipulating through the live handles, the forceps.

"Don't pull," Sato said gently. "Don't pull . . . *draw* . . . yes, *draw* . . ."

The crown of the head—as if a wet plastic coat lay over it and over some minute, startlingly black lines—filled the space that was the distended vagina and perineum. The minute, startlingly black lines suddenly could be seen to be hair.

Lew watched and moved gently, drawing almost motionlessly . . . He had absolved himself of time, of living, of everything but doing . . . doing almost motionlessly . . . and watching, watching . . .

Sato said, "Now a little help for the shoulder . . ."

Then Sato had taken the forceps and Lew was holding the baby head down by the feet—the baby so light he thought he'd dropped it, so heavy he thought he might—and Sato had cut and tied the cord and the baby was yelling, crying with more fury and indignation and righteousness and plain orneriness than she would ever again be able to allow herself.

"If you have a mother who can take it," Sato said with respect, "not giving a general anesthesia will give you spontaneous respiration every time."

Bobbie took the child.

"Spontaneous respiration, Doctor," Sato said. "You should be very proud."

"Let me *see* . . . Let me see my beautiful baby!"

"Congratulations," Bobbie said, holding the baby for her to see.

"Oh, isn't it wonderful," the girl said, crying now with tears. "Isn't it wonderful?"

"Everything's fine now," Bobbie said.

"Oh I know; you're all so wonderful." She looked as Bobbie held the baby up.

"A girl," Bobbie said. "A tiny little girl."

"Oh," Ellen said, crying harder, and smiling, and crying harder still. ". . . how happy I feel . . . I always knew it was a girl."

"Like natural childbirth," Sato said.

Lew delivered the placenta, poured antiseptic, and after Sato had examined and placed the placenta aside, began suturing the perineum.

"Almost a natural childbirth," Sato said to the mother.

"Relax," Lew said, "I want to sew you up."

"Oh, isn't she beautiful!" she said, trying terribly hard now. "Oh sweetheart, oh my baby," only her head able to move, her arms strapped and unable to reach out to the baby girl the nurse was holding up squalling by the side of the table.

"Relax, dear," Lew said.

"What's wrong with her head?"

"She's dirty from the table," Bobby said, carrying the baby over to the readied, sloping, V-shaped receptacle.

"What are you doing to her?" the girl said through her crying, turning her head to see.

"We're just putting a few drops in her eyes," Phyllis said, "so she'll have good shiny eyes always,"—Bobbie dropping into the infant's eyes the solution prescribed by state law in all births in order to prevent the child's eyes from contracting gonococcal infection that might have been picked up, if present, on the way through the birth canal.

"There," Bobbie said, "*there* punkin, there sweetheart," carrying the baby down to the foot of the table as Sato gave the girl an ergot injection to keep the uterus contracted and help prevent hemorrhage.

Lew didn't look up. Bobbie said to Sato, holding up the baby, "I see so many of them"—and very seriously—"but they're all so cute."

Sato said, "One moment," and Lew withdrew his hands while Sato dried the vaginal area with towels and poured more antiseptic. Lew held his hands out and away from his body, again in the effeminate gesture of waiting, and noticed for the first time ever how brilliantly yellow his gloves were under the light.

Sato said, "I'll break more stitches." Phyllis was given the baby and took it out to the nursery. Lew continued to suture. They had been in the delivery room for twenty-one minutes.

Bobbie said, "How can you see through those glasses, they're so dusty?"

Lew said, suturing, "They are not."

"I can see the dust from here."

"Do you know what her name is?" Ellen said.

"No," Bobbie said. "What's her name?"

"Sylvia."

"That's a beautiful name."

The suturing continued. The girl had fallen asleep.

Suture. Sponge. Suture. Sponge.

Phyllis came in beaming. "*Thirty-six sixty-five.* Your baby weighed eight-one; eight pounds, one ounce."

"*Oh*," the girl said, waking, "oh, how perfect that is," and began to cry again.

Worship looked up grinning. "How do you like that? Only sixty-five off. Pretty good, hunh?"

Bobbie said, "Dr. Worship, I believe Dr. Granchard is likely to chew your tail worse than ever."

The anesthetist left. Occasionally Sato and Worship exchanged remarks. The nurses carried on a full conversation, and every so often, when the girl became wakeful, comforted her without even really noticing that they were speaking to her. But the girl had now fallen into sleep almost entirely, a mild snoring passing from her lips. Sato was saying, "Gut at the edge, small, bite small, take small bites . . ."

Lew began tying the sutures—they would never have to be removed, being made of a thread that eventually allowed itself to be absorbed. Tying—a long pull, holding the thread with the scissors, then wrapping the thread around the scissors, then in again and tie . . . Over and over . . .

The girl awoke and said, "My mother told me they came very fast for her," then went back to sleep. Ever so often her legs extended, became rigid again and shook within the braces. Then Sato placed a hand gently on one leg and both legs gradually relaxed.

She woke again. "Everything's over," Bobbie said. She slept again.

Lew completed the last tie.

Sato nodded approvingly. "Beautiful."

"Come look, Bobbie," Lew said, casting away what had been an absolution from time.

"I've seen . . ."

"I don't do so many you can't take a look."

Phyllis said, looking, "Isn't that nice?"

Bobbie came over. "Yes, sweets, it's beautiful," she said and tousled his hair through his cap . . .

. . . Sato stood back and allowed himself, and Worship, the slightest of smiles. He looked at Worship more closely, intently, studied the intern's euphoria; but the object of his attention was not Worship, but a little boy—how old had he been? nine? ten? it was so many years—transfixed with both horror and fear, and an old woman, so old, in fact, she was hardly able to move at all. And there was another figure: a young woman in the agony of labor, no one to assist her, screaming at him to help, please, many times, help . . .

He had known the young woman all his life. He could recognize that this was her. But it was not her. She was nothing of his world. She was a threat. He had almost run from her. But the old woman's voice addressed him, unexcited, calming him, telling him what to do . . .

He had done it. And the child had been born alive and the mother had become suddenly, happily and tearfully, again the young woman he had known all his life. Then the little boy had stood in the center of the room and also cried—cried with such intense happiness he thought he would never cease crying. And then the old woman had laughed at him and complimented him and laughed more and told him more things to do.

The boy had gotten himself, through many difficulties and among many difficult people, into and through school, and college, and then to America for medical school and internship and residency until such time as he could return to Japan and try to lessen the incidence of deliveries assisted only by an old woman and a frightened boy.

The boy had experienced that intense happiness more than several hundred times since. It had not changed at all. The desire to cry had never been stilled. Nothing had changed from the boy's original experience except that the doctor who had been the boy was now able to control his feelings . . . He *had* to, of course. After all, after every successful delivery, it would not be very professional for the brilliant young obstetrician to stand in the middle of the delivery room and bawl . . .

Lew placed a length of white absorptive material along the vagina.

Phyllis wheeled a bed in. They woke the girl and she moved herself onto it. Then the two nurses wheeled her off to the recovery room while Sato and Lew threw their gowns and gloves underneath the table, dropped their masks, and scrubbed up. Then they went into the recovery room to congratulate the girl. Phyllis, as recovery-room nurse, had begun massaging the girl's abdomen, and thereby the fundus uteri, to keep the fundus uteri contracted and thus prevent the hemorrhaging which its sudden relaxation could cause. They each shook the girl's hand and congratulated her. "It's my first, you know," Ellen said.

It had happened again, though he'd known it was impossible for it ever to happen again. Not again *and* again. Human emotions just didn't work that way . . .

But he had begun to sob inside again anyway; sobbing at a beauty and a joy that could climax itself again and again, never diminish, always provoke these sobs of joy in him . . .

They had gone into the delivery room forty-six minutes before.

30

"You know," Mason, a resident, said to Fishbein and Sato and Suzie-Jane, "you know, this man here"—tapping Worship—"if he hasn't seen it, it probably doesn't exist. That's how vonduhful huh vonduhful doctuh *he* is."

Lew said, "All I said was . . . What *did* I say?"

Fishbein said, "You made it sound like the greatest delivery of all time."

"Well, I didn't mean it that way. It was mostly Yuky. You've got to be awful good to be able to guide someone else through a good delivery."

Sato said, "It was *your* delivery, Doctor."

Lew laughed. "It *was* a great delivery, wasn't it? I mean, *spontaneous* respiration!"

"Vonduhful," Fishbein said.

"It really was. Listen, let me tell you . . ."

"You already have," Mason said. "She's been delivered ten times already."

Bobbie came in. "Dr. Mason, you're up. Mrs. Ramonez has decided to have a baby."

Sato said, "You can tell Dick that as far as I've been able to determine, Mrs. Ramonez is eligible for all the good heavy *cyclopropane* he feels like giving her."

"Hunh?" Mason said.

"He should skip that nitrous oxide junk again," Lew said.

"Some interns," Mason said, starting off with Fishbein, "are having too many deliveries for their britches."

Alone in the lounge, Sato lit one of his rare cigarettes and looked across the room at Worship and said, "It's not just to *pull* the baby out or just catch it—any policeman or cab driver can do that: and the mother may be all right, the baby may be all right. But that's not *obstetrics*. There's a way of holding, a way of doing, that makes obstetrics an art, a *beautiful* thing as well as a functional thing."

Lew nodded, and nodded again.

"Some people say there's a lot of mess and filth around a delivery room, but, you know, when you see what comes out you don't feel that way. I would describe it as beautiful," Sato said.

Lew nodded again. "Seeing somebody come out of somebody else . . ."

"Yes," Sato said, the slightest smile again, the voice peculiarly distant again, "yes."

Lew had looked at the board in the nurses' station and found that he was now on second call behind Langley. In a couple of hours, and around three, he'd be called again, so it wasn't worth going back up to his room. On the board next to his name he chalked up the extension number for one of the cot rooms behind the lounge. Then he went to the room. Langley was sprawled out, still in a scrub suit and quiet as the room itself, on one of the sheeted but unblanketed cots. Worship sank down on the cot opposite.

At almost any other time in any other place, Lew Worship would have been a farmer. Farming had been the birthright, legacy, and demand note presented to every male Worship from his day of birth through seven generations in America and probably seventy more generations in England.

Now it was no longer quite so

. . . All of the clichés, he was thinking . . . Life . . . Death . . . all of them . . . Her silly words . . . my response . . . That feeling of sobbing . . . of elation, joy, as before great beauty. If it's this way . . . every time . . . but it can't be . . . it can't be . . . it can't *possibly* be this way every time . . .

But it is. I had to be sure. But it is . . .

Worship had decided he couldn't leave it, and thereby had chosen his specialty.

31

Alicia Liu was up until after midnight writing a letter to Dr. Harvey Bonny. She had applied to him at Century Veterans for a residency in psychiatry. She knew, of course, that Century, being a veterans' hospital, was a highly unorthodox place for a woman to apply to for a residency. She had expected very little to come of her application, though at the same time she was unable to determine her exact future except in terms of Bonny and Century.

Unaccountably—for no one as yet had even received notice of an interview—she had received a letter from Bonny asking for information pertinent to her long-range plans in psychiatry.

She wrote him that she had become interested, through the work of a young psychiatrist in Cambridge who had published several papers on the subject, in a new field which the young psychiatrist had termed and described, "Cross-Cultural Psychiatry." After completing her residency, Alicia wrote, she planned, if possible, to go to the Far East and, through psychiatric, anthropological, and sociological investigation, begin work on making feasible the transference and adaptation of psychiatric treatment to Eastern cultures —the principles of which treatment and techniques, she particularized, were, of course, Western in nature and therefore, without adaptation based on study, likely to be inapplicable in an Eastern culture. She then planned—she continued—to take a personal analysis in order to become a psychoanalyst and work at integrating the principles of analysis with a culture to which it might be, and probably was, entirely alien. Eventually she would like to work with Easterners having a difficult time adapting to this country and also explore the cross-cultural and psychiatric aspects of brainwashing with Americans who had suffered it in the East.

When she finally went to bed around two, Alicia was almost too exhausted to remember to call the operator and leave a call for herself for six fifteen.

32

Jim Aptshult had also written a letter before he'd gone to bed. The letter was to his wife Louise, and its substance was again an offer of the five thousand dollars Jim's father would confer on her after a divorce. Jim wrote, "As we both know, he hasn't *got* that kind of money, but he can arrange to borrow it to settle this thing. I hope you will consider this offer and appreciate its fairness. Again, I apologize to you for having been so irresponsible as to have pressured you into

marriage with me. I now hope that we can finally settle this
thing without making it more difficult than it ought to be."
He signed the letter simply, *Jim*.

For a moment he considered rewriting the letter and de-
leting the part about apologizing for having pressured her
into marriage. Then he thought, *No, damn it*. That said what
he wanted to say, even if it sounded foolish, even if she
thought it was foolish.

This was beginning to worry him, this old business with
Louise, and too, this new business with Alicia. And his worry
worried him. Nothing of the outside had intruded upon him
or bothered him since he'd started his internship. Even very
little *in* the hospital bothered him. In Surgery, of course, he
had worried over certain patients. But it hadn't really even
been the patients so much as it had been just being worried
about how to manage and treat them, figuring out what the
best thing to do was and then worrying about how to do the
best thing . . . And then, too, he remembered he'd been quite
concerned over all those kids in TB when he'd been up
there on the TB service. All those kids, three, four, five, and
six and seven years old. Coming in one at a time. And
staying up there on that floor in that ward for one, two, even
three years . . . That had bothered him considerably. But
nothing outside had gotten to him . . . not for months . . .
and now it wasn't going away or even just staying the same,
it was getting worse, getting more complicated . . .

—

33

By one o'clock, Conny Mercouris had found his angle for his
residency.

He sat at his desk bent over two large, open, paperbound
books. One book listed the staff members of New North, the
other book listed the staff members of Century Veterans. By
comparing every name in the New North listings with every
name in the Century listings, Mercouris had eventually, in the
W's, found a name listed as a member of both staffs—a man
who was an attending at Century and a staff associate at New
North.

The man's name was George Wexler and he was a surgeon.
Mercouris cursed. A *surgeon*. Of all the God damn luck.

He sighed and closed both books. All right, so he hated surgery. So he'd just have to go ahead and do what he'd planned to do anyway. He'd arrange to scrub with this man Wexler, get to know him, and see what he could work through him.

A *surgeon*, Mercouris thought again with disgust, and called the operator to leave his name for a six o'clock wake-up.

34

Dr. (practicing provisionally) Amos Sprague was awake and reading when his telephone rang at one thirty. His roommate, Conny Mercouris, had gone across the hall to shower, and Sprague was thinking of doing the same thing. He was on call for the night, but since his service was Gynecology, there was very little chance that anything would come up. Nothing ever happened on GYN at night. Or rarely happened, anyway. Not like Surgery or OB.

He had finished all the studying he was likely to do that night. And a shower would sure set him up, maybe even a blade shave, too . . . But the damn phone. He knew it must be for him. Conny wasn't on call. It was a certainty it was ringing for him. And because of this certainty, he was able suddenly to appreciate how entirely exhausted he was.

Wearily he got up from lying on his bed and went over to the desk and picked up the receiver. "Sprague," he said, wanting very much to hear the voice on the other end say, *Dr. Mercouris, please.*

But it didn't. The voice, that of GYN's night-charge nurse, said, "Dr. Sprague, we have a new admission. Emergency just sent up a twenty-six-year-old white female with a chief complaint of uterine hemorrhage."

Sprague said, "Shouldn't a resident look at her?"

"I called Dr. MacDonaugh and he said I should get whatever intern was on call to see her and then call him."

"All right," Sprague said, "I'll be right over."

Jesus, he thought. That MacDonaugh is undoubtedly the laziest bastard alive. But *good,* he thought. You should be so good. Well, good when he got started. But he almost never gets started. Not after midnight, anyway . . .

The nurse, Ann Wafford, took him from the fully lit, glassed-in nurses' station down a silent, night-lit corridor to a semi-private fully lit room in which the new patient, Mrs. Josephine Ritchy, was the only occupant.

The nurse said, "Her driver's license has her down for the same name, but as *Miss*."

Sprague nodded.

They entered the room.

The patient had been undressed and then reclothed in a hospital-issue nightgown She lay turned away from them in the bed. Sprague couldn't determine whether she was crying or moaning. But the sounds seemed to come from a long way away.

Mrs. Wafford said, "This is Dr. Sprague, Mrs. Ritchy. He's going to examine you and find out what's wrong. Roll over, dear."

Mrs. Ritchy didn't move, the sounds didn't change.

Sprague went around the bed to the side the woman was facing. She looked at him, but didn't move, didn't quiet. "Please," he said, "lie on your back, Mrs. Ritchy."

"I asked her to before I called you," the nurse said. "Now she's gotten off the pads and messed up the bed."

There was a great deal of blood on the bed. The nurse held out a glove she had broken from a pack. Sprague gloved his hands and went over to the patient. Holding his hands away from himself, he said to the nurse, "Help her turn, please."

Mrs. Wafford gently but insistently helped the woman to move on to her back. The woman kept her legs raised almost against her stomach and tightly together. The absorptive napkin that must have been put on just minutes before in Emergency was already soaked with blood beyond its ability to absorb and had fallen to the bed. The woman herself was pallid beyond any pallor Sprague had ever before seen. "What's her B.P.?" he said.

"Eighty over forty," the nurse said.

Sprague began examining the patient for a vein he could get a needle in, found none, realized the veins he was looking for had probably all collapsed, and knew he'd have to do a cut-down to find a vein for an I.V. procedure.

He said to the nurse, "Get me an eighteen needle, a cut-down set, and saline."

While the nurse was out, the patient didn't move, and when the nurse came back, Sprague realized he had not moved either.

The nurse readied the I.V. apparatus. The patient was held so that she was immobilized from the waist down. Sprague took the knife and made an incision inside the ankle where there was a bigger vein than in the arm. He said, "Maybe we can slow the hemorrhage by contracting the uterus." The nurse handed him a small plastic tube which he proceeded to insert into the vein. "At least we can try," he said. "So get some pitocin into the bottle. One ampoule." While he attached the I.V. tube to the plastic tube already in the vein, the nurse introduced the pit into the saline. Then Sprague closed the incision with two sutures.

"She's very cold," the nurse said.

"Put a blanket over her above the waist," Sprague said. "And get me a blood-sample tube. I'll take it directly from the vagina, it doesn't look like she could stand having any more taken than she's losing just naturally."

The nurse went out.

When she returned with the tube, Sprague said, "You'll have to help me keep her legs apart while I examine her."

The woman tried with sudden strength to protest the examination by rolling away. With difficulty Sprague and the nurse held her in position. After disinfecting, Sprague began the examination. The distant, faraway sounds became slightly louder, slightly more intense, but somehow no more immediate.

He abandoned the examination almost at once, and the woman rolled over on her side again and drew her legs up against her stomach. The increased intensity of her sounds continued.

Sprague said, holding out the tube half filled with blood, "No record of blood type on her, I suppose . . . ?"

"No," the nurse said.

"No, there never is. Get this typed and cross-matched for five pints. Tell the lab *stat* and damn stat."

The nurse nodded and left. Sprague followed her, both of them moving quickly, out of the room and down the corridor to the nurses' station. "After you get rid of that," he said, "get someone to try and ring up her home in case she has anyone who can give us information. And it might be a good idea to have the glucose and saline I.V. ready."

In the nurses' station he picked up the phone. "Dr. Mac-Donaugh," he said. Then, "Sprague. Uterine hemorrhaging. She must have been at it for a long time, maybe twenty-four hours. She's white as paper and cold. It's almost impossible to examine her, she keeps her legs up tight. Pulse about sixty. I can't tell for certain, but she seems pretty damn well torn up inside, and in this condition a terrible operative risk. I'm trying to get her typed. She needs a transfusion just as soon as we can give it to her, she seems to have lost more blood than I knew you could. I'm treating her for shock."

MacDonaugh said, "I'll be right over. Go try and talk with her. Find out anything you can. All you can."

They hung up and Sprague went back to the woman. He could see no sign of response. "What B.P.?" he said.

The nurse looked up from the blood-pressure machine. "Sixty over zero," she said. "I can't get a diastolic pressure at all."

"Ampoule of Levophed. *Hurry.*"

She didn't look at him. She seemed to have hunched herself even tighter. She said, "I don't want to die, don't let me die, I didn't mean it . . ." The voice had come from so far away it seemed that it came from something no longer alive. Then the sounds started again, and after a few seconds she began speaking again over the sounds, or through them, but at the same time.

Sprague shouted, "Where the hell is that Levophed?"

Looking at her mouth, as if he could *see* what she was saying—her voice was still so far and distant—Sprague saw that she had put lipstick on her lips very recently. As if she had done it to be looking her best at the hospital. No other make-up, just the lipstick, bright and crimson against the pallor of her skin, though it was a dark lipstick.

"Please," she said. "I didn't mean it. I'll never do it again . . ."

"*What?*" Sprague said. Then, seeing what was happening to her, the change and horror moving behind her face, as if all the motion were subcutaneous, he thought, *No. No! Please, don't tell me. Please!*

But she was crying out, from very far away now, "I didn't mean it. *Oh God,* I didn't mean it, forgive me . . ."

MacDonaugh hurried in. Then, without touching the patient, he said, *"Write it down,"* and ran out, the woman saying, "I just wanted him to take the baby away . . . It wasn't a baby yet . . . It wasn't, it wasn't, it wasn't . . ."

"Who?" Sprague said, "*Who?*" the trained part of his mind searching to find if it had ever learned the legalities of the situation or whether it had just forgotten them: What was his responsibility? What was he supposed to do medically-legally? But already he was calling, "Wafford! Wafford!" just to have a witness. "*Who?*" he yelled at the woman. "*Who?*"

"I'll never do it again . . . I'm sorry, I'm sorry . . ."

His mind remembering, *A statement made to a physician by a dying patient aware of imminent death is evidence admissible in court dependent upon the character of the physician as presented to the court by physicians who shall recommend themselves by . . .*

Wafford came hurrying in with a tray on which there were several instruments and two hypodermic syringes. She said, "Dr. MacDonaugh is going to . . ." But Sprague waved her silent, was writing as fast as he could in the pocket notebook he always carried with him, saying over and over, loudly, "*Who?* Tell me *who* did it." The nurse stood there, the tray placed on the empty bed. She stood and stared at the woman and bit her fist . . .

Sprague looked up. MacDonaugh and another resident stood there. Sprague capped his pen and put it back in his breast pocket. The nurse left the room. "I'll call," she said. The other resident stood back from the bed again. "For fair," he said. "Fix up the chart and I'll take care of the rest." MacDonaugh picked up the chart and handed it to Sprague and nodded him out of the room.

"I don't ever want to see that again," Sprague said.

"Come up to my room. We could use a drink. I'll get someone else to cover for you."

"I don't ever want to see that again!"

"C'mon, man. Fix the chart and we'll get a drink upstairs."

"Yeah," Sprague said, his voice gone as small as the woman's had been.

"Did you get anything from her?"

"Nothing," Sprague said. He looked around as if he might find something he wanted. "*Nothing!*" he called out.

35

In another city, Dr. Herbert L. Grumbacher was working late.

Dr. Grumbacher, who was medical superintendent of the Interfaith Hospital of Internal Medicine, had before him on his desk (until they could be placed alphabetically on his shelves) two hundred and twenty applications for residencies for the coming year commencing July one. Each of the two hundred and twenty had excellent or near-excellent records—they had been sifted from well over five hundred.

In addition to the two hundred and twenty with excellent or near-excellent records, there was a file of thirty-one applicants who were of interest to the hospital for reasons other than and in addition to excellent records—special interests and services, special recommendations (without excellent records), and special intents of practice or research.

A staff group of seven, supervised by and including two assistant medical superintendents, had gone through the original batch of over five hundred. As medical superintendent, it was Dr. Grumbacher's job to reduce the number of acceptable candidates at least to one hundred and fifty—these one hundred and fifty to receive personal interviews before the number was cut further.

A committee of seven staff members would then pick and choose among the remaining one hundred and fifty. But *any* staff specialist could have anyone he wished, even if the applicant had been dropped on the first sort-through.

Dr. Grumbacher put out his cigarette and sighed or, more accurately, wheezed a grunt. They *all* had excellent records. But what made it worse, they were *all* zealous as well.

At first, years before, he had *thought* they were all zealous. Then, later, he had thought he had been disabused of that belief. Still later, and permanently, he had discovered they *were* all zealous, no matter what their records showed before or what might be added to their records later.

The question was, assuming their zealousness (which was beyond question, or else Grumbacher might have had good cause to reverse his decision not to retire, a decision he had made two years before when the question had come up officially), which ones of them were the most *capable*—for some of them might not *be* capable; in fact, some of them

(Grumbacher knew just from experience) certainly were *not* capable. Which ones, and how to know? And then, which ones were most capable, and how to know? He'd never been able to formulate any rule or standard test.

Grumbacher lit another cigarette—all right, he would die of cancer; at least the disease would be of his own choosing. His derrick-claw-like hand pulled down a group of seven folders at random. He opened one. Five letters of recommendation were requested. There were eleven. A three-thousand-word autobiography was requested. This one was at least six pages extra in length. That might be grounds for turning down the application, depending on the contents. But they were *all* like that; and each one confused the reader's standards more than the one before or the one to be read next. There must be a better way . . .

Sure as hell, Grumbacher decided, he'd retire immediately after settling this, this, *this*—his mind was incapable of finding a noun derogatory enough. But he'd retire immediately after.

He'd felt exactly the same for the last eight years, the first five decisions having been in favor of resignation from the office and return to nonadministrative work rather than retirement. The lovely vision of retirement gave him the strength to work.

Immediately after the work was finished, the vision would be neither lovely nor acceptable. He was not a geriatrics case *yet*.

36

Tom Elwood heard the ring of the telephone through his sleep, and then, slowly, drifting, moved away from it, shut it out, shut out the sound of his roommate's voice answering and saying *Okay* and *Thanks* for the wake-up.

Six fifteen, his roommate's voice said.

Had he said anything? had the telephone rung? No. A dream. Nothing real. Not for hours yet. He had hours yet. He had reality niched for all time right in that part that had moved away from the sound of the telephone that hadn't really happened at all . . .

Did he hear an electric razor? no. It was a bee, a swarm of

bees outside his window in the sunshine, and anyway, they were gone . . .

Hey, man. Twenty to seven. You won't have time to catch breakfast before rounds.

He never understood why that voice bothered to speak to him. But it was gone now. There had been a click, and it was gone, like the bees had gone. Had there been bees? no. Had there been a click? no.

He opened his eyes. The room was still. It was dark, didn't that mean it was still night? He had hours yet. He wouldn't move for hours . . .

Upon his arrival in the city (two days late) he was an M.D. and nothing more, though within the hour, once he had gotten himself to the hospital, he would be—at least provisionally—a *practicing* M.D. In the cab going up to the hospital he composed himself accordingly. The prospect had numbed his imagination too thoroughly for him to be afraid.

He had taken the train up from Georgia. He was not afraid of flying, but neither was he convinced of its safety. The train had taken twenty-eight hours and he was too numbed *generally* to be aware of his own numbness or of any specifically localized numbness. He was rather, actually and almost totally, disassociated—not only from reality, but from himself also. Things, people, passages of action, made an impression, but only in the way in which an exposure of an *n*th of a second makes an impression on a light-sensitive film. The film still needs to be developed before the impression has a reality. Because the rhythm and the enclosed atmosphere of the train had worked so thoroughly, this state was more the result of the train than of the impending experience of being a practicing physician.

He was driven uptown through heavy afternoon traffic. After the time in the train, the flush of sunlight and of new sounds, of smells and of sights, was unaccustomed. There was no newness in the world. Therefore, what seemed new was not new and had therefore been experienced before. And the whole experience of being in a new place under new conditions breathed past him as if familiar beyond recognition. Certainly familiar beyond response.

He had said to the cab driver, "The New North Hospital, please."

And the cab driver had said, "New North it is." Then the

driver had said, "Helluva place for a white man to be going."
The driver was white.

Tom was too disoriented and numb to mark the unique-
ness of this kind of remark in this part of the country. Where
he came from it would have been a passing of the time of
day. He himself did not pass the time of day in this manner,
nor indulge in phrasing his views publicly, but he agreed
with the sentiments.

He had come to New North because it was big. So big the
interns had plenty of work, plenty of chance to work. Not
like at med school where all you did was sit around on your
tail all day memorizing and memorizing and memorizing.
Not like the private teaching hospitals where an intern was
given almost no opportunity to do anything but paper work,
no opportunity to do anything but draw blood samples and
listen . . . At least at New North he'd be *doing* for a change,
putting his training, his memorization, to practice . . .

After a while, abstractedly—because he thought one was
obliged to talk to cab drivers in this part of the country—he
said, abstractedly, "Why y'say that?"

"Hell," the driver said, "you'd never get *me* in there, no
matter how goddam sick I was."

"How come?" Tom said.

"The place is filled with colored and Puerto Rican," the
driver said.

At first Tom had thought the driver was German—a slight
touch of an accent, no more. But now he realized the man
must be Scandinavian, probably Swedish.

"I live near there," the driver said in his funny accent.
"But you wouldn't catch me in there with all them colored
and Puerto Rican if it took every cent I saved in twenty years
of drivin' a cab. No sir. And I got a wife and a daughter
that ain't married and another daughter that's got me a son-
in-law that don't work to take care of."

Tom watched the cars manipulating themselves among one
another at thirty-five miles an hour with only one or two feet
to spare. He had never seen driving like it. He was too impressed and numb to even be afraid. "I hear they got good
doctors there," he said.

"New North? They got good doctors, I guess. But you don't
get me in there with all them colored and Puerto Rican." The
driver was silent for a few blocks. Then he said, "I'd damned

sure catch something worse than what I went in there with, you make no mistake."

Herunh, Tom thought, considering the prospect with his train benumbed consciousness. Well, this was a northern city and he'd have to accustom himself to lots of colored and Puerto Rican. When in Rome. It wouldn't be any great problem. They were put together the same physically, anyway.

Two hours after his arrival, having been shown his room, which he was surprised to find he had to share with someone, issued six whites, and packed in—though not unpacked—he reported as directed to Male Surgery, Ward B, and to Dr. Grenatti for afternoon rounds.

Dr. Grenatti was only a resident and, Elwood had discovered, not even the chief resident. Grenatti was not at the nurses' station when Elwood reported. Three other iterns lounged there like youths on any street corner in the country—rather unkempt (anyway, two of them needed shaves), holding cigarettes at dramatic angles and using four-letter words often and as unthinkingly as they might a stethoscope. One of them was a Negro. They didn't even bother to look him over. A Negro nurse went by him and out as if he were an inanimate object. Another nurse, after a while, looked up from a notebook she was reading and said, "Dr. Elwood?" It was the first time he had been called *Doctor,* but it didn't give him the thrill he had expected. Incongruously, he was noticing that the nurse wasn't even pretty. She looked, in fact, as if she should have been retired sometime earlier.

Elwood nodded to her question. "Yes," he said. "Yes, I am." The nurse started to say something about having been expecting him, but one of the lounging youths in white came forward and offered his hand and said, "Jim Aptshult, fellow body mechanic."

The Negro said, "Ted Eckland, nice to meet you—even if it *does* mean I won't have the room to myself any more."

Elwood shook the third hand and heard, without registration, the voice saying, "Parelli, Joseph, Joe to you—except in front of patients. Have to call me *Doctor* then. I'll do the same for you."

He didn't really hear Parelli. The Negro had been specific. It was impossible. Fate had taken too exacting an interest in him. Yet it was only for a year, only a year. When in Rome

. . . When in Rome, he said to himself. *When in Rome, when in Rome* . . . He smiled around the room— *When in Rome.* Who could he talk to, ask about, get things changed? But that would make it worse in this environment, he could see that. He understood Rome. They might even have done it on purpose . . . Rome, Rome, Rome, Rome . . . (Even later when he discovered that roommates were usually teamed and assigned alphabetically, it was *Rome.*)

At the doorway to the nurses' station there stood a slightly older than young man—though the mark of youth was still rather disconcertingly on him—wearing only the white, buttoned-across-the-shoulder tunic without the customary jacket. He said, "If you jokers are ready, we might make sure the patients are still alive."

The three filed out past Elwood, one of them, the first one —Aptshult?—picking up a metal clipboard from a rack of them as he went.

As Elwood started to follow them out, the one at the door said, "You Elwood?"

Elwood said, "Yes, sir."

"Not sir. *Doctor,* if anything. And Grenatti if not that. Put the two together and you may get along here," he said from the corner of his mouth. He didn't offer his hand. Elwood had never heard anyone talk from that area of the face before. He must have paused, staring or bemused, because Grenatti said, "Shake your ass, *Doctor.*"

They went through the ward, hot with summer heat. They saw thirty-seven patients. Two of the patients were in private rooms. The rooms were heavy with heat and stench. On stands in these two rooms there were bottles filled with essence of peppermint which were supposed to deodorize the atmosphere. They merely made it more sickening. Elwood wondered whether it was his numbness or whether he really had a strong enough hold on himself not to react.

The rounds took twenty-one minutes, and except for a single incident, consisted of, *"Mr. Bitena, how are you feeling this afternoon?"*

"Okay, Doctor, but I don't get much food, Doctor."

"What diet is Mr. Bitena on?"

"Du Bois," Aptshult would say, *consulting the metal clipboard.*

"Milk, Doctor. All I get is milk. Every meal. A man can't live on just . . ."

"He seems to be recovering. Change it to soft."

"Thank you, Doctor . . ."

"Mr. Rentner, breathing more freely . . . ?"

The incident took place in the third room they came to, Grenatti leading the way, Aptshult following immediately behind and writing the notes in the metal clipboard, the others following according to their spirits.

In the third room there was an old man with facial lacerations. He had received them while trying to remove his granddaughter's spouse from his own—the grandfather's—house during a period when the grandson (in-law) was resenting the world. The grandson had taken a plaster statuette to the old man.

The old man was a new admission, having come in earlier that afternoon. Aptshult, called down to Emergency, had sutured him, and Eckland had admitted him and taken his history. The two of them were uninterested. But Parelli was interested. The lacerations passed up-and-down the forehead, through the eyebrows, and up-and-down the cheeks. Two different grades and types of sutures had been used. Parelli began asking Aptshult about it. Grenatti said, "Hold it a minute."

"Mister . . ." Grenatti said, picking up the card at the end of the bed, ". . . Symington."

The patient, eyes closed, said, "Yes, yes."

"Mr. Symington, can you sit up?"

"Ahh," he said, "I can do whatever you want."

But he had trouble, he was an old man. Grenatti said, "Elwood, put him up and hold his head."

Elwood raised the rear of the bed with the crank and went to the patient and moved his hand tentatively toward the patient's head. He found himself waiting out the time of the world before actually getting his hand to touch the patient. On his hand, suddenly, he felt another hand placed angrily and forcefully and unarguably. He felt it place his hand firmly and unarguably on the base of the patient's cranium and then lever both his hand and the head up.

Once his hand was placed, he was unable to shrink from doing as he was supposed to. The hair was dry, the scalp wet with perspiration. Grenatti had not even looked at him, had not apologized with a look, had not disclaimed or understood with a look. Grenatti was saying, ". . . lacerations of differing characteristics though received from the same instrument, but because of the differing characteristics . . ."

Afterwards, no one even mentioned the moment to him. He knew it hadn't gone unnoticed. Grenatti had seen to that. But if not an apology or an explanation, he thought at least he could have expected a lecture, something—*anything*. You can't just forget a moment like that. Not even in Rome.

But nothing was said, not even an allusion made.

And later that day he waited with the others for the chief resident to show up so they could start late afternoon rounds. When the chief resident, Eugene Duane, arrived, Parelli introduced him.

Duane shook hands curtly. "Couldn't be bothered to get here on time, hunh, Elwood?"

"My father died."

"I see. Sorry. The hospital supplies you with a number of things and replaces free of charge all bulbs and batteries for your ophthalmoscope. Blood-pressure machine and so forth is on the floor, ask the nurse. The hospital also supplies anything you need for a sterile procedure. Parelli can show you where to pick up your batteries and junk after rounds . . . Ah . . . You need assume no responsibility unless you want to. There is always a resident available who will take over whatever responsibility you feel inadequate or unwilling to assume . . . That's the speech. Except for one thing. In a hospital like this, there's very rarely even an attending around, except on occasional rounds. The chief resident runs the whole show and pretty much the whole place, too. So keep on his good side. And when he's not around, the charge resident runs the show. Remember that and you may get out of the year alive . . . All right, *Doctors*, let's go see how many patients you can refrain from distressing today."

. . . It had become fully light in the room. Gray. As light as it ever naturally got in rooms in this northern place with its cold and wet and sounds of steam and of radiators clunking.

Duane, he thought, Grenatti, Rosen. Kalik. Granchard. All of them. He got up, an irresistible energy born of his own indignation levering him up almost like a physical force. He dressed, the indignation lending him more strength than he'd felt for . . . He couldn't remember in how long.

TWO

THE WARDS

37

By six fifteen A.M. van Wyck was in his whites and standing in front of the mirror in his room running his electric razor up and down his face. It never gave him a completely satisfactory shave, but, like most of the other interns, he used an electric razor because it was faster than a blade razor, and because, no matter what he (or the others) used, he always had to shave again around five in order to keep looking the way a doctor was supposed to look. He knew his face couldn't take two blade shaves a day—it could barely take two *electric* shaves a day.

His roommate, Courtney Walters, said, still lying in bed, "There damn well better be some answers in the mail today."

Van Wyck unplugged the razor and blew it clean. "Why?"

"*Why?* Because I'm getting damn nervous. That's why."

"It's still early."

"Listen, Pete, even Elwood and Mercouris and Otis have gotten at least one request for a personal interview."

"Yeah. But look at the jerk places they applied," van Wyck said.

"Yeah," Walters said, a little less pained. "It's something to bear in mind, isn't it?"

"Sure," van Wyck said, transferring his stethoscope and ophthalmoscope and pens and pad from the jacket he'd worn the last two days to a starchy clean one. "And don't forget Lew Worship. If you're worried about *you*, just give a moment's thought to him. That oughta cheer anybody up."

"Worship?"

"*He* hasn't even written anywhere yet."

"Oh, yeah, sure," Walters said, not at all impressed. And then, as he thought about it, he got up on one elbow in bed and looked as if he was going to smile, though he didn't. But he did say, "Yeah, Worship. Nowhere at all . . . And those others, just jerk places . . . Pete . . . ?"

"Hunh?"

"It's something to bear in mind, isn't it?"

Van Wyck's first stop, after taking an elevator down, walking across, and taking an elevator up, was Male Surgery B. It was his morning, together with Conny Mercouris, to draw blood and test urine from specified patients as listed in the doctor's order book.

The night nurse was still on duty. "How were things?" Pete asked her.

"No trouble at all. Except that Murry boy. He got up once. No idea what he was doing; I don't even think he was even seeing anything. But I got him back to bed and he didn't give me any more trouble."

"Who could give you trouble after falling off a three-story building?" Conny said.

"That was three days ago," the nurse said. "Maybe he's going to be all right."

"Did he talk to you?" Pete said.

"Nothing I could understand. Not real words."

"I talked to him yesterday," Conny said. "Maybe he's beginning to get oriented. I asked him who was President."

"Well, what'd he say?"

"Truman. Anyway, he was close, so maybe he's getting oriented."

"Did they find out yet how it happened?" the nurse said.

"Some other kid pushed him off," Pete said.

"Twelve years old," the nurse said.

"Okay, sweetie," Conny said, handing her a tray. "All duly

marked and labeled and waiting for your tender touch."

The breakfast rush hadn't started yet. Except for a few interns who had had order-book duty, the tables were unoccupied and there was no one in line.

"*Hey,*" Pete said, as they started in, "wait a minute."

He went over to a man in a plain blue business suit who
was putting up a poster on the wall. The poster solicited
membership in a nurse's aides' union. The man was taping
it to the wall, not even in the area of the wall reserved for
notices and posters and therefore faced with cork.

Being an intern and thereby having very little else with
which to comfort himself, van Wyck had an intense pos-
sessiveness about his hospital. He said to the man, "You're
not supposed to put that there."

The man turned and looked at him. "Move along, buddy,"
he said.

Van Wyck said, "You authorized to put that up?"

The man went on putting it up.

"You authorized to be in this part of the hospital?"

The man had completed the taping job. He walked up to
van Wyck. "I suggest you shut up and mind your business,"
the man said.

Van Wyck bowed slightly. "Thank you. As a member of
the staff of this hospital, I'm authorized to ask for your
pass. And to see it, if you have one."

The man said, "You're interfering with the union. What
are you, just an intern anyway?"

"In other words," van Wyck said reasonably, "you
don't have a pass and you don't have authorization to put
that up."

"What the hell are you talking about? This is *union* business. Not yours, *comprunch?*"

"No comprunch," van Wyck said, and went to the poster,
tore it down, and ripped it into several pieces. Then he
nodded to Conny and they went into the dining hall, the
man in the blue business suit calling threats after them.

In a while, other interns and residents, some nurses,
and a large number of student nurses came in. Joe Parelli
and Lew Worship came over and sat down with them, and
then a nurse asked if she could have her coffee with them.
The girl made van Wyck uncomfortable. Like the others, he

knew her, and knew *of* her—someone had dated her a couple of times and had said that she was willing, but that there was nothing particularly inspiring about her either in bed or out. Looking at her, van Wyck could not have cared less. The way in which she went out of her way to be *just* a nurse overwhelmed by being with real doctors had always made him feel not only uncomfortable, but disgusted and a little angry. She seemed to have no pride in her profession, and after every meeting with her, she left him, temporarily, with a little less pride in his own. He tried to remember her name . . . Petschek, he thought. Yes, she was H.N. on Male Medicine A, and if he drew that ward, he'd have to work with her. He hoped not.

When she had left, Joe Parelli said, "That one is sure looking to get laid."

"I'd rather sleep with a sputum culture," Conny said.

"Those oh-so-modest, dew-heavy eyelids," Lew said.

"Maybe she's looking to get married," Pete said.

"To an *intern?*" Joe said.

"I guess you're right," Pete said.

Otis put his tray down on the vacated spot at the table. With his eyes he followed the nurse moving out of the room through the now fully occupied tables. He turned to the group at the table. "I resent the old implication there, Joe. 'To an *intern!*' There really isn't anything low about being an intern. Take me, for instance. I, for one, have prospects."

"That makes *exactly* one of us," Joe said. "If I got my ideal residency, I'd be making one hundred bucks a month next year. Period."

"There're residencies that pay a helluva lot more than that," John Paul said.

"They're few, they're far between, and mostly they're lousy or in the army," Joe said.

"I suppose," Conny said, "I *suppose* she might be interested in getting married on just prospects. I mean, it's *possible*. If the prospects were good enough."

"It's possible, anyway," Pete said.

"Sure it is," John Paul said, setting down his empty juice glass. "But I tell you. Nothing works like what you can give them *now*. *Now* is always it—no matter what you're after. You put it on the line now, you can get anything you want."

"What do you suggest, Doctor? I mean for *right now*," Conny said.

"There are ways," John Paul said.

"Like spending every night with them, hunh?" Lew said.

"Hey. *Buddy*. What's got into you? I thought you were muh pal. You got a mad on at me—cause you covered for me?"

"Forget it."

"No, I won't, Lew. What's up? For godsake, *you* were the one who . . ."

"I know, I know. Forget it, John. Wrong side of the bed, I guess."

John Paul snapped his fingers. "That's it!"

"What, for godsake?" Parelli said, startled out of a half doze over his coffee.

"Lew's trouble," Otis said. He turned back to Lew. "Bed. That's the whole thing. You work too hard, Lew. Don't spend enough time in bed. As a result, you don't keep your body in shape. Or certain parts of it, anyway. The specific part I'm thinking of'll atrophy if you don't give it exercise."

"So'll your brain," Lew said, "if you don't give it exercise."

"Jesus Christ, what'd I say?"

"Just shut up, hunh?" Lew said.

"Hey, *Lew* . . ." Parelli began.

"Listen, Lew," John Paul said, "nothing was meant that you oughta get sore about. Listen, I've got you to *thank*, not . . ."

"So you have. So how about just maintaining silence on the subject?"

Otis put his fork down and looked at Worship directly again. His voice had quieted, become emotionless. "What're you riding me for, Lew?"

Lew had the impression that John Paul had asked because there was a damn good reason to ask, because there was a damn good answer to the question and Otis wanted to find out if Lew knew it. But he didn't, so he said, as emotionlessly as Otis, "I don't know," thinking, I don't know the answer, and I don't know the question really, but now I know there are both; and rose and said, "Excuse me," and left the table.

"What was that all about?" Pete said.

"Search me," Otis said. "I think he needs a girl."

"Write 'im a prescription and send him to the dispensary," Joe said.

"Maybe I will. He sure looks like he needs *something*."

"He looks like he's exhausted, period," van Wyck said. "And you don't look so hot yourself, John Paul."

"You don't," Joe said. "Really. You . . ."

"Forget it. I'll be fine as soon as I've done my daily good deed. And I'm about to," he said, getting up. He crossed the room, but not toward the exit.

Van Wyck said, getting up too, "You ready, Conny?"

"Yeah, sure, I always skip my first cup of coffee . . ." But he got up and followed Parelli and van Wyck out.

Bobbie was one of the last night-tour head nurses to come in for breakfast. She had not yet even had a chance to change from her scrub smock. Through the strain of the night, her face had acquired the pale, drawn, cosmetic-less appearance that resembled nothing so much as the face of a woman after several hours of labor.

She usually had breakfast with Didi Loomis, a teaching nurse she had known since they'd both been to school together. She saw Didi across the room and started over to her. She was stopped by John Paul Otis—"Say, Bobbie— got a minute?"

"I don't know," she said, indicating her tray.

"Here, let me hold it for you."

"Thanks," Bobbie said, relinquishing the tray.

He put it on an empty table and said, "Siddown a second, hunh?"

"Listen, *Doctor*, I'm meeting a friend . . ."

"Just a second."

"All right. What's your problem?"

"Not mine, a friend's."

"So why's it yours?"

"I . . . Hey, I dunno." He shrugged. "I guess, just cause I like the guy. I don't think he likes *me* very much, though . . ."

Bobbie patted him on the arm. "Listen, maybe you oughta see a psychoanalyst, I'm not licensed along those lines, you know . . ."

"Big joke. Listen, Bobbie, I'm serious. It hit me a few minutes ago this guy oughta be fixed up with a girl."

"And you're fresh out of spares, hunh?"

"Right."

"Sorry," she said, starting to get up, "I'm married."

He put his hand on her arm and she sat down again. "I thought maybe you could fix him up. I'm really serious, he's been acting a little wacky lately. Anyway, I've known him for a long time, we went to med school together, and we've always been friends, but, like this morning, he took my head off for nothing. I think he's just lonely for a girl, only I don't think he's the kind who'd even realize it. Or if he did, he wouldn't exactly know how to go about it. Anyway, what he took my head off about was sort of about a girl, so I figure he's a little . . . well, envious, maybe. Anyway, the girl business was what triggered him. So I figure he could do with a little feminine companionship of his own."

"Who is this lonely child?"

"Lew Worship."

"*Really?* He hasn't got a girl?"

"No."

Bobbie's face softened. "What a waste." She nodded and picked up her tray. "I'll see what I can do."

Didi was seated at a table, her breakfast dishes pretty well cleaned, an empty cup and saucer to one side, a nearly full cup of coffee in front of her.

Bobbie, putting her tray down, said, "Not with your students yet? I thought you'd be gone by now."

"Flo's taking my class through a surgery floor this morning so I can go to a CPC I'm interested in at De Witt later."

"Anything interesting?"

"Well, Riccio's conducting it."

"Ah," Bobbie said. "Mein son de vitch doctuh."

"He's all right."

"If you can handle him. He once threw a knife at his scrub nurse during an operation."

"It was the wrong instrument," Didi said, equably. "And he hasn't done it once, he's done it several times." She sipped her coffee. "As a matter of fact, he managed to stab two girls in the arm that way."

"Boy, if anyone ever hit me with a forceps . . ."

"It happens all the time on Surgery. Occupational hazard. The girls get used to it. They even expect it."

"What happens?"

Didi shrugged. "Nothing. If he misses, you keep passing instruments. If he doesn't, you wipe the blood off and disinfect if there's time—but anyway, you keep passing instruments. You don't make the same mistake soon again, though," Didi said equably.

"No, I guess not. *He* wouldn't make it *once* with me."

"Things're different in an O.R. OB—the delivery room— well, things aren't as tense. Or as brutal . . . Besides, something sweeter is happening . . ."

"Oh sure. Sweeter. Like the woman last night who . . . Never mind," Bobbie said, buttering her toast. "You're right." She bit into her toast and it crunched as she chewed it. "As a matter of fact, I've got a classic example of OB-itis right now. An intern. He's more excited than the mother."

"He'll get over it."

"No. Not this one. Every so often you get one like this. The ones who go *into* OB. Haven't you ever wondered who goes into OB? Well, anyway, this one's so excited by it all the only thing that'd calm him down is prolonged I.V. sedation."

"Impractical."

"Exactly."

"So?"

"So, I think it's fine. He'll be good; he'll make a *fine* OB man. He's already got some of the gentleness."

"Well, anyway, that certainly means he'd never make it in Surgery."

"I'd like to do something for him," Bobbie said.

"Just exactly *what* did you have in mind?"

"Fix him up with a girl."

"Why?"

"I don't know . . . something about him . . . he seems sort of a little out of balance."

"A girl would balance him?"

"Maybe," Bobbie said.

Didi said, "You sure he *wants* you to do this thing for him? A hospital is not *Tea and Sympathy*, you know."

"Okay, all right. Laugh. But I have a feeling. I'd like to see him fixed up with a nice, reasonable girl . . . I mean, I'd *like* him to keep his head in the clouds. But I'd also like to see his feet on the ground at the same time."

"So to speak."

"So to speak."

"And a girl would do this?"

Bobbie looked disgusted. "Well, I don't think a *boy* would."

Didi watched the smoke from her cigarette dissipate itself above her head. Then she looked back at Bobbie. "I have the girl for you," she said.

"Who?"

"Gloria Mead. She's a senior in one of my classes. College educated, poised, and lovely-looking too."

"Yeah? If she's such hot stuff, why hasn't someone else grabbed her?"

"Don't think they don't try, kiddo. But this one's got other ideas."

"If she's a student, she's the *only* one."

"True," Didi said. "But you can't stay a virgin forever."

"It is my impression," Bobbie said, still munching toast, "that around a hospital you can't stay a virgin at all. You'd think it was considered septic, or something."

"The girls bring it on themselves."

"Did I say *No?*"

"What's this paragon's name?"

"Which paragon?"

"The one who gets more excited than the mother and needs a girl to balance him."

"Lew Worship."

"An intern, you said."

"Yep. And smart."

"He *is* unusual for an intern. I thought they were all just sex-starved."

"This one is too, but he doesn't know it."

"Listen," Didi said, lighting Bobbie's cigarette and her own, "I don't want to throw this girl away on just *anyone.*"

"I thought you indicated she does her own thinking."

"She does. But your boy sounds as if she'd be a perfect setup for him. Defenseless. An emotional intern who loves mothers. It'd bring out *her* mother instinct."

"So?"

"So there's no use her being a real mother right away."

Bobbie snorted. "I'll give them a lecture on prophylactic procedure right after we introduce them." Bobbie quickly looked back at Didi. "Is this girl *really* that innocent?"

"Not innocent, exactly. No. But just too sweet. For a nurse, anyway."

"So's my boy. For an intern, I mean . . . Well, when'll we arrange their nuptials for?"

"Let me speak to Gloria first. I'll let you know."

Though they had more respect for her than for one another, Gloria Mead's classmates were not overly fond of her. She was older than they by two or three years because she had gone to college and gotten herself a B.S. before entering the nursing school for an R.N.—where she was given credit for a number of her college science courses and so was able to save a year.

Aside from the age difference, she was quieter than her classmates, more mature and comfortable in herself than they. She no longer needed an intense social life in order to be aware of her own existence and reassured of its worth. Thus, she did not take part in many of her classmates' social activities—their frantic flirtations, frantically boisterous parties, and frantically sophisticated double and triple and quadruple dates.

Because they admired her, her classmates resented Gloria's absence from the activities they thought she ought to share with them; resented her absence because it seemed to reflect on these activities, devalue them, passively censure them. It was only this that kept them from having a warmer regard for her.

Gloria was a little troubled by her classmates' aloofness in their dealings with her. In reaction to this distance between herself and the other girls, Gloria had developed a manner of amused detachment. It was the same manner she employed to gently rebuff, without insult, the rather frequent advances she received from interns, residents, and younger attendings.

These advances, of course, were often made publicly, and their frequency did not endear her to the other girls either, since most of them actively encouraged such attentions.

Thus, Gloria had had to resign herself—only temporarily, she hoped, for the length of her training—to having nothing but a professional existence—which made for a rather unbalanced total existence since she not only trained in the hospital, but lived in its student-nurse annex. Most of the social life in the hospital was not to her taste—she thought it was too superficial and brief, and far too physical for its brevity—and she had even less social life available to her outside the hospital since she came from another city and had little opportunity to make friends except through her professional life. In fact, her only immediate friends *had* come from her professional life—girls more her own age and temperament, like Didi Loomis, with whom she would see a movie or a play or have an occasional drink.

She was standing at the window of her room in the annex, just about ready to go off to class and noting that the sky had gotten gray from the beautiful blue it had been when she'd gotten up and it was going to be another ugly day, and she was trying to remember whether she had washed her hair *two* nights before or *three* nights before, and the telephone rang and she thought, Oh Lord, I must be late, my watch must be slow . . .

"How's your sex life?" Didi said.

"About on the level of the patients'."

"You mean *prone?*"

"Ha, ha. Believe me, it's no life for a girl. How's yours?"

"Up and down," Didi said. And then, *"Now stop that!* This is not a course in differential diagnosis."

"All right. What is it then?"

"It's a plan afoot to get you a man."

"Do I *want* one?" Gloria said, bewildered.

"Don't you?"

"A man, yes. But not one of those satyrs with an M.D. instead of horns."

"My, my, *my,*" Didi said.

"My my my," Gloria mimicked. "Did you ever go out with someone who closed in at the end of the evening by suggesting that maybe you hadn't had a vaginal recently?"

"All *right,*" Didi said. "As a student, though, let's just show a little more respect for the teacher."

"He didn't even care whether I said yes or no, he just figured I ought to be given the opportunity."

"Gloria."

"Yes, m'am."

"Do you or do you not want this date?"

"Tell me about him."

"He's an intern."

"I do not want this date."

"He's different."

"They're *all* different. That's the trouble. Any relationship to gentlemen living or dead is purely coincidental."

"I'll vouch for him personally."

"Yes? This one I would like to meet. Where do they keep him, in a bottle?"

"Gloria, you have one second to say yes or no."

"Do I know him? What's his name?"

"Lew Worship is his name."

"I don't know him."

"Yes or no?"

"All right."

"Talk about being *difficult*," Didi said. "You'll receive instructions as to time and place in a plain manila envelope," she said, and hung up.

In the nurses' station, their chatter incorrigibly buoyant and also inconsistent with the miserable quiet of the corridors, there were already gathered—waiting for the chief resident—three other residents, seven interns, two nurses, and an orderly.

Pete and Conny elected to wait in the corridor and avoid the splendid conversation of their colleagues. An immense woman in a nurse's uniform but wearing the cap of the teaching staff came toward them from the other end of the ward, shaking her head wearily and unhappily as she came. She paused by them, gathered her breath, and said to van Wyck, "Doc, you seen any students? Any on the floor yet?"

"They're all in my bedroom, Flo."

"I know," she said, starting off again, "but let me know when they come up for air."

"They don't have to," Conny told her. "Pete gives them oxygen after wreaking his masculinity on them. He's got the only private oxygen tent in the house. It was presented to him by Dr. Wohl out of recognition of a permanent emergency situation. He . . ."

"She can't hear you any more," Pete said.

"I know. Hey, listen, Pete. Tell me what your setup is with that cute type down on OB."

"Who?"

"What's her name. The one that had a crush on you. Joan. Yeah. Joan Feldman."

"I just went out with her once—when I was on OB."

"Yeah? I mean, what was your relationship to her?"

"Very simple, Doctor. Medically basic, in fact. We worked hand in rubber glove together."

"I see," Conny said. "You're sure it was *hand?*"

"That basic an anatomical mistake I do not make."

"Yuh huh vonduhful doctuh," Conny said. "Thanks."

"Don't thank me too much," Pete said, thoughtfully.

"We've got that nurses' party at Didi Loomis' New Year's Eve . . . At least I have. Did she ask you?"

"Yeah . . ."

"I've been thinking, maybe I'll take Joan if she's free."

"My usual luck."

"Want me to see if she can fix you up?"

"No. I'd rather go stag and do my own picking. Then I just have myself to blame."

"All right, Doctors," Duane's voice suddenly announced to the room. "Let's go see how many patients survived breakfast."

They trooped down the corridor and into room after room, stopping briefly at bed after bed, Duane commenting directly to Courtney Walters, and Walters noting in the order book the chief resident's new orders for each patient—change of medications, treatment procedures, changes of diet, orders for tests to be run. The patients looked up numbly as if they felt they had no positive existence.

Outside a private room, Duane stopped the entire group. "This next one is interesting," he said. "Thirty-six-year-old Negro male, admitted last night. Chief complaint—the entire right leg is ulcerated. He's signed a consent to amputate. Has a long history of alcoholism. Claims the leg developed within the last month. If it did, it might be one of the collagen group, so take a close look. The braver of our young doctors might palpate. Dr. Riccio's operating at five o'clock."

They went in. The stench was terrible and huge. The man was sitting up in bed, a metal, elongated urine receptacle in his hand. He grinned and said to Duane, "Can't pee, Doc. Been tryin' since breakfast."

Duane turned to Walters. "My first order is, get a deodorizer in here."

"Essence of peppermint," Walters said dreamily.

"When you get through in the treatment room, catheterize this man if he hasn't been able to urinate yet."

Duane pulled down the blanket. The patient pulled up his nightshirt to reveal his leg. It was a third thinner than the normal leg and striated with open, red lesions appearing irregularly and pulpously in tissue that was in some places purple and in others absolutely black. In still other places the white of bone showed through, the bone itself being palpable in several places where the tissue had degenerated entirely.

There was not a single vestige of healthy tissue on the entire limb from a point several inches above the knee down to just above the ankle.

The patient grinned almost proudly. "Some mess, hunh, Doc?" he said, exercising what little mobility the leg had left. There was no articulation at any of the joints.

With the bedcovers pulled back, the stench had become even worse. Mercouris looked at the leg, smiled tentatively at van Wyck, and then withdrew from the room. The others moved in closer and began arguing the origin and nature of the condition.

Van Wyck looked at the man grinning around the attentive circle, listened to his easy amiable joking (as if he possessed something extraordinarily desirable), was impressed by the incongruity of the appearance of the rest of the man's body. Van Wyck looked at the leg. It was so heavily ulcerated that it no longer seemed a leg at all. The man would be in the O.R. at five o'clock. Soon after, he'd lose the leg. Soon after that he'd lose his life.

At least in hours, at most in two or three days. The leg was so bad that amputation was almost certain to be unsuccessful—for the infection *inside* the leg ran too far up. Yet left alone, the leg would kill him in, Pete guessed, probably about ten days or two weeks. Less if the progress of the condition moved at the rate the patient reported. There might be one chance in a hundred he'd recover from the operation. There might be. But Pete didn't believe it. And he knew no one else did either.

The patient was about nine hours away from the O.R., and, except for his leg, impressively alive, impressively happily oriented. Pete wanted to ask him, *Do you know you're going to die today? What does it feel like being young and so alive today when you're not going to be alive tomorrow, when you'll be buried the day after, when you've eaten your last meal already except for tea, seen all you're going to see of life outside the hospital already, and going to see just nine more hours of this, going to be just nine more hours . . . ?*

To Pete it felt unbelievable. A person can't just cease. Not when the world is the place where it's so easy to laugh and where you're having a fine time right now only nine hours before ceasing. A person can't just cease—not without some more appropriate psychological prelude than this . . .

But a person can. Is is Is. This man he was looking at, hearing the man laughing, would probably not *be* when he, Pete, reported for rounds this time tomorrow morning. This same time. Is is Is. It could only turn to horror if you denied it.

Pete examined the leg and then scrubbed up. Then he was out in the corridor and found himself walking next to Conny again. Conny said, "Boy. I'm used to just about anything. But that got me."

"It didn't make me feel too good either," Pete said.

"That was mine."

"Your what?"

"My one case in a thousand I wasn't ready for. The way I was warned."

Pete nodded. He had been warned too. That doctors are not special people, not always impervious . . .

The first time he had reacted to something emotionally that he hadn't expected to react to emotionally, he had worked out a theory for himself in detail. The theory explained, and by explaining it helped exorcise or dispel the reaction he'd had to his very reacting—for he had considered that manner of reacting a frightening weakness. And the theory had helped mitigate that fright, had made it possible for him to accept without fear the ever present possibility of reacting that way emotionally again to some patient's condition.

He had decided that: Doctors are not special people, not a species emotionally apart. It is the attitude toward them that is special. But not they themselves.

He had decided that: One is revolted by the handicapped or diseased or injured out of fear that the same condition may happen to oneself. It is not sympathy. Sympathy is a matter of making your own revulsion more acceptable to yourself. It is a way of masking your own revulsion for your own benefit every bit as much as for the person whose condition revolts you.

He had decided that: One is revolted out of fear that the same condition might happen to oneself. But you forget that the handicapped, say, has made a much larger adjustment to his condition and acceptance of his condition than the person seeing him and fearing can possibly even *imagine*. No matter how slight that acceptance and adjustment is in

terms of the psychology of the handicapped person himself.

He had decided that: The doctor is fairly immune to fearing and thereby becoming revolted because his experience
gives him a perspective which mitigates the unreasonable
parts of the attitude—just as the average person is not revolted by a splinter or a cut thumb. For he knows what can
be done for the condition and how to do it; and thus,
it does not represent a mysterious and unknown danger to
him. And just as the average person never gets *used* to a cut
thumb, so too the doctor never gets *used* to disease and
injury. But, out of knowledge (*not* familiarity) both the average layman and the doctor learn how to be fairly well at
ease.

But doctors are not entirely immune, the way the special
attitude towards them supposes them to be. Knowledge is
not an impervious or total or constant shield. For the doctor is still a human being. And each one will have a weak
point that knowledge can't protect—a sight or smell that
may make him suddenly and unexpectedly nauseous.

He had decided that: The immunity to this kind of reaction (when the immunity exists) is not, as he'd always
thought it to be, toughness or callousness. It is the simple
result of knowledge and understanding gained through experience. But there was that simple danger of depending
upon these factors to be always efficacious. And that kind of
dependent expectation could be and was incalculably dis-
astrous. *That* was the aspect of it to avoid.

"Mr. Quieno is another prospective amputee," Duane said
for the benefit of those who had not seen the case before.
Duane was standing by a bed in another six-bed room. "Mr.
Quieno has extreme frostbite of the large toe of the right
foot. He got it while sleeping on a park bench while quite
drunk. His history is also long and alcoholic. Right in all
particulars, Mr. Quieno?"

"Right," said Mr. Quieno, clear and direct.

"Mr. Quieno is a stickler about particulars and details.
Right, Mr. Quieno?"

"Right."

"He just doesn't bother to be a stickler about taking care
of himself. He figures we'll do it for him and keep him on
welfare at the same time . . ."

"Right," said Mr. Quieno, unasked.

"This is his third NNH visit with us this year. I believe he manages some of these things on purpose. I believe he likes to stay on welfare," Duane said.

"Right," said Mr. Quieno.

"Here's a paper for you to sign, Mr. Quieno. It's the consent to amputate."

Mr. Quieno took up glasses from his bed table, put them on, and read the paper through. After long, careful study he looked up. "Amputate *what?*"

"The large toe of your right foot, of course."

"Then put it in so it reads that way, you cutthroat. And when you get through, if I'm missing any more than that large right toe, *I'll* cut *you* for a change. And I'll just leave enough of you to be thrown out of the profession. *Understand?*"

Duane regarded Mr. Quieno benevolently, took the paper, fixed it and handed it back. "All right?" he said. "All right in all particulars, Mr. Quieno?"

Quieno studied the paper again and then signed.

Duane said amiably, "And if I see *you* in here again I'll cut you up so much you'll be a walking vacuum. How do you like that, Mr. Quieno?" Duane said, no longer amiable.

"Not without a consent to amputate, you won't," Mr. Quieno said, glaring at Duane. "Now beat it. I want to sleep."

Duane nodded and smiled and moved on to the next bed. Walters handed him a chart from a wheeled rack of them Donnecker had been pulling along.

Duane studied the chart and began reading. "Mr. Horace Markham. White, male, age fifty-two, first NNH admission. Admitted through Emergency five o'clock this morning. Lacerations and incised wounds of the head, seventeen stitches, various contusions, fractures negative by x-ray . . . uh . . . brought in by prowl-car team . . . found lying on sidewalk . . . probably attacked and robbed after leaving bar at closing time . . . no personal identification . . ."

"They took my God damn wallet," Markham said.

"Change his bandages and check that he was cleaned up properly."

"*The hell,*" Markham said. "I don't want a God damn intern, I want a doctor."

"Everyone here is a doctor," Duane said. "With, of course,

the exception of the nurses." He handed the chart back to Donnecker and moved toward the next bed.

Markham got up swiftly and grabbed Duane's shoulder. "*Listen,* you'd better . . ."

Duane turned around. "*Get back in bed!*" he shouted. "*Move!*"

Markham hardly hesitated. Safely in bed, the covers pulled up and held like reins in his hands, he said, "I want my own doctor. I don't belong here. I want my own doctor and *his* hospital. I don't know why the stupid cops brought me to *this* place. I'm not a bum. But no one's gonna touch me. No God damn intern is gonna even take my pulse. You touch me and I'll sue till they take your license away . . ."

"You through?" Walters said. "At five o'clock this morning when they got me out of bed to keep you from floating away in your own blood, you didn't seem at all averse to having an intern touch you."

"You were only doing your job," Markham said. "So don't play hardship with me."

All Walters could manage was to shake his head with disbelief.

Markham said to Duane, "They shouldn't have brought me here in the first place. I told you. I would like my own doctor and I would like to get moved from here."

"If you'll give me your doctor's name I'll call him and give him your message," Duane said. He stared at Markham. "*Well?*"

"Thank you," Markham said, by no means mildly. He gave his doctor's name and turned his back.

"Mr. Dowling," Duane said at the next bed, "have you made up your mind yet?"

"I'll know this afternoon," Dowling said carefully.

"We can't keep you around here forever," Duane said. "I want to know by three o'clock."

The army moved on. Van Wyck paused. He stared at the man. Forty-four years old, a big man, and so full of guilt that he was tentative and humble, sickeningly humble, and very careful in front of the youngest intern.

The man looked up at van Wyck tentatively, a tentative smile trying to display itself on his face. "I woulda known by now," the man said apologetically, "but I think it's a question I oughta discuss with my girl. I mean, I think she

oughta have a say. Hunh, Doc? I mean, I been tryin' t'get in
touch with 'er," the man said apologetically, "but, you know,
sometimes I can't reach 'er just right away. I mean, just off
like that. I mean . . ."

Van Wyck knew (and understood why) it was imperative
that the doctor never make a value judgment, never make
a moral evaluation of a patient. But this one disgusted him
beyond all intellectual consideration. He had been in clinic
twice, on the floor just a month earlier. He had been offered
psychiatric aid. He had refused it. He had been warned
about his condition. He had ignored it and purposely made it
worse. Van Wyck was disgusted by him.

"Listen, Mr. Dowling," van Wyck said. "You don't *have*
to have your stomach removed. We told you. All you have to
do is stop drinking. We know you can. You go for months
not drinking. But whenever you feel like drawing that welfare
check, you just drink your stomach into a storm and come
into clinic and get us to put you on relief. All you have to
do is decide not to try to freeload that way any more and you
can keep your stomach. Personally, I don't think you will.
I think you'd just as soon have your stomach cut out. *I'd* just
as soon not bother with you; I didn't take up medicine to spend
my time treating gutless freeloaders who make *themselves*
sick, there's plenty of others who . . ."

A voice behind him said, *"That's enough, van Wyck."*
Grenatti said, "Get into the treatment room."

Van Wyck started out. Behind him he heard, "I'm going to
report that man." "No, that's not necessary, Mr. Dowling."
"I'm going to report him, you can't stop me . . ."

In the treatment room—tile-floored, two tables, several
instrument stands, two sinks, cabinets, and lit by two large,
circular, frosted-lensed operating fixtures—Mercouris, gloved
and at work, was feeling his usual reaction to postoperative
evidence of surgical procedure.

Looking at the various incisions he was helping to re-
dress (as he did daily) he felt castrated, at least sexless, a
great hollowness, as if he had voided his sex.

The old man on the table before him had been cut from
above his abdomen straight through his genitals, and all non-
essential organs had been removed. He even urinated through
a catheter into a bottle strapped to his side.

Conny reached into the incision—which extended laterally

under the skin on each side for two or three inches—and removed the absorbent dressings that he had packed there the day before. The man could not be sewed up until these pockets had healed without infection. It was doubtful that he would live that long. In the meantime, the treatment room procedure prevented infection from setting in.

The old man moaned, over and over again, crying to himself and expecting no surcease from the pain or from those attending him. Conny had given him as large a dose of Demerol as he thought the man could safely manage, but Demerol did nothing but make you feel drunk. The pain was still there.

These old men made him uneasy. They looked at you, it seemed to Conny, with such jealousy. These old ones, postoperative, sick and with so little chance of recovery it was hardly worth the operation—these old ones, who before their operation had been so strong (how otherwise could they have survived the operation?); the way they look at you, wanting to have youth again, *your* youth if they could get it, if it were possible, wanting to be youthful again and not oblivious of its value, wanting to suck it from you with their eyes, almost like a vampire . . .

Duane said, "Cut all that black out, or scrape it out," and moved away.

The old man continued to moan, louder with every touch.

Conny thought of the cigarette he'd have out in the corridor as soon as this was finished. He continued to re-dress the incision.

Two interns from other services, Aptshult and Parelli, stood behind him with Walters. Walters was saying, "I tell you, you'll never see anything like this again. Didn't I tell you? Look. The whole goddam peritoneum's exposed . . ."

"Did you scrub on it?" Aptshult said.

"No."

"Jesus, how I'd love to have scrubbed on that."

Van Wyck and Mercouris went back to the nurses' station and lit cigarettes and waited for the residents and/or calls from Admitting.

The immense nurse named Flo was surrounded by a number of young women in the royal blue shirts of students. The white, high-necked jumper-aprons they wore over the shirts sprayed out stiffly at the hem from starch and moved as if held by wire as the girls bent over charts. Three stripes on their sleeves indicated they were near graduation.

Some more interns returned and, much quieter now than earlier, sat around the station waiting.

Pete said, "I'll be damned. That one there has a bite on the back of her neck. Human-type bite."

"Which one?"

"Look." Pete went over and touched the girl on the nape of the neck. The girl didn't even look up from her chart.

"Jesus. I wish I'd put it there," Conny said. She was a very attractive girl.

"There's your date for New Year's."

"Too young."

"Don't be silly," Pete said. "She's lovely." He said to her, "How old are you?"

Flo sighed wearily. "Even while I'm trying to teach them something?"

"Only take a minute," Pete said. And to the girl, "Will you tell me?"

The girl looked up, flushed but not entirely displeased by the attention, and not without her own control of the situation. "Twenty-two," she said. "And I'm busy New Year's Eve."

"My luck," Conny said.

I *am* complacent, van Wyck thought. I do these things too easily.

The immense nurse said, "All right, we'll go see the patients now. I want you each to give your patient seventy-five cc's of TLC."

A girl said, *"TLC?"*

The interns laughed.

"Tender loving care," Flo said, and led her brood into the corridor.

Duane returned and said, "Dr. Riccio is having a Clinical-Pathological-Conference over at De Witt at ten. Grenatti and Baker will cover for anyone who wants to go, and I think it's worth your time. Who's up?"

Van Wyck said, "Yeah."

"Okay," Mercouris said.

"I'll scrub," Walters said.

"Anyone else . . . ?"

At the elevator Mercouris said, "Man, like I'm going back

to my room and sack. Four hours of sleep a night is just not enough. Make sure I'm up when you get back?"

"Sure," Pete said.

De Witt, New North's teaching affiliate, was twenty blocks south and several blocks over. The teaching staff of both hospitals was identical, but most of the teaching, including the CPC's, was done at De Witt since De Witt also embraced a medical school. Men who were on the staff there and also taught had also to be on call as attendings at New North in order to teach.

The room in which the CPC was held was a regular classroom in the hospital itself. It was equipped with chairs that had wide arms for note-taking and its floor was slanted so that those sitting in the back half (the back five rows) could see the blackboard and the x-ray backlight.

The first five rows were occupied—but not very fully occupied—by men in suits who seemed to be executives lounging in their own offices. The rear five rows were tightly occupied by a number of young men in whites, some with the black shield and letters *D.H.* of the Department of Health stitched on their sleeve (these from New North), and some with red insignia and the words *De Witt Hospital* on the sleeve. Van Wyck and Walters nodded to De Witt interns and residents they knew and sat down to look over the mimeographed histories they'd been handed on coming in.

A gray-haired staff man in whites who had admitted the two cases to be discussed read a history. Two lab doctors in scrub, a man and a young woman, read their determinations and presented x-rays. Dr. Riccio, who had operated, outlined his procedure and the reasons for the particular procedure, both operative and postoperative.

Then the other doctors, those in the first five rows, began their questions and, in some cases, their lengthy criticisms. The criticism sometimes bordered upon insult, but van Wyck appreciated its objectivity. It was interesting, though; especially when an older man cut and reduced a younger man to incoherency—it was interesting to see that competition seemed to reach full bloom *after* an established practice rather than before. No one in the rear five rows asked a question in the two hours the CPC went on—except for Duane. When he had stated his question, several men in the front of

the room turned and nodded agreement. Van Wyck was
impressed beyond any respect he'd ever before had for
Duane or any other resident he'd worked under.

Walters decided to stay and have lunch at De Witt and
van Wyck drove back alone. The hospital parking lot had
a chain across its entrance. Van Wyck blew his horn. The
attendant stuck his head out of his shack and shook his head.
No. The man withdrew again. Van Wyck put his hand on the
horn and held it there.

The attendant came out and walked over leisurely. He
stepped over the chain, did not take it down to let himself
out. He came to the window of van Wyck's car. "No room,"
the attendant said.

"What, exactly, do you call that *over there?*"

"That's for doctors," the attendant said.

Van Wyck patiently opened his overcoat and displayed
his whites. "Doctor," he said. "D-O-C-T-O-R, *doctor.* For
chrisake, you know me, you know this car."

The attendant shrugged. "I said it's for doctors, not interns.
No room," he said, and walked away.

"Why you sonofabitch!" van Wyck yelled. "There's room
for *twenty* cars! Hey, listen. I have to be in clinic in half an
hour and I still haven't eaten."

The attendant shrugged but didn't turn around.

Van Wyck checked to see if he was in first, took his foot
off the brake, slowly released the clutch, and pressed the
accelerator to the floor.

The chain snapped satisfactorily without the slightest
tremor inside the car. He parked and got out. Seeing the
attendant running at him and hearing him yelling furiously,
van Wyck took out his notebook, wrote his name, tore out
the page, replaced the notebook and pen in his pocket, handed
the page to the still-yelling attendant, and went across the
street to the hospital.

He had lunch with Jay Fishbein, who was currently on
OB and was surprised at how light things were lately, but
exhausted anyway, and with the anesthesiologist, Dr. Bloomberg, who stated, "I can't escape the conclusion that it is
the opinion of the powers that be in postgraduate medical
schooling that one cannot learn unless one is either tired,
browbeaten, or hungry, and preferably a combination of

all three. TBH, I call it. Tired, browbeaten, and hungry. TBH. The intern's syndrome; see *Syndrome, intern's*. First described by Gower Bloomberg, a New York anesthesiology specialist attending at New North Hospital quote unquote. Quote, *The systematic degradation of the individual,* unquote, *Bloomberg's Dictionary of Morbid Disease*. Meanwhile, the man who's getting paid for a particular case—at least in a voluntary institution—is, not infrequently, home sleeping because he lives so far away he couldn't possibly get there in time anyway. The story of my life. I interned at a voluntary hospital."

"Mine, too. The story of," van Wyck said.

"You know what I object to?" Fishbein said. "I object to the systematic undercutting of whatever ideals you bring into internship."

"My life," said Bloomberg.

"Mine," said van Wyck.

"The three of us ought to get drunk together some night," Bloomberg said. "Only I'm afraid it wouldn't do any good. Drinking is only analgesic."

"You know what the usual attending says when you ask him why internship has to be this way?" Van Wyck looked around.

"I went through it, why shouldn't you?" Fishbein said.

"You get so sick of it after just a few weeks. All I do is draw blood, write charts, change dressings, suture scalps, take histories, test urine, and remove splinters just about," van Wyck said.

Fishbein looked at the ceiling as if, as he was, so tired of voicing the same complaints ineffectually over and over, he was bored with his own now meaningless words. "Attempt, usually successful, to break ideals. The hell with ideals. Drop you on your ass the first sign of an ideal you show . . . Penal servitude, forced into work far beneath your ability because . . ."

Bloomberg said smartly, as if on parade or, anyway, recitation, "Because and for the *privilege of learning*. Wonderful phrase, isn't it? Mark, gentlemen, how it rings in the ears: *privilege of learning*. Wonderful phrase. Absolutely beautiful. Covers a multitude of sins and saves the hospital money at the same time." He went peacefully back to eating.

Van Wyck, working up to real heat again such as he'd felt

outside the parking lot, quoted, *"We had it rough, you'll have it rough, too!"*

"TBH. First identified by Bloomberg of New North Hospital. The intern's syndrome. Price of the privilege of learning," Bloomberg said.

"On the job training," van Wyck said, with real disgust. "Hell, GM has an executive-training group. Every other kind of organization has one. And *pays* them. Pays them damn well for what they have to offer. *We* have four years of college *plus* four years of postgraduate work and what have we got?"

"Not an executive-on-job-training group," Fishbein said.

"Damn right," Bloomberg said pleasantly. "You've got forty a month as an intern and maybe an average of a hundred a month as a resident."

"In any other profession you get *paid* while you learn," van Wyck said.

"The public is so used to getting free medical care, they don't expect to pay for it on any level. You're an intern? That's your job—of course, *job* doesn't indicate pay in this context. The other professions are less professional. That's why they pay more," Bloomberg said reasonably. "Less technical, too, most of them."

Fishbein shook his head. "I don't know. They say we're getting trained. But that's not *why* they should pay us almost nothing . . ."

"Don't knock your head against the wall," Bloomberg said. "If there's gonna be any changes, it'll have to come from the licensed, practicing physicians, *you* can't do anything about it. Except, of course, remember how it was later when *you're* practicing." He nodded at them and got up and left the dining hall.

What van Wyck didn't like in the day, what he didn't like particularly in Surgery, what, in fact, bugged him the most always, but certainly and particularly in Surgery, was clinic.

Some of the people who came to Surgery clinic were fine people, people who deserved to be treated and treated unstintingly—*most* of them. The rest, maybe one out of five, were not fine people. They were like Mr. Dowling and they disgusted him. And they *deserved* to be treated accordingly. Yet he always managed to treat them as well as the others.

He had been told that some of them came to Medicine in a self-induced diabetic coma—that is, they were diabetics who drank until they became comatose and got carted off to the city hospital, there to live on the city, and thereafter, for a couple of weeks anyway, to live off the city on the outside.

And then there were cases that came into Surgery with a peripheral leg ulcer—an ulcerated condition that had been brought under control just two or three weeks before upstairs in the ward, an ulcerated condition kept active on purpose. A mistreated peripheral leg ulcer that they could die of when so many people wanted to live, when so many people who wanted to live were suffering from conditions contracted unwillingly. A mistreated peripheral leg ulcer mistreated just to get back on welfare and relief.

All you could do—as a responsible doctor—was be disgusted and give them hell and make it so miserable for them that they couldn't bring themselves to come to clinic at all but know they need the clinic (and the doctor) to stay alive. So that when they finally do come back, they pay attention for a while and don't mistreat themselves on purpose. Until they've been out for three or four weeks and the old desire to get on welfare and relief returns again, until they return again with the same condition now complicated by abuse beyond anyone's recuperative ability and beyond any doctor's ability to repair. Like Dowling. The sonofabitch. Month after month, year after year, until they died—and were replaced by two new identical cases for each death.

And when welfare and relief checks came in on the fifteenth of the month, the load on the clinics and the Surgery and Medicine wards doubled. They cashed the checks at the liquor stores and spent them there. Or in bars. And then got drunk or fought or got drunk *and* fought—and became the responsibility of the hospital and the city. But particularly, the hospital. White or black, Spanish-speaking or English-speaking—you couldn't, at least, find grounds for discrimination in New North's histories.

He walked down the long, extremely wide corridor with benches lined up in front of the different service clinics like companies, each bench filled, every bench surrounded by standees who had arrived too late to get seats.

He said to the orderly, "Open the dikes."

It was one o'clock. By four, he'd see, diagnose, treat, and dress or re-dress thirty-five to sixty patients and he'd give each (or *try* to) as much attention as ideally he would in a private office—even the malingerers. And there were four other interns and two residents working in partitioned booths next to his.

At *four thirty*—since nothing ever worked out on schedule for an intern—van Wyck went back up to his room and shaved again. The telephone rang. He was admitting intern for the day, and the head nurse for his ward had a new patient for him to look over. He wearily put his white jacket back on and left his room . . .

Admission data, the standard form, the whitish aluminum clipboard with the drop front that became the chart when it had papers in it . . . Chief complaint . . . white male . . . seventy-one years . . . admitted at: by: to: . . . Patient's History . . . # of hospitalizations . . . Family History . . . where born . . . important that he'd never been in tropics, note you noted that . . . HPI (history of present illness) . . . Habits—smokes how much, drinks how much, takes no drugs . . . Review of All Systems . . . eyes, ears, nose, mouth, chest, lungs, heart, GU, GI, neurological, skin . . . eyes, sees well, no pain, uses glasses . . . admission by staff doctor, referred to Surgery for probable presence of carcinoma of the rectum, rectal carcinoma established . . . HISTORY IS EIGHTY PERCENT OF DIAGNOSIS . . . ears, no ringing; nose, no obstruction; mouth . . . neck, no swelling; chest, no pain; lungs, no cough; heart, no chest pain, no history of coronaries, no palpitation; genitourinary, no . . . metabolics, lost fifty pounds in two months, 170 to 119, 10/5 to 12/5; skin, no . . . rashes, no . . . bloody urine . . . PSYCH, no hist of hallucinations . . . WNWD (well nourished, well developed) white male in no acute distress . . . pulse equals . . . B.P. equals . . . NOTE: operative risk irregular pulse . . . ORDER . . . EKG, Chest x-ray, BUN, FBS . . .

Van Wyck was thankful for one thing: he wasn't interning at a hospital that demanded a *ten*-page history for every patient whether the patient warranted it or not. But he thought of the kind of patient he would have, at the moment, welcomed: the good man who came in at night in a coma and couldn't talk. There would be no need for an admitting intern then.

This new one talked plainly and quietly in a gentlemanly

manner, but—if you were admitting intern—the trouble was that they talked at all.

Five-o'clock rounds took only twenty minutes. He had fixed his new admission up with all the care and attention the man might himself demand were he a private patient in a voluntary hospital; and he had advised Baker, the charge resident, that it was probably a case of C-a of the rectum.

"Did you examine him?" Baker said.

"No," van Wyck said, "I just saw him on the street and asked him in."

"Don't get funny with me, boy. Did you *feel* this C-a of the rectum?"

"I did."

"You felt it."

"I felt what felt like one."

"*And?*"

"*And,* I figure him for five years if he's not operated. Maybe a couple of months if he is. Maybe less. Among other things, he has a very irregular pulse."

"Not, in your opinion, a good operative risk."

"I'd like to see the lab reports on the tests I ordered before I committed myself the way you want me to."

Baker nodded. "That's a good idea, van Wyck. The way I want you to commit yourself is the same way the patient wants you to commit yourself. Let's go see him."

On the way out of the patient's room, the old man called van Wyck back and whispered to him.

Outside, Baker said, "Something personal, or can we all know?"

"With great dignity, my quiet old gentleman in there just told me, *quote,* I just shitted without blood for the first time in two months, *unquote.*"

Baker said, "With study you'll develop the perfect bedside manner, van Wyck. In here two hours and he's cured after just seeing you long enough for you to take his history."

In the nurses' station, the head nurse said, "Page for you, Dr. van Wyck."

Van Wyck picked up the telephone and said to the operator, "Dr. van Wyck."

"One moment, Doctor," the operator said. There was a click and then another click

Then still another click and a female voice said, "Dr. Wohl's office, Dr. van Wyck. Please tell your resident you're wanted here immediately."

Mrs. Lawrence looked up just long enough to say, "Knock."

Van Wyck knocked, and Dr. Wohl's voice said, "Yes."

He went in. Wohl said, "Well, van Wyck."

Van Wyck faced a somewhat pompous man of immense proportions who spoke with the rapidity of a machine gun in a voice pitched somewhat higher than one would expect of such a hulk and, of course, than one would expect from such a face, for the face was always an angry face. Though his subordinates often found him pompous, or at least gratuitously resplendent, Dr. Wohl acquitted himself and his office duties in nothing but the most admirable fashion. He worked an average of fifteen hours a day and managed to accomplish twenty-four hours' worth of work in that time—running the hospital, supervising its financial arrangements, interviewing prospective personnel, interviewing personnel with outstanding problems, testing new materials, drugs, biologicals and mechanical equipment, and still managing to drop in on the staff in all stations from the wards and clinics to the kitchens and from the solarium to the boiler room. Van Wyck had a great respect for him.

Wohl studied van Wyck reservedly. Finally, he said, "From what I gather—or rather, from what has been called to my attention by various sources—you've had quite a busy day, as I understand it, Dr. van Wyck." More study and more reservation. Then, in a tired, unhappy voice, *"Please,* Dr. van Wyck, don't fight the unions *all* by yourself. And please, try to treat our parking lot a little more gently. Those of us who for years used to drive round and round here with a patient waiting inside in an operating room—we take a certain amount of pride and comfort in our little parking lot. We'd like to see it stay in one piece . . ."

More reserved study. Finally, as if coming awake from a long hurtful weariness, he said, "Ah, my dear fellow, please be seated. I understand you've been playing God, *never mind"*—holding up a hand—"I'll do the talking. A patient named Dowling complained—and correctly so.

Justifiably so. Please remember that this is a hospital, not a religion, and you are a member of a profession, not a cult. Bearing this in mind, you may be able to avoid scaring the patients out of what little wits they are able to display to us. While you're here, is there any other personal problem you'd like to discuss with me? No? Then thank you very much for coming by and I'm sure you'll be interested, if you can find the time to attend, in hearing Dr. Jenkins next Tuesday in Room two eighty . . . Good day."

Van Wyck went directly to the dining hall for dinner. On his way in he was stopped by Tom Elwood.

Elwood shook his hand and said, "Thank you. Thank you so much."

Van Wyck said, *"What for?"*

"Thank you," he said, shaking his hand again. "Just, *thank you.*"

He sat with Ted Eckland and Alicia Liu and Jim Aptshult. "You know what just happened to me?" he said to them. "I met Tom Elwood and he stopped me and he . . ."

"Thanked you," Eckland said.

"Yes," Pete said, nodding. "That's what he did."

"He *kissed* Lee," Eckland said. "He thanked Jim. And after months of not talking to me, he shook my hand *and* thanked me."

"For *what?*" Pete said.

"Who knows," Aptshult said.

38

Dr. Fishbein had had a relatively light thirty-six hours in OB. He had been involved in only six work-ups and four deliveries—along with the usual rounds on the *post partum* floor. He had been able to get quite a lot of reading done for the oral boards he would have to take at the end of the year before he could settle into his residency. *If,* he reminded himself, he *got* the residency. He thought only in terms of two or three of them (out of the ten applications allowed). These two or three were the important ones, the ones where he could see the work done he wanted to see, and be closely involved with it too.

His specialty was to be a new field which was just being explored—neuro-ophthalmological surgery. At least four years residency. But he was certain he would be unable to satisfy himself with anything less than six—four years in one place, two in another. There was too much to learn in just four years. It would be a starting all over again. But he wasn't depressed about it. He felt good enough to walk all the twenty blocks home, get some fresh air after the hospital. And the walking made him feel better still. The future was encouraging—he was sure to get at least one of the three residencies he wanted, and the years involved, he felt, would be fascinating beyond anything he could now imagine them to be . . .

He had a beautiful wife who could cook like a French chef with almost nothing at all to work with. She kept the world balanced for him—worked as a secretary to pay the bills and rent he couldn't on his forty a month, loved him, made him feel they weren't really living under hardship. And he was going home to her now. The only thing that distressed his high spirits at all was passing a florist, and then another, and then, two blocks from home, still another. Lois loved flowers. He kept having to fight himself to keep from going in and buying her something, if only one flower. But she had every dime, *actually* every dime, figured and allotted, from his bus fares to and from the hospital, to the one-tenth of a dress she figured she could buy herself each month. Even so, Jay thought, he couldn't remember her getting a new dress—or a new *anything*, for that matter —since they'd married a year and a half before . . . If he brought her anything, even one flower, she'd be more likely to be furious than pleased. *Women*, he thought. But there was pleasure in his thought, and a warm appreciation of Lois. And at the same time he no longer felt so assured of the rewards of the future. He need *not* get any of the residencies he wanted so badly . . . And even so, even if he did, just the basic residency was so desperately long . . .

39

He walked up the four flights to the top-floor apartment that always scared him because there was no fire escape, only another flight outside their front door up to the roof, from which you could get to another building. But flames had a way of following a draft straight up a stairway, so that escape that way in case of fire would be the least feasible. It frightened him that Lois slept in this building, its walls cracked, its floors and stairs of old, creaking wood, its wiring old and uncertain . . . Because he was an intern. Because the room and kitchen and bath had the wonderful advantage of being priced within the range of Lois' salary as a secretary. It was so simple. He was an intern. Therefore his wife had to live in a place where one had to consider and reckon with the equally simple factor of the possibility of a fire—a fire from which one equally possibly might not escape.

Lois barely kissed him. "I haven't started dinner," she said. "You didn't call."

"Oh, God, honey, I'm sorry. I forgot. When I got off I just put on my coat and left I was so glad to be getting out."

"It won't take long, anyway," she said. "It's hash. I'm sorry, but that's all I could afford—I had to pay a big cleaning bill today, I couldn't wear anything to the office any more, all my things had gotten so dirty . . ."

"Don't be such an idiot," he said, holding her. "You don't have to *explain*, for godsake." She relaxed a little and rubbed her cheek against his and then kissed him. "That's a whole lot better," he said.

"It's nice to have you home."

"Me too," he said.

She grinned and stood back from him and straightened her dress. "Anyway," she said, "I really am sorry about the hash . . . But I'm going to bake it with garlic and ketchup and some of that sherry we still have left . . ."

He held her as tightly as he could. "I don't come home just to eat, you know."

"I'm glad. In that case you can take your overcoat off now."

He hung the coat up and said, "As long as everyone is apologizing *and* explaining, you know if I stay around long enough to call you, it's even money someone'll grab me for something and I'll be busy for another couple of hours."

"Well, you could go up to your room to do it . . ."

"Yeah. I never thought of that. Thanks, Sam."

"My pleasure. There's enough sherry left for you to have a drink before dinner."

"Mmmmm. We'll split it, Sam."

"You have it. I'm so hungry one sip would knock me out."

"Can't have that," he said, pouring himself a fruit-juice glass full.

"Everything's all ready, though. I just have to put it in the oven."

"So put."

"I'm putting." She looked up. "And what do you think *you're* doing?"

"I'm *patting*. You know drink always makes me lascivious, Sam."

"Sam is busy fixing dinner. Lois, your wife, will drop by after the dishes are done."

"I'll be waiting for her." He lit a cigarette and gave it to her. She took a single puff and handed it back and went on fixing dinner. "What's new with Lois, by the way?"

"She got a letter from her sister Caroline."

"And what *of* Denver's most beautiful bride-to-be?"

"Denver's most beautiful bride-to-be is upset because I won't be at her wedding."

"Oh," he said, the sound of the word quiet and different from the way he'd been talking up till that instant.

"I'm sorry," she said. "I'm really sorry I mentioned it, darling."

"No, *I'm* sorry."

"Forget it, Sam."

"I am sorry. Maybe we can work *something* out . . ."

Lois suddenly slammed the oven door and stood straight and looked directly at him. *"How?"* she said, accusing.

"I'm sorry. It was a stupid thing to say."

"It was, indeed, a stupid thing to say," she said. "We just *can't* manage it, that's all . . ."

"Look, I'll try writing my parents . . ."

"Jay, how can you? How *can you* stand there and talk that way? They told us not to get married till later. I won't have you ask them for a single cent . . ." She carefully put her pot holders down on a cabinet top and stood not looking at him, her back toward him.

In a moment, watching her back move, he could see that she was crying. He put his glass down and went to her and put his hands on her shoulders tentatively, a little afraid. She shook herself from his touch and he stepped back.

Then she turned and dabbed at her eyes with a paper napkin. "How long can we keep living like this?" she said soberly and quietly. "How long can we just *subsist*? We can't even-afford to go to a movie once a month. How ever did you think we could pay for me to go out to Denver?"

"I.. ."

"My only sister is getting married," she said again soberly and quietly. "Do you remember our wedding?"

"Yes . . . but . . ."

"There's no connection," she said. "I just suddenly thought of it. I'm not going to Caroline's wedding, and that settles that. She's not going to call off the wedding just because I'm not there. Nobody's going to die from it. But Jay. How can we keep living like this? Four and a half more years like this . . ."

"Don't you want me to be the kind of doctor I want to be?"

"*You can ask me if* . . ." She suddenly looked directly at him again, her voice almost without tonality. "I don't know any more."

He nodded. This whole conflict was so easy to understand. He picked up the glass of sherry again and sipped from it and carried it into their only room and looked out of their only window and lit a cigarette and then put the cigarette out in an ashtray that bore an almost worn-off decal and words reading *University of Colorado* and walked back into the kitchen.

Lois closed the oven door quietly. "Dinner will be ready in about five minutes," she said.

"Look, honey," he said, "I can probably get a direct commission into the army, take my residency there in some other field. Langley arranged a voluntary induction like that. And you get an allowance for wives. It won't be luxurious living, but at least it'll be better than . . ."

"*No!*" She stared at him furious and helpless. "That won't help us. Can't you see anything? That would just make us richer paupers. It's a *half* measure. We'd still be paupers. We'd still be living like animals. And then what afterwards? Back to your *four*-year residency? Oh, don't try to figure anything out. Just go on doing your doctoring, while we . . . we . . ." She began crying, angrily, and would not let him touch her.

An anesthetist can make almost twenty thousand dollars a year in almost any hospital in the country immediately after completing his residency. It is usually one of the shortest

residencies, two years; and it can be served in the United
States Army, which pays doctors (who are officers) the
same amount it pays all other officers of equal grade—
that is, considerably more than the average resident makes.
Twenty thousand is both the bottom *and* the top for most
anesthetists. There is relatively little opportunity to expand
the income. But the income begins relatively early in the
physician's career.

The next morning, in free time he created by skipping a
CPC, Jay began writing letters of application for residencies
in anesthesiology, his first letter being an inquiry to the
Surgeon General of the Medical Corps of the United States
Army. And after all, he told himself, it *is* still part of surgery.
A major part, an unappreciated part usually, but a major
part . . .

40

Mildred Donnecker did most of her grocery shopping for one
person's appetite rather than for two. Because of his schedule
at the hospital, Fred was only home for every seventh and
eighth meal. Mildred ate breakfast, lunch and dinner alone.
Then she slept alone. Then she got up alone and ate another
solitary breakfast and another solitary lunch. Fred's thirty-
six hours theoretically ended at six P.M. But even though the
the apartment was only ten minutes from the hospital, he
was rarely able to get home before eight.

On the day of the once every other day that Mildred had
dinner with her husband, she stayed in bed as long as she
could bear to. Then she put off having her lunch for as long
as possible so that she wouldn't be hungry—not too hungry,
anyway—until Fred got home; so that she could last without
food until she could have the meal with Fred. After her late
lunch she usually washed her hair and did her nails, taking
as long as possible with each task. Then she chose what she
would wear, taking as much care in her choice as she would
have were Fred a college date rather than a husband. She
usually tried to plan something a little elaborate for these
dinners—not because either of them was particularly conscious of the food they ate, but because an elaborate dish
took more preparing and therefore more *time* to prepare

than a plain one. She could busy herself for an entire hour chopping things and laying them out for when Fred got home and she put them on. And an hour was a very satisfying unit of time for Mildred to get rid of.

But by five-thirty or six she usually had nothing more to do. If she could think of something to do, it was a blessing and she did it. She didn't particularly like liquor, but drinking one drink took up some time and some attention. So did listening to the fifteen-minute-long six-o'clock news. So, occasionally, did letter-writing but every day it seemed she had already written to her mother only yesterday. In fact, she had written to just about everybody she knew at all well. Sometimes they were interested enough to answer within a week. Sometimes it was several weeks, and sometimes not at all. But she always got off her reply immediately upon receipt of any mail.

On the days when Fred wasn't home at all she made herself go to museums. In the evenings she saw a movie. She wasn't too interested in books, but she did a lot of reading, mostly slick magazines and occasionally a newspaper—all of which bored her, but at least it seemed to her to have a purpose beyond just filling time. She felt it improved her mind and made her more interesting to Fred whenever they got a chance to talk at length about anything that wasn't the hospital. She had tried to read some of his books, tried to learn just a little bit about medicine. Unfortunately, though, she was able to understand very little, and what she did understand usually repelled her so much that she was unable to continue reading. She was very proud of Fred's being a doctor, but she herself was unable to stomach most of what he dealt with or did daily.

She was usually alone, and, if not *resigned* to being alone so much, she at least avoided resenting it. It would be over, she thought, when Fred's internship was over July first. Five and a half more months. One hundred and eighty days. And if afterwards he couldn't give her as much time as other men in other professions were able to give their wives . . . Well, that had to be expected. That had to be put up with. At least it wouldn't be as bad as this internship business, this next five and a half months, those last six and a half months.

Mildred had met Fred while he was at Harvard Med. She was twenty and finishing up her second year of junior college. He courted her—when he had the time—and she found herself, as the result of his attentions, newly and happily at ease with herself. Not that she'd been unpopular, but neither had it been unusual for her to find herself without a date on a Saturday night. Also, of the two or three boys who had professed to love her, Fred was the first one she'd respected, even admired. She was entranced with his being a doctor, entranced with the impressive and mysterious words he and his friends used so casually—*laryngoscopy, osteoporosis, edema, encephalogram, fistula* . . .

They got married as soon as they both had graduated. They had no time for a honeymoon. They came directly to New York and stayed for two days at a hotel while they looked for an apartment. On the second day they found the apartment, and on the third day Fred's internship began.

Fred's family was supporting them through the internship and so Mildred didn't have to go to work. For a month she had occupied herself quite happily with decorating and furnishing the apartment. Then she spent another month unhappily with nothing to do. She decided to get a job and then discovered that she wasn't trained to do anything that she was even vaguely interested in doing. She spent another month in a secretarial school, but the experience depressed her so much that she couldn't bring herself to finish.

She had known no one in New York at first. And although she had since made several friends, they were friends through Fred. Mostly other interns, and most of them without wives. The few wives she did know had full-time jobs and rarely felt like even just visiting in the evening. So Mildred went to movies alone or started projects (which she abandoned at the first obstacle) like learning to play the ukulele or knitting a sweater for Fred or making some of her own clothes. Thus, she owned a ukulele, a sewing machine, two sets of needles and several balls of yarn, and twenty yards of assorted materials—all of which were carefully and unreachably stored on the uppermost shelf of the hall closet.

41

Lew Worship had not gone to dinner. He was so tired he knew he could not hold anything in his stomach, that if he ate, what he ate would turn hard and come up. He had gone back to a cot behind the lounge, not to sleep—because he knew he was too tense to—but to get rid of the feeling in his stomach, the need for food, a hunger in fact, and his stomach's inability to accept food. The feeling did not go away. And in the dark his mind faced him again with what had happened during the day, and his tension grew . . .

"Dr. Tyssen," he had said, just a few minutes before, "I know I'm very late about this . . . but, well, you see, I didn't really make up my mind till last night."

"Yes? Well, Dr. . . . ?"

"Worship. Lewis Worship."

"Oh, yes. Have it written right here in front of me. That's what happens at my age. What's on your mind, Doctor?"

"I'd like to apply for a residency here."

"Nothing stopping you. Get the form from Dr. Wohl's office, nothing I can do till I see your application in order."

"Yes, sir. I realize that. I wanted to see you personally to explain why I'm applying so late."

"Yes, you certainly are. Well?"

"Well, you see, I just didn't know what I wanted to specialize in . . ."

"But now you do."

"Yes, sir."

"Made up your mind last night, did you?"

"Yes, sir."

"I see. Sudden, wasn't it?"

"Not exactly . . . I'd been thinking about it for some time."

"I should hope so."

"And I'm finally convinced I know what specialty I want."

"OB-GYN."

Worship nodded.

"There's a place on the form for giving your reasons for OB-GYN, and also for giving your reasons for wanting a residency here. So I won't bother asking you now. You realize, of course, that you are terribly late."

"Yes, sir."

"We've already tentatively filled what few openings we have."

"I see."

"However, those decisions are, as I say, purely tentative and depend upon the results of personal interviews we haven't conducted as yet . . . On the other hand, Dr. Worship, you must be aware that it is not the practice of this hospital to encourage applications or select its residents from its intern staff."

"No, sir. I didn't know that."

"It strikes me that you haven't done much looking into the matter." He shook his head. "Never mind, I'll look at your application. Yes?"

"Well, I was just thinking, Doctor . . . if my application *should* interest you, well, maybe you might talk to Dr. Sato about me. I know it's not standard to consult a resident about this sort of thing, but I think he might give you a favorable impression of me . . . I mean, after being so late with the application and . . ."

"Dr. Sato, eh?"

"Yes, sir."

"Mmmmm . . . let's see, Worship . . . That would mean that Dr. Granchard is your chief resident, wouldn't it?"

"Yes, sir."

"Mmmmm . . . Why then, since he's your chief, didn't you suggest my talking to *him?*"

"I thought . . . well, I think Dr. Sato has a . . . a more, uh . . . *favorable* impression of me."

"I see. And why would that be, Worship?"

"Well . . ." And he remembered the scene with Granchard that afternoon:

He was on fourth call, and things had been light all day and still were. He could have been sleeping. Maybe even should have been. But instead, he'd sat waiting in the lounge behind the nurses' station for Granchard. He'd come in, have to come in, for a cigarette eventually. But Granchard, in his usual perverse way, had not stopped by for a cigarette, as he would have had Worship not been waiting for him.

He had been waiting for over an hour, almost two. Could have been sleeping. Could have made the encounter in the corridor—but he had wanted it to come off at some time and in some place where there would be leisure to exploit the situation fully. I am not a sadist, he had thought. I do not kick a man when he's down. Just so long as he hasn't done it to me first, he told himself. Anyway, Dr. Granchard, I may be an intern, but oh you sonofabitch, I have my pride. Which you have beat upon and which is now going to beat upon you.

Otis collapsed, exhausted, into a leather chair next to him. "Worship, why the hell aren't you sleeping?"

"Cause I damn well don't feel like it."

"Oh boy, here we go again."

"Hey . . ." Worship looked up slowly. "Am I on fourth call because of you?"

"Well, look, you covered for me last . . ."

"I don't *give* a damn! I take care of *my own* responsibilities."

"Don't be a child, Lew. You took care of yours in advance —last night. I'm taking care of mine tardy—today. What the hell are you being so perverse about to me?"

"Perverse?" Lew said, startled by the word.

"Yes. Perverse, damn you. Did I do something to you?"

"No . . . You didn't, John. I'm sorry. Really I am."

"Forget it." He looked at Worship carefully. "I just wanted to make sure it wasn't something . . . *personal.*"

Worship became aware of something again. Something John Paul was questioning him about. "No, nothing personal." But something. And then he asked himself, Why are you suddenly a watchdog? And was so embarrassed by his attitude toward Otis that he couldn't bring himself to do anything when Granchard came in.

"Still on your ass, hunh, Worship? Every time I come in here you're sitting on your ass."

"You know another part of me I should be sitting on?"

"You can stand on your head for all I care. But don't do it where I can see you. I see interns sitting around, I get *itchy*. Know what I mean?"

"I was just gonna sack out," Lew said, getting up.

"What call you on?"

"Fourth."

"Well, now. *That's* nice and safe. Who put you there—our friend Dr. Otis here?"

"No, I . . ."

"Yeah, he *did*. So what?"

"So nothing, Worship. If Otis wants to knock himself out taking off every night and doing double duty every day to make up for it, it's okay with me. As long as he keeps up the quality. Personally, I don't think he can much longer. So he'll get *his* soon enough . . . But you're another case. You're such a hotshot doctor, I can't see you taking it easy sacking out. Hell, man, you could be up in the O.R. right now watching a section . . ."

Worship sat down again, knowing that he was going to

do something to Granchard. "How's your wife? Get that martini last night?"

"Yeah. I did. What's your point, Worship?"

"Just wondered how your wife was, you talking about her so much last night and all."

"She's fine." Granchard cocked his head. "Just don't get personal, Worship. You'll find yourself specializing in being a wrong-end barber."

"Sure. So what I want to know is, when're you gonna pay me the ten bucks you owe me?"

"Did I borrow ten, Worship? I don't recall . . ."

"Seen Ellen Davis's chart today? You were so hot after seeing her chart last night I figured the first thing you'd do today . . . Anyway, it's all written up very nicely. Including the weight of her baby."

"Ah hah," Granchard said quietly.

"Ah hah," Worship said quietly. "Ten bucks."

Granchard seemed about to say something. Then he went into the locker room, was gone a moment, and came back and handed Lew a five, four singles, and some change.

Otis looked startled.

"Thank you," Lew said.

Granchard stood looking at him, a quizzical look on his face. "Worship, words escape me."

"It's the first time," Lew said equably. He put the money in the tunic pocket of his scrub suit. He looked up at Granchard directly. "For a second there I thought I'd feel guilty. You know—taking a skirt away from your wife?" He relaxed in his chair. "But then I figured, the guilt's yours, not mine, right? I mean, *you* risked the money that was for her, not me, so . . ."

Disastrously quiet, Granchard said, "Enough, Worship."

"Right." He got up. "I think I'll sack out now."

"You do that. And you know something else, Worship?"

"No."

"I take back what I said about your tender ego." He sat down and picked up a magazine. "You belong up in Surgery."

But he hadn't sacked out. He'd called to see if Dr. Tyssen was free. And then he'd gone to see him. And he'd just been asked why he'd given Dr. Sato, instead of Granchard, his chief, as a reference. And then been asked why Dr. Sato should have a more favorable impression of him than Dr. Granchard.

He said, finally, "Well . . . I just think Dr. Sato has a less cynical attitude, I guess."

"Mmmmm. All right, Worship. You know the chances of an exception being made. But, of course, I can't prevent you from making application. I suggest, though, that you investigate other residency openings."

"It's pretty late," Lew said, unable to stop his words, "and the ones that'd still be open . . ."

"There are always hospitals looking for residents, Dr. Worship. And, I'd like to point out, a serious student can profit from *any* training, no matter what *you* may now think." He nodded.

Lew said, "Thank you," and left.

That was the way it had gone, Lew thought. Good old Jack Tyssen. The fool who wouldn't let Ellen Davis have a spinal course.

And then, coming back a few minutes before, Lew, his stomach sick with tension and the fatigue of his body, had been stopped in the corridor by Bobbie, who had said, "Why don't you have a girl, Lew?"

"I don't know."

"Want me to fix you up?"

"I don't care."

And now he lay on a cot in the dark waiting to be called and thinking, I don't care because I've waited too long. It was the darkness that did it, probably, he thought. Lying there, not sleeping, looking up into—nothing. Just darkness.

I don't care, he thought, because I've waited too long. There was no longer the need. Like a stomach that unfed for a long time shrinks beyond the physical point of letting the body know it is empty of food. It ceases to demonstrate need, and so the body no longer possesses appetite.

Yet he wanted to need a girl. He wanted to have a girl. But no longer out of physical hunger. Now it was out of emotional hunger. He thought, I have *everything* ass-backwards . . . No physical desire. But an emotional one, a need to love someone. And he thought, Yes, that's it, there's all this love that wants to spend itself before it bursts or bursts

me . . . And he thought, Yes, ass-backwards, I have to find a
girl I love emotionally so that I will get to love her physically,
but the physical hunger won't happen until after the other
has. Which isn't right, he thought. It isn't. I don't want to
be built this way . . .

I want to be normal . . . But it doesn't work that way for
me, my God damn ego isn't affected if I don't have a girl.
Like some of the others. Like Otis maybe, but anyway,
Mercouris and de Traunant, having to have a girl every
night so they can know they're men, ego-dependent on
having a girl, but at least they're normal. Nor do I have to
force myself not to have a girl so I can concentrate my
energies, like some of them; but at least they have the *need*,
even if they won't let it dominate them, but at least they have
it, they're normal. Nor is a girl a second-class citizen to
me to be had or not had as it strikes me, like van Wyck, but
at least he isn't empty of need, he's normal. And so I'm
more emotionally generous than he is maybe, and I don't
have to discipline myself like Parelli, and I'm not ego-dependent like the others . . . But what I'm not isn't normal. Why
can't I just have the need, instead of just the love . . . ?

He found the darkness oppressive, yet he couldn't get
himself to leave it. He was waiting for the darkness to make
him disappear, as if it were some chemical atmosphere
he would rather be destroyed by entirely than leave . . .

The telephone next to the bed rang. "Dr. Worship," Bobbie's
voice said.

"I'll be right out," Lew said, not even wanting to wait to
hear what it was about.

42

In the interns' lounge—a large, not often cleaned room in
the old North Hospital building, a room containing a record
player but no records, a lot of chairs, a TV set, a Coke
machine, and two always-*already*-being-used ping-pong tables
—van Wyck settled himself on a camp chair in front of the
TV set to digest his dinner.

The man next to him, Joe Parelli, said, "You wanna
know the plot?"

"I've seen the show before."

"Then *you* tell *me* the plot, I've seen it about five times and I haven't been able to discover a plot once."

"I thought you were on OB."

"I am," Joe said. "But like people aren't having babies any more."

"They had 'em all when I was down there."

"Shut up," Rosconovitch said, "I'm trying to get some sleep."

"Sack out in your room, for chrisake," Parelli said.

"I can't. My roommate, a guy named Peterson—who shall remain nameless—has a nurse up there."

"How is he having her?" Otis said.

"Sunny-side up," Rosconovitch said.

"Is it true that GYN recommends scrambled?" Worship said.

Van Wyck turned up the volume on the TV.

"Jesus Christ!" Rosconovitch yelled. "A guy could die of exhaustion . . ."

"It's therapeutic!" Alicia yelled back. "After a while you can't hear *anything!*"

"What?"

"Then you can sleep *anywhere!"*

The telephone rang. Sprague picked it up while everyone watched him warily, not wanting to hear the name or names he would announce. "Joe," Sprague said, holding out the receiver. Parelli cursed, took the phone, listened, said, "Okay," hung up, said, "It's my duty to announce that people are having babies again," and left.

Worship said, "Anybody mind if I change the program?"

"Hey, no, don't, it's getting interesting . . ."

"That's the *commercial,* stupid . . ."

"Change it . . ."

"Turn it off . . ."

The telephone rang. The voices quieted. Sprague said, "OB wants Liu, Otis, Rosconovitch, and Worship *stat.*"

"Granchard must've found the mother lode," Otis said angrily. Then the four of them left.

Sprague said, "Just what the hell does 'stat' *really* mean?"

"Latin," van Wyck said. *"Statim.* Immediately."

"They couldn't be bothered to *say* 'immediately'?"

"It wouldn't be professional," Donnecker said. "We'd sound just like anybody else."

Sprague said, "I hear you had a little chat with Wohl today. How'd it go?"

"The usual. I couldn't tell whether he was chewing me out or patting me on the back."

"You'll find out. After he replies to inquiries from the places where you've applied for residency."

"You mean, when I get *their* answers to *me*."

"If you get *any* answers at all, Wohl hasn't been disturbed by you."

Aptshult came in. He looked around and said, "Anyone seen Alicia?"

Van Wyck, watching the TV screen again, said, "She scrubbed."

Aptshult sat down. "What's the plot?"

"For godsake," Sprague said. "Can't *anyone* recognize a commercial?"

A figure stood up from a chair on the far side of the room where the light from the screen didn't reach and where it was fully dark. The figure came over to van Wyck and stood there until van Wyck knew someone was standing by him and looked up. It was Tom Elwood. Elwood put out his hand.

Van Wyck said, "What is this—a new game you invented, Tom?"

Elwood just grinned at him and continued to hold out his hand. Van Wyck took it finally and shook it vigorously. Elwood said, "I just wanted to thank you." He turned to the others. "All of you," he said, and punched Donnecker lightly on the shoulder. Then he went out.

The telephone rang. Sprague said, "Walters. Walters here?" He looked around the room. "Not here," Sprague said, and hung up.

"*Wonderful,*" Donnecker said. "I love to see that thing take a beating every so often."

In OB-A, Granchard kept Otis with him and watched him carefully. But all Otis did wrong was forget to put on the rubber-soled white bucks that were supposed to be worn in the delivery room to avoid sparks and electric conduction that might explode the heavier anesthetic gases like cyclopropane. But, given the original fault, Otis changed his shoes fast enough to suit even Granchard.

Granchard was paying such strange attention to Otis

that Worship found himself aware of it and began watching Granchard carefully. Then he was watching both of them carefully. Watching them not separately, but as a unit, the one watching the other, each making transparent pretenses at being unaware of the other, and Worship watching them both.

Finally Otis said, "You want me to build you a papoose-carrier, Granchard? Then you can ride around on my *back*."

"I already am, Dr. Otis. I find you much more interesting even than Worship."

"You mean you've replaced me?" Lew said.

"Only temporarily, Doctor. You'll be back in the line-up soon enough."

Then, later, while Otis was delicately sewing a hemorrhaging perineum that had ruptured before an episiotomy could be performed, with Lew as his first assistant and Granchard standing across the room watching, silent, yet making his presence and watching known very carefully and subtly and as if by telepathy, but actually by maintaining an uninterrupted stare—Otis had looked up, sweating, from the delicate, minutely demanding procedure and had said, his voice tense with control, "Get that bastard off my back."

And from across the room, Granchard's voice, emotionless, had said, "Worship, you've got your own troubles. You better stick with 'em, they may be the only friends you've got." Then he left the room.

In Male Surgery B, the charge resident, Baker, had just looked at a patient sent up from Emergency Admitting. The chief resident was away and the patient didn't look like he'd keep for more than a couple of hours without operative procedure. And Baker was not going to take it on himself without first consulting the charge attending. Riccio had operated that afternoon—the ulcerated leg amputation. As expected, the patient had died shortly after being taken into the Recovery Room. Riccio had gone home, so Baker called D. L. Riccio's home number.

The voice he got was not that of Riccio but of Riccio's answering service. The answering service wanted to take a message. Baker identified himself and described the situation, but the service still insisted upon taking a message. Baker threatened with every law he could think of. And then he threatened with every law he could improvise on the spot to fit the situation and intimidate the voice of the answering service. The girl finally told him that as far as she knew Dr. Riccio was still at De Witt and please remember whose responsibility this was now and . . .

Baker hung up and called De Witt and got Riccio immediately and described the patient's condition. Riccio said he'd probably have to do a laparotomy and call and get an O.R. readied and he'd need Grenatti to assist and he wanted Mrs. Hughes as his scrub nurse as usual, and oh yeah she's off by now get anyone, and yeah get that intern, what's his name—van Wyck?—to scrub, tell him to get on the floor stat and take a look at the patient for himself; Riccio would discuss the case with him before they operated if they operated . . .

Van Wyck took the receiver from Sprague, his eye on two cowboys who were about to draw on each other but were taking a helluva long time about it.

Baker's voice said, "Get your ass up here, Riccio wants you to scrub with him." Van Wyck put the receiver down and ran.

Mercouris said, "It's my theory we're not paid to run."

Sprague said, "We're not paid, period."

Mercouris said, "But run you will, or licensed you will not be."

Donnecker said, "Knowledge I am not getting here. But muscular legs I am."

43

Baker had said to him, "Go take a good look at the patient and at his chart too. And you'd better come up with some hot ideas, because for some reason Riccio plans to have a private CPC with you."

The chart told him that the patient was a seventy-three-year-old Negro male in acute distress with a chief complaint of abdominal pain. The admitting physician had noted a two-day condition of anorexia coupled with nausea, and that the patient had stated that he had had no bowel movement nor passed flatus for at least that length of time. Temperature was two degrees below normal, pulse weak. The

patient's name was stated as Samuel Johns, his present oc-
cupation retired postman, and this was his first NNH admission.

Van Wyck completed a physical examination, and, then,
expecting the necessity of a rectal examination, went to get
a glove.

When he passed the nurses' station on the way back to
the patient's room, Baker called him in and told him Riccio
was in with the patient and Riccio said to wait right here.

In a few minutes Riccio came in. He said to van Wyck,
"Did you examine the patient?"

"Yes, sir."

"And?"

"I found a palpable mass low in the right upper quadrant
in roughly the position of the liver. I'm not sure that it's the
liver itself, though. If it *is* the liver, it might be anything
from a carcinoma to a stone obstructing the bile duct,
maybe jaundice that's just short of manifesting itself clinically . . ."

"Procedure?"

"Well, I'm not sure. The *entire* abdomen is distended. I'm
not sure that an incision at the site of the palpable mass
would necessarily discover anything more than a symptom . . ."

"You wouldn't do an exploratory lap then?"

Van Wyck was becoming more and more uncomfortable.
He had a sure impression that Riccio's quietly leading
questions were leading him directly into making a fool of
himself so that Riccio could be his usual rude and crude self
at van Wyck's expense. Van Wyck said, "Well, with the
entire abdomen distended, I'd want the results of some tests
before I decided where to go in, even for just an exploratory lap. A white blood count, a hemoglobin, a bilirubin,
cholesterol and esters . . ."

Baker said, "His hemoglobin tested out normal, his WBC
is high, about sixteen thousand high."

Riccio said, "While you're running all these tests and
waiting for results, what's the patient going to be doing about
staying alive?"

Van Wyck was silent.

"And?" Riccio said.

Van Wyck pushed himself on. "With the abdomen that

distended, I'd at least go in with a sigmoidoscope and make sure I could rule out . . ."

"Dr. van Wyck," Riccio said—and van Wyck thought, *Ah*, ah, here it comes, here it is—"Dr. van Wyck. We have a patient here in a condition sensitive enough already without ramming a stick up his ass. Tests may bring on shock, and the lab takes too long anyway. Too long for *this* patient. Elapsed time could easily result in a fatality. A definite diagnosis is virtually impossible under these conditions. And would be conditional at best, certainly incompatible with the time factor. Very simply, Dr. van Wyck, the patient's major symptom—the palpable mass in the RUQ you so perceptively noted—that symptom necessitates an immediate exploratory lap *at that site*. That operation will be a straight up-and-down laparotomy and will begin in thirty minutes. So, if you have no other immediate plans or suggestions, you might go down to the O.R. and get into a scrub suit and take time for a long careful scrub."

Van Wyck, angry, but convinced that a sigmoidoscopy ought to be done before any such operation, paused. And as he paused, Riccio, with obvious dissatisfaction that van Wyck was still within conversing distance, said, "We have quite enough information, I assure you, Doctor. The patient has a hard belly. Whether he has an anal obstruction or a deviated septum or an Oedipus complex can hardly concern us in our consideration of the belly. The belly demands immediate exploratory surgery. And since it is the belly we are after, *that* is where we will operate. We proceed with abdominal surgery, not rectal or anal surgery, no more than we shall ask the patient about his relationship with his mother."

"But, Dr. Riccio," van Wyck said, committed now to pressing his argument for as long as Riccio left him coherent and in one piece, and also, at the same time, noting that Baker was being vastly amused by the entertainment Riccio was providing him with. "But Dr. Riccio," he said slowly and carefully, the way you might speak to a child whom you fear you're not communicating with, "might there not be a rectal condition which at least is the principal contributory factor to the abdominal distention?" Then he waited, resigned to being entirely overrun by the next assault.

He waited. Riccio just looked at him, saying nothing, regarding him as if he were some species of animal about to become extinct, and there was nothing anybody could do about it, and who cared, anyway?

The silence was worse than the worst assault he had prepared himself for. To counter the silence, he started talking again. "Another condition we don't know anything about might be causing . . ."

"Yes, Doctor, it might be. But the patient's *abdominal* condition indicates surgery immediately. *That* particular condition is the one that may kill him, not possible contributory conditions. There are two kinds of surgeons, young man. There are *cutting* surgeons and there are *delaying* surgeons. I suggest that there are more fatalities due to delaying surgeons and the accompanying elapsed time they allow in various diagnostic procedures than there are fatalities due to cutting surgeons who treat symptoms a first-year student would recognize rather than spending hours ruling out possible syndromes and conditions that a specialist would find hard to identify much less diagnose."

Mentally, van Wyck closed his eyes; but out loud said, "Then no sigmoidostrophy, Doctor?"

"My *dear colleague,* I appreciate your commitment to this *vision* of yours, or anal obsession, or whatever it is. But I should like to point out to you once again that diagnostic techniques are brilliant on paper in the textbooks and in theory and, of course, in the minds of the diagnosticians. They are also sometimes useful in practice. But in this case, as with many like it, we run the risk—using a sigmoidoscope—of traumatizing the patient. We would move him from pre-shock to shock, and I assure you that in this sort of operation, as many fatalities are due to shock as to hemorrhaging. If you want to go by the books, then I suggest you consider not only the diagnostician's attitude, but also the anesthetist's. As you may know," Riccio said with offensive patience, "the anesthetist feels that a number of operative fatalities are due to the patient being in shock when he's brought *into* the O.R. The anesthetist claims he can minimize operative fatalities due to shock if the patient is at least only in *pre*-shock when he's brought into the O.R. The anesthetist's computations have to be based on the assumption that the patient is *only* in pre-shock. Otherwise he would not be able to administer anesthesia at all.

"Those are your textbook opinions. My own is that I

am a surgeon and as a surgeon my duty is to cut; to get in and find out what's wrong and cut accordingly; and if nothing is wrong to *prevent* something from going wrong; and if there is nothing to prevent going wrong, then to sneak out as carefully as I can, close the patient up, and turn him over to Medicine. But remember, please, Dr. van Wyck, you are in Surgery now, not in a textbook. Textbooks do not treat individuals."

Van Wyck started out to go to the O.R. Riccio said, mildly, "By the way, van Wyck, I don't suppose you've given any thought to supportive therapy?"

It was a question for a first-year student. Van Wyck turned around angrily. "I.V. electrolytes and a Levine tube," he said, and walked out.

Riccio raised his eyebrows. He said to Baker, "If we could get him to curse, we might turn him into a surgeon yet . . . After all, there's no use wasting good material on another service."

Van Wyck got back to his room at eleven fifty and went immediately to bed and to sleep.

The telephone bell rang suddenly and loud. He rolled sharply over. *Three forty-five.* Walters wasn't back yet. Van Wyck sat up and reached over for the phone in the darkness.

"Hello?" he said, half asleep and as if he didn't believe there would be anyone on the other end of the line. "Van Wyck."

He listened. It was something about Mr. Quieno. "Not passing water," he said over to himself. The fact had no significance. It should have. He said, "Hold it, let me think . . ." his free hand pressed against his forehead, his head bent studiously. The fact must have some significance . . .

He said, after a moment of silence, "All right, I'll come over and catheterize him."

He got up numbly and put on his whites. The walk over would wake him up. He had to rely on the walking doing it, because his mind didn't seem to be able to.

After he finished in the ward, he decided to go down to the Surgery Recovery Room and see how Samuel Johns was getting along. They had opened him up and found an obstruction in the bile duct which Riccio had been able to correct immediately.

He disliked the R.R. It was the only place in the hospital

that unnerved him. It gave him a feeling of strangeness and unrelatedness, as if he himself were part way under anesthesia. But as long as he was up, he might as well check on Johns' recovery progress.

The R.R. made him uneasy because it is always the present, an immediacy that is endless, a time unit that is separate but continuous.

He stood in it and looked around at it.

The Recovery Room seems a vacuum. On three beds, widely separated, out of forty beds, three patients lie in stages of post-operative recovery or coma. In the well-lit long emptiness, only the sounds of breathing and of gathering progressive consciousness are heard. The patients have been so fitted that they may not move in any way that will harm the sutures they have received, the gauze and bandages they have been packed with—or disturb an oxygen tent or a needle and tube which is supplementing them intravenously or draining them intra-abdominally. Occasionally there is a moan, a cry, the sound of a nightmare from a waking consciousness, or the sound of a motion on sheets abruptly halted by restricting bandages, tractions, splints, or straps. But mostly there is just the silence of breathing, for breathing is a very silent sound, a private sound one dares not even hear when listening for it: the nurse on duty rarely has to look up from where she sits at her desk charting—none of the sounds are new to her, even the desperate ones. Here one feels as if in a vacuum, soundless, yet there are things to hear. The atmosphere is that of the slowness of pain, the eternity of a single heartbeat, the infinity and finality. It is a vacuum; yet in it, one feels exposed to the stealth of God.

. . . Van Wyck examined Johns just enough to assure himself that he was coming along satisfactorily . . .

Then he was outside of it, parted from it, and he had no overwhelming feeling of the presence of *is* any more.

He walked down the corridor toward the elevator and sighed. He had to be up again in less than two hours and he still wasn't back in his room and in bed again yet.

44

Because of the emergency admission of Josephine Ritchy to GYN two nights before, and the subsequent fatality, Chief Residents MacDonaugh (of GYN) and Granchard (of OB-A), called a meeting after morning rounds of all OB-GYN interns, the other residents to cover the labor floor and GYN ward. Kalik, who believed in doing rather than talking, sent only half his staff of interns over and didn't come himself.

They used a conference room high in the new building, thirty-odd interns sitting around a table far too small for the size of the group, Granchard sitting off to the side at one end and MacDonaugh standing next to him doing all the talking, lecturing on the history of and differences between therapeutic abortion and criminal abortion.

After about forty-five minutes, MacDonaugh nodded and the meeting began to disperse itself. Granchard had said nothing the entire time, had made no gesture to add his own comments. He had just sat and listened to MacDonaugh and kept his eyes attentively on one intern.

When the last intern had left, Granchard didn't get up. He just sat and reflectively tapped the end of a pencil against the surface of the conference table.

"You coming down?" MacDonaugh said, waiting for him.

Granchard looked out the window at the somber, gray, December sky. He looked out and continued to tap the pencil on the table and said reflectively, "You know, Jack, a funny thing happened to me a few weeks ago . . . I was on duty Thanksgiving Day." He looked over at MacDonaugh. "Not too happy about it, you know—wanted to be home with my wife and the kids . . ." He looked out the window again. "Anyway, one of the patients had been in labor so long I decided to pit her . . . Funny thing, the box was empty of pit, and ergot, too—had to get a special order filled. On Thanksgiving Day." He looked over at MacDonaugh. "No easy matter, you know?"

He swiveled around to face MacDonaugh fully. "So I bawled hell out of the head nurse and she bawled hell out of the orderly for not calling it to her attention—and he swore up and down this was the first he knew we were even low, much less out . . ."

He lounged back in the chair and reflectively lit a cigarette. "Well . . ." he said, blowing smoke out, "I thought about it, and I figured what the hell, you know? Just one of those things. So I apologized to the nurse and she apologized to the orderly, and everybody forgave everybody else."

"Very interesting," MacDonaugh said. "But I've got to get down to . . ."

"Anyway," Granchard said, going on easily, now looking out the window again, "it's been on my mind ever since. Just sort of stuck there." He turned his head back to MacDonaugh. "Funny thing to happen, don't you think?"

"Yeah. Yeah, it is. But I . . ."

"And you know, we've been low on pit and ergot a couple of times since. Unexpectedly low . . . No one seems to know what happens to the stuff . . . just disappears . . ."

MacDonaugh looked more carefully at Granchard.

Granchard looked up. "Jack . . . you ever seen a woman after an ergot-induced criminal abortion? Say after the first trimester? I mean, one that didn't work out?"

MacDonaugh's face remained completely inexpressive. He just stood unmoving and looked at Granchard.

Granchard was looking out the window again. Easily, unhurried, matter of factly, he said, "Sort of messy. Saw a couple on GYN where I went to med school. Not at all nice. The uterus sometimes ruptures—that's how strong the contractions get. Hell of a lot of hemorrhaging. Respiration begins to go, but usually it doesn't go fast enough and they die in spasms anyway."

Granchard looked up at MacDonaugh. "You could use pit to induce an abortion too. You know?"

MacDonaugh still didn't move, still didn't relax his stare.

45

Van Wyck finished with his last clinic patient a few minutes after four. At six thirty he had an appointment downtown for drinks and dinner and the opera with some friends he'd gone to college with. In the meantime he figured he could get a full hour's sleep.

He went up to his room and lay down on his bed. He was one of the lucky ones—he could go to sleep in an instant and sleep fully for whatever length of time was available. At least three quarters of the other interns he knew—for example, his roommate, Court Walters—either hadn't mastered the trick (if it could be considered a trick) or simply weren't capable of going to sleep without a long, time-consuming approach first. As a result, someone like Walters usually went close to thirty-six hours without any sleep at all—and then collapsed immovably for the next twelve.

Van Wyck closed his eyes. He could see the blackboard in front of him getting larger and larger, closer and closer, closing him in protectively . . .

The loud, shrill bell of the telephone broke the blackboard into fragments.

"Van Wyck," he said.

"Grenatti. Get your ass down to Emergency, you're scrubbing."

"Oh *Christ*, Don. *I'm* not on call."

"You are now. The cops just brought in eight kids that've been cutting each other up with knives. Everybody's working tonight. *So shake it, hunh?*"

Eight guys . . . They'd be in the O.R. at least till midnight.

He didn't even have time to call and break his appointment.

Waiting for the elevator, he heard the page system calling, *"All surgical interns to Emergency . . . All surgical residents to . . ."* Christ, it must really be something if they were calling out the residents, too . . .

When he got to Emergency Admitting—a series of twenty booths surrounding a corridor—he found his way to the proper partitioned cubicles by the lines and spatters of blood on the floor. He heard someone say, *"It took three ambulances to bring 'em in, three, for godsake . . ."* There were a number of cops standing around. He recognized several of them from the dining hall, they came in for free meals every so often when they were working the immediate area. Three residents—Duane, Grenatti, and Baker—were already covering. Walters, Mercouris, and Donnecker were also already there.

"Just get some gloves on," Duane said to him. "When they're ready for the O.R. you'll scrub with me. In the meantime close everything in sight and get the two in this booth ready for the table, and yeah let me know if anybody needs to get put in the O.R. fast . . ." And he had turned his back and gone into another cubicle.

Behind him, van Wyck heard Donnecker saying, "*Jesus,* they've all got stab wounds of the belly, two of them pulled the knives out themselves . . ."

Every belly puncture would mean a laparotomy. Open them up and look for internal bleeding, if there was any blood, find out where it came from and sew it the hell up. *If* you could find it. *If* the guy didn't die on you first. And if they had to resect the intestine they'd be at it all night . . .

He had pushed aside the curtain and gone into the unit Duane had indicated. Two boys about fifteen or sixteen lay on tables a few feet apart from each other on opposite sides of the booth. Both were still bleeding freely from slashes around the head and face. In both cases blood was running onto the sheet-covered tables and then dripping from the sheets into pools on the floor. One boy's shirt had been torn—or slashed—open and he had taken slashes across the chest and abdomen. He was alternately crying and coughing.

Behind van Wyck a nurse was breaking a prep tray on an instrument stand. Van Wyck gloved himself quickly and went over to the boy with the chest and abdominal wounds. He could see bone exposed twice on the chest area, and the thought crossed his mind that it couldn't have been a razor, the incision would have held itself closed, it must have been a pretty dull knife. There was also an abdominal puncture wound. If the knife had caught the bowels, chances were the kid had had it. But it was impossible to tell what angle the blade had taken inside, what it had caught and what it hadn't caught. In two places there were little fountains and squirts of blood rising from the wounds.

Van Wyck said, "How soon will we get into the O.R.?"

"Ten minutes," the nurse said. "Fifteen at the outside. They're setting them up now."

"Tell Duane this one ought to be first, probably *the* first."

He went to the tray and got some Kelly clamps and returned to the table and began clamping off the bleeders. Duane came in followed by the nurse. Duane took a quick look. "As soon as they get the second O.R. ready," he

said. "We got one down the hall with his guts hanging out."
Then he was gone again.

Van Wyck finished clamping the most profuse bleeders
and then went over to the other table. The second one had,
by comparison, only superficial incised wounds. "Break
me some stitches," van Wyck said. "Four-O silk." He went
to the instrument table. "Where the hell are the butterflies?"
Then he found the package, broke it and taped closed the
facial wounds on both patients, saying, "It's sure as hell not
going to be their faces that'll give 'em the trouble. What's
this?"

"Three-O, I'll have to . . ."

"Forget it. Get me some more clamps and an I.V. set, saline
with a number eighteen needle so we can switch to blood
if we have to." Then he yelled after her, "And a hemoglobin set, I'll have to read it right here," beginning to
bite the curved needle into the flesh along the edge of the
deeper incisions on the second boy. Before the nurse had
returned he had finished the suture and gone over to the
tray for more silk.

What warned him while he was at the tray was nothing
more than not hearing the crying and the coughing any
more. He turned around quickly and saw the boy with the
abdominal wounds moving across the cubicle toward the
other boy, his body half bent and an arm pressed tightly
across his abdomen, but with the other arm raised un-
believably high, the hand of the arm making a fist around
a gleaming surgical knife he must have lifted from the instrument stand while van Wyck's back had been turned to
him.

The boy with the knife was so close to the other boy that
all van Wyck had time to do was throw his whole body
toward the attacker. At the instant of collision there was a
scream, and then van Wyck was rolling away on the floor
and getting up almost blindly, his hands protectively in front
of himself . . .

The scream had come from the boy with the knife. He
lay on the floor screaming still, holding himself and screaming, the knife lying harmlessly on the floor several feet
away from him, and the other boy on the table cursing
viciously and trying to move himself up and toward the
boy who had just tried to kill him. But the one on the
table didn't have the strength to do more than curse at

van Wyck when van Wyck without effort pushed him back down to a lying position.

Duane, the nurse, and an attending in a scrub suit were already in the room, Duane and the attending lifting the boy on the floor carefully back onto the table.

"Jesus Christ! *Do we have to strap 'em down too?*" Duane said.

"Around the throat, if I had a chance," the attending said.

"You all right?" Duane said.

"Yeah, yeah," van Wyck said. "Yeah."

"Shaky?"

"I'll do."

"Then go scrub, I'll be in in a minute and Walters and Donnecker can take over with these two."

"Tell your boys to take their time getting in here," the attending said. "Maybe these two'll bleed to death if we give 'em a chance."

Van Wyck said, "This one's not ready for the O.R., yet. Give me a few minutes."

"Christ," Duane said. "Get with it!" and left with the attending.

He placed additional Kelly clamps and then began the standard pre-operative procedure. He drew blood and gave it to the nurse to have it typed and cross-matched and told her to call the bank and have a thousand cc's standing by stat because they were going to the O.R. stat. Then he started the hemoglobin test, drawing the blood by a needle through a pipette and into a tube containing hydrochloric acid. He shook it up and matched it against a color chart and went back to the patient and took his B.P., found it at sixty over thirty, the sonofabitch was in shock, what the hell if he had a kidney shutdown in the O.R.? He yelled for some Levophed and got it set up almost immediately and began titrating, counting the drops, drop per drop, minute by minute, taking the B.P., then taking it again, then again, watching the drop feed and the B.P. every second . . .

"He's in shock," van Wyck said.

"That'll be the anesthetist's worry. Get'm into the O.R.," Duane said.

With a nurse's assistance, he wheeled the boy, table and I.V. stand, into the O.R., titrating and taking the B.P. every step of the way. In the O.R. he turned him over to the anesthetist. From then on any fatality was the anesthetist's responsibility. If the anesthetist told them to close him up, they'd have to, no matter at what point in the lap they were. The anesthetist ran the show in the O.R., and van Wyck thought, *Thank God*. It was no longer his responsibility. *Thank God*. Because it looked like this one wasn't going to last. The anesthetist had taken over, was titrating as van Wyck went to scrub.

Donnecker was just finishing. "Jesus, you should see him. Compound lacerations, organs all the hell over the place . . ."

In the O.R., Duane nodded to him. He prepped and draped the patient, shaving his abdomen clean, cleansing it with PhisoHex, and hanging the cut-out sheet. The scrub nurse moved an instrument table in on Duane's side and her assistant, the circulating nurse, moved a Mayo stand over the feet of the patient. In a few moments there were also instruments clipped and lying on the sheet itself. After using them, Duane didn't even bother to hand them to either him or the nurse but threw them across the room to get his hands free of them quickly.

They found no blood internally. *"Lucky sonofabitch,"* the circulating attending who had been supervising said. Then he left the room to look in on the others.

"Why the hell there's no blood in this belly, I don't know," Duane said. "I thought sure as hell we'd have to do a bowel resection."

Van Wyck was sewing almost immediately behind Duane's progress, leading the gut in a tight continuous suture for strength—in contrast to the interrupted suture he'd used externally on the second boy. He looked at it, saw himself doing it, and at the same time saw the gut dissolving in three weeks as if he'd never been there, never touched . . .

"For chrisake!" Duane yelled. "That's not a face, get a move on, there's no cosmetic consideration intra-abdominally, van Wyck."

The scrub nurse laughed.

"Gut," van Wyck said, not allowed to talk directly to the circulating nurse.

"Chromic," the scrub nurse instructed the circulating nurse. The circulating nurse left the room.

They finished with their first one in about two and a half hours. Then they moved to another O.R. and started on one of the lesser casualties, a boy whose problem was merely incisions and lacerations that needed debridement and suture.

46

Fred Donnecker was well pleased with himself. For one of the rare times in his life, he had been first assistant on a major operation—putting a compound laceration case back together again. And the procedure had been successful. Surgery was not Donnecker's proposed specialty—ear, nose, and throat was—but even an ENT man could take satisfaction from having performed successful surgery with a difficult case.

It was eleven o'clock when he left the hospital with Grenatti (whom he'd assisted), and he had headed straight home in spite of Grenatti's extremely tempting offer of a couple of drinks at the Park North. Even Grenatti was quite pleased; in fact, pleased enough to pay for the drinks himself if Donnecker wanted to join him.

But Fred had gone straight home. That one time stopping off for beer hadn't gone well with his conscience at all. He didn't know why it shouldn't have, but it hadn't.

He was exhausted. But he'd be funny for Mildred. He'd be *fun* for her. Why the hell was he not, hard as he tried, *fun* for her any more?

She said, "Exhausted, sweetie?"

"Not at all, I'm dead. Like they could perform an autopsy on me standing here and never know the difference." He remembered he had to remember not to tell her about the operation. She didn't like hearing about that sort of thing.

"Maybe a drink would revive you?"

"All of a sudden I think a drink would pickle me. I could use another kiss, though. Very good stimulant. Oral, too. Very easy to take."

"Okay, Doctor. But who's going to administer?"

"We'll take turns. Like in med school."

After a moment, he said, "You know, I think I'll let you do all the administering. You have the touch."

"I have to go administer to a pound of hamburger . . ."

"Hey!" he said, grabbing for her as she got up.

"Dinner in half an hour. You sleep . . . then maybe you'll
be able to do a little administering of your own later."

"Hmmmmm," he said.

"Is that your considered opinion, Doctor?"

"Hmmmmm," he said, and got up and whacked her on the
bottom and said, *"That* was my considered opinion. I'm going
to stand in the shower till dinner's ready."

"Well don't steam up the whole place," she said, rubbing
her haunch and going to the kitchen, "and in the future please
treat my behind with a little more respect. Gentleness, anyway."

"What?" he yelled from the bathroom.

"Gentleness."

"I can't hear you, what'd you say?" he called.

"Forget the whole thing."

"What?"

"NOTHING!" she said, and turned on the oven and decided he really had whacked her more sharply than he
should have.

At dinner, Mildred said, "Guess who just *called* me awhile
ago?"

"Sidney Wohl," he said promptly.

"Oh, you're an idiot. Christine Kenady!"

"No!" Fred said, enraptured. "Not Christine Kenady! Not
the Christine Kenady!"

"Yes."

"I don't believe it. Who is she?"

"Oh, you're terrible, Fred. You *are* an idiot. Don't you
remember the girl we doubled with on our first date? She
introduced us."

"You mean the gorgeous dyed blonde?"

"Don't be catty, she's very nice."

"I know. She has bigger breasts than you do."

"That was uncalled for."

"I agree. But it's okay, hers sag."

"Fred!"

"Marry a doctor and get the facts of life."

"You know I don't like that kind of talk."

"Oh, for Christ's sake, honey."

"Please," she said, "as a favor to me, just don't talk that
way when you know it offends me."

"All right, okay. What'd she have to say for herself?"

"Well. She's in town for a week and she wanted me to have dinner with her tonight but I said I couldn't because of you . . ."

"Thanks piles."

"Fred . . ."

"Loads. Thanks loads."

"Anyway, then she wanted to come up here, but I said she couldn't because of you . . ."

"You *could've* just explained about me being tired . . ."

". . . and she said, well, why don't I have dinner with her and some friends tomorrow night?"

"Well, why don't you?"

"I said I'd check with you first. Is it okay?"

"Sure, honey. For chrisake, you don't need my permission to have dinner with some friends."

She said quietly and apologetically, "Some of the friend's friends are boys."

"As long as they're not men, everything's under control."

"You *mean* it, darling?"

"No, I don't mean it, I'm giving you a false diagnosis in order to spare you the mental pain of knowing you only have a few days to live. *Of course I mean it.* Could I be *married* to you and not trust you to have dinner with a friend and the friend's friends?"

"You're a darling," she said, and kissed him and pranced away delighted. "I'll call Chris right now."

"Give her my love and tell her some dyes make your hair fall out."

"She doesn't *dye* it, darling, she just *tints* it."

"Some tints make other things fall out."

"Fred!"

"Okay, okay. Christ, Shakespeare would've ended up just good old Bill, Stratford's town drunk, if he'd been around you."

"*Just what do you mean by that?*" she said, putting the telephone down.

"I *mean* . . . Never mind, I don't know what I mean. Forget it."

"Yes you do."

"All right. I mean Shakespeare was bawdy as hell. *He* delighted in living," Fred said, letting his anger color his words, "in just *being* alive—and all the *natural* functions that go with it. Cut that out and you wouldn't have Shakespeare, you'd have a professional moralist, a goddam tract writer."

"Well *thank you*. I suppose you mean I would've turned him into a tract writer just because I like to preserve a little decency around the house."

"Decency, *hell*. Is being unashamed indecent? Is enjoying things indecent?"

"*Enjoying* them isn't indecent. Sometimes talking about them *is*."

"I see. There's a difference between talking and doing."

"*You don't even do!*" She automatically put her hand to her mouth. "I'm sorry, Fred. I'm sorry, darling. I didn't mean that."

Fred relaxed. "Yes, you did. You did mean it. I'm sorry too. For giving you cause to mean it."

She came to him, still angry, still ashamed, but wanting to make it up. "Please, darling. Please. I didn't mean it."

He sighed. "Mildred, don't be ashamed of what you know is so. Don't be ashamed of anything you know is so. I said I'm sorry, and I mean that. Don't say you're sorry about something you really meant, we'll wreck us if you keep that up . . . if either of us do. Come sit down and let me explain."

She allowed herself to be led over to the couch and deposited in his arm.

"I just can't. When I get home I'm so exhausted I'm operating on sheer nerves. It's not that I don't want you . . . sometimes I want you so bad I don't even know where I am. It's just that I get home and I'm tired and I want you . . . but there's just no way of telling my body to *have* you. Understand?"

"I think so, darling."

"Really?"

"Yes."

"Well, kiss me. Administer to me."

She pecked at him and said, "I've got to go see to the dishes," and stood up and straightened her skirt.

"*Do* you understand?"

"Yes, I do, darling. *Really*. Now I've really got to go inside and see to the dishes."

"Sure," he said, and lay back and put his arm over his eyes and went almost immediately to sleep.

47

Van Wyck had been wrong. It wasn't midnight when he finally got out of the O.R., it was after one. Walters had just broken from his O.R. too, and they stood together in the now silent, now empty corridor and lit cigarettes.

Walters said, "I don't know, on something like that, eight hours standing at a table. I just don't know. I don't know what keeps me going. I don't know what keeps me from doing things by rote in a trance or something."

Van Wyck said, "It's a funny thing, Court—I think it's the sight of blood that keeps *me* going. It shocks me every time. Anyway, shock or whatever the word should be, it gets to me enough to keep me wide awake."

"Yeah. *Yeah.* Maybe that *is* it. The sight of blood. I'll be damned."

Duane came out of the scrub room, nodded, and went off toward the parking lot exit.

"How do you like that?" van Wyck said. "Scrub with a guy for eight solid hours. More than eight. Side by side at the same table. And all he can do afterwards is nod. Not even, 'Good night.' Man, I'll *never* understand residents."

"I don't know about Duane . . . I sort of admire him, the way he handles patients. Sort of old school, like Riccio. He blasts 'em, he doesn't hoodwink 'em. They can call him a bastard, but they can't call him negligent. I guess he's the kind of doctor I'd like to be, you know?"

"You can't curse that hard."

"What say we stop off in the lounge and get a Coke?"

"Yeah. Good idea."

Usually the lounge was empty at this hour except for one or two die-hard movie fanatics entranced by some midnight rerun. But van Wyck and Walters walked into a group of twenty-odd interns—a group oddly low-voiced and restrained, just sitting talking.

". . . It's an incidence of one case per year per class of interns here. One like that, and then one TB."

"You sure?"

"It's a matter of record."

". . . That's fine. You been on TB yet?"

"No. You?"

"Yeah."

"Have the TB shot, BCG vaccine?"

"Sure. A helluva lot of protection that junk gives you."

"Feeling tired, run down?"

"Oh shut up . . ."

Walters said, "What's up?"

Aptshult looked up, "Where you two been?"

"Emergency O.R."

Parelli said, without inflection, "Elwood went nuts and tried to kill Riccio. Met him in a corridor and just tried to strangle him."

Van Wyck put his Coke down. Parelli nodded slowly *yes.* "The thing is," Parelli went on, "the thing is, they figure it's a nervous breakdown and that he's been this way at least since yesterday. And nobody noticed."

Alicia said, "And nobody noticed."

48

Worship had been there when it happened. It was in one of the basement corridors to the dining hall. He had been walking along a few paces behind the small figure of Dr. Riccio, watching the short Riccio legs stabbing down and cutting forward and covering so much ground so fast that Worship found himself walking at a swifter tempo than he was used to in order, for no particular reason at all, to keep the distance between himself and Riccio the same. Then he'd seen the Riccio legs, both of them, stab down, and not move forward, but seem to straighten up against great pressure, and by the time he'd looked up the entire figure was being forced back.

At first Lew didn't even recognize Elwood; but as he ran, he did, and his naked lack of understanding—the naked lack of logic in what he saw—kept him, for an instant, from doing anything. At least he thought it did, but actually, he was still running, had not paused, and grabbed at Elwood's body and then, seeing Riccio's face, left off on Elwood's body, and concentrated on Elwood's arms and releasing the grip of his hands.

He did. Riccio moved or fell or disappeared backward, and then, with so much pain he thought he would just shake his head and cry, he saw Tom Elwood's face just looking at him, the figure not moving, the face unstrained, relaxed and gentle even, looking at him, as if with a question, like a woman in delivery when she is too exhausted to do anything else and the pain is no longer pain for her, but something lacking any reality or connection with her, and all you can see in her face is exhaustion and *asking* . . . He found he had his arm cocked—what was he going to do with it? hit Elwood? . . . and he couldn't, his arm just fell limp to his side, and he wanted to sink to his knees and cry, Elwood's face there before him, no tension in it, weariness and exhaustion only, passive even to being hit, defenseless, and not waiting but just *being* and *asking* . . .

All this in the instant it took him to realize it wasn't necessary to hit Elwood, and Elwood saying, "Thank you," and walking over to Riccio and saying to Riccio, "Thank you, thank you," and holding out his hand and—Worship thought he had been struck and must be unconscious, unrelated to reality—Riccio accepting it and shaking it . . .

And then had realized Riccio was paying no attention to him on purpose and so had gone over and touched Elwood on the shoulder and had said, "Tom, we've got to go upstairs," and Elwood had said, "Sure, Lew," and had said again to Riccio, "Thank you," and they had shaken hands again, and then, without his even having to direct it, Elwood had followed him along the corridor and Worship had said, "We better go up to *my room*," and in a few minutes Riccio had come in with two psychiatric nurses . . .

So that he'd found himself alone with Riccio and Riccio had said, as if quoting something, "How many more are there at home like you?" but had not said it to Worship.

"Dr. Riccio, I . . ."

"Got any booze around here?"

"We're not supposed . . ."

"Cut the crap. What's your name?"

"Worship. Lewis Worship." And then, because he'd saved the man's life and, because of this man, Elwood had looked at him in that way, he'd said, "Lew."

"Lew." Toneless. "You got some booze?"

"No."

"Jesus Christ. I think the rules and regulations are beginning to turn out the kind of doctors we pretend to everyone we want." Then, "Aptshult live around here?"

"Few doors away . . ."

Riccio turned around. "C'mon. That sonofabitch'll have some. He probably keeps it the same place he keeps the instruments he lifted off me."

"Jim Aptshult?"

Riccio turned around. "Aptshult is going to be a damn fine surgeon, and don't you tell him I said so."

Worship began to laugh.

"Listen, you, Worship. One a night is all I can take."

Worship continued to laugh.

"You bloody well be careful, Worship."

"Sorry, Dr. Riccio," Lew said, still laughing.

"I don't actually know it was him. But he was the best of the lot and he *is* going into surgery."

They went into Aptshult's room. Jim was lying on his bed in the dark. Riccio switched on the light.

Jim sat up in bed and said, "Dr. Riccio."

And Riccio said, "Hospital life is *full* of surprises, isn't it, Doctor?"

"It shor is," Jim said, and managed himself out of bed. He grinned, still befogged by sleep. "Can I help you, Dr. Riccio? Or was you just browsing?"

"Aptshult, you may be half asleep, but you damn well better remember *who* and *where*."

Jim came totally awake. He said, wide-awake now and not only carefully, but tentatively, "You wanted something, Dr. Riccio?"

"*Yes*, God damn it!" Riccio thundered, now fully exasperated. "Where's your God damn booze!"

Jim pulled out a drawer and, from it, pulled out a two-thirds full bottle and held it up proudly. "Bourbon," he said, proudly, in his shorts, holding up the bottle like Liberty holding up the torch.

Riccio said, "All right, Aptshult. I'm not gonna reach."

Jim discovered himself, looked up at the bottle held two feet above his six-foot frame, and, a cautious expression on his face, handed the bottle to Riccio.

"The last time," Riccio said, pulling the cork out of the bottle and sitting down on a bed, "I saw a look like that, it was on a plastic case that turned out to be a failure."

"Yes sir," Jim said.

"Lost your southern hospitality, boy?"

"Just tired, I guess."

"Well you take some Dexamyl and wake up. Worship here, and I, we had quite an experience tonight, and we mean to finish off this God damn bottle of yours if it kills you. God damn hospitals anyway," he muttered, taking a swig. "No bars, what's the use of asepsis?"

"Gimme that bottle," Jim said, and then he was told about Elwood.

Later, the bottle finished, and Lew drunk from drinking or lack of sleep or lack of food or some of each, he couldn't tell which, he said to Dr. Riccio, who, he had discovered, didn't even know Elwood's name, "You didn't even thank me for saving your life."

Riccio grinned. "Would you thank anyone for saving Riccio's life?"

"What?"

"You'd be the only intern around these parts who would ... Well?"

"Well?" And he suddenly became sober and realized the risks he was taking and thought, The hell with it, but then figured he couldn't be that sober after all.

"Shit or get off the pot," Riccio said, now reclining on a bed.

"I've got a problem, Dr. Riccio, and you could help me if you would."

"All right, boy. We're all as plastered as you are. What is it?"

"I'm applying for a residency here. Only they're against taking guys from their own intern staff."

"On what?"

"OB-GYN."

"You think *I* can help you?" Riccio said wearily.

"I can't think of any other excuse."

"Wisdom, you've got what they call *hutzpuh*."

"My name's Worship. What's that word?"

"*Hutzpuh*, Wisdom, *hutzpuh*. Aptshult here'll explain it to you." He got up. "When I begin to get propositioned, it's time to go home." He held out his hand. "Thank you, Jim. I'll send you a *full* bottle tomorrow. I get bigger fees . . ." He managed his way out of the room without shaking hands with Worship.

"He doesn't look too used to drinking," Jim said.

"No. He doesn't . . . Jim? What's *hutzpuh*?"

"It's like *savoir faire,* only with an edge on it."

"Try again?"

"It's a Jewish word meaning you took an unconscionable gamble and got away with it."

"Yeah?"

"Yeah. You got away with it. The sonofabitch'll help you."

49

It was like . . . it was like . . . Court couldn't think of *what* it was like. He was . . . He was . . . *Fuzzed.* That's what he was, *fuzzed.* And over there on the other side of the room there was this statuesque type. Too bad she was married. To his old friend, what was his name? Harkland. Tooey Harkland. What kind of name that, *Tooey?* What kind of name that, *Courtney,* for that matter . . .

Tooey. Worked for . . . Worked for . . . Boopey Doopey Boopey Doo. Advertising agency. Oughta be. Anyway, you remember the name. Booby Dooby Cooby Doo. Name not likely to forget. Espesh when attached to a frame like that statue by association. She was looking at him. Wasn't she looking at him? Maybe it was just because he was looking at her. Better not look at her. Look at wall above her head.

Anyway. Thick abdominal wall. Difficult for listening to fetal heartbeat.

Should've gotten it when could in college. Well, not quite true. Tried. Didn't make it. Made it for a while. Sort of. Then Tooey made it. Permanently. Had the touch. Bedside manner. Should've been a doctor, not work for Gloop Gloop Gloop and Doop, advertising.

Old friend Tooey. "I think it's just wonderful, Court. I wanted to be a doctor too, you know, Court. But all that *time.* Hell, I figured I'd lose eight or ten years just gettin' ready . . . And you know me. I wanted to be *doing* something. But hell, if you're built so you don't mind losing all that time . . . well . . . why I think it's just wonderful if you can do it. Personally, I just couldn't see shooting that much of my life." Old friend Tooey.

Successful. *Doing* things. What things? Any things. Things you can see you've done. Things that're there after you've done 'em. Things you can see in a paycheck or even just in what people say to you . . . Living good, own apartments, afford ninety-cent drinks all evening without going into next week's pay much less next month's . . . And got a future too. A future you can *see*. Not a future you still have-ta magine like a kid dreaming about when he's grown up.

. . . Jesus, my twenties shot. Am I ever gonna have *my* girl insteada just a lay? . . . some respect insteada just . . . ? *Am I ever gonna have my twenties again?*

Am I . . . ? I'm supposed to have fun now, but I'll be in my thirties before I even get to be *myself*, much less what myself wants for myself which isn't really so much, just doing what I want to do and having my share of fun sometimes . . . Some share . . . Why I gotta lose my twenties to be a doctor in my forties?

"I bet you guys sure have it made with the nurses, hunh, Court? I bet that must be a real ball, all those nurses droppin' their pants?"

Court looked over and brought someone into focus. "I don't know," he managed. He sounded surprisingly sober to himself out loud. "I don't know. None of 'em dropped their pants around me yet."

"Aw, c'mon, Court," the someone said with a wink. "*Everyone* knows about nurses."

"I don't."

The someone smiled understandingly. "What you givin' me, Court? Professional loyalty?"

"Profe . . . Look . . . Look . . . Soma girls sleep with soma boys. Okay? It's a old custom. Girls're girls, an' boys're boys, an every so often they get together in bed. Same ina office. Same ina college. Same everywhere. So same ina hospital."

The someone smiled more broadly. "Same, except more so—right, Court?"

"Wrong, you sonofabitch! You wanna hear what I can tell you about it? You wanna hear from someone ina hospital? Or you just wanna crap along believing what your own sex . . . obsessed . . . *sex-obsessed* mind wants to believe? Hunh, Carsons?"

He had no idea how he'd gotten this way. He hadn't been drunk since a beer party his freshman year. What the hell had gotten him drinking and *willing* to get drunk? Hunh? What?

The statuesque one was looking back at him again, returning his stare at her. The one married to Oooby Dooby Oooby Dooo. In the well-cut suit . . . Good old Tooey . . . Old friend Tooey . . .

So even if she wanted to jump into bed with him, he didn't even have a bed for her to jump into with him. Or without him. What the . . . was he going to let *her* pay for the hotel room . . . ?

"Court, *boy*, you should hear this. Alex was just telling me his office expects just about *everything* to go up two points this year . . ."

"As I was telling El, Court, it looks like a wonderful year to get in on. I mean now. I tell you, both of you, now's the time to sink everything you've got . . ."

Court said, "Seventeen dollars?"

"Aw, c'mon, Court. Make it twenty. Like a sport. No, seriously . . ."

"Sounds great," Court said, and wandered away. He sat down next to a young man he'd only vaguely known in school. The young man was all smiles. His wife had just had a baby. Babies and wives and families . . . Well, it was the greatest. He knew it was trite and clichéd to feel that way, especially in a sophisticated gathering like this, but it was *true*, it *was* the greatest . . .

Court was thinking how it would be to go home to Mrs. Ooofy Doofy Boofy Poo every night. Well, that is, every *other* night . . . Have her make your eggs for you in the morning. How would that be? A bit of all right, hunh? Have her worry about you, take care of you, want you to be around . . . Someone to *want* you around . . .

He woke up. On *what?* Forty a month? Away all the time. And no money too? How long could a girl live like that? Yeah. And have it happen like Jim's wife. Someone'd turn up to be there when you weren't, spend money you didn't have to spend, have the *time* to spend it too, have the time just to talk to your wife and be with her . . .

With one factor settled you might have a chance—money. But nothing ever made up for the *time* you didn't have just to keep things going at their simplest and just plain subsistence level. That too would be the girl's problem, the wife's problem. Money *and* that too.

Court raised his glass and drank to the wives he knew who were doing it, taking it all on themselves and making it work

when even their husbands didn't know it wasn't working.
Lois Fishbein . . . Even Mildred Donnecker, who had the
money thing solved for her . . . But she was still sitting
around on that beautiful behind of hers losing her twenties
too, just like Fred, when she could be making it with any kind
of life she wanted, getting her full count for her twenties
. . . *Christ,* he thought, women are so wonderful . . .

He had a not unexpected and not unfamiliar longing
for his own wife. Why couldn't she be with him *now* instead
of not only not with him, but entirely unknown to him? Why
was he ten years behind anyone who was normal?

He was very sober now. His want had sobered him. He
hadn't even known that it was possible to want so badly. It
was amazing . . .

The investment type had come over and joined him and
the young-married type and was saying, "Really, Court, I
had to tell you this . . . and you too, Mickey . . . I've got an
awful good one for you, I put money in it myself. Anyway, I
know how tough it is for you doctors just beginning,
but . . ."

Court left him telling the young married how he could
do it on just . . . And then he found himself standing next to
the statuesque type in the tight black sheath. She said,
"You don't really remember me, do you?"

"I *do.* I thought you didn't remember me."

"Why would I forget you? We kissed almost a whole night
once, just . . ."

"Five years ago. I counted up when I saw you here.
Donna."

"Donna." She nodded. *"Court."*

"Sure. Then you and Tooey started up."

"You weren't very attentive, you know."

"I know. I was a grind."

"You certainly were, you used to call me once every
three weeks. Like clockwork. You called me once every
three weeks on Monday for a date on Saturday. I thought you
had a lot of other girls you were seeing in between during
those other weeks. And then I discovered you just *studied.*"
She laughed warmly. "Every three weeks like clockwork."

"Well, you see," he said, embarrassed, "I'm not . . . I
don't *study* very fast. I had to grind just to keep average
marks. So I could get into med school."

"I know. That meant a lot to you. Did you go where

you wanted to? Did you get in where you wanted to?"

"Not quite. But a place almost as good. Better, in a couple of departments."

"I'm sorry. I mean I'm sorry you didn't get in where you wanted to."

"Oh, the place I went to was fine."

"I'm glad." She looked at him and studied him and smiled. "You look a lot more . . . oh, I don't know . . . *mature* now. Yes, that's it. You look awfully mature now. A lot more than just about anyone in the room."

He nodded. "Thanks. I guess . . . I really don't know what to say to that . . . You're looking . . . very beautiful. Even more beautiful than I remember you. I remember you very beautifully," he said, laughing.

She curtsied. "That's the kind of compliment a mother of two likes to hear."

"Two. No, really?"

"Five years," she said. "Tooey wants lots of children. So do I."

"I do too," he said, surprising himself. He couldn't remember having thought about it before.

"Why don't you get married? You must have a head start with all the girls just by being a doctor . . ."

"Sure. Don't you want to hear about the nurses? How we don't need to get married because it's so wonderful with the nurses?"

"Oh, is that *really* true? I've always heard, of course, but . . ."

"Forget it," Court said. "I was making a joke."

"No, now don't shy away. You were the one who brought it up. And you know all women have an insatiable curiosity about . . . well . . . about the kind of women who . . ."

"Forget it. I told you, I was making a joke. What hospital did you deliver in?"

"Now don't change the subject, Court. We have a very good subject already . . ."

"How about money? Don't you want to tell me about all the money Tooey's making now?" Again he was surprised. He wasn't bitter. He didn't have bitter things to say. "Excuse me," he said, and put his empty glass down and started toward getting his coat.

Someone grabbed him. "Listen, Court. Sylvie's been telling me about this great job she has researching for . . ."

"It's not *really* so great, but I get to travel . . . I went to Europe last year and I'm going again in about . . ."

"Excuse me," Court said, "excuse me," and pulled away: I *wanted* to hear about it, I did, I *know* I did, but . . .

"Court, I'm sorry if I said anything just now. I mean, I didn't want to . . ."

It was Donna. He liked Donna. She was a lovely girl. What was it a lovely girl was apologizing to *him* for?

"Tooey and I are thinking of going out to dinner in a few minutes. Won't you come along with us? We'd really love to have a chance to talk to you."

He had done something that had made her have to apologize to him. *He* had done that.

"No," he said. "No." Why didn't he? Why wouldn't he? He had the money now. *No. No. No. No.*

What has gotten into you? What are you being so goddam sensitive about? "No," he said again. "No." And got his coat and took the subway back to the hospital and left a call for six thirty and lay there thinking, *But I'm doing what I want to be doing . . . Aren't I doing what I want to be doing? Or do I have to wait for that too?*

50

They sat down to a Sunday night dinner of soup and chili and Mildred said, "I'm sorry dinner's so uninteresting, but we were out so late last night I slept all day and I didn't even have the energy to go out and shop."

"Umhhh," Fred said, his mouth full of soup. "Tastes good to me. What'd you do? Where'd you go?"

"Well, Christine had this boy friend Sam, and Sam brought along a friend of *his*, Terry. It was very funny. Terry didn't know I was married."

"I hope you told him."

"I showed him the ring. First he said, 'Take it off,' then he said, 'No, leave it on, it makes me feel like a real cad, a real helluva man.' "

"He sounds utterly charming. And a real wit, too."

"Oh, Fred. Anyway, we went to the Copa for dinner."

"You don't mean the Copacabana by any chance?"

"Fred, be serious."

"I am. It's just that I'm not used to having a wife who lives so high. *Copa*, hunh? Fan-*cee*."

"Oh, the show wasn't so good. The girls weren't *that* pretty."

"Sagging breasts, eh? I know, I know," he said hurriedly, holding up his hands in a stop signal, *"Fred!"*

"Yes. Anyway, they did. Some of them."

"What I want to ask is, how come yours've stood up so long?"

"Fred . . ."

"Yeah, yeah, sure. So, dinner at the Copa. Then what'd you do, rob Tiffany's?"

"Don't be an idiot. We went to the Latin Quarter."

"Oi vey!" he said and clapped his hands and laughed with complete delight.

"I wish you wouldn't use those Jewish expressions."

He stopped laughing. "And what, pray tell, is wrong with Jewish expressions?"

"Nothing. Nothing, when Jewish people use them. But otherwise it's just sort of common."

"Thank you," he said. "I think your language is impeccable, too."

"Fred, *please,* do you want to hear about last night or not."

"I can hardly eat my chili, such is my anticipation."

"Well, then, as I told you, we went to the Latin Quarter . . ."

"How many Latins did you count?"

"Do you want to hear about it or not?"

"I'm sorry. Go on."

"Well, we went to the Latin Quarter and saw the show." She giggled. "Terry noticed *my* breasts, too. He said I shouldn't wear them in public."

"One helluva wit that Terry. Remember," he said, pointing a finger at her, "remember I said so even before you told me about that particular remark."

"Anyway, he said I was built quite a bit better than most of them were."

"I agree, not even having seen the show. Tell me, just out of idle curiosity—what were you wearing?"

"My black dinner jersey."

"Oi and *vey.* No wonder. The poor guy."

"You wouldn't say that if you knew what happened later," she said primly.

"Knew what happened later? So *nu?* what happened later?"

"Well, we went to a bar and talked until it closed and then he took me home in a cab . . ."

"Such *class,*" Fred said, continuing his Jewish accent.

". . . and he tried to kiss me and feel me up all the way back."

"I trust you fought fearlessly."

"Well," she said, though it wasn't true but because she wanted to see Fred's reaction, "I let him kiss me on the cheek. Twice."

"Good for you. One for each chorus line. No tip for the drinks at the bar?"

"Fred, you're not being fair."

"No, you're right, I'm not. I'm a thorough brute. Any husband would delight in his wife letting a stranger smooch her all the way home in a cab."

"Twice," she said. "Only twice. That happens to me at a party with *your* friends *all* the time."

"I can vouch for *my* friends, they have Wassermans daily."

"That's a disgusting thing to say."

"I apologize." Then he said, "I mean it. I do, really. I apologize."

She said nothing. Then she smiled softly and said, tinkling her water glass, "He wants me to go out with him again."

"Good for him," Fred said. "He's got taste. I revise my opinion."

"Shall I?" she said, coquettishly.

"Naturally. That's what all married women do. Go out with feather merchants all the time."

"He's a leather goods manufacturer. He's got his own plant or factory or something. And he's very attractive."

"Good. I hope you two will be very happy together."

"Oh Fred. Silly. Don't be sulky. I just meant he was nice, all right?"

"Okay." He sighed and stretched. "Now how about some coffee before I fall asleep in the chili?"

"Coming up," she said, standing and gathering the plates.

He reached out his hand to her arm and pulled her arm down so that she had to put the plates back on the table. Then he managed her over to him and sat her on his lap. "I'm jealous," he said, "if that's what you're bein' after findin' out. I don't like me wife off in the horrid taxicabs with the

daarlin' young men." He kissed her. "Perhaps *I'll* administer
to *you* tonight."

She smiled at him and stroked his hair. "Not tonight,
darling. Your *wife* is exhausted for a change."

"Maybe sex would fix her up."

"Sex would probably kill her."

"All right," he said.

"Don't sulk."

"I'm not . . . All right, I am. I'll stop." He grinned. "Now I
know how you feel sometimes."

"Now you know," she said, and pecked him on the forehead, and stood up and started carrying the dishes into the
kitchen. Then, as she poured the coffee, she decided that
perhaps she had been a *little* unnecessarily severe with him,
and went back into their dining foyer and kissed him on the
mouth, but thinking, I *am* too tired.

51

Fred wanted to insist. But he remembered that *she* had always
been fair and avoided embarrassing *him* by not insisting.
He, at least, owed her equal acceptance with respect and
without argument.

But he was angry. And as he thought about it, he realized
that he was not angry at her refusal to have intercourse with
him, but at her refusal on top of having spent the previous
evening with another man—in circumstances which befitted a
husband, not an acquaintance.

Then he remembered that she had not known about the
"date" in advance.

It was all right. She hadn't accepted a "date." It was just
that the friends of the friend were men. All right. There
was nothing for him to be angry about.

Except her letting her "escort" kiss her on the ride home.
Well, only on the cheek. But still . . . But. But he knew her
well enough to suspect that she had made that part up to
see his reaction; make him wake up to her.

Well; she had succeeded. But why had subterfuge been
necessary? Why had she had to go about it in *that* way?

Because she was unhappy. Obviously. She had to be

unhappy to have to make a presentation of that sort to him. Unhappy enough and unsure enough to have to make the presentation indirectly. (I should be going into psychiatry instead of ENT, he thought.)

Well then. Well. Well, number one, that took care of the anger. He had found out what he was really angry about and had fairly well understood the thing that had caused the anger. And well, number two, the fact was, things weren't too hot for them as a married couple, and *that* had to be dealt with. There should be no necessity for Mildred to make that kind of presentation to him. Therefore, he had to remove the necessity. Therefore, he had to make her happy. And therefore he had to bring them together—so they could talk. And yes, he had to fill in the empty spaces in her life so that an evening like the evening before wouldn't be so important to her—or to *him,* for that matter, he thought.

He went into the kitchen. She was doing the dishes. He started untying her apron.

"Hey!" she said.

He was tying the apron behind himself. "Research," he said. "I want to see what it's like to do dishes. Only way I'll ever *really* understand housemaid's hands."

She just stared at him as he edged her out of the way and took up what he considered a professional stance at the sink.

Suddenly he repented all sham—was *unable* to sham. He took her in his arms and held her and said, "I love you, darling." He kissed her neck and locked his arms around her. She held him in return, but without ardor, he thought— not tightly or responsively. He said, "I can't love you more than I do."

She squeezed him. An instant. A token. Then pulled back and looked at him, and smiled and shook her head and said, "Such a silly."

He smiled, thinking, what is it she's actually saying to me? and started on the dishes, still smiling—for himself, not for her, because she had left the kitchen, just gone away without saying anything more.

Later she refused him again; and he felt he had done the worst possible thing—had *twice* done the very thing she never did to him: embarrassed her with insistence. As a re- sult he lay awake next to her experiencing a new exquisitely uncomfortable emotion. Remorse. An emotion which angered him because he felt that it was unnecessary for him to have to feel it. After a while he tried to talk to her, but she said, "Please, darling, I'm so tired I can't even think." So he lay unsleeping, his body tense, his mind probing and exploring this new and painful presence in him.

52

Worship and Walters settled down into the two chairs in the room and van Wyck went to his bureau and took out a bottle of Scotch. He stopped and weighed it in his hand. "Feels a little light," he said. Then he held it up toward a lamp. "My God. It's half gone."

"Guilty," Walters said.

Van Wyck looked at Worship and shrugged his shoulders. "*Guilty*, he says . . ."

"I'll replace it."

Van Wyck uncorked the bottle and began pouring. "Don't be a jackass. It just surprised me." He looked at Lew. "My roommate has been keeping steady company with every bottle I bring in."

Walters grinned.

"The trouble is, I haven't got the logistical organization necessary to keep up with the replacement problem."

"Buy two at a time," Court suggested, watching the light come through the liquor in the glass in his hand.

Pete nodded, sitting down on a bed. "Yeah. We'll call them *yours* and *yours*."

"I could always go on the wagon."

"Don't do anything rash," Lew said.

"He hasn't really got a drinking problem, you see," Pete said to Lew. "It's just that whenever he finds himself with nothing else to do, he whiles away the long hours with short shots."

"Anyway, it's company," Court said.

"It makes him talk, too," Pete said. "And that's something. Lately, having Court for a roommate has been like rooming with a statue."

"Silence is golden," Court said.

"Then you oughta be rich as Croesus. Tell me—do you ever talk to the *patients?*"

"Only if they talk to me first," Court and Lew said in unison.

"You oughta get out more, Court," Lew said. "I mean, don't give up drinking, or anything like that, but try drinking *outside*. It's healthier."

"Nothing outside," Court said. "Besides, look who's talking."

"Yeah?" Lew said. "Well let me tell *you*, Courtney—like Dr. Otis says, *I've* got prospects."

Pete said, "How was the reunion?"

"Great."

Pete looked at Lew. "See what I mean?"

Court grinned.

Someone knocked. Pete said, "Yes?" and Otis came in. "Have a drink," Pete said, getting up.

John sat down on a bed. "Not on duty, I might get called any time."

Pete said, pouring, "If you get a call, just eat some toothpaste."

Court said, "Pete's the only guy I know who uses two tubes of toothpaste a week."

"Big joke," Pete said, offering the glass to John.

"No, really. It makes me nervous." John settled back against the wall.

"Nervous?" Pete said.

"Yeah. I guess I haven't got your kind of confidence, Pete."

"Yes? What's that mean?"

"I mean, if I know I've had a drink it makes me nervous that I'll make a mistake. And then I do, just out of being nervous that I will, not out of being high or anything."

"So?"

"So apparently you don't get . . . *aware* of yourself that way. So you function okay after a couple of drinks. I just can't. I get inefficient as hell thinking I'm gonna bollix something."

Lew cocked his head. "John Paul, you startle me. Startle and amaze me. I keep thinking you're the real cavalier spirit around here. And then you come up with something like that. I'm really impressed."

"Me, too," Pete said. "I thought you could handle anything. With one hand tied behind you."

"Well, for example," John said, "I can't handle Granchard."

"Who can?" Walters said.

"Lew can," John said.

"Once," Lew said. "He still on your back?"

"Not only on it, but I think he's filed his spurs."

"Sweet man," Pete said. "Milk of obstetrical kindness."

Court said, "Has he got a *reason*?"

John pursed his lips. "Well, maybe it's the impression I give. Like the impression you guys have of me. For some reason people take whatever I do as a personal insult. Just normal things."

"It's your cavalier attitude," Lew said.

"Yeah, maybe . . . And also, people jump to conclusions about my motives."

Pete nodded carefully. "John, we have underestimated you."

"Yeah," Court said. "We thought you were shallow."

The telephone rang. Pete took it. "Dr. van Wyck." Then, "Yeah, he's here . . . Lew?"

Lew took the receiver. "Worship . . . Oh, hi, Bobbie . . . I'm off tonight, you know . . . Yeah? The night after tomorrow? . . . Fine. Okay . . . Pick her up at the students' annex . . . Sure . . . And thanks." He hung up.

John said, "That's quite a grin you have on, Lew."

"So Lew's got a big date," Pete said.

"Maybe I ought to tell him about the facts of life," Court said.

"You don't know that many words," Pete said.

"Stop grinning, Lew," Court said. "You frighten me."

"Tell you the truth, I frighten me."

"Well, you're sure not acting like the mature young professional," Pete said. "You look positively adolescent."

"All right. Enough."

"You sure you don't want the facts of life?" Court said.

Lew's face, in spite of the control he tried to subject it to, grinned again.

"You know," Pete said, "I think he's looking forward to this date."

"Liquor is safer," Court said.

"*Anything's* safer than a student," Pete said.

53

On his Saturday night date with her, Art Rosconovitch was unable to proceed with Alicia in any way that was satisfactory to him. She was warm, humorous, and gentle; she took his arm and laughed with him. But she failed to outwardly notice—much less accept—the least of his carefully understated suggestions, even that they go out together again very soon.

He had decided—from pride—that she was exactly like the other hen medics. Sexless. So dedicated to the *physician's art* that sexual differentiation was only an interesting biological phenomenon that must, of course, be taken into account physically in diagnosis, but had no further significance, certainly no further interest for her.

His pride had told him that. His intelligence and his emotional response to her had told him entirely the opposite. He couldn't afford to get mixed up with passion, much less *unrequited* passion. He had enough to do just acquitting himself sufficiently well to earn the esteem of the medical staff that would convene in a few months to decide whether he was eligible to make application for a license to practice medicine.

So he thought, The hell with it. Not with her. *It.* The distinction comforted him and allowed him escape from a certain part of himself at the same time. That part of himself was the part that was the adolescent, the part he was fighting all the time. He was ninety percent mature, and a doctor. But he was, to his own mind, still ten percent an adolescent thrust into a world of adulthood by his own professional aspirations—after all, a doctor was an adult thing to be, and he felt he was only getting away with it. He felt he had thrust himself unready into an adult world. For he felt that this ten percent of himself had not yet unlearned the desires and emotions which do not exist—supposedly—in the mature individual.

An adolescent believes that life and suffering are the same thing. But the adult rejects that idea. And that rejection leads him into the belief that they are mutually exclusive. Which did he believe? For Rosconovitch felt that this was *the* test question. When he could answer he would know, finally, whether he had fully gained maturity and defeated the adolescent.

54

His response to Alicia's lack of response had openly forced this question upon him. On Monday morning he reported to GYN for rounds at nine o'clock as usual. But the question of his own degree of maturity (and thereby his fitness to practice medicine) preoccupied him to the virtual exclusion of the patients he saw. Later, realizing this, he returned to have a second look at most of the patients he was directly responsible for. One of these patients was somewhat exceptional—a lovely, twenty-year-old blond girl. He had to remember not to give in to himself. He had to remember not to spend an inordinate length of time with her.

She had one of the doubles alone to herself. And while he sat on the empty bed talking to her, one of the other doctors passed her open door.

"Who is *he?*" she said.

"Who?"

"The one who was just outside the door talking to Dr. Sprague."

"Oh. That's Dr. Ford. He's one of the residents."

"Oh."

After a pause and looking at her, he said, "Why?"

"Nothing."

"Must be something, Phyllis."

"He said I was going to die."

"I don't . . ."

"He told a nurse. They were standing right outside the door there, like just now. He said it to her this morning. After he saw me."

"You don't . . . You don't believe . . . You feel a lot better, don't you? A lot better than when you first came in?"

"Yes."

"Then forget it. He probably wasn't talking about you at all. Even if it was true, you don't think he'd stand right there and say it where you could hear, do you?"

"I . . ." she started; but if she was going to say something, she was either unable or unwilling to complete it.

"He's a responsible doctor, Phyllis."

"I don't want to die, Dr. Rosconovitch. Am I supposed to die?"

"Phyllis, you're . . ."

But she went ahead. "All I did was make love. I loved him. Even now I know I loved him. That's how much I loved him."

"Phyllis, you . . ."

"But I don't want to die . . . Can I tell you something?"

"Sure. Of course."

"The last time I made love was just a month ago . . . Don't you see? I was all alive just a month ago. I was all alive just *last week* before I . . . before I tried . . ."

She had looked away. "Yes," he said.

"But I was so alive just last week!" she cried at him, looking at him so desperately that he was almost unable to keep himself from looking away from her.

She had made fists of her hands and she looked down at them, her whole body as tense as the fists, her face staring at the fists, but her eyes squeezed closed.

"Phyllis, you ought to be lying down, you ought to be giving yourself some rest."

He started to get up to make her lie down, but she suddenly relaxed and looked at him with so little apparent strain in her face that he sat down again. Her voice was equally without strain, almost conversational. "I went to a party with my friends just last week and I was all right. I had fun. I had a lot of fun. Just talking with people . . . just being with people . . . And the day before . . . I came here I sat in the park. It was almost warm, there was so much sun and it was so nice. I started a dress, too, just before . . . It was going to be a nice dress . . ."

He could see the tension beginning to grip her again, and he thought, this is no good, I better get her some pheno, and said, "You'll finish the dress," and was going to get up and get the pheno except that she went on and he remained seated.

"No I won't. But it was for spring. It was going to be scooped. Here. Just a little. And sleeveless. For the spring."

"Phyllis, I told you . . ."

"I got the idea sitting in the park that day. I thought the

air smelled like spring. And I started thinking about when it got warm and how nice it would be to go walking and looking in the windows of the stores and I thought up this dress and got right up and went and got some nice material—cotton, with little flowers on it, just tiny green flowers on this pale yellow material—and I took it home and started making the dress. It was going to be very pretty. I think I would have looked pretty in it."

"Phyllis, listen to me for a minute. Let me tell you again . . ."

"I won't be alive in the spring. I won't even be alive in the new year . . . When it gets to be the new year, I just won't be at all . . . Where will I be?"

Rosconovitch said, "We're going to settle this right now. I'm going to talk to Dr. Ford. *I* know you're not going to die; you're recovering just fine. I'll just find out *exactly* what he said and who he was talking about. All right?"

He had to say it again. "All right?"

"You'll tell me the truth?"

"I'll tell you every word."

But it wasn't all right and he wasn't going to tell her every word. She was going to die. The next day, the day after. Within a week, certainly. Whenever her infection outstripped her body's ability to be. Nothing could be done, either by her or for her. Whatever could be done had been done already, first when she had introduced a knitting needle through her cervix—as if the needle were a curette—in an attempt to abort her pregnancy and had thereby ruptured herself into primary massive hemorrhage and begun an infection already so malignantly established twenty-four hours later that antibiotics did not even seem to slow its spread; and it had been done later for her by the doctors attending her who, having looked at her and administered to her, attended her not only without expectation of success, but also without even hope of success.

55

Ford said, "We've been running every goddam test in the book. And at the rate she's filling herself with toxic substances, she won't live more than three days. We can't take her blood out, can we? We can't take everything in her abdomen out, can we?"

Rosconovitch had known she was going to die. So had everyone else in GYN. But they had just never mentioned it to each other. They had said that she was suffering from this and that, and that her course of treatment was to be this and that, and that she was to be given this and that, and that her condition was this and that: up till this statement by Ford, every statement had been diagnostic, for everyone had wanted to and had somehow managed to avoid prognosis. But apparently it wasn't even worth the effort any more. He just nodded at Ford.

He himself hadn't really realized before that he hadn't bothered to admit the prognosis to himself, had, in fact, avoided thinking about it altogether. But just now, the ninety percent of him that was the doctor had informed the ten percent of him that was still the adolescent that this lovely young girl who was making a dress for herself to wear in the spring was not going to be alive in the spring, was not, in fact, going to be alive next week, was, in fact, probably going to die in three days.

It just couldn't be, the adolescent wanted the doctor to say. It just couldn't be, the adolescent said. It won't be. I don't know, the doctor wanted to believe, I *really* don't know. The adolescent insisted. The doctor thought, Well, maybe.

"Back me up," Rosconovitch said. "Anything I say, back me up." He wasn't even asking. He hadn't even thought of making it a question.

"Sure. Anything. Art . . . I did a damn fool thing. I'm not excusing myself, but just remember you could have done it too. You can't watch yourself a hundred different ways *every damn second* . . . I'm just sorry it had to be her . . . I like her a lot myself . . . Listen. I'll go in with you. I'll tell her. It'll sound more believable that way. All right?"

"That'd be good."

56

So Ford was saying to her, "You see, I was talking about a patient down the hall the nurse had just seen and was asking me about. Nothing to do with you. I'm sorry you

heard it, doubly sorry it upset you, that you misunderstood
. . . I shouldn't talk about *any* patient when another patient can overhear . . . Well, so don't let on you know, all
right?"

"Thank you," the girl said. "Thank you for telling me."

"Hell. Forget it. My fault to begin with. Well. Things to
do, I'll look in later."

"Thank you," she said again.

Rosconovitch stood up from where he'd been sitting on the
empty bed. "Okay now, Phyllis?"

She said to him, "Why am I alone? Why am I in a room
alone?"

"So you won't be bothered, so you can get some rest,
like you ought to be doing now . . ."

"No one else is in a room alone."

"Who's the doctor here, Phyllis?"

"Why did Dr. Ford keep smiling so hard at me? He
doesn't look that way usually. He *never* acted like that
before . . . Please, please, Dr. Rosconovitch, please help
me not to die."

"You're not going to die, Phyllis!"

But she was already going on. "Maybe I won't even be
alive at *Christmas*. That's not so far, that's only . . ."

"You'll be home by then, Phyllis. You'll be resting up . . ."

"*Please* keep me alive."

More than anything he wanted the girl to believe that
she was going to live. He wanted it for himself—almost as
much as for her, as if believing it was going to be so would
make it so, even though he knew it wouldn't. But he too
wanted to believe the girl was going to live. She would be so
much fun just to take out to dinner: to believe that she
wasn't going to live would make her dead already. He would
never be able to talk to her again . . .

He said, "Phyllis, do you like me?"

"I don't understand, of course I like you; you've been so
nice to me, you . . ."

"I don't mean as a doctor. Please, listen close. I mean,
do you like me as . . . Listen, call me Art. All right? Just for
a few minutes. Art." He was saying all this very quietly,
directing his eyes to the open door every so often to see
that no one was around or could overhear, because he *really*
wasn't supposed to be doing this—for about ten different
reasons, all of them good and all of them doubly good now.

He kept his voice so low that he had to wonder whether she could hear him.

"Art?"

"Yes. Say it again."

"Art . . ." She looked at him questioningly.

"I mean . . . Do you like me . . . Do you like me *as a person?* No. Don't . . . I don't mean as a person. I don't mean that way at all. I mean, do you like me as a . . . male? Do you like me the way a girl likes a man?"

She looked at him uncertainly and said nothing.

"I want to know if I'm attractive to you. If *Art* is attractive to you, not your doctor."

"Yes . . . I *like* you . . ."

"Not just as a doctor."

"I like you, Art." She was smiling, but her voice was serious.

"Could you be interested in me? Outside of here?"

"You mean, seeing you—outside the hospital?"

"Yes. You know, I could get bounced for this. They bounced a guy last year for dating a patient." He managed to grin. "It's not supposed to be ethical or something."

She finally laughed. He hadn't seen it happen before. "*Ethical?*"

"Yeah. It's not supposed to be . . ." He looked quickly to the door again. Then, even more quietly than before, he said, "Please. You have to tell me something honestly. If I asked you for a date, would you go out with me? I mean, the way you would with another guy?"

She was uncertain again. He was afraid he might even have offended her. She said, staring at him without expression, "I don't know if you meant what you said then this way—but I wouldn't just go to bed with you."

"I didn't mean that at all, I . . ."

She was still talking to him. "I only slept with one person in all my life. I don't . . . Well, I'm not . . . you know."

"I wouldn't be talking about—what I'm talking about if I thought that. But Phyllis?"

"Yes?"

"If I went out with you and kept liking you, I'd want to go to bed with you; I'd probably at least *try* to sleep with you— I don't want you to think I wouldn't."

"I couldn't tell you *now* . . ."

He laughed. "I don't expect you to. I just wanted you to

know so that you wouldn't be expecting that I was going to be . . . well, *disinterested*. If I liked you a lot . . ."

"I know. Art, if I liked you a lot, I'd want you to . . . to at least *want* to."

"Then fine. Now we've established that we don't have to be just doctor and patient forever. So . . . So, what I want to know is, well, if you're rested up enough then—and you ought to be, the way you're coming along—well, would you be my date New Year's Eve, there's a party over at a nurse's I know and no one would snitch, and, well, would you?"

She considered it for a long time, Art thought. A terribly long time. And not *it*, not his question, it seemed to him, but *him*. She was considering *him*; just looking at him, seeing him and not his question.

She said, so quietly he almost didn't understand, "Really? Really New Year's Eve?"

"You're very beautiful," he said. He had to light a cigarette. "I'll be very proud of you."

"I want to. I want to so much . . ." She was excited now, as eager as a child who has forgotten that the one night the circus is going to be in town is a school night.

He tried hard not to let her remember. "You'll have to let me kiss you, you know. At midnight. Even though it's a first date. And I might take a long time at it."

She began to smile. "Would you?"

"Well?"

"I want to . . . Can I be sure?"

"I'm not in the habit of asking girls out I expect to stand up."

"Yes. Yes, I want to so much."

"Yes, what?"

"*What?*"

"Yes, what. Yes, I want to, *what?*"

She laughed now. "Yes I want to, *Art*."

"Good. And unless I tell you otherwise, it's back to *Dr. Rosconovitch* now, and don't forget, or else you'll be going out with an out-tern."

"Yes, *Doctor*," she said with great seriousness.

"Now get some sleep. You have to be rested up so you can go out that night."

In a very quiet voice, as she lay down, she said, "Art, *Art*, I'm hurting again."

He managed to smile. "I cut my hand last week. See? It hurts, too. But it's getting better."

She smiled a little again.

"But since you're a patient and not a doctor, you rate medication. I'll have a nurse give you a little Demerol. All right?"

She nodded.

"And then you sleep."

Outside her door and far enough down the hall so that she couldn't possibly see him, he had to stop and lean against the wall and shut his eyes to stifle the nausea that he knew might in an instant have him vomiting.

He was thinking, *If she's going to die she shouldn't have to live with this this way. If she's going to . . .* And then he thought: *I made a date with her, so she's going to be all right . . .*

He didn't know if it was the doctor or the adolescent speaking; or both. But he was able to open his eyes and start moving again.

57

Also on Monday, before going to lunch, Jim Aptshult stopped by the mailroom to pick up whatever might be in his box. Unlike some of his colleagues who very nearly managed to live in their mailboxes, Jim rarely went near his more than once a week. He had found it unnecessary to stop by more often. His only correspondence consisted of two or three letters a month from his father or an occasional answer from a hospital he'd applied to for a residency.

There was one letter in his box. It was addressed in an irregular feminine script. His wife's script. He ripped the letter open without moving from the spot he was already in.

Dear Jim,

About my consenting to a divorce, you are my husband. I didn't get married to get divorced. There are appearances to think of. Just remember, you are my husband.

I have been talking to a lawyer, Mr. Emory Harrison, about a legal separation. He has been working out how much money you should pay me and we both agree on a set percent of your gross yearly income, though your pay-

ment to me is never to be less than $200.00 per month to
be paid monthly. He will write to you I am sure.
  I hope you are well.

Louise

Since it was lunch hour, Jim went directly to the dining
hall. There he found a friend who agreed to cover for him for
the afternoon, found his chief resident and got her permission
to have someone cover for him for the afternoon, and then
searched out Mike de Traunant. Mike was eating with some
other interns.

Jim said, "I gotta see you a minute, Mike."

"Well, use your eyes, son, here I . . . *Hey!*"

Jim was tugging him up out of his seat.

"Jesus," Mike said, being led bodily out of the dining hall.
"You got Elwood's Disease or something?"

In relative privacy outside the dining hall, Jim said, "Your
father's a lawyer, isn't he?"

"Yeah . . ."

"Personal type lawyer, not corporation."

"Yeah . . ."

"Well, would you fix it up for me to see him this afternoon?"

"You got your jet ticket?"

"Hunh?"

"He's in Europe."

"Shit!"

Mike started to walk away. Jim grabbed him. "Someone
else. Someone else in his office? Can you set up an appointment for me with someone else in his office this afternoon?"

"I could try, I guess . . . What's the rush?"

"Never mind. I'll tell you when it's settled."

"Okay. I'll call right after I finish eating."

"Now."

"Jesus, Jim. Everyone's out to lunch."

"Try anyway."

"Can't I just . . ."

"Please, Mike."

"Sure. Okay. I wasn't hungry really, anyway."

At four thirty Jim was in the office of Mr. Arnold Dykes of
Thorn, Dykes, de Traunant, Attorneys at Law.

Jim shook hands, sat down, and said, "I want a divorce. I

have five thousand dollars all told to spend on expenses and whatever settlement may be involved. I hope it won't come to that much." He then explained his grounds, the history of his marriage, and his relationship with his wife. Then he handed the lawyer two bundles of envelopes: his correspondence with Louise over the past two years and correspondence from various friends who had written him about his wife's activities.

Mr. Dykes said he would get in touch with the firm's associates in Jim's home area and would call Jim the following week. As Jim got up to go, Mr. Dykes said, "Considering your previous opinion that it was your mistake and your responsibility to remain stuck with it, what suddenly changed your mind?"

Jim thought and shook his head, and then finally offered, "I guess I no longer believe in perpetuating or prolonging a hopeless situation."

"Yes," said Mr. Dykes, "but what *brought* you to this new attitude?"

Jim thought immediately of Alicia Liu. But he realized that his letting himself feel something for her was a result of his new attitude, not the reason for it.

He sat down again. "I guess," he said, "I guess it's been getting this way for a long time. I mean, *I* have. I see people die, and I wonder what the hell they ever did with their lives. They let themselves in for so much they didn't have to. And then suddenly they're dead and they might just as well have never been born. So, anyway . . . I guess I got started thinking about what the hell the *living* are doing with their lives. Particularly me . . . And it occurred to me that just about everybody seems to putz their life away in lousy situations they think it's immoral to change, or that they're too afraid or gutless or lazy to change. So I didn't want it that way— only it took this letter I got this morning to make me see I was right. Or rather, make me see I ought to *do* something about it aside from just intellectualizing about it . . . I mean, what's the use of being if you're not allowing yourself to be alive? There's no sense in just being for being's sake, is there? So why perpetuate something that's hopeless or no good? Why not end it and try for something positive instead of negative?"

He had asked a question which Mr. Dykes was surprised to find had not been intended as mere rhetoric. Mr. Dykes said, "Why not?"

Jim went back to the hospital and wrote his father to make arrangements for the five-thousand-dollar loan from the bank. Then he went back on duty—the evening Pediatrics Clinic.

58

When the telephone rang—unexpectedly (her telephone always rang unexpectedly)—Mildred was trying to decide whether to go to a movie, read the new *Mademoiselle*, give herself a permanent, or just decide.

She said, *not* unexpectedly, "Hello?"

"How's the married woman?"

"Who's this?" she said, almost giggling because she knew.

"Bob Hope."

"Oh, c'mon. Who is it? I hate telephone games."

"You mean you really don't know?"

"Sidney Wohl?" she said.

"Who? *Who?*"

"You mean you're *not* Dr. Sidney Wohl?"

"No. *Now* who's playing telephone games? Maybe I should hang up."

"Oh, stop it, Terry. I knew it was you all the time."

"You did, hunh? You sure didn't sound like it."

"I'm sorry." He said nothing. She said, "Your nickel. I mean, your dime."

"Yeah. Well. I just called to see if maybe you'd like to see a movie with me tonight, that is if you're not stuck with your husband."

"I'm never *stuck* with my husband, and it just so happens I *don't* want to see a movie tonight."

"Oh, c'mon, Milly . . ."

"I told you, I don't like being called *Milly* . . ."

"Okay. *Mildred*. I forgot. So sue me. I mean, c'mon, we'll just go see a movie."

"No."

"Please, Mildred. What the hell. C'mon. I'm alone and you're alone, what's wrong with us seeing a movie together? I'll even let you pay your own way."

"Then I *positively* won't go with you."

"Okay, *I'll* pay your way. And buy you a drink afterward to boot."

"And keep your hands to yourself in the cab coming back."

"Cab? *Cab?* What cab?"

"And keep your hands to yourself in the *cab* coming back."

Terry groaned. "And keep my hands to myself in the cab coming back," he said.

"What time will you pick me up?"

"Pick you up? Jesus, *cab, pick you up?* I thought maybe you'd meet me at the Paramount."

"Good night, Terry. Thank you for calling."

"Okay, okay. Don't hang up. I'll pick you up in half an hour."

"Forty-five minutes," Mildred said.

"Yeah, yeah, forty-five minutes."

"Hands to self?"

"Yeah, sure, hands to self."

"I'll be waiting. And Terry?"

"Yeah?"

"Thanks for calling."

She carefully dressed in her beige jumper and a white blouse. The jumper did not fit her tightly and the blouse was discreet without being unfashionable.

Terry was very good in the movies and only held her hand, and, of course, *had* to be good in the bar because there were a lot of people around and there was an entire table between them even though it was in a booth, but at least he didn't try any leg business. And then in the cab he was just as good except that he made a few pointed, though funny, remarks about her coming up to see his apartment. She half excused him though, because she felt that he was honestly and sincerely proud of his apartment and *wanted* her to see it.

It was just that he tried to kiss her good night. He was not funny, he was just pointed. And, very strong. She slapped him quite properly.

"Well, thanks," he said. "Thanks for a wonderful evening."

"Don't bother to call again," she said.

59

Now . . . I am *not* a child, Lew told himself, trying to get to sleep. I am grown up and mature and I have an M.D. to prove it.

Then he waited. But it didn't get him to sleep.

He kept thinking about the girl. In spite of not getting to sleep because of thinking about her, he would not have been so upset had he had an image to look at in his mind. But he hadn't met her yet—their date was for the next night. So he kept thinking about her, and yet he had nothing to think about *about* her—not even a face. He found this not only discouraging, but uncomfortable. Because it showed what a fool he was. An adolescent, the way Pete had said. Being kept awake thinking about a girl he hadn't even seen a picture of, much less met or talked to.

You *are* a child, he told himself. And waited. But it didn't get him to sleep.

Well, why don't you worry about getting a residency? he thought. Because if you don't get this one here, you're going to be stuck out in some small, second-rate place where they probably don't have any interns and only one other resident, where all you can learn from the staff, you can learn in a couple of months. It would be like interning another year . . .

No, he thought. I'm not going to get to sleep thinking about that, either.

The girl came back to his mind, and he found himself thinking, No, I'm not like Pete or the others, I don't know how to just jump in and out of bed with a different girl every time out. I'm not against it, I just don't know how to get myself to go about it. And, with the girl still in his mind, he thought, So please . . . Because I don't know any other way and I want to love . . .

Still he didn't get to sleep, and still his mind would not let the idea of the girl go, and he found himself wondering if Donnecker and Fishbein and Granchard loved their wives very much and if the wives loved them back and if John Paul Otis loved his girl very much and if she . . .

He was surprised and discouraged when he saw light outside. He'd wanted to be fully rested and relaxed for his date so that he could enjoy it and the night out, God knew when he'd get out again and have a date at the same time . . .

60

Tuesday morning, when Conny Mercouris got to the locker room, he was much too early. But that was all right. He had planned it that way. He wanted to make a good impression on Dr. Wexler. Dr. Wexler was to be his entree to Dr. Harvey Bonny and Century Veterans and the wonderfully non-physical specialty of psychiatry.

But Conny was forty-five minutes too early to even change. He sat down on the bench in front of his locker and stared around the empty room. Except for there being no smell of sweat, it was all quite like getting to the gym rather too early to suit up for a football game. He began to tense up in his stomach just as he had before a game or before an examination. He had as little business in an operating room as he did in either of the others.

After a while he lay down on the bench . . .

A voice above him said, in a moderate tone, "You're going to be late."

He sat up violently. The voice belonged to Dr. Wexler. It continued. "We were supposed to be in the O.R. ten minutes ago."

Conny hurriedly got into a scrub suit and followed Dr. Wexler into the operating room. It was an O.R. for minor operations, and its scrub sink was in a corner rather than in a separate room. He and Wexler stood together at the sink and began scrubbing with nail brushes.

Wexler looked over at him and said, "Put some elbow grease into it, Doctor, it's not *that* late in the day."

Conny thought, Jesus, *I'm* not the one who's operating; I'm not even first assistant; he's got a scrub nurse to hand him his junk; what the hell do *I* have to scrub so hard for? But he did, anyway, because Wexler was still watching him.

"The idea is asepsis, Doctor," Wexler said. "Not a beauty treatment."

As he dried his hands, Conny heard Wexler, behind him, say to someone—the nurse or the anesthetist—"I don't know what the hell anyone wants to see a *bursitis* operation for. For chrisake, it's nothing more than lancing under anesthesia."

Conny couldn't bring himself to turn around. Instead, he pretended to continue to dry his hands.

"Helen, *where the hell is the patient?*"

Helen laughed. Conny turned around. She nodded at him. "I thought *he* was the patient."

Wexler and the anesthetist laughed. Conny thought, The *bitch*. But he couldn't say anything. She was probably Wexler's permanent, favorite scrub nurse. Which meant she could get away with anything.

"You were late, so I didn't send down for her till I saw you. They'll have her up in a minute."

"Prepped, I hope," Wexler said. The anesthetist laughed and this time the nurse flushed.

She said, "Of course."

Wexler turned to Conny. "The patient is a sixty-year-old white female suffering from inflammation, severe pain, and subsequent loss of mobility of the right arm. There's probably a fairly large calcium deposit that's putting pressure on every muscle, tendon, and nerve in the area. It's probably the usual subacromial bursa. I'll open it, clean it, and close it. I don't know what the hell you want to watch *that* procedure for, but suit yourself. I swear, interns get stranger every year."

Conny occupied himself with getting out a pack of gloves. Wexler said, "What the hell are *you* gloving up for, *you're* not operating. Just stand over there and you can see everything. If you wanna puke, get out of here fast." He turned to the anesthetist. "One of 'em puked all over the place during an appendectomy last week. An *appendectomy*, for chrisake!"

The patient was wheeled in and transferred to the table. She was plainly holding a great deal of fear in check. Wexler leaned over her solicitously. "Now, Mrs. Sapper, you don't have to worry about a thing. In about five minutes you'll be asleep, and in about an hour you'll be awake again and your arm won't hurt you any more when you move it. You just relax now and listen to what this young man tells you to do, he's going to help you to get to sleep." Wexler nodded at the anesthetist. The anesthetist began turning dials and watching lights. Then he made adjustments so that he could keep a constant check on the patient's heartbeat and blood pressure. Finally he took the mask in his hand and explained to the patient how to breathe and what to expect as she went under. The patient nodded. The anesthetist placed the mask. The patient's arms tensed and half raised themselves. But after a few seconds they relaxed, and after a moment or two more, the anesthetist said, "All set."

There were almost no preliminaries. After prepping the area, Wexler just said, "Okay, sweety," and the nurse handed him a lancet.

Begrudgingly, Conny admired the man's technique and ability. There was no inflammation or discoloration on the surface of the skin. But Wexler seemed to know precisely where to go in without palpation. An incision perhaps an inch in length about five inches directly above the nipple in the infraclavicular region. Then he went deeper. There was very little bleeding. Then some paste-thick white substance began coming up out of the incision. Wexler put pressure around the area of the incision. "Look at the damn stuff come out," he said. "Just like toothpaste."

"Not my brand," Conny said, trying to make a sound like a laugh.

Wexler said, "It is fundamentally impossible to please an intern."

The area around the operating table began to smell foully. Conny automatically stepped back. Wexler looked up, "Puking I expected," he said. "This is my first experience with even an intern shitting in his pants."

The nurse said, "I think the patient has had a bowel relaxation, Dr. Wexler."

"Perfect working conditions," Wexler said, and went back to draining the bursa. "You follow professional football, Mercouris?"

"Hunh? . . . Oh, no. No, not much."

"Saw a *helluva* good game Sunday. Jesus, what a game." He described the game. Meanwhile, he cleaned the incision. He finished describing the game. Still cleaning the incision, he said, "You hear the story of the two mice in the nose cone?"

Since no one else said anything, Conny said, "No, I haven't."

"Hell bent for outer space and one of 'em's complaining like mad. Finally the other one says, 'What the hell are you bellyachin' about? It's a damn sight better than cancer research.' "

The nurse laughed. The anesthetist laughed. Conny pretended to laugh. How come the sonofabitch was suddenly being pleasant to him? The sonofabitch! He's cutting, he's happy. What a bastard. whatever he was, he was certainly at the moment pleased with himself.

Wexler looked up from getting rid of some cotton and gauze cleansing pads and said, "Okay, nursy, hang on me the suturooni."

He waited with his hand out and then received a scissors and needle. *"Well where the hell is the suture!"* he yelled.

The nurse said, "It's . . . it's not here, Doctor."

"Well, get it! What the hell am I supposed to do, *close it up with my teeth?*" The nurse started to leave the room. "Triple O nylon," he yelled after her. He stood looking glumly at the patient. Then he said to Conny, "You know why I'm using that?"

"Cosmetic reasons?"

"Yeah," he said, still looking glumly at the patient. "So the scars'll be as small as possible in case this old bag ever decides to wear a low-cut evening gown, God forbid."

Ten minutes later they were in the locker room changing. Mercouris remembered that he wanted to make an impression on Wexler. Ask questions, he'd decided. Sound interested. But what the hell kind of questions could you ask about a procedure like that? A first-year med student wouldn't have to ask any questions. Well. Well, there was always one safe question to ask—safe because there was rarely any unarguable answer to it. Conny said, "Uh, Dr. Wexler, one question I'd like to ask?"

Wexler looked up from his buttons. "Well?"

"How come you used a transverse incision rather than an up-and-down one?"

Wexler just stared at him. Stared at him till Conny thought the man had suddenly gone catatonic. Wexler dropped his arms to his side as if stupefied. "Doctor, that is surely the most damn fool, stupidest, pointless question I have ever been asked in my entire medical experience. And I have been asked some dillies, let me assure you."

Conny started to speak. Wexler cut him off. "Now, Doctor, considering how far back from the table you were standing, and considering the length of the incision, I'm very much surprised that you could see the incision at all, much less what direction it took . . . You know, Doctor, I've been wondering just why the hell you wanted to see this operation anyway."

"I . . ."

Wexler kept talking. "Now, considering the other operations of immensely more significance and interest that the inquiring mind has available to it in a hospital of this size, why exactly does the inquiring young intern choose a *bursitis* operation to watch?"

Conny was thinking, *Because it was the first one you had scheduled*, you sonofabitch! But all he said aloud was, "I was interested in it."

"Why? What interested you about it?"

Conny stared at him.

"I'm interested in knowing what interested you about it, Doctor."

Conny was within a fraction of hitting him.

"What the hell interest does it have for *anyone?*" He became sarcastic. "Come now, Doctor. Is it something private or personal you don't feel you can tell me? You can tell me. I'm your friend. I'll keep it secret. Privileged conversation, you know. Maybe you have an unnatural obsession with bursitis operations?"

"My mother is having a bursitis operation next week and I wanted to see what would be going on. *You sonofabitch!*"

In a calm voice, Wexler said, "I don't believe you. I suggest you don't pull a line like that on anybody in this profession ever again. And as to the sonofabitch part, well that's private and personal between you and me," and he took one step forward and hit Conny hard enough in the face to knock him over. Conny lay on the floor, holding his hand over his mouth. No teeth broken. But his lip must have been cut, his mouth was full of blood. Wexler said, "Grab your pants and get out of here till I finish dressing."

61

Lew felt very good. He'd gotten off at four precisely. He'd come up to his room and sat on his bed and wished he'd made the date for dinner too. Hell, he *should* have made it for dinner. He wanted to be with this girl. She didn't even have to be somebody he could love, he also suddenly discovered. Just a girl. Just a girl to sit with and talk to someplace outside the hospital.

He felt like laughing and clapping his hands—he didn't know how else to go about handling the excitement he was feeling. He hadn't realized, for instance, he wanted a change of food so much. It was a discovery that delighted him. He felt suddenly rich. He hadn't realized he was this other person too—this other person who wanted to get out for a while, wanted to feel *alive* the way he was feeling now. He hadn't realized he hadn't been feeling alive lately. That's what came of getting your kicks from OB. You could stifle the whole rest of yourself.

He got the operator to ring Gloria Mead at the students' annex. Then they switched him to Male Surgery A. Then Male Surgery A said Miss Mead's group had gone off at four. Then they switched him back to the students' annex and he left a message for Miss Mead to call him when she got in.

He lay down. And went immediately to sleep. And woke suddenly and looked at the clock and saw it was ten till seven and remembered his date was for eight and figured, what the hell, wherever they went he could eat there, and went and luxuriated in a long shower and a slow, careful razor shave.

As he fixed his tie, he looked in the mirror and complimented himself on his shave and the way he looked.

The telephone rang. Great. They could still get started a little early. He hoped that maybe she hadn't eaten yet.

"Worship," Granchard's voice said, "I've got three Caesarean sections going at once and no one to spare, you better stick around tonight."

"Hey, but . . ."

"No hey-buts, if one more woman in labor comes in, I'll need you. Period, Doctor. So stick in your room or tell the operator where she can get you right away."

"Yeah. Okay."

Then, "I'm sorry, Lew. Bobbie told me you've got a big date tonight; she wanted me to try and get someone else." Then, as if it pained him, "I tried. But everyone else who's got the night off has sense enough to get the hell out of the building as soon as they could."

As soon as Granchard had hung up, Gloria Mead called. "Listen," Lew said, his voice sounding to him as if it were something he was listening to rather than producing himself, "I can't make it tonight, but . . ."

62

Mercouris knew he could have hit him back. He could have damn near killed him. Without even getting out of breath. That was his consolation. Damn little consolation. No consolation at all.

He spent the day making excuses for his bruised and swollen lip and jaw. He was not on call that evening, so he thought he'd save himself from appearing in the dining hall. Though what he actually told himself was that he was sick and fed up with New North's food, so he'd eat out. But he found himself drinking instead. One after another, rye after rye. What the hell, as long as he was drinking, it might as well be whiskey, not that piss they called beer.

So Wexler was a shit and a bastard; that was plain. That had been plain to him even before the locker-room scene. A shit, plain and simple. Forget him. Bastard.

But let's get onto some clear thinking. Without Wexler, without *some* angle, Harvey Bonny was pretty damn unlikely. Well, so what? There must be thousands of psychiatrists who never worked with Bonny and made out all right. Yeah, but you gonna end up taking second best again?

Okay, *no*. So, you gonna hold out for Bonny? And screw yourself into accepting second best when he turns you down? Okay, *no*. So what're you gonna do?

He thought about it through a couple of more drinks. He considered dermatology. No one knew what the hell went on there anyway. He'd seen an established dermatologist with a pretty fancy reputation diagnose the same condition in the same patient two different ways in two days and when asked about it check both previous diagnoses and come up with a third. Hell, you could go on like that for years. That's the way it is in dermatology. No one can say you're doing the wrong thing. No one could be *sure*.

Except. Except for one thing. In dermatology you got exposed to some pretty mean conditions. Mean-looking, mean-smelling. And that's what he was trying to avoid. And working with people and their disgusting conditions and body odors all day. And that's what he was trying to avoid. So dermatology was out. So he had another drink.

Then he thought of it. The perfect one. Better even than psychiatry. Hell, he'd hardly have to even see patients, just other doctors most of the time. And *he'd* be the expert and they'd do the listening.

Radiology. Give 'em a dose of radiant energy. Click on, click off. And diagnostic roentgenology. Click on, click off. Take a picture. Spend the rest of the time alone, *away from patients,* just sitting around interpreting the plates, looking things up, talking things over with the doctor who called you in. No sweat. All the time *alone*. Chance to check everything out with the books. Or even the therapeutic aspects of radiology. Get out the old slide rule. Figure. Read up on the disease and never ever have to go near the patient much. Just operate a machine according to the rules. And *hell*—he could *learn* the rules. The rules couldn't be too terrible just to take pictures or lay on a little ray. He was good at math; he was good at physics; he just might be pretty damn good at radiology.

He was beginning to get excited. He ordered another drink. No fooling around with patients. None of this business of having to smell them all the time or see their lousy conditions all the time. In, out. Click on, click off. Look at pictures. Discuss pictures. Lay it on. Click on, click off. In, out. Maybe not more than half an hour a day with patients. Maybe not that much most days. Great. Perfect.

It was, let's see, a three-year residency. Yeah. Something like three. And afterwards those guys made Money with a capital *M* once they got set up. And there was this new field—*Nuclear Medicine*. Sounds exciting as hell. And impressive, too. Just count up fallout all the time. Figure out what to do about it, or something. All part of radiology. *And man, that is IT, with a capital* I *and a capital* T. *Radiology is for me.*

He ordered another drink. Celebration.

He tasted it. Something wrong. He called the bartender over. "Hey," he said, "listen, Mac. I may look drunk. But I'm not all *that* drunk. What's the idea of ringing in watered whiskey on me?"

The bartender said, "Sir, we don't serve watered whiskey." He took the glass away from in front of Conny. "Why don't you go outside and take a little walk and think it over. Okay? Maybe come back later if you feel like it. Or go home and get some shuteye. Tell me about it tomorrow if you're still mad, and we'll talk it over then. Howsabout it?"

Conny looked at him and nodded slowly. "You think you're a pretty clever sonofabitch, don't you?" He started laughing. "Come back tomorrow, hunh? Pretty clever. Goddam bar probably won't even be here." He laughed harder. Then he stopped. "Okay, you sonofabitch . . ."

He got up and left.

63

He felt a helluva lot better. At least the bartender hadn't beaten him down. The bartender couldn't hide behind being an established doctor like Wexler or Riccio.

Sprague was out, so he had the room to himself. He drafted a letter to Harvey Bonny in which he said that he was afraid the setup at Century Veterans—after much mature consideration, of course—didn't quite offer him what he wanted. Then he wrote it out, hoping that Bonny would realize that the tone of the letter was that of uncontrollable condescension. That ought to knock some wind out, do a little impressing. The great Harvey Bonny condescended to. *Wham!* Who would *ever* believe that? Hah! and *double* wham! He addressed, stamped, and sealed it, and took it downstairs and mailed it in the box in the new building's lobby.

Back in his room he got out his copy of *The Directory of Approved Internships and Residences* that the *Journal of The American Medical Association* published.

In the *Directory,* under Medical Specialties, he looked up Radiology to see what the length of residency was and what he'd have to be doing. Everything he read delighted him. Lots of lab work and technical study and comparatively little direct contact with patients. At least not the way it was in other specialties.

The last section was headed Examinations, and the last sentence of the last paragraph read: "The applicant is also examined in 'professional adaptability,' in an attempt to ascertain his attitude toward his fellow practitioners and his patients."

This amused him. It was the funniest thing he had ever read in anything medical. It amused him because *he* knew his own weaknesses, *he* was pretty damn objective about himself (he probably *would have* made a pretty good psychiatrist), and he knew this would be the toughest part of the radiology examinations—no matter *what* else they threw at him. He closed the *Directory* and started laughing. He'd be ready. They weren't going to get him on *that.* When they got through with him on that examination they'd finally think they'd found the ideal radiologist. He'd see to it.

64

Christmas was the next day. Yet the rhythm and activities of the hospital remained relatively unchanged—remained almost the same as they had been on July second or October eighth or April nineteenth. People *talked* about Christmas, but that was just about all. Interns who had elected Christmas as their day off discussed going home or just sleeping. Some presents had been bought in off hours during the weeks before—the presents that had to be mailed home. A lot of presents were bought on December twenty-fourth in the hospital gift shop. Some of the nurses brought in mistletoe and ribbons and holly and hung them in the nurses' stations. Pediatrics had been heavily decorated and some of the members of the staff made sure that certain patients got small gifts or at least a card. Jim Aptshult organized a party for the kids in the children's TB ward. Alicia Liu and her roommate made several gallons of eggnog and invited all their fellow interns up to their room for a midnight celebration. But that was about all. Christmas at New North was largely just a matter for discussion—something theoretical that was pleasant to talk about. During another season it would have been the World Series or what July Fourth was like at home. Just something different to talk about. A change in conversational subject matter.

Art Rosconovitch wanted to get his patient, Phyllis, a present. He had kept putting it off because he felt uneasy about making a commitment to the future. It would somehow be bad luck to buy a present for her . . . *in her condition,* he said to himself evasively. He had grown adept at using phraseology in his mind that avoided any exact statement of her condition. The present had been on his mind for several days. But if he bought it on Monday, he was quite frightened of . . . *of what might happen* on Tuesday. A present bought on Monday would tempt the fates too much during the days before Christmas when he'd finally be able to give it to her.

Now, on the twenty-fourth, he desperately wanted to get her a present. But he was going through agony trying to get himself actually to do it, actually to *decide* to do it.

Theoretically it was against the hospital rules. Theoretically he could get into a good deal of trouble by giving a patient a present (for the hospital had to worry about the *other* patients and charges of favoritism or discrimination or even neglect). But he'd toss the rules over in a second.

He wanted to get her a gift. Desperately wanted to. But it would mean being dishonest in a way that appeared to him to be nothing but malignant. For he felt that the gift would be meaningless, and therefore evil, if she didn't live.

She was still alive, though. And he knew that if she was still living he would not be able to bear not giving her at least *some* sort of Christmas.

He agonized through it all day, weighed it against not giving her any Christmas gift the next day, avoided her room both morning and afternoon until a nurse told him she had asked about him and wanted to know how *he* was, was *he* all right, she hadn't seen him all day.

Ten minutes before the gift shop closed at six o'clock, Art skipped a GYN meeting he was supposed to be at (where his absence would certainly be noted and examined) and went down to get a present for Phyllis.

As soon as he saw the display he knew he was wrong, he shouldn't get her anything, the whole idea was sick. All the gifts seemed to imply a future. All the gifts seemed to imply the existence of time in which to enjoy them: books, sewing kits, even dolls and games. He could see the doll . . . still there . . . alone in her room, the same bright, little-girl expression on its face . . . but the doll alone.

He bought her some ribbons for her hair. And a tiny artificial Christmas tree to put on the table next to her bed. He started to leave the shop. They were just about to close. Then he bought the doll. It looked like something she would love. He suddenly felt better. It was going to be a *happy* Christmas. The woman asked him if he didn't want a card. He looked at the cards. They all said *Happy New Year* as well as *Merry Christmas*.

But the purchase of the doll had done something. Given him some sort of faith maybe; for by buying the doll, he felt he had done something positive. So the cards that also said *Happy New Year* didn't upset him as they might have. He just didn't buy one. He'd give her the gifts and just say aloud, *Merry Christmas, Phyllis.*

65

Joe Parelli spent Christmas Day sleeping.

A patient named Kronkauer ate a piece of plum pudding his wife smuggled in to him and felt no ill effects from having eaten it, but noted again (as he had several times during the past few days) that perhaps his tongue was losing a certain amount of mobility and that certainly he had lost a good deal of control over his right eye and the right side of his face and that indeed he had completely lost all sensations of temperature and touch in that side of his face.

He wished his wife wouldn't come to see him. At least, not so often. Not just because he disliked her having to face the symptoms of his disease (distressing enough in themselves, but probably quite horrifying and destructively depressing in a loved one), but because he knew his condition was terminal in terms of two or three months and felt that she should not condition herself to living with the condition of dying. Emma was healthy, Emma was alive. She had the prospect of many more years before her. She should be gathering her strength for those years, not wasting it on a situation that was hopeless anyway. She should be using this time to build a transition into living a full life alone. Instead, she was devoting herself so entirely to him that she was even blocking off the possibility of such a life after he was gone. Her devotion was certainly admirable; but the extent of it was frighteningly unhealthy for her; and after all, she was the one who had to do the living.

Jim Aptshult gave Alicia Liu a large, beautifully wrapped box which when unwrapped turned out to be a cardboard file for, he said, ". . . your voluminous correspondence." Inside the file there was also an envelope containing two tickets for the theatre for New Year's Eve and a note that suggested that perhaps it would be polite for her to ask him to share the tickets with her. She said nothing at the time, but that evening he found, slipped under his door, a formal invitation (in her handwriting) requesting the pleasure of his company on New Year's Eve. He decided that hospital life could be beautiful, and later, that it *was* beautiful when his roommate told him that Alicia had been not only impressed by Jim setting up the party for the TB kids, but also apparently quite touched and had not been too guarded about saying so.

The subject of conversation had already changed. The new topic was New Year's Eve. *That* was something about which something *could* be done. The residents were obligated by tradition to cover for as many interns as chose to take that evening for their off day. An intern couldn't do much about the lack of pay, the abundance of scut work, or the long hours, but he could do something about New Year's Eve. He could get drunk. Or even better, he could get some other interns each to buy a bottle apiece, he could promote a nurse into lending her apartment for the occasion, he could bring the interns and the bottles into the apartment, mix well with a liberal supply of nurses, and finally, and in short, *he could have a Ball, Wohl* . . .

66

In the week preceding New Year's Eve, Jim Aptshult alternated between states that seemed to him to be either entirely manic or entirely depressive. He was manic about his date with Alicia. His expectancy was further brightened by her new and warmer attitude toward him, as if she had just seen him for the first time and was attracted by what she saw; and was brightened by the plans they had made together—to leave as soon as they could get off and go for a long walk in real air, to eat dinner Dutch at whatever restaurant they found when they got tired walking, to go to the theatre, and then go up to the party at Didi Loomis' where all their friends would be.

He was depressed when he thought about his wife. Dykes hadn't called him about how the divorce was shaping up, though Dykes had said he'd call and call this week. Jim charged it off to its being a holiday week. He'd probably hear from Dykes soon after the first. But not hearing continued to depress him. He found himself excited and restless in the evening, either flushed or chilled, or so exhausted he had to go to bed right after dinner, and, after a nap, so full of energy he couldn't sleep an hour the entire rest of the night. He took his temperature once. One-o-one on the line. He was very sick. Hot flashes alternated with cold flashes. He was going through menopause. At twenty-six. More likely, he was going out of his mind. For godsake, if only New Year's Eve would get here, if only Dykes would call . . . In the meantime. God, the meantime. He seriously considered taking up drinking seriously. What seemed to prevent him most was just the lack of money to finance the project.

Dr. Granchard, Chief Resident of OB-A, was also looking forward to New Year's Eve. Though not in quite the same way as most of his interns. Granchard had to be on duty that night. But he was looking forward to it anyway—though with a certain amount of uneasy expectancy. He had, he felt, reason to believe that New Year's Eve would be his last opportunity to solve a problem that had been on his mind since Thanksgiving: the missing ergot and pitocin, how it was *getting* missed, who was responsible, and why. On the first of January, the interns would be changing services. And Granchard believed that one of his interns would prove to be the individual responsible for the missing drugs. If so, Granchard was certain, the responsibility had to be proven before the change-over. For he was equally certain that *after* the change-over, there would be no more opportunity to prove *anything*. The ergot and pitocin would merely stop disappearing.

Since he had informed her that he had elected to take Christmas Day off and work New Year's Eve and would therefore not be able to take her out that night, Cynthia James had refused to speak to Parelli. Joe had bought her a black nightgown for Christmas. It was both lovely and expensive as well as sheer; and it was a present they had been looking forward to his giving her. He had tried to give it to her in the hospital on Christmas Eve, but she had refused it. He had mailed it to her, and she had had it left for him in the hospital—unopened. He was beginning to be unhappy about the whole situation. He was, in fact, so unexpectedly unhappy that he was beginning to suspect that he might have (unknown to himself) begun falling in love with Cynthia. And her reaction was certainly violent enough to indicate at least *some* sort of strong emotion on her part. *Christ!* he thought, *what a mess.* The intern-nurse relationship had been just fine. Why did it have to get complicated with something it was going to take a helluva lot of emotional energy to cope with? He had enough trouble managing enough energy just to fulfill his duties. He had no business handing part of himself over to the pursuit and adoration of Cynthia James. Or of anyone. If he started splitting himself up now, he'd fall apart. So he wouldn't. He just wouldn't. Let Cynthia hand out trouble on her own time or even someone else's time. He didn't even have time enough for himself.

Didi Loomis sent out reasonably formal invitations to Mercouris, van Wyck, Walters, Liu, Fishbein, Worship, Sprague, de Traunant, Eckland, Rosconovitch, Aptshult, and enough nurses to cover the males who weren't bringing females. Everyone else she could think of to invite was either a pure fink or going to be on duty that night. Her invitations read:

Commencing four o'clock in the afternoon, the Thirty-first of December:
    The First Formal Meeting of
    THE ASEPSIS CLUB
    (By invitation only)
        at
The Private Ward and Clinic of Dorothy Loomis
    (sole owner and proprietor)
Address:
ANESTHESIA: local, liquid, oral,
             and bring it yourself.
PROCEDURE: Drs. will provide selves
            with own scrub assistants
            except as otherwise already
            noted; all procedures will
            be sterile, and also pro-
            phylactic if necessary.

Pre- and Post-operative supportive
care will be provided in the form
of various edible nutriments; therapy
will be provided by scrub assistants

as they see fit. The management assumes
no responsibility for such therapy or
any issue thereof.

Various Members of the Permanent, Senior
New North Staff Will Be Cut Up for the
Amusement and Enlightenment of Those Present.

TILL: seven hours after midnight New Year's Day

Didi congratulated herself on the prospect: it was going
to be an all-day, all-night *picnic*.

67

On the morning of the thirty-first, Fred Donnecker got up
so late he had to take a cab to the hospital to be on time.
He would have preferred to have stayed in his room at the
hospital. But he had been worried about Mildred; her tone
of voice over the telephone the night before when he had
called to sound her out about staying over at the hospital
had been anything but sympathetic. It had been a *Just do
as you please, I couldn't care less* tone.

He was angry, and he was thinking, Now why should I
have to sound her out on something like that? Why couldn't
I just assume that she'd want what was going to be most
comfortable for me? Why should I have to feel guilty if I
call her and say I've had such a hard day and have to be on
duty so early it would be easier for me to stay at the hospital?

What angered him most was her making him feel guilty
when he saw no logical reason for him to feel guilty. And
his own ability to feel guilty made him even angrier. He
had thought things had gone so well on Christmas Day—
brought them closer together.

He had elected Christmas Day when the notices had gone
up about electing a holiday off. Christmas was for families
to be together. New Year's was fun, and all that, but Christmas had a meaning to it whether you were religious or not.
It was *the* day to share with the person you loved.

They had gotten a tree and decorated it and sat up late

Christmas Eve looking at it and drinking a milk punch he
had made.

The next day they had gone to church and she had held
his arm very possessively as they went in and came out.
They had walked. They had fed the pigeons. They had had
some drinks. And then they had gone to a restaurant and
had a huge turkey dinner and gotten the giggles and walked
and gotten more giggles. They hadn't made love, but that
was just because *she* had looked tired when they'd gotten
home and the day had been so "successful" (the only word
he could think of to describe it) he had not wanted to endanger it by bringing up something she had not brought up
or encouraged herself. It was then that he felt fear—that
they did not know each other now, were not as intimate now
as they had been when they'd been at the dating stage.

He'd try hard to remember to call her at midnight if he
possibly could.

68

Rosconovitch's patient, Phyllis, died early in the morning of
the thirty-first. Around one A.M. she had suddenly begun
hemorrhaging again. Around two thirty she became comatose. At four thirty-eight she died. Rosconovitch was asleep
at the time; he didn't learn about it until he came on duty
at nine. He had asked to be called if there were any sudden
developments in her case; but the night staff had been too
busy to remember. When Rosconovitch reported to the nurses'
station for morning rounds, one of the residents—Dave
Ford—was sitting on the desk shelf thumbing through a
chart he had propped on his thigh. "Miserable day," he
said. "Supposed to sleet later." He didn't look up from the
chart. "By the way, Phyllis died last night. Secondary
parenchymatous hemorrhage." He still didn't look up.

Rosconovitch said, "Oh." He just stood there.

Ford didn't look up. "Rounds in a few minutes, as soon as
Sprague and de Traunant get here."

Rosconovitch said, "Oh," as if it were unexpected but
uninteresting news. He looked at Ford, just because he was
already looking at him. Ford continued to examine the chart.
Rosconovitch thought—rather numbly, as if he'd just gotten

up—*Well, that's surprising, I thought it would bother me a lot more. Funny, its not having any effect at all.*

He couldn't just stand there looking at Ford. So he went out into the corridor. Then he walked down the corridor. He decided to stop and look in at Phyllis' room. Naturally, it had been cleaned up already. The bed she had occupied had been tightly made up with clean sheets. It no longer had any personality. It was just a perfectly made bed waiting for a patient. The doll was gone. The ribbons too. And the kit she had brought in with her.

But somehow the tiny Christmas tree had been overlooked. It still stood on the table between the two beds, though the glass and decanter and tissues had been taken away. He looked at the little tree and vaguely wondered what would happen to it now. It began to seem like a major question. After all, what *does* happen to little Christmas trees when the owner leaves them and doesn't make provision for their care. Maybe they grow up to be *big* Christmas trees, he considered, completely unaware of any humor in the thought. He just stood in the doorway and looked at the tree.

He saw a hand, an arm, reach out, take hold of the tree, and move it off the table. He looked up a little to see where the arm had come from. There was a new patient in the other bed. He hadn't noticed before. Well, not *new* patient. He knew her. She'd been in and out of the ward a couple of times. A lined and beaten forty-five-year-old prostitute and drug addict named . . . He couldn't remember her name.

She took the tree and held it at arm's length up toward the light from the window by her bed. Then, still at arm's length, she began to move it in a slow small circle, over and over again. She began to hum as she moved the tree. At least it sounded like humming. Then the hum became a laugh. Louder and louder. Hoarse. Rough. The tree still being moved in the slow, small circle, the laughter becoming hoarser and grosser.

Rosconovitch turned and walked down the corridor, came to the stairs suddenly, and walked down the stairs. Somehow he was still walking. It was too much effort to stop. Through the lobby. And outside. He wasn't thinking about anything; he wasn't even thinking about *not* thinking anything. He was just walking. In fact, he was only vaguely aware of doing *that*. He was only a *little* less vaguely aware that to stop doing whatever he was doing or not doing would cost him an effort beyond any the human body was able to will.

The only thing that he was at all aware of was that the exertion of stopping whatever he was doing or not doing would crumple him entirely. He continued to walk and forgot even about the problem of exertion that had just been vaguely on his mind.

It was two hours before he became even dimly aware of himself again. He was only aware of a change of state. He tried to trace it to what had caused it—for he couldn't understand why he hadn't remained so peaceful.

It was the cold. He was very cold. After all—he discovered almost with surprise—he didn't have an overcoat on. Then he noticed that people on the street were staring at him. He wondered if what he was feeling—the thinking about Phyllis that had started again—showed so clearly on his face that people were startled enough to stare. He walked another block wondering about this. Then he realized that he was in his whites and that that was why people were staring. He must be quite a sight sauntering along in the midst of winter with no overcoat on and wearing of all things hospital whites, and to top it all off, a stethoscope sticking out of a side pocket and an ophthalmoscope stuck in his breast pocket.

He became embarrassed and looked around to see where he was. Figuring the crosstown streets, he was about forty-odd blocks from the hospital. He must have walked in a pretty wide circle to use up that much time, he figured, looking at his watch. He'd better take a cab back. But when he reached in his pocket to see if he had enough money, he found he had no money at all.

He could ask a cop—but a cop would want to see his credentials, want some sort of explanation. He had neither. Certainly nothing he could convey in less than an hour or two. He decided to walk back. He began to walk back.

It was almost twelve thirty when he got back to the hospital. He wasn't hungry, so he didn't feel like going to the dining hall. He didn't really feel like sleeping, so he didn't go up to his room. He decided he might as well go back to the GYN nurses' station and read up on the morning's charts before he went to clinic at one.

Ford was in the nurses' station. Maybe he hadn't left it.

Maybe it was nine o'clock and he was just coming in to report for morning rounds. He almost looked at his watch. But he knew that was silly.

"The return of the goddam prodigal," Ford said, spitting the words at him.

"Yeah," Rosconovitch said. It was all he could manage. It was all he could think of.

"You fool," Ford said. "There's an automatic dismissal for this."

The word *dismissal* appeared in tiny letters way back, far away in his mind. It grew, slowly loomed closer and closer, growing larger as it came. When it was so close he couldn't see it any more, his mind had grasped it, wrenched it into a thought rather than a picture. He felt as if he'd suddenly come out of a long drunk he hadn't even known he'd been on. *"Dismissal?"* he said. *"Dismissal?"*

"You're God damn right."

"God," he said, sitting down. "You think so?"

"You . . . you . . . I know so!"

"Oh God . . ."

"Yeah. Oh God. *Now* you bother to think."

"Oh God . . ." He sat entirely still.

"What brought you back at all?"

Rosconovitch didn't answer.

"What brought you back at all, I said?"

Rosconovitch remained entirely still. Then he raised his head. Then his body sagged. Then he made himself light a cigarette. "When will they?"

"When will they *what?*"

"Dismiss me."

Ford looked at him with disgust. "They're not going to. You're a lucky goddam bastard, Rosconovitch. I saw you take off this morning. I yelled at you even."

"I didn't hear."

"No," Ford said sarcastically. He looked malignantly at Rosconovitch. "As I said, Rosconovitch, you're a very God damn lucky intern. I just didn't report you."

"Thanks," Rosconovitch said. "Thank you."

"It happens again, I'll not only report you, I'll drag your bloody carcass into Wohl myself."

"It won't happen again."

"Now go get some lunch. And don't go to clinic; report to me here this afternoon."

"I'm not hungry."

"Apparently, you don't understand, Rosconovitch. From now on, when I look at you, you jump. Go eat. And you damn well better get enough coffee into you so I can hear it slosh around. *Jump!*"

"Yeah. Sure," Rosconovitch said, getting up. He was beginning to really feel he was back in the land of the living. Permanently.

"And when you get back here, Rosconovitch, you're going to work your bloody little ass off." He smiled at Rosconovitch. "You may think you know what scut work is, but you have no idea how scutty it can get. You'll have to look up and strain your eyes to see an orderly." Kindly, he said, "Now remember, Art. This afternoon. We have a date. Jump!"

Rosconovitch took off. Ford got up and went to the door of the nurses' station and watched Rosconovitch hurry down the corridor. Ford went back and sat down. Sourly, he complimented himself, "You sure are one hell of a psychologist."

69

New Year's Eve began desolately. The wards were overcrowded. At the last minute—even with all the residents, as was traditional, standing duty for the interns—many interns had to remain in the hospital, most of them on duty, a few just on call, though being on call kept them from leaving the premises. From some of the windows, the black, icy water of the river could be seen, the white streaks from the lights on the opposite shore seeming to lie on the water and stab at the hospital.

Surgery would be busy—there would be excessive numbers of automobile accidents, knifings, and fights. Contagion and Medicine were already overcrowded with the midwinter high incidence of contagious disease, which resulted from people spending so much time in closed atmospheres together.

A fierce wind struck the windows. Some patients complained of drafts. And complained again. The steam heat was turned up unbearably high for a healthy person. The coffee machine broke down at dinner. The switchboard was closed to personal calls—coming in *or* going out. The lines at the pay phones were too long to be practical if you were on duty.

Surgery put more interns on call and several more on duty in Emergency Admitting—the streets were beginning to ice up from the sleet and even pedestrians were injuring themselves just walking along on the sidewalk.

OB—and there was no reason why it should happen on New Year's Eve; it just did by coincidence—had suddenly become so crowded with women almost beyond the first stage of labor, that even Granchard was allowing interns to make deliveries unassisted. Was forced to. And where practical was even slowing the contraction rate with mild depressants in order to give himself and his staff time to catch up and begin practicing obstetrics again. For it was no longer obstetrics, it was no longer an art, it was a factory system under pressure.

Interns and residents alike—and even attendings who found themselves unfortunate enough to be immediately available in the hospital—were brought in from other services to double on OB, Surgery, and Medicine. Even GYN was getting better than its average number of nightly hemorrhage cases.

Class distinctions temporarily disappeared. Interns found themselves doing everything *but* scut work. Full attendings finished with a patient, found themselves free to go on to the next case, looked around to see where they were needed, and suddenly found themselves working with an intern who was already halfway through a case but needed assistance to finish up.

It was, in ways, worse than a disaster. In a disaster, at least, most of the cases are similar (burns, shock, suffocation) and can be treated accordingly, each largely upon the basis of the nature of the others. But these cases were diversified beyond any but the most superficial similarity or interrelationship.

By eight o'clock, every intern who was still in the building had been notified not to leave it. Only a few, a lucky (*blind lucky*) few, who had left immediately after afternoon rounds had escaped to enjoy the holiday.

And then the telegrams from a few thoughtful attendings began to arrive. *Happy New Year Stop,* and a name.

At four o'clock, Jay Fishbein was in delivery. When he
came out he was told he'd be needed again in about fifteen
minutes and not to plan to have the evening off, God knows
when they'll stop coming in.

Personal calls hadn't been made *verboten* yet, and after
a wait, he managed to get an outside line and reach his wife.
He told her quickly he was all tied up in umbilical cord,
didn't know when he'd get cut free, and she should go on
ahead to the party at Didi's and he'd meet her there later,
whenever he got off, it was a lucky thing the damn party
was scheduled to run straight through to doomsday. She said
all right, don't fall in, Sam, and he went back and found himself delivering with another intern as assistant.

It was two hours short of midnight. Didi hoped her party
wasn't contagious. For instance, there sat Olga—Olga Bjorg,
a nurse from De Witt General, who was Didi's surprise hors
d'oeuvre for the party. A better break than Olga a bunch of
bastard interns couldn't get. Olga's opening remark to a male
was almost always, "What they say about Swedish girls is true
in my case."

Didi decided she would never understand interns. She had
decided the same thing several times before, but this time she
felt a certainty about her decision. There sat Olga, about
whom it *was* true, in a low gown with high breasts and
apparently no underwear, and no one paying her any
attention.

Didi circulated. "Spend your first year at Tyler," she
overheard. "See some good brain work. Lots of private
patients."

Fascinating conversations one overhears at an interns'
New Year's Eve party, she thought.

". . . Lots of surgery. That's the saving grace of the place."

"Yeah, but the residents're on twenty-four-hour call *all*
the time."

"So?"

"So suture. How many amputations have you had?"

"Four. But I haven't been lucky."

Didi didn't bother to swat either of them. She changed her

image. The party was a complete prolapse. It might be true
about Olga, and it might be true about nurses, and it might
be true about interns, but anyone who was worried about it
just had to look in on this party. She consoled herself with
another Scotch and thought, Fortunately, I'm fascinating
company for myself.

71

In Emergency Admitting, in one of the treatment cubicles,
Donnecker's patient stopped breathing. The patient, drunk,
had fallen down a flight of stairs and was suffering cerebral
concussion, fractured skull, and probably cerebral hemorrhage. Donnecker was busy prepping him for the O.R. and
didn't immediately notice the lack of respiration until the
blood pressure suddenly began to fall. Donnecker went for
the heart with his stethoscope, hardly bothered to listen, yelled
for assistance and, unable to think of any other immediate
technique of stimulation available to him, raised his arm,
made his hand flat and stiff, and brought the side of it down
violently like an axe blade on the region immediately over the
heart. He chopped viciously again and again, as hard as he
could. An attending who was suddenly standing next to him
was calling for oxygen. Then the attending was preparing
a needle, and Donnecker was manually duplicating the
patient's normal abdominal respiration. The attending introduced the needle into the heart. Donnecker continued his
manipulation. The needle was put aside. The attending said,
"Good, Doctor. Scrub up." And then, "We'll have to use a
local to minimize the strain on the heart." And then, "And
start an I.V. now."

Scrubbing, he remembered that during the rush of the day
he had forgotten to send Mildred flowers. Now he'd be in
the O.R. till five, six, seven in the morning. God he loved her,
God it was a mess—they'd fix it up right finally for sure
when he got home the next evening. He'd see to it. He'd long
since gotten over having to look at the clock to make sure
he'd scrubbed properly. He stopped automatically almost at
the exact proper second, dried his hands, and went into the
O.R. and got gloved and gowned.

The operation lasted thirteen hours. The patient lived.

Olga spoke of going home and getting some sleep. Didi said, "Don't be silly, you haven't anyone to go with yet." Olga sat down. Pat got herself another drink. Might as well be drinking paraldehyde.

Then Eckland yelled, "Everybody over here to join the editorial board of my new magazine. Its impressive title is, *The Saturday Evening Post Partum!*"

Sprague yelled back, "Ted, you're drunk as a *skunk!*"

Eckland yelled back, "Skunks don't get drunk, but they do rhyme!"

Sprague yelled back, "Man do they *ever* rhyme!"

And of such innocent and frankly juvenile exchanges, Didi discovered, are great parties born. Interns' parties, anyway.

Pete van Wyck kissed Joan Feldman. "It's not midnight yet," she said.

"I'm practicing."

"I'm glad you invited me."

"Why?"

"I like practicing with you."

"Wait till later. I'll practice *on* you."

She sighed—without appreciation for the remark. But then he looked so uncomfortable because she hadn't laughed that she really did laugh and took his hand and kissed it and said, "It better not be *practice*"—it must be the drinks, she told herself.

Mildred received a call from Terry. He was drunk. "I'm slightly high," he said.

"And at a party."

"A *terrific* party."

"If it's so terrific, what're you calling me for?"

"All it needs is you to be a *perfect* party."

"I thought I told you not to call me again."

"All it needs is you. I'll pick you up. In a cab, yet. Right away."

"Happy New Year," she said, and hung up.

Didi discovered that her real hit was not Olga (who was

batting okay, just the same), but Gloria Mead. This worried Didi, and worried her consciously. She reminded herself that she was a teaching nurse—an instructor. And because Gloria was one of her students and was still five months away from graduation, and because Didi had taken a special liking to her, Didi felt responsible for her until she graduated. Of course Gloria could take care of herself. But these were *interns* she was dealing with, Didi reminded herself. The poor girl could be *sixty* and she'd still be out of her league. Unless she knew how to handle them. And it was Didi's considered opinion that Gloria hadn't been around long enough to know how to handle them. So whenever Didi saw the conversation getting intense, she steered Gloria away from whatever youthful physician she was talking to and planted her among whatever group seemed to have the largest number of females. Protective coloring, Didi figured. But she was exhausted keeping an eye on Gloria, and she'd run out of groups. And Gloria was a girl that apparently no coloring could protect. She wasn't built along the unlikely proportions of Olga, but she was built with precision and with apparently severely enticing proportions. Didi gave up. Whatever else, the loss of hymen had never, to Didi's knowledge, proven fatal.

Jim and Alicia arrived. They received more than passing notice because Jim had his arm around Alicia's waist and every so often Alicia put her hand on the hand on her waist and caressed it.

There was, of course, speculation. But on learning that they had been to the theatre, seen the entire show, and enjoyed it, it was generally agreed that there hadn't been time. Van Wyck studied them for a long time and then finally led Joan Feldman to a corner away from them. "I think they're volatile," he said.

Everyone wondered where Rosconovitch was. Nobody had any suggestions. Everyone seemed to be enjoying themselves so much, Didi decided it would be worth while to make an effort to enjoy her own party. So she went into her bathroom, shut the door, and removed her bra, stockings and girdle. Immediately afterwards she forgot about playing hostess except to make one rather unnoticed announcement about where the food and coffee was. De Traunant arrived.

Olga told him that in her case it was true. De Traunant knew better than to pay attention to any girl who *talked* about it, and moved on to investigate other breasts. Sprague refused a drink. Eckland said that the goddam party must be breaking up. Walters arrived. Things were rough at the hospital, things *had* been rough on Surgery, but all of a sudden things had quieted down to next to nothing on Surgery and he had been let off. He was made to chugalug half a glass of bourbon so that his hands would remain steady for more important manipulation. Instead, he almost immediately collapsed from exhaustion. Someone changed the records and turned up the volume. Van Wyck forced Walters to get up and dance—as a scientific experiment to see if it was really that bad. Walters danced with Didi. He discovered it was really not that bad. He discovered she had no bra on, and then, with a little judicious backhand, discovered she had no girdle or panties on either. Didi asked if he wasn't interested in finding out about her stockings too. Walters discovered it not only wasn't so bad, but he could probably keep going for as long as Didi was willing to provide bodily friction. He also decided that van Wyck was a true dear roommate for having gotten him up to dance. Rosconovitch arrived perfectly sober, refused a drink, wandered around for a while, and then asked Gloria Mead if she would please just dance with him and no one else for the rest of the evening. Gloria didn't know what to make of him, but thought he was very unhappy, and so said yes. Eckland announced that he would be the first Negro in history to be the first person to bring up the Negro question at a white party, was applauded, announced that he had achieved his purpose and brought it up and been the first Negro to be the first person to do so at a white party and that they might now discuss it quietly among themselves and got down off the chair he'd been standing on and took Didi away from Walters. Walters took Joan away from van Wyck. He discovered she was wearing underwear and switched to Olga. Olga discovered Walters' condition and suggested a truss until later. Walters was insulted, grabbed the first person he saw, and discovered he was dancing with Mercouris. Mercouris cut out and began dancing with Lois. Lois suggested he fast find himself a girl who wasn't married. Mercouris was insulted and cut out and cut in on Eckland to get at the remarkable Olga, who, he saw, wasn't wearing a wedding ring. Eckland danced with

Lois. Olga told Mercouris it was true in her case. Mercouris knew better than to believe any girl who *talked* about it, and went to open a window. The smoke was stifling. Olga cut in on Lois and took Eckland. She said it was true in her case but nobody would believe her. Eckland knew better than to listen to any girl who *talked* about it, and cut out to get a drink. Van Wyck shut the window because Joan was cold. The smoke began piling up again. Someone turned up the volume on the phonograph. Jim danced almost motionlessly with Alicia. Rosconovitch said he'd like to dance now, and he and Gloria began to dance. The whole thing was wrong and he felt cumbersome and maybe he'd better go home. Gloria said that was all right and began to teach him as if he'd never been on a dance floor before in his life. Didi told Cynthia she was sorry about Cynthia breaking up with Joe Parelli. Cynthia stood as high as she could in her stocking feet, said she couldn't care less, kissed Conny Mercouris violently for a long period of time, burst into tears, went off to the bathroom, found the bathroom occupied, went off to the bedroom, found the bedroom occupied, and finally shut herself in a closet and cried into Didi's summer dresses. Didi danced with Courtney Walters some more, thought it would be fun to take *everything* off, thought of her professional reputation, and dissuaded herself. Olga was less thoughtful. She had been drinking straight rye for twenty minutes. She had been drinking gin before that. She unzipped her dress, pulled it off, and asked if *now* someone would believe her. Conny said he would and did, but made her put her dress back on. Didi decided the party was a success. Van Wyck decided Olga had a stunning figure. Joan decided van Wyck had seen enough and he should close his eyes and try *oral* sensation. Van Wyck complied happily. Sprague announced that the illustration for the cover of the first issue of the *Saturday Evening Post Partum* was now on the bathroom floor and that it was nonrepresentational. Walters said for chrisake if this party had been going on just since four, what was it going to be like at noon? And Didi said stick around and see and put his hand on her behind. Cynthia came back from the closet, her eyes red and the skin around them puffed. Mercouris said he didn't know that kissing him was *that* bad, and Cynthia burst into tears again and went back to the closet. Didi went to comfort her. Walters went to comfort both of them. Rosconovitch had a drink and decided, the drink not touching him, that since he was still alive, he owed Phyllis a debt to make something of his life. Didi and Courtney found themselves alone in the closet, and decided to stay there for a while. Cynthia decided that Joe Parelli was a fool. Gloria decided that Rosconovitch was pretty dull even if she did feel sorry for him. De Traunant decided that Gloria was the girl to go after and that he'd been a fool not to take Olga at her words' value. Joan took off Pete van Wyck's tie. Eckland danced Lois into giggles. Didi thought this damn closet isn't big enough. One of the nurses announced that the second edition of the *Saturday Evening Post Partum* was out. Some people from De Witt arrived. One of them was drunk enough to clean the bathroom—Didi was brought out from the closet to show him where the mop was. Walters decided he could hardly wait for noon, decided he wouldn't wait for noon, and tried to throw everyone out immediately. Mercouris put on a hat and introduced himself as an attending with prostate trouble. Didi put on shorts. The people from De Witt introduced a new game called Let's Do It. Everyone pretended to have to learn the rules. Van Wyck began attempting a lecture on Introductory Reproductive Biology. No one listened. The window was opened again. Shut again. The phonograph turned up. Lois couldn't stop her giggles. The people from De Witt were still trying to get their game started. Walters was trying to get Didi back into the closet. Didi wanted to know what people would think. Cynthia got the giggles from Lois. Lois looked at Cynthia and lost the giggles. Joan borrowed a pair of shorts from Didi and remembered to keep *her* panties on underneath. Everyone danced. The people from De Witt tried to explain their game. Someone turned on the radio, then turned it up to full volume. By the time anyone heard it, it was no longer New Year's Eve and had become the new year. Everyone kissed.

73

It was already the new year—had been so for almost twenty minutes. As if the change of calendar had had some mystic effect, the labor floor had begun to quiet. One by one the residents and interns were finding themselves with nothing immediate to do. Soon, Granchard figured, he'd be able to let some of his people off to sleep or, if they had the night, go out and celebrate. The thought depressed him. He hadn't found the person responsible for the missing ergot and pitocin yet. Once he started letting people off, he might lose his last chance to discover his man. Because his man would no longer have the opportunity to be discovered. His man might be among those already off duty and so off OB entirely, but Granchard didn't believe it. He thought he already knew who his man was. If he could just catch him at it. Once Granchard caught him, the man could give up living. Granchard was going to arrange for him to feel that way.

It was a sophomoric way to go about it, but it was the only way Granchard could figure out to possibly provoke his man into showing himself, and showing himself in a way that breached excuse or explanation. He unlocked the drug cabinet and left its door open wide enough to be seen by anyone in the corridor passing the nurses' station. Then Granchard went away. But not too far away.

74

Otis saw it, went away, had to pass it again, saw it again, fought himself about risking another time, fought himself harder, and went back to his patient, finished temporarily with her, and, with no other place to go, decided that the lounge and nurses' station would leave him too vulnerable to temptation and so just stood in the corridor and smoked.

He had three cigarettes (without chain smoking) before he thought he ought to go back and check his patient again. He went through the routine examination. Nothing had changed. She had been waiting a long time. A very long time. Almost twenty-four hours—with her contraction rate constant and just short of being rapid enough and strong enough to deliver, for she had long since reached sufficient dilatation. Except for the inadequate strength and frequency of her contractions, she should have delivered much earlier. It would be practical to give her a minim of pitocin to stimulate the contractions. It would be not only practical, but medically *advisable* to pit her, and pit her immediately. If he didn't, he would be needlessly allowing an unfortunate condition to persist that was within his power to rectify.

Go ahead, pit her, he thought. Except for one thing. If you go and get some pit for her, you'll take some for yourself. Even though you know it's so dangerous, even though you know if you get caught you're finished. For life. As a doctor, anyway. And if they tied it up legally with what they'd tie it up mentally with, you might be through for life as a person. If they could tie it up for a court instead of just some medical board of review, it wouldn't mean only no more medicine, it would mean prison. Two to twenty. According to what they could prove.

Remember *that*.

But this woman needs pitting. And you ought to pit her for the same principle you've been operating on to do the other things: *that it is within your power to rectify an unfortunate situation.* Well hell, that's a lot of bunk, he thought. I never *really* believed that was the reason. How could I? I've got a mind. For the *money*. To keep going to bed with the girl I wouldn't otherwise be able to keep going to bed with because I wouldn't be able to hold on to her without the money. Because we're each the kind who needs money the way a diabetic needs insulin. Because that's the way we live —with each other or without. God knows the money's going to run out soon enough. Even with her plan to stretch it. Even with her wanting to make it last for us as much as I do. And God knows that right this minute or all during this time she could have a lot more than I'm giving her. She could have it just for the asking. That's how beautiful . . . just for the asking . . . She choked men up. She didn't have to go to bed with them or even touch them. She just had to be where they could see her and she choked them up and they begged to do things for her, give her things, *anything* just to be able to be in the competition. So she was used to the things money could buy. She hadn't asked him for the things that were the impossible things for him, but just for the things that had become the minimum things for *her*. The restaurants, theatres, night clubs. Just the things that she had come to *subsist* on, the things without which she became only half alive, a thing only half existing. And, of course, the apartment. Which by virtue of what they had worked out was now as much his as hers. And, of course, the clothes of his that hung there—the clothes she had cajoled him into buying, and which she had helped him choose; and which he had always insisted to himself he would someday wear anyway; and which he was now wearing a little bit sooner than he'd expected; and some of which still needed paying for.

Not much, really; not any of it. Except when you did it the hard way. Not what you'd call the real high life. Not what she could have without him. But enough. Enough to make some more pit awfully important. It would be like money saved and put away. A bank in the future. Not too much of it could keep them going till June, till his internship was up, till . . . Not that the stuff was expensive or valuable in itself particularly. But it had its uses; and the stuff from the hospital couldn't be checked up on—unlike stuff from a drug store, say, where you had to leave a prescription behind; where you'd leave a trail behind. It certainly did have its uses; and getting it from the hospital left no trail. There was nothing to sign. You just took it when you wanted it. And as long as you didn't take too much at one time, no one would even have a *chance* to notice there was less in the drug cabinet than there should be. Because how was anyone ever to know how much there *should* be available? How, when it was being used all the time? Just taken out and used?

What a bank not too much more of it would make.

Sitting on the floor, late at night, at the party when he'd first met her, she had said to him, "Are you really a doctor?" and he had assured her that really he was and she had said, "That's very funny. Because, you know what? I'm pregnant and I'm not married and maybe you could do something about it." He had laughed and said, yes, there was something he could do about it, he could marry her. "Something more practical, darling." He had asked her if she'd tried falling down stairs or anything like that. She said, "You wouldn't like me to, would you?" She had been serious. Everything had been serious, really, he realized. He'd said no, he wouldn't like her to. "What then?" He didn't know.

Not then, anyway. Not out loud to himself. Not yet. But after he'd seen her twice more and she'd asked him twice more, "Well, darling?" he'd said, well, maybe there was a way, but he'd have to think about it, think about it a lot. She'd nodded and taken him to a cocktail party where he again watched the choking sensation appear in the faces of other men. From the hospital he stole an ampoule of pitocin and a hypodermic syringe; and several ampoules of Demerol and scopolamine to use as depressants just in case. He explained to her: He would give her a minim of pitocin. This might or might not stimulate her uterus into contracting. He didn't know—in fact, he didn't even know that *much* about pitocin. If it did, the contractions might or might not be strong enough to expel the fetus. If the contractions were strong, they might or might not be strong enough to rupture her uterus and cause massive hemorrhage, severe shock, and death. If the contractions reached such strength, he would try to depress them with Demerol and scopolamine. The depressants might or might not bring the contractions under control. A hospital would probably be able to do something about the hemorrhaging. The uterus, if ruptured, might or might not infect. It probably would. If it did, she might or might not die. Under such conditions, she probably would.

She only wanted to know if it was likely that contractions would be caused that would be strong enough to expel the fetus. He said he didn't know, such things varied with the individual, but with the amount he was going to give her, it would be unlikely. She said to make it more. He said no. She said, "Then go ahead, do it your way, but you'll just have to try again later. You'll just have to make it more *some other time* . . ." He said no he wouldn't then or later, and she said, "Well, *do* it, then."

Her contractions were dangerously strong, but brief. He had already begun to prepare the other injections when the contractions ceased. There was some bleeding. It continued for several hours. But it finally ceased also. The fetus had been expelled.

Afterwards—both immediately and later—it was more as if she were taking care of him than he her. He didn't find this strange or even unlikely, because he was able to see how much she wanted to. She never mentioned money, she never made him feel responsible when, for instance, after a party, they were asked to join a group going out for dinner and had to refuse because he couldn't afford it. Or had to turn down going to the theatre with her friends for the same reason. After several weeks she only suggested that, being unable to reciprocate, they stop accepting cocktail and dinner invitations. She no longer saw any man but him. On nights when he was on duty, she merely stayed in. On such nights it was rarely even possible for her to see girl friends. They would be with escorts, and since she refused to be escorted—even "platonically"—by anyone but him, she felt better not going out at all rather than being alone among couples.

She had a small income from her deceased father's insurance. Enough to pay the rent on a modest "luxury" apartment. Enough for food, a certain amount of liquor and the designer clothes she wore, gas, electricity, taxis, magazines, and incidental entertainment. But that was all—*all* in that it could not provide the lavish extras which she cherished and which she had grown used to and which were only available to her through the desire of her admirers to out-court each other. She had an additional source of income available to her as a bathing-suit and photographer's model. She had tried it for a while, but disliked most of the people it brought her in contact with. She had once tried fashion photography herself, but found that she didn't have enough patience for or interest in the more technical side of it. So she provided her food and shelter and clothing with her own income; and received the lavish side of her life as an offering from her admirers. She was not a prostitute, nor even a démimondaine; nor even a coquette. She went to bed with a man because she wanted to—very *much* wanted to—and not because she was free with her favors.

So she never mentioned his not having money. And she never made him feel responsible for what he knew was the narrowing circle of her existence. Nor did she even allow him to feel responsible. She said, "It's *my* choice, not yours." He asked her if it was because he had helped her out. She slapped him. He saw he was not to apologize. She would never have seen him again. Eventually she said, "You're a fool," and that was the end of it.

Sometime later in the fall, having gone out in the park because she wanted to smell the leaves, they were sitting on a park bench watching a cooing cluster of pigeons peck at some broken, stale bread an old woman had thrown them, and she said, "A girl I know who's a model is pregnant. She's a very successful model and she doesn't want to get married. And she doesn't want to lose the fees she would when it starts to show. That's about seven months she'd lose, and even a very successful model's life is only about four years. But mostly,

she's worried about losing her figure—for modeling, anyway
—if she goes ahead with the pregnancy. It doesn't take much
distention to ruin those girls, you know. Not in high fashion.
Not with the kind of figures they have to have." He said
he'd done it for her, but that was different. It had been for
her. She said, "All right, this is, too. She's willing to pay a lot."
He looked at her. She said, "Yes, it's that pure and simple."
He understood exactly what she meant: *when the money
hadn't been available she hadn't said a thing. Now the
money was available.* He said no. She shrugged. She hadn't
refused him that night, either. She had allowed no change
in herself at all. Not in her outward attitude toward him,
anyway. But he had seen that it was a matter of will, intent,
on her part—and not something natural. They were together,
the day had begun in a certain way, it would end that way.
But when he got up at five the next morning to leave her and
go back to the hospital, he had known instinctively that she
would not allow him to see her again. When he left her
that morning he would have to—and the word came to him
easily—debride her existence from his mind, or he would
make himself sick. He knew also that it would do no good to
think about it. Even if he decided to do it, and called her
and told her so, she would not then—later—accept his decision. Or him. He knew that much about her. He woke her and
said all right. He said they'd talk it over and arrange it his
next night off. She apparently didn't even have to woo her
mind from sleep. She said, "When I went to sleep last night I
thought, 'Look at him now because it's the last time,' and I
did, and then I turned the other way. I wasn't going to wake
up when you left, either." She had put a nightgown on before
going to sleep, and, as she sat up in the bed with her arms
straight at her sides, both straps had come down and he was
looking at the whiteness of the one exposed breast, the whiteness of it and its shape in the dawn light that made everything
a grayish blue, the nipple erect from the chill of the air. She
said, "I want you, too, and I'm not going to because you
had to wait to say all right, you couldn't say it *at the time*.
I'm not *paying* you to say all right, I'm not bargaining with
you; we're not that kind of people." He said he'd had to think
about it, it was his career, it was his profession. She said, *"Individual conscience.* Are you familiar with the phrase?
Which of us do you plan to honor?" He said after all she

couldn't expect to be his conscience for him. She said, "I made my decision wholly and entirely. I made it before I asked you that first night. I made it before I even *asked* you. You never even had to flirt. I *decided. Period.*" She was very angry, and becoming angrier he saw. "I asked nothing. Except that you be to me what I am to you. I didn't think I had to *ask* that. I didn't think it needed *words*. I didn't think I had to *mouth* it for you." She wiped her mouth. "I didn't think we had to *think* about it." He said he thought it had more meaning having made the commitment after testing it with his mind and having his mind overrule him and then give in. He said that way it wasn't just blind emotions. She said, "Bullshit! you make it sound like you gave in to your filthy prick!" He said nothing. His mind was a long time at work on what he wanted to say. Then he said he wanted the money, for them, he wanted it. She said, "Yeah," with disgust. He walked over to her and slapped her. When she stared at him, her face blank and just staring at him, he slapped her again. He said she hadn't put in four years of college and four years of med school sweating for one thing. He said she had no commitment to anything but putting her behind on expensive furniture, so how the hell could she know about making a commitment with her head as well as what she called her emotions, though he thought it was her ass, what the hell else did she know about him except his looks after talking to him for half an hour? She said, "You *bastard!*" almost crying but not letting herself. "I didn't know that then either." She started calling him *bastard* over and over again. He'd stood there until she stopped. Then she'd said, quietly, "You better get the hell out now." And with disgust, "Are you planning to come down your next night?" He said yes, the next night was tomorrow night. She said, "Swell!" and turned away from him, pulling the covers up so he could see only the back of her head.

Afterwards, he'd blamed it on having to go back to the hospital. The way it was there. What he had to take. How it demeaned him and how the demeaning part was on purpose and unnecessary and fuck them all. But he'd known, even as he tried to tell himself this, that it was bunk. He'd made his own decision. He told himself that he had made the decision because he wanted to keep being the self that he liked. The self that had her.

The following night he told her that just because it had worked for her, that didn't necessarily mean it would work for her friend. She said, "I'll tell her that." And the stuff about the danger, too, he told her to tell her. "I'll tell her that, too." And not over the phone he told her. "I'm not a fool," she said. He asked her what she'd do if something went wrong in her apartment, if the girl died. "She's not going to," she said. "But that doesn't mean we have to do it here." We? he asked her. "Christ, I don't know why the hell I have to tear myself apart being with you," she said. "We'll do it in her apartment. And you'll show me everything I ought to know to be able to help."

So they did it in the friend's apartment. Then the friend didn't work out, but she paid anyway and got assistance elsewhere and recommended a friend to him and told the friend it was the easiest way if it took and if it didn't there were other ways. The friend of the friend worked out. So did, eventually, a friend of the friend. Meanwhile there were others. He always stayed with them till all danger was past. And if something happened, he had committed himself to staying with them till proper assistance arrived. He always went to them with the telephone numbers of the nearest hospitals. They paid well, and it was really a slight effort, except for the implicit danger involved and the equal danger involved in stealing adequate supplies of his materials. The two of them, on his nights off—and sometimes even on his nights on when he could get somebody to cover for him—began living her old life again. Neither did *this* change her toward him. He enjoyed this kind of life, though, he discovered. Enjoyed it immensely. He began becoming expectant about getting enough new "patients." During a fight once, she even told him he was getting corrupted, they ought to stop, he wasn't doing it the same way she was any more. They stopped. Then they needed money. He felt they did, anyway. He couldn't stand her sitting around the apartment with him. She said, "Am I being difficult, *am I complaining?*" He said no. She said, *"Am I any different?"* He said no. But the following week they accepted a new "patient" anyway.

75

If the man made a move, Granchard was thinking, *if the man just stood around in the place Granchard had in mind, the man could give up living.* Granchard would see to it that he *had* to give up living.

Granchard thought: That's a *fine* attitude for a doctor, okaying getting rid of life. That makes two of us, Granchard thought.

Two to twenty, Otis thought. Remember it. Remember *that.* And remember it good. But this woman *needs* pitting. All right. But you don't have to take some pit for yourself. You can get *her* pit, but none for yourself.

That's two to twenty *years.* In *prison.* And you're almost out of it. Tonight's your last night on this service. She doesn't know enough about the setup here to *expect* you to be *able* to get any more of the stuff. And that takes you off the hook with *yourself* even though she never knew any better. You won't have to expect it of yourself if she doesn't know you could still work it. *All right,* he told himself, *I'll leave it alone.* I'll just go get what I need for the patient. But for myself, *I'll leave it alone.*

Then Granchard was suddenly frightened. *Will I call him on it?* It's one thing to suspect him and hate him for it; and it's another thing to actually be the one who manages him out of the profession, maybe into jail.

I don't have the guts, Granchard thought. I just want him not to do it. So I won't be forced to be an executioner; *that is not my function.*

Nor *his,* Granchard reminded himself.

But he's a good doctor. He's good at what he does, and God damn him for some of what he does, but please don't make me be the one to be the hand of Your Damnation.

And if I catch him at it and don't call him on it because I hate that kind of responsibility and am afraid of it and will never be able to clean my mind of having done it, then will I be able to live with *not* having done it, with having been a coward because of fear of having to live with knowing that I am responsible for a man being in jail . . . ?

Yes, *God damn him*, Granchard thought. For doing what he's done. And for making me be the one who has to mete out justice to him. God damn him for doing to me what he's doing.

Granchard felt physically ill. I'm a doctor, he thought, *not* a policeman. God damn him for making me into a policeman when it's not my responsibility to be one. And God damn him for making me into judge and jury too. Because if I call him on it, I'll be all three, the verdict included, just by calling him on it.

He was still frightened. How can I get myself to call him on it even if he does it right in front of my eyes when I know what I'll be sending him to?

76

The labor floor seemed suddenly deserted. There was no one in the corridor, or in the nurses' station. The door to the drug cabinet was still open. Well, that happened when things were heavy and rushed. He ought to know. The circumstance had served him often enough before.

He removed an ampoule of pitocin from the cabinet and felt its reality in his hand. There were many more like it in the cabinet. Row on row of them, standing up in lines in boxes; small, the glass vaguely bluish. Like the light that vaguely illuminated a room in early dawn. The ampoule in his hand felt like success, surety, money, quiet, a world of being at ease with himself. Six months of being at ease with himself, anyway. His hand closed on the ampoule it held—not tightly, not greedily, but respectfully. Very respectfully.

If you do it this time, he told himself, *you can't blame it on her. Not this time. Back during the beginning,* he remembered, *she hadn't complained when there hadn't been any money, when the money* hadn't *been available. She hadn't said a thing. Not till the money was available. Now she wasn't saying anything either. She had assumed and decided that that part was over.* So, if he took some now, he knew and told himself, it was and would be for *himself,* not for her the way it had at least partly been up till now. If he took some now, it would be because *he* wanted to, not because *she* wanted him to. *I want to,* he decided.

A box had already been started. He removed about half of the remaining ampoules. Twenty or so. He put a few in the breast pocket of his scrub tunic, and a few in each of the side pockets. He went to another cabinet and got down a syringe with which to pit the woman who had been waiting so long. He started to go out into the corridor. But Bobbie, the night head nurse, in her blue scrub smock, her hair damp and flat against the skin of her forehead from the heat of the delivery room, came scooting in and he had to stand back to let her pass through the door.

"Hi, sport!" she said happily, and whacked him on the behind. *"Twins,"* she said happily. "Male and female." She began fighting her lighter viciously. "Damn it! it's a new one too, my husband gave it to me for Christmas."

"Here," he said, and took out a book of matches and lit her cigarette.

"Thanks, sport," she said, talking, and blowing out smoke, and smiling all at once. *"And Happy New Year.* You can kiss me—no one's kissed me yet."

He said, "Happy New Year, love," and kissed her on the cheek.

Jay Fishbein came in. "Hey! *I'll* scrub."

"Make it lingering, then. I like them *lingering."*

Fishbein gave her a lingering kiss on the forehead.

Bobbie said, *"Boy,* when you pulled out that second one! I'd only heard *one* heartbeat."

"Me too," Fishbein said, grinning.

Otis started out the door again, but Granchard and Worship were coming in and he had to stand aside again.

Granchard remained in the doorway. He leaned against its frame and lit a cigarette. "Whatcha got there?" he said to Otis, looking at the syringe and the closed hand.

"Pit. For Mrs. Kramer."

"Ah." Granchard blew out some smoke and spat a speck of tobacco from his lips. "That all?"

"You mean the syringe?"

"No, I don't mean the syringe," Granchard said, stepping forward. Otis tried to step around him. "I mean," Granchard said, reaching at a tunic pocket, *"in there."*

Otis stepped back again. Bobbie, Fishbein, and Worship looked over with interest. Otis tried to get by Granchard.

Granchard was crowding him. He shoved Granchard out of the way. Granchard went off balance for an instant, recovered himself, and grabbed him from behind, trying to pin his arms. Otis whipped around, got loose, and swung. He hit Granchard on the upper part of Granchard's left arm. Granchard stepped in close and tried to pin him again. Bobbie, Fishbein, and Worship watched silently, suddenly perplexed. *"Grab him,* for chrisake!" Granchard yelled. None of the others moved, but they had stood up from various seats, confused, now realizing that something bad was happening. *"Grab hi—"* Granchard started, but was cut off by Otis' managing to hit the side of his face. Fishbein and Worship rushed forward, caught Otis as he got to the door, and held him, though so tentatively that he kept almost breaking free. *"Settle down a second,* for godsake," Fishbein said. "What the hell's goin' *on* between you two?" Worship said.

Granchard stepped toward Otis. Otis tried to kick out at him. Fishbein and Worship held Otis tighter. Granchard relaxed and stepped back slightly. "Look in his pocket, Worship."

"Hunh?" Worship said.

"Look in his God damn pocket, Worship!"

Otis struggled violently.

"Worship!"

Worship managed to reach into a side pocket. He brought out a handful of ampoules. Otis almost broke away and Worship dropped the ampoules. Two or three broke on the floor. He and Fishbein now locked Otis between them so he couldn't get any leverage, much less move at all.

"Now what do you think he needed all that pit for?" Granchard said.

"You lousy little bastard!" Bobbie screamed at Otis.

Otis had stopped struggling and now stood alone, Fishbein and Worship at the ready behind him. He said, "There are some laws that are God damned particular about what's evidence." He said it very carefully. Mildly. He lit a cigarette.

"You'll damn well never practice medicine," Granchard said also carefully and mildly. "I'll run you so far out of the profession you won't even know you're alive," he said. "Maybe you'll wish you weren't alive when I get through with you. That much I can promise you right now." He looked at Otis for a long time. "About the courts and evidence . . . Well, we'll just see what we can dig up."

Otis looked at his cigarette and then looked up. Mildly, he said, "And Happy New Year to *you*, Granchard."

77

The people from De Witt were trying to get a practical demonstration of their game, Let's Do It, going on the living-room floor. Didi, overwhelmed with giggles, was trying to stop them. She was *so* overwhelmed with giggles that she found herself being set up as one of the participants—and because she was giggling too hard to get a word out, unable to protest. Walters finally got her away. Eckland announced that they had run out of vodka. Didi said that they'd never *had* any in the first place. Eckland said well that explained it then. De Traunant was trying to establish a working relationship with Cynthia. Mercouris was trying to wake Olga. Rosconovitch was trying to remember *exactly* what Phyllis looked like; but the harder he tried, the more her face eluded him, though he had started his concentration with a pretty accurate image in his mind. Gloria made herself a sandwich. Olga woke up and announced that she was ready to drink again. Eckland brought her a glass of water. Olga poured it down de Traunant's back. De Traunant took off his jacket and shirt—still not getting up from talking to Cynthia—wiped himself with a bundle he made of the two pieces of clothing, threw them in a corner, carefully tied his tie around his naked neck, and quietly went on trying to establish his relationship with Cynthia. Van Wyck put on a new set of records. Six couples began trying to do the Charleston in an area big enough for just one of them. People who fell down defaulted the contest and were not allowed to get up. This made it more difficult for the couples still dancing. It didn't do the people lying on the floor any good either. Gloria made a number of excuses to a number of young men to avoid dancing with anyone but Rosconovitch. But Rosconovitch didn't want to dance. He didn't even seem to want to talk very much. It was a damn stupid promise to have made to *anyone* on New Year's Eve. She con-

tented herself with having another sandwich. The last of the
couples finally tripped and fell down on the floor. None of
the couples were bothering to get up. It looked like the
people from De Witt had finally gotten their game started.

Lois Fishbein, who had been sitting on the couch quietly
talking with Pete van Wyck, suddenly said loudly, "It's not
true!"

Van Wyck looked surprised. "I *think* it is," he said. "I
thought you knew."

"Well I don't."

"I'm sorry," van Wyck said. "I didn't mean to upset you."

"It *can't* be true!" she said, getting up suddenly. She
stamped her foot furiously. "Are you *sure* it's true?" She
looked at him angrily.

Other people were looking around. Van Wyck was quite
uncomfortable. "Yes," he said. "I'm sure."

"Listen," she said *at* him angrily, "I didn't get married for
this. I haven't put up with being a med student's wife and
an intern's wife and damn near anything but a wife for this!"

"Hey!" van Wyck said, getting up fast. "Where're you
going?"

"*Home!*" Lois said, pulling her coat viciously out of a
closet.

Van Wyck ran after her. "What'll I tell your husband
when he gets here?"

She stopped and turned around. "*Tell him to go to hell!*"
She turned again and slammed the apartment door behind
her.

Jesus, van Wyck thought. What'm I gonna tell Jay?

78

At midnight Fred didn't call. That was all right, Mildred
knew he must be busy, she knew how things got at the hospital sometimes. But then at twelve fifteen and at twelve
thirty he didn't call either. Not at quarter of one or at one.
She looked away from the clock. *All over town people are
having fun,* she thought. She had been thinking it all evening.

Shortly after one, Terry called again. "I've been kissing
some very pretty girls," he said.

"Congratulations," she said.

"None as pretty as you."

Mildred smiled. "Tough luck," she said.

"I'd rather just *be* with you than kiss *them*."

"You're full of something my husband would have a bad word for."

"I mean it."

"So do I."

"Why don't I pick you up, say in . . . like as soon as I can get a cab and get up there?"

Mildred said nothing. In a few seconds her eyes went to the copy of *Vogue* that she'd been reading and that she'd thrown down on the floor, losing her place, when the telephone rang.

"*Well*," Terry said, "how about it?"

Mildred was still looking at the copy of *Vogue* lying on the floor. "What time is it?" she said, after a pause.

"Time? *Time?* Hell, time for me to pick you up!"

"No, I'm serious. What time is it?"

"Jesus," Terry said, disgusted. There was a pause. "It's . . . *it's one seventeen*," he finally said smartly.

"Call me at quarter of two. All right?"

"Quarter of *two?*"

"Never . . ."

"All right. All right. Quarter of two."

"Happy New Year," she said.

"Happy New Year," he said.

Between the time that Mildred hung off with Terry at one seventeen and the time that he called again—quarter of two— the phone did not ring at all. Mildred said, "What kind of a party is it?"

Terry said, "*A terrific* party."

"I know, but what are people *wearing?*"

"Well," he said thoughtfully, "everyone is wearing clothes. The boys are wearing suits and . . ."

"Not the *boys*, silly, the girls. What are *they* wearing?"

"I take it back. Some of them are only partly wearing clothes . . ."

"Cocktail dress, dinner dress, or evening dress, dope?"

"I'd say . . . *cocktail* dress. Yeah, that's it. Cocktail dress."

"All right. Come whistle at my window."

"*Whistle . . . ?*"

"Don't be more of an ass than you are. Come pick me up is what I mean."

"I'll whistle at other things . . ."

"If you don't get off the phone, New Year's Eve will be over before you get here."

"Right, right, right, I'm on my way."

She chose a black, silk evening blouse that was scooped low enough to show—if she bent over at all—the organdy trimming on her half-cut, strapless bra. With it she chose a black, silk skirt and decided not to wear a girdle, just a garter belt and panties. She was going to conquer the party. The girls were going to be jealous of her, and the boys were going to leave their girls to talk to her. And Terry was going to have a terrible time controlling himself. But if he couldn't control himself, she'd do it for him.

79

Lew just told them, that was all. All there was to tell about Otis. And he was watching a girl he didn't even know the name of; or was *with* her, he could not tell; she was near him and he was watching her and she did not go away from his watching. And Pete van Wyck was saying, "What's it about?" and someone else he didn't know saying, "Someone at New North made a booboo," and another one behind him saying, drunk-happy, thinking it was the funniest of all, "And got caught at it."

So he told them, wondering, How does John's girl feel about it? He wondered what she was doing now. Was she staying home alone waiting for him? Being alone New Year's Eve for him? Just staying alone for him?

Did she know about John? what he'd been doing? what had happened to him as a result? Was she home alone now and did she know about it or not by now, there alone? and did she love him very much? at all? were they going to get married? Had John done it for her? had it hurt him and did he love her that much?

Lew wondered if he'd ever love anyone that much, was he capable of it? And he wished he knew who John's girl was so that he could close her off from ever having to know about John—if it were possible. Would he ever meet anyone he could love that much? He wanted to, but it frightened him that it was possible to love so much that you could do what John had been doing. *Love.* It was supposed to be the purest of human emotions. And would it get you to do what John had done?

Van Wyck said, "What're they doing about him?"

Lew shook his head. "It's crazy," he said. He had no comprehension left. "It's crazy. They don't know what to do with him. No one knows. They caught him and they don't know what to do now."

"What about Wohl?" Pete said.

"They couldn't get in touch with him. He's supposed to show up any time now, they left word for him. There's no one around who knows what to do now."

"What about *him?*"

"They've got him in his room. He just sits there and smokes. Two guys staying with him because no one knows what else to do and he just grins at them and smokes and makes kind of funny remarks at his own expense. I was up there with him for a while. They were waiting for Wohl to get the message and get there and do something."

"You don't look very right," Pete said, and handed Lew his drink.

Lew took it and held it but didn't even look at it, and went on and on, explaining—explaining without comprehension. "They'll wait till they hear from Wohl," he said. "He should be there by now, they thought he'd . . . If they can't get evidence to bring him to court, they'll just be stuck with settling for dismissing him and keeping him from practicing."

"Yeah," someone said. "Big deal. You goddam city hospitals, you're not happy unless you're being dramatic." Then, swinging around, "So where's the fun and games? What happened to the New Year's Eve spirit?"

80

And it was as if the other had not happened, as if he had just walked into the party.

He was not by nature sentimental. But he seemed to have

been getting that way lately. The symptom worried him. At twenty-five, he felt that perhaps he was too young to be set upon by middle age. But he couldn't seem to be able to *do* anything about it. He just couldn't help himself. The Otis business, the long day when he was supposed to have been off . . .

But he was at the party, and, even after Otis and the long day, he couldn't help himself. He fell in love. He couldn't understand why every male there wasn't making a play for her, an immediate play. But only two or three were. It shocked him. And, of course, her date was being attentive. Rosconovitch seemed to be her date. Maybe the date explained the lack of attention he felt she unmistakably deserved. But the relative lack continued to shock him. Maybe the rest of the guys in the room were trying to be very casual in their approach. Maybe the girl was so desirable she embarrassed them. Maybe they were all homosexuals.

Lew was unable to help himself at all. He went directly to her and asked her for a dance.

She said, "No." Then she looked at him and said, "I have to explain that I . . . Well, it just *can't* be explained. But I promised Art—do you know Art? Anyway, I promised Art I'd only dance with him tonight." She looked at him closely again. "He *insisted*," she said, looking uncomfortable.

Lew started, "Hey, Art . . ."

Rosconovitch put out a cigarette and stood up. "It was kind of a silly promise, wasn't it?"

Lew said, "You mean it's okay? If I dance with her?"

Rosconovitch said, "I'm a jerk."

Lew brightened. "That's great. Thanks, Doctor." He put his hand on the girl's arm to lead her off to dance. But then he looked at Rosconovitch again and no longer felt so bright. "Hey. Art. You okay?"

"Yeah. Sure. Just tired."

"I mean, I don't want to take your girl away from you, or anything like that."

Rosconovitch looked perplexed. Then he laughed and shook his head. "Gloria's not my girl, she was just being nice to me. Gloria Mead, Lew Worship. And vice versa."

Lew said, "Gloria Mead?" and stared, and caught himself, and remembered he had status to live up to and said, seriously, "Really, you okay, Art?"

"I'm really beginning to feel better. Really." He laughed. "I've been involved in waking up all day."

"Maybe you need some coffee," Lew said.

"I need some fun. And I think I'm at the right party." He took a good long swallow of his drink, made a horrible noise of distaste, slapped Lew on the back, and went and cut in on Alicia and Jim.

Lew took the girl near the phonograph and held her tentatively. She was blond, almost a small girl . . . and was *beautiful* . . . and smiled at him as graciously as he'd ever been smiled at in his life.

He couldn't help himself at all. "I love you," he said. He startled even himself.

She said, "Pay no attention to it, it's probably just physical."

"Maybe so, maybe so," he said hurriedly, "but I've got to find out, and right away, because . . ."

She interrupted. "The record's over," she said. He was still dancing with her and there was no music.

"There'll be another," he said desperately.

"Good," she said. She disengaged herself. "Send me a copy."

He caught her quickly and kept her from walking away. "Please," he said, because he couldn't think of anything else to say. And then just, *"Please."*

She said, looking at him closely again, "I think you're serious."

"I am. I am." Quietly, forlornly, he said, "I am."

Her eyes still scrutinized him closely. He saw her brow tighten slightly. "No," he said, for it was the only thing he could think of saying, "I'm not sick, I'm not psycho, there hasn't been any insanity in my family for generations."

"That's comforting."

He went on hurriedly, "I mean, there is in every family, almost, at one time or . . . look, let's talk, I've *got* to talk to you."

"Before you turn into a pumpkin?"

"Yes. No. I mean, I've *got* to *talk* to you."

"To find out if you love me," she said, amused and maybe sarcastic at the same time.

He was utterly and completely deflated and exhausted and unhappy. He sighed at length and his shoulders sagged. "Yes," he said, quietly, with his last energy.

She leaned forward and sniffed at him. "You haven't even been drinking!" she said, as if the last excuse in the world he might have for himself had been exhausted and her patience along with it.

"No," he said, miserably, thinking, there must be *some* reason.

She stared at him, he felt, as if he were something that was supposed to be nonexistent. Then she took his hand and started to lead him over to some unoccupied pillows on the floor. "Come," she said.

"I'll be God damned," he said simply. And then to himself, I'll be simply God damned.

She got down on the floor and pulled her skirt over her crossed legs. "Sit," she said.

He sat.

"Talk," she said.

He talked very fast, thinking she might get up and leave at any instant, like a bird startled from its perch. "I'm an intern," he said, "and I go back on duty at six tomorrow evening and I have to get back to get some sleep before then, so I . . ."

"Love doesn't make any difference?"

Still talking very fast, he said, "Sure it does. But if I'm going to marry you and support you I have to be in a position to make a living and that means reporting to the hospital on time tomorrow so I can be in a position to be making enough money to support you in . . ." He counted on his fingers, *"Six months."* Quickly, he amended himself, "That is, if you don't mind living very simply at first."

"You're sure there hasn't been any insanity in your family for generations?"

"Positive."

"Well, I think it's just reappeared." But she laughed. "Doctor, I think you need a drink."

"No. If you want to get rid of me, just say so."

"I don't want to get rid of you," she said, standing up. "I'm just going to get you a drink. I wouldn't dream of not coming back. I'd never know if you were real or not then, would I?"

81

Jay Fishbein arrived. Van Wyck got up immediately and went to him. Jay had looked around the living room and was starting off toward the rest of the apartment, his face looking nothing but worried. "Where's *Lois?*" he said to van Wyck.

"She went home."

"Home?" he turned to face van Wyck. *"Why?"*

"I'm not sure."

"Didn't she say anything?"

Van Wyck cleared his throat uncomfortably. "She said for you to go to hell."

"Me?"

Van Wyck nodded.

Fishbein left him immediately and went to the phone. He dialed. "Hello," he said angrily. "Why aren't you here?" He listened. "This *instant?* Listen, Lois, what the hell's the matter with you?" He listened again. "All right. *All right!* I'll come right home. You sure can pick the perfect times to make life miserable, the one God damned party we've gotten out to since . . . *Yeah?* Well if I'm a disappointment to *you,* just at this minute I wish I never married you!" He listened. "You're God damned right I mean it!" He listened. Then softly and intently, he said, "Just don't wait up for me, baby, the lack of sleep'd kill you." Then he hung up.

A few minutes later the telephone rang. Didi crawled to it, put the instrument on the floor, and, prone, with Court Walters coming at her on all fours, picked the receiver up and said, "Hello?"

In a moment she started to say, "I'll get hmmmmm . . . Court! *stop it mmmmmm,"* and rolled about on the floor under Court's oral embrace, the receiver dropped and left lying by itself and Didi quickly forgetting it and slowly putting her arms around Court's neck.

Olga rolled over to the untended receiver. "Yah?"

Mercouris followed at a fast crawl, levered himself on his elbows, and ran his right index finger down Olga's cleavage.

Olga grabbed his hand viciously and placed it firmly on her left breast. Mercouris subsided with contentment. Olga said, "Yah, sure." Then she yelled, "Fishbang! *telephone*." Then she too dropped the receiver and directed her attentions to more immediate diversions.

Van Wyck, who, while exploring Joan's mammary regions in a prone position nearby, had been hit in the head with the receiver, reacted instinctively, turned over, took the receiver in his hand, and put it back in its cradle.

Less than sixty seconds later, the phone rang again. Eckland found he had trouble even hearing the phone through the music and voices. But he kept hearing it, and no one else seemed to. He thought perhaps he was going crazy. He decided to find the phone and assure himself that it really *was* ringing. He had trouble enough seeing through the fog of smoke itself, much less finding something in it. But he followed the sound. Finally, he could swear he was standing right *on* the damn thing. But he was surrounded by a log-jam of couples lying on the floor and he was still unable to see it. He got down on the floor, crawled about, turned right at Olga's cleavage, then left at Joan Feldman's, stopped, listened, backed up against Didi's posterior, pushed van Wyck's head aside, and found the phone. Eckland put his ear down to it. Sure enough, it was ringing. He *wasn't* going crazy, there really was a telephone and it really was ringing. Reassured at last, he stood up and went and got himself a drink.

The telephone stopped ringing. The telephone started ringing. Van Wyck said, "Jesus Christ!" and picked up the receiver. "Asepsis Club," he said, "Nobody here but us rabbits . . . Oh. Jesus. Lois! I'm sorry . . . Yeah, yeah. He's around here somewhere, I'll get him." He held the receiver away from his mouth. "Fishbein!" he yelled. *"Jay!"* He looked around. "Hey! For chrisake! Fishbein! The God damn *telephone*." Fishbein loomed over him.

Fishbein had had four fast bourbons in twenty minutes. He didn't bother to raise his voice to be heard through the din. But van Wyck heard him quite clearly. "I'm not scrubbing," Fishbein said. Then Fishbein walked away.

"Jesus Christ!" van Wyck said. And then, "Lois? Your friend's getting himself clobbered. In the most professional way, of course. And he won't come to the telephone. I'll . . ." He looked at the receiver, shook it, listened again, shrugged, and replaced it in its cradle.

Lois arrived within fifteen minutes. She didn't even bother to take off her coat. She immediately saw her husband drinking alone in the kitchen. She went in, picked up a bottle of bourbon, and, grabbing his arm forcefully, said, *"Come!"* and dragged him off to the bedroom.

There, several couples were arrayed in variously decorative positions. Lois said, "Everybody *out!"* There was no response. She went around poking them viciously with the bottle of bourbon. "Out! *Out!"* De Traunant looked up from lying on the bed with Cynthia. "Hey. Lois. *Just when . . ."* he started unhappily, and then found himself *pulled* off the bed. "Okay, *okay,"* he said, and led Cynthia out of the room. Lois slammed the door and turned on the lights. She stood with her back against the door and the bottle of bourbon held by the neck as if it were a weapon. Jay, on his sixth drink, speculated that this woman could not possibly be his wife. "Sit down, Sam," she said. Then, *"Sit!* damn it!"

Jay sat.

The woman who was masquerading as his wife threw the bottle at him. He just managed to catch it before it fractured his skull. "Drink," the woman said.

"I've already got a . . ." Jay started, pointing to the glass he'd put down on the bed table.

"Drink!" the woman instructed. "You wanted such a God damn party, well, you're gonna *have* one. Right now. And not with water in it, either. *Drink."*

He drank again.

She went over, pulled the bottle from him, tipped it up, swallowed a good amount, and pushed the bottle back into his hands. *"Now what's this I hear about you switching to anesthesiology?"*

"Well . . . Well, it's a good . . ."

"That's right. That it is. For them what are drawn to it. *How do you explain you?* The great neuro-ophthal surgeon."

All of a sudden he found himself on the defensive about it. And he didn't understand how that could be. After all . . .

"Well, Doctor?"

"You see, Lois . . . Well, you can make more money faster being a . . ."

"Give me that bottle!" she drank again.

This woman certainly wasn't his wife.

She shoved the bottle back at him again. "And why have

you suddenly become so interested in making money fast?"

"Now wait a minute! That isn't fair. You yourself said . . ."

"*When?* When did I ever?"

"When you got that letter from your sister!" he said angrily.

"So? So aren't I allowed to bitch occasionally? It's recreation, it's therapy, *Sam.* But that doesn't give you the right to go out and cut off our nose to spite *your* face. Not without consulting *me*, it doesn't. I haven't stuck it through this long trying to help you to get what you wanted to be . . . for . . . for you to not even *consult* me when you decide to be something *else!*" She started to cry.

He stood up to comfort her.

"*Sit down!*" she yelled. She actually pushed him. "You didn't even *ask* me," she said, still crying. "You didn't even *tell* me." She sat down next to him. She was the one who was crying, but *she* was the one who took *his* hand. Jay found the whole thing very confusing. He drank from the bottle. She held his hand between hers. She said, softly now, and still crying, "I decided a long time ago that if I wanted to hold onto you, I had to hold onto whatever you decided you wanted to do and help you to do it. And I want to hold onto you, darling, darling Sam. I don't want someday for you to stop and look at yourself and find out you're not what you wanted to be and decide that it was my fault. I'm just being selfish. Period. It's just selfishness on my part and nothing more, and my selfishness makes me want you to go ahead with the neuro-ophthal residency." She sniffled. "Understand, Sam?"

He nodded. He couldn't think of anything else to do, so he handed her the bottle.

Lying next to Mercouris on the floor, his arm under her head, a glass in one hand balanced on her stomach, Cynthia was feeling ill-used and maltreated and sorry for herself and was becoming increasingly angry with Joe Parelli. She thought she had already felt what could only be her highest pitch of anger at him. But the more she found herself *trying* to enjoy the party, and the more she found herself joining in with the general gist of things and *trying* to be affectionate to someone like Conny or Mike de Traunant or others, the more she became angered at Joe. She *wanted* to be with *him*.

But he was such a bastard. Purposely *working* New Year's Eve. She wanted him. But how could she have any respect for herself if she traipsed after someone who didn't even show her basic common consideration?

She felt she was going to cry again, and just then Conny moved suggestively close to her, and in pushing him away and getting up she spilled her drink over Olga and Olga's partner. She certainly would have cried again then, but neither one seemed even to have noticed having gotten drenched. And so she didn't cry, she almost even laughed, and went and sat down on the couch. Very soon Mike de Traunant was again talking to her about the aesthetics of love and intercourse and she didn't have the chance to cry.

She held it in her arms like a baby and sniffled again and then smiled at him. "I think we ought to get drunk together and talk. We'll drink the whole thing, Sam," she said, holding the bottle up to the light. "We don't have to portion it out and figure how much we ought to save in case someone should drop in. The whole thing, Sam." She held it to her lips and drank and then handed it to him. "Bottoms up, Sam."

"You know," he said, smiling. "I did a stupid thing. I didn't cancel the ophthal applications."

She smiled at him. Tenderly, she said, "Bottoms up, Sam."

He nodded. "So why don't you take off your coat and stay a while, Sam?"

In the living room, on the floor, Mercouris was thinking, Here I am lying down with a nurse again. With no particular interest in her except what she covers with underwear. So here I am lying down with a nurse again. And this one isn't even particularly interested in *me*. I must be nuts, why do I involve myself in a relationship like this that isn't even a relationship?

The answer was easy. Well, I couldn't very well just *give up* women during internship and residency just because prospects don't pay bills. So therefore, due to my professional aspirations, I am enabled to allow myself to settle for superficial relationships. A *great* profession, he thought. Simply great. In which you learn to content yourself with this kind of thing.

Conny said, "*Hey.* She's the pretty one with the bite." He and van Wyck were standing over a group of throw pillows that Lew and Gloria were sitting on. Lew had his arm around her and she was nuzzling her cheek against his.

"What bite?" van Wyck said, drunk and thinking of snakes.

"The bite on the back of her neck."

Van Wyck stared. "Jesus Christ. So she is."

Worship looked up. "What bite?"

"Bite-size and ready to eat. *Mmmmm!*" Conny said.

"What bite?" Lew said again.

"The bite she had on the back of her neck. Human-type bite," Conny said.

"I *got it* from a *ten-year-old* in Pediatrics. That was her idea of fun."

"What a disappointment," van Wyck said.

"The medical profession is a constant flow of disillusionments," Conny said, and he and van Wyck walked away.

A nurse said to an intern: "Tell me, when you were born, back in the days before resuscitators, did they slap you on your backside or on your *head?*"

An intern said to a nurse: "So I've got halitosis. So it's a lot better than no breath at all."

And de Traunant was saying intently to Cynthia—who still had not been given even a *chance* to cry and really only wanted to go to the bathroom anyway—"What's your primary purpose in life . . . It's got to be one of four things . . . to be happy, to make other people happy, to bear children . . . What I'm getting at is what's your *moral* outlook . . . ? Are you *true to yourself?* Your own physical instincts? . . . and then there's the ethereal . . . the long silences when two people meet above the stars . . ."

Lew Worship was very drunk, and, lying with his head in Gloria's lap, was trying to explain himself to her, ". . . and even love the love the mother has for the child that excludes him . . . I mean, me . . . like the way you're what that woman is makes me love you even more than you can . . . than you could ever unnerstand . . . without, that is . . ."

Gloria just said, "There, there," and rubbed his forehead and kissed him every so often until he had gone to sleep, his head still in her lap, the strained look he had gotten trying to explain himself and thinking that he *had* to explain himself gone from his face, and, slowly, as he became more deeply asleep, a smile, somewhat of recognition, in its place.

Van Wyck was saying ". . . Inter-County General mit der auto haccidents from der zuper highvays . . ."

Alicia Liu was saying, "No, no, it isn't right that way at all. It should be exactly the *other* way around. It *should* be *her*-terectomy and *his*-nia."

Didi was saying to Conny ". . . If you're not pickin' cotton, *get your cotton-pickin' hands off me!*"

83

He was going back to his room. It was damn near eight o'clock. And Parelli was disgusted. With himself, with Flynn, with Bonny, with Otis, with OB, with the hour, with New Year's Eve, with people, with medicine, with life, and with . . . But mostly with himself. The night had been so God damned hectic, he hadn't had the slightest chance to go up on *post partum* and talk to Head Nurse Flynn. Much less even *see* her. Sure, medically and practically, the night had been valuable. But so too would have been Christmas. And then he would have had New Year's Eve for Cynthia. *Well the hell with her.*

He unlocked his door, switched on the light, and shut the door and just looked at it. *What a hole*, Parelli thought, for the *n*th time. What a putrid hole.

He couldn't bear to change the room, though. Any improvement, any touch of decoration, would only have served to blatantly point out—by contrast—what a despisable, despicable hole he was living in. He could not have borne that—no more than he could have borne continuing with Cynthia if she was going to make him look at how things could be different.

When Terry arrived, shortly after two, he gave her a very chaste New Year's Eve kiss. It hardly brushed her lips. And then he was very good in the cab. Slightly *drunk*—but very good. And funny. And because he was very good and very funny and because she found that she was enjoying herself, she decided he wasn't drunk, but just slightly *high*, and she decided that she wanted to get that way too and also decided that she had a certain amount of warmth in her heart for Terry and that if Fred knew him and especially if he saw how chastely Terry was taking care of her, Fred would be warmly disposed toward Terry too.

At the party he didn't leave her alone. Fred would have. Fred would say afterwards, "For chrisake, honey, don't we get enough of each other at home? It's *fun* to be with other people . . ." But Terry stayed with her all the time, brought her drinks, put his arm around her—not in a *bad* way, but just affectionately—and said nice funny things to her that she couldn't remember *when* Fred had said to her.

Afterwards, when people started leaving the party—around four—and the host and hostess looked like they were doing things out of hospitality rather than enjoyment, he took her to Reuben's for breakfast. Afterwards she had him take her for a walk, along Fifth, into St. Patrick's, across to Rockefeller Center, where there was the seventy-foot Christmas tree all lit up and poinsettias in the garden row.

It was already light above the buildings, though still night on the streets. They looked up at the Christmas tree and he said, "Let's go up to my place, anything may happen, even a drink." She giggled and they took a cab up to a very nicely appointed room and a half (it had a dining balcony as well as a kitchenette, bathroom, and two closets) where she sipped brandy because he said it was the only thing to do at this hour except something else that she would like and he would too but that she might feel was a little too sophisticated after St. Patrick's.

She stretched out on the couch to smile and listen to him talk, and after a while he was sitting by her and then he put a hand on her waist and kissed her and she put her arms around his neck and felt like a girl again, not like a wife, felt as she hadn't felt since cars and necking and college. When he put his hand on her breast and felt for her nipple and caressed it with his fingers, it was just too good to give up, too like when she'd been so happy before getting married, when things had been *exciting,* and, besides, she could always stop. But when he pulled the blouse out of her skirt and raised her and pulled it over her head and undid her bra and pulled the zipper down on her skirt, she didn't stop, she pressed him to her.

85

Mildred awoke early at eleven A.M. Because they'd gone to sleep where they'd lain on the studio couch and she had been pressed between him and the wall, she felt stifled. When she got up, he didn't awake, and she became angry at him suddenly.

She felt not quite as if she were there. Or anywhere at all. But she managed to dress herself. Then she quietly left his apartment.

When Fred got home at eight, she was in bed. He said, "You sick, honey?"

"No," she said. "Not really. I just think I'm getting the curse early. It feels like it anyway."

"You want something," he said, sitting down on the side of the bed and putting his fingers in her hair. "Some Trigezic?"

"No," Mildred said, and turned on her side away from him. "I think I just want to sleep."

"Okay," he said, "you go ahead. I'll just fix myself something to eat, then I'll sack out too."

She pretended to be halfway asleep already.

THREE
THE PATIENT

86

New Year's Eve was gone—even as a subject of conversation. They were back within the confines of the closed atmosphere of the hospital. And with June still almost six months away, the various interns found themselves once again seemingly cut off from *both* the past and the future.

87

On the morning of January second, Dave Rosen, Male Medicine A's chief resident, brought all of his interns together and gave them the word on his service. It was not so much indoctrination or orientation as it was a half-hearted attempt to give the new group a sporting chance.

Ward A of Male Medicine had a normal complement of forty-eight beds in six six-bed rooms, five two-bed rooms, and two one-bed rooms. On January second it had a patient occupancy of sixty-one. Extra beds and cots had been placed in all the six-bed rooms and behind movable partitions in the corridor.

Fifty-five of the patients were directly the responsibility of Medicine; the remaining six belonged to Neurology, the Neuro service never having many in-patients and therefore sharing Medicine's ward facilities—and, sometimes, of course, Surgery's ward facilities when a neuro patient was operated on.

By far the largest number of Medicine patients were cases of cerebro-vascular accident—"strokes." On January second the ward was bedding twenty-seven such CVA's. Owing to the nature of their conditions—neural complications and impairments resulting from cerebro-vascular accident—a number of these CVA's were also under associate treatment by the Neurology service. The CVA was always New North Medicine's most common patient and was usually in his late fifties.

Medicine's next biggest single group of patients was the diabetics—usually forty to fifty years of age. Rheumatic fever patients in their teens were a much smaller but equally consistent type of in-patient. Ulcer, coronary, and cirrhosis victims were also regularly present.

On January second, Male Medicine A had in addition been dealing with one case of drug addiction (heroin) and one case of alcohol habituation. They did not have proper facilities for treating the addiction case, and were therefore trying to transfer him to an institution that had such facilities. However, the addict preferred to stay where he was rather than undergo the same sort of deprivation in some place unknown to him where the regime might be, he felt, as horrifying as his worst hallucination. He was therefore being very difficult about signing the necessary papers, though he had amazed the staff by accepting complete withdrawal in the ward.

The case of habituation was slightly different and, in the difference, directly a responsibility of Medicine. Whereas the addict could withdraw without anything more than negligible harm to himself *physically* (his condition being one of pharmaco*psychosis*), the habituate had undergone such physical changes as the result of his habituation (which thus made it *habituation* rather than addiction) that his body was now the subject of an entirely new kind of fluid-balance environment. Treatment by withdrawal could easily wreak such physical havoc within him as to be fatal. Medicine was slowly trying to reconstruct the fluid-balance environment to match normal findings, or, at least, to approximate normal findings to an extent that would make it possible for the patient to be no longer physically habituated to the alcohol. But the chief resident instructed the new intern group that Medicine allowed itself only very little hope.

Many of the patients—of whatever chief complaint—who had been confined to bed for any appreciable length of time —*weeks,* say—were suffering from decubitus ulcers—"bed sores." This was particularly the case among the older patients who were able to move very little anyway. Constant pressure upon a single area of their bodies—especially where flesh was normally thin and taut over a protuberance of bone—could not help but irritate and eventually open and infect the area thus mistreated. What little motion and articulation these patients were capable of was often more harmful than no activity at all. And such ulcers were relatively impervious to treatment. The condition could not be expected to respond to treatment until the causal agent (confinement in bed) had been itself substantially or entirely removed. Thus, treatment was largely ineffective.

Occasionally a case of tetanus would come in; or Dermatology would send up its rare patient who needed full hospital care. Among the coronaries, CVA's, alcoholics, addicts, and rheumatics, pneumonia (usually lobar) was not an uncommon secondary development, even under a hospital course of treatment, after they had been sufficiently weakened by their primary complaint. All cases of infectious disease, the interns were told, were to be transferred to Contagion immediately upon confirmation of diagnosis. Contagion would then deal with them almost autonomously, though the staffs of all three services—Contagion, Medicine, and Neurology—were mostly interlocking, attendings and chiefs doubling on both floors. Among the adult Neuro cases, meningitis was the most common infectious disease they would be dealing with.

Neuro had only one case presently on the floor of such exceptional significance that it would pay them to familiarize themselves with it immediately and completely while they had the opportunity. A patient named Kronkauer whose diagnosis was syringomyelia. Neuro's chief, Dr. Samstog, would himself shortly present the case to all interns and

residents interested—of whatever service. Since they were
immediately responsible for this patient, the chief resident
suggested that it would be wise of them to attend and, oh
yes, *pay attention.*

The group broke for lunch. All except Aptshult. He went
back to his room and slept. He wasn't very hungry, but he
sure as hell *was* tired.

The one thing Rosen had been unable to tell them about
properly was Kronkauer. There was just no way to tell them,
no way to prepare them. He had to happen to you before you
could learn how you were going to adjust to him . . . You
had to spend nights on the floor and hear him . . . Talking
about it would have been futile . . . Rosen didn't know the
words that would tell them what he wanted them to know
and which they would learn soon enough just through simple
exposure . . .

Old Kronkauer, dying of syringomyelia, but not dying
fast enough to suit himself, wanted to die right away, wanted, in fact, somebody to knock him off. "Just a small over-
dose of something, Doctor. Please, Doctor." Or, "My wife,
Doctor, she can't bear the expense, all our savings are going,
what we were going to live on in our old age. If I live an
extra two or three months, what's she going to do, go to the
poorhouse? There's no one to take care of her, so, Doctor,
please, if you'd just . . ." Or, in the middle of the night,
just two words: *"Doctor! Please!"*

It was unbearable pain, which Kronkauer could bear only
because he was still alive. *Bear?* Hell, he wasn't bearing it
—he couldn't help it if he was still alive—he was suffering
it every moment. *Suffering* wasn't it either, wasn't Kronkauer's kind of pain. Kronkauer was *living* his pain.

It made no difference that through progressive neural degeneration Kronkauer had lost all physical, all sensory pain.
Kronkauer's pain was in a knowledge of what was happening to his body, what was going to happen even more rapidly
and destructively now. The pain was in this knowledge and
the horror it stimulated rather than in any sensory manifesta-
tion—for Kronkauer had long ago lost sensation, just as he
was now losing, through progressive paralysis, not only mobility, but the slightest physical articulation. Soon he would
probably not even be able to speak. His body was locking
his mind in a vegetable prison from which there was no

escape nor even any possibility of communication. Eventually the neural degeneration would affect his respiratory system and he would just stop breathing. The whole system would go. Just before his mind would. It was possibly too bad that the mind couldn't be one of the first things to go. Then there wouldn't be those two words at night, *"Doctor! Please!"*

And he—a scholarly man, though apparently unschooled in any formal sort of way—would say "Doctor, please, a little extra something. So I might live another month? This is not life, this is torture. If a man was dying at the hands of torturers and the torturers were keeping him alive just to torture him more until they tortured him to death, and there was no hope of relief, wouldn't you help him to die? Wouldn't you? Won't you?" or, exhausted, and in this far reach of pain unable even to cry, would say, "The good Lord gave us death just like He gave us all the other good medicines. Death is His pain killer. Did He withhold it from the physicians? Did He, Doctor? *Did He?"*

Lew Worship missed OB. There was nothing on Medicine that gave him a sense of fulfillment, much less happiness. Except, of course, Gloria Mead. That counted for a lot. It particularly accounted for a lot of time he spent on the ward nights when he didn't have to when Gloria had the twilight shift. But it wasn't at all the same as OB. Everything was slow and old. Nothing was ever conclusive. Nothing ever happened.

Including getting a reply to any of his applications for OB-GYN residencies. He *was* late. He knew that. But not *one* reply? Not *one* request for a personal interview? That frightened him. And, he knew, frightened him with good reason.

Pete told him, "You can always take your tour in the army. Get that over with."

"Sure," Lew had said. "Sure. And get stuck in orthopedics or ophthalmology or dermatology or some damn thing for two years. What good's *that* gonna do me?"

Pete had shrugged.

"You're damn right," Lew said. "None whatsoever." Then he half smiled. "But you know what, Pete? If I get an OB residency and get myself deferred till I finish it, then I go in *as* an OB-GYN man. They keep you on it then, see?"

"Yeah, I see."

"Well don't look so morose about it."

"It's your own goddam fault," Pete said angrily. "Not applying for *anything* till December."

"All right."

"All right, all right," Pete had mimicked. *"You* brought the cruddy situation up. Listen, you better damn well hope you've got *something* working for you. Anything. And right here at New North. Because those other places you applied are divided into two groups—the good ones, and they got filled before formal applications were even opened, and the other joints where they never even heard of half the techniques you used your first week here in OB. Jesus, some of those places you applied couldn't teach you to deliver a package."

"They were still accepting applications."

"So you better hope you've got an angle here."

"I do. Riccio."

"Yeah. And that's the most insane yet. He's enough to queer alcohol."

"He said he'd help. At least, I think he did."

"Listen, Lew. I don't want to scare you worse than you are, but you said he said it that night. *Someone'd just tried to strangle him.* If you don't think Riccio was a little off his own nut after that, just remember what he did. He came up to an intern's room for a drink. Now think that one over."

Lew was quiet for a few seconds. "I am."

"Okay. Then think over that he was thinking it over too. The next morning."

Gloria Mead reflected that this was the first time the mutually protective artificial gulf between her and patients had been removed by the powers of the hospital and, particularly, of nursing education. Since the beginning of her training she had been kept at a safe remove from patients—except for sporadic and infrequent, minutely supervised supportive care. Everything else had either been lecture, study, demonstration, or play-acting.

Essentially, this tour of regular duty just before graduation was meant to be the student's final test. For she had already been taught and tested on everything that could be taught or experienced in a learning situation. The final months were not so much *to teach* as they were *to test* in order to inform her superiors whether she was indeed eligible to be graduated and licensed as an R.N.

Gloria surprised herself by discovering that, except for having to adapt to the specific routines of the ward and the specific conditions of the patients, she was far better prepared to fulfill the requirements of her profession than she had known.

It was only that one patient, Kronkauer, who still, at times, was able to make her feel both vulnerable and inadequate.

88

The window behind Dr. Tyssen's desk faced an airshaft, and Dr. Tyssen had never done anything about it. When he'd taken over the office the blinds had been up and he'd left them that way ever since.

He was a thin, gray-faced man, the face, in spite of its grayness, giving the appearance of being not only smooth in spite of age, but powdered, in spite of the grayness. The desk and chair, being of normal proportions, were much too big for him, and he compensated for this by sitting very stiff and erect and so uncomfortably that Worship found it impossible to sit comfortably in his own chair while this stiff, gray discomfort sat in his view.

In contrast to Dr. Tyssen, Dr. Granchard—over to one side—sat, loose, *sprawled* in fact, sideways, one leg over the arm of his chair, the other leg balanced perfectly on its heel on the floor. An arm hung down loosely, its hand loosely holding a cigarette, the cigarette within a few centimeters of scorching the floor.

Dr. Tyssen nodded almost motionlessly at Lew and said, "We're quite impressed that you were able to enlist the aid of Dr. Riccio in your behalf."

Lew felt his body give an involuntary start the way it did sometimes when he was almost asleep. He swallowed, equally involuntarily, and had almost gotten himself to say something—what, he had no idea—when Granchard said, "Impressed isn't half the word."

Dr. Tyssen looked at Granchard in a way that failed, on

purpose, to see him. Granchard seemed unaffected. "Some going, Worship," he went on.

Dr. Tyssen said, "Did you think that Dr. Riccio possessed enough influence in OB-GYN to gain you one of our residencies?"

Lew said—watching Tyssen and unable to find a position in his chair that was even remotely comfortable—"No, sir . . . that is . . . No."

"What then?"

"I thought . . . well, Dr. Riccio being on the staff and all . . . I thought his saying something might counterbalance my making the application so late."

"And might make us consider taking someone from the intern staff? Against policy?"

"Yes, I guess so. I guess I thought that."

"Did you know that Dr. Granchard was accepted from our intern staff?"

"No, no I didn't." Moving only his eyes, he looked at Granchard—involuntarily, and trying not to even as he did it. Granchard was grinning at him quizzically. As if, perhaps, he were in a cage in a zoo and Granchard was a Sunday stroller.

"As I believe I mentioned to you before," Dr. Tyssen said, "you don't seem to have looked into the matter very thoroughly."

"I know I want OB-GYN," Lew said defensively.

"That, Doctor, is apparent from your application." Dr. Tyssen's eyebrows seemed to raise themselves of their own accord and remain there to think things over and decide what to do next. "If I may say so, Dr. Worship, should you ever wish to supplement your medical income, you might do very well to look into the market for purple prose. You have an unmistakable talent." The eyebrows remained effortlessly suspended rather high above their usual position.

"People tell me I'm sometimes pretty emotional."

The eyebrows came down.

"Sometimes pretty sharp, too," Granchard said, grinning.

"I hope you appreciate," Dr. Tyssen said, "that our decision was made purely upon the basis of your scholastic and internship records. It would be unfortunate for everyone involved, and particularly for our future relations, if you felt you had received the residency due to influence rather than qualification."

Lew thought, I'm supposed to say something.

Granchard said, "Of course, fortunately for you, you also played your other cards right, too. Though they're only important if you *don't* play them right."

"Poor cards," Dr. Tyssen said. "Dr. Riccio almost left the office when he realized I didn't know him and he had to introduce himself . . . But we decided, upon Dr. *Granchard's* recommendation, to make an exception in your case."

Lew thought, I'm supposed to say something.

"One break," Granchard said. "For *you,* anyway. I'll be gone and Yuky'll be chief next year."

"I'd like to point out now before you make your decision," Dr. Tyssen said, "that when we *do* appoint a resident from among our own interns, we are doubly jealous of his professional conduct. You will receive no favor."

"Exactly the opposite," Granchard said. "I know. Believe me."

"I don't know," Dr. Tyssen went on, "how ambitious you are, or if you are. But, regarding whatever ambitions you may be nurturing, I would also like to point out that it is extremely unlikely that a former intern here will make chief."

"I know," Granchard said, "believe me."

"Dr. Granchard made it by exhibiting the unique ability to be everywhere at once. Well, Dr. Worship? Or would you like time to think it over?"

"Yes," Lew said. "I mean, yes, I accept."

Dr. Tyssen nodded, almost motionlessly. "You must realize that your appointment is unofficial and will remain so until the proper time—and that your acceptance in no way binds us should we find any cause in your conduct, professional or personal, to make us reconsider."

"I understand," Lew said. "And thank you." He got up and shook Dr. Tyssen's hand, and then, embarrassed, faltered an instant, so that Granchard gave him the stroller-in-the-zoo grin again, and then almost broke his hand for him.

They went out together. In the corridor, Granchard shook his head and said, "You're a *lucky* sonofabitch, Worship. But really."

"I know."

"I wonder if you do . . . I really do."

"I think I do."

Granchard shook his head. "If you did, you'd be out cold now." They walked down the corridor. Where they were about to go in different directions, Granchard said, "Word of advice?"

Lew nodded. "Sure."

Granchard wasn't smiling, wasn't being sarcastic. "Conduct yourself like if you jiggled you'd get a red-hot poker up your ass."

89

De Traunant had drawn Female Medicine, and being fresh up from GYN was maniacally and stubbornly in favor of the vaginal rather than rectal routine examination. His chief resident was equally stubborn and confirmed in his opposition to de Traunant and the vaginal approach. But stubborn and confused as he was, the C.R. was the weaker of the two opponents in that he found it as exhausting to talk *at* de Traunant as it was to listen to him. Finally he relented— from fatigue. "Just *once*, de Traunant. Just so you can't ever claim my mind is closed to the, ah, more progressive aspects of the profession."

"Just wait and see, man."

"Yeah. Well. New arrival just up from Admitting." He flipped open the metal chart holder. "Might help if you knew something about her. Thirty-one-year-old white female; married, no children, lives with husband; chief complaint, abdominal pains and anorexia of three days duration, in no acute distress . . . no vomiting . . . ah . . . rule out appendicitis, appendix removed May two years ago by Dr. Duane . . . ah . . . ah, note: part time hooker and full time D.A."

"What's she on?"

"Yeah. Ah. H."

"Long?"

"Doesn't say. Maybe you're interested in her name, too?" De Traunant cringed. "Yeah."

"Mrs. Cooper Watkins. Stella."

"Christ, why are all these hookers D.A.'s, or vice versa?"

"It's vice versa. For the money to support the addiction. This one was in an institution eight months ago, came out supposedly cured. Which is exactly when the pusher hits them. He hangs around and offers it to 'em free until they finally take him up for one reason or another. Then they're hooked again—or else he keeps 'em on it *free* till they're hooked again. Then they start looking around for money cause it stops being free. The easiest way for a man is just to take someone else's money or property by force. The easiest way for a woman is on her back. So she starts hustling . . . Ah . . . when they're in the ward and can't get the stuff, we feed 'em up a little on Thorazine."

"Thorazine?"

"It's an ataraxic."

"And it works with an addict? It calms him enough so he doesn't . . ."

"For a while. We can't give 'em too much. But it calms 'em a little, even with the dose *we* give. And it's pretty effective against depression . . . ah . . . Well, shall we see the patient?"

They went to her bed. "Just the usual examination, Stella," the C.R. said.

"What, hey, *again?*"

"You want us to fix you up, don't you?" de Traunant said.

"Yeah, hey. But for chrisake I wanna get some *rest* too like. Dig?"

"Cool," de Traunant said.

Stella started slightly and then smiled. "Cray-*zee!*"

"Yeah, hey," de Traunant said. He and the C.R. pulled closed the curtain that hung on an aluminum tube above and around the bed.

"Like we're gonna have an orgy, hunh?" Stella said.

"Like pull up the drapery and assume the position like," de Traunant said, rather disinterested in his own phraseology except to assist him with the patient.

"*Crazy,*" Stella said. De Traunant put on a glove while the C.R. prepped her with PhisoHex. Stella got the idea immediately. "What're you, a *fingersmith?*" she said cordially.

De Traunant explored with one hand introduced into the vagina and the other palpating the abdomen outside. "This hurt?"

"Like negative."

"Now?"

"Same."

"This?"

"Like you just are not making it, fellow."

"Now?" But he stopped. "Hey," he said. He began slowly withdrawing his hand from the vagina.

"Ayuh, *what's up, Doc?*" Stella said, and began roaring laughter at them.

De Traunant held a small wad in the fingers of his gloved hand. His fingers began working at it. He held it up. The wad had become a twenty-dollar bill.

Stella stopped laughing. But she grinned at him. "I see you've found my secret hiding place."

"Jesus," de Traunant said.

"Only place my husband wouldn't look."

"*Yeah?*" de Traunant said disbelievingly. "I'd think it'd be the first place he'd find it."

"That's all you know. But thanks for the thought."

De Traunant went back to his examination. Eventually he found what might or might not—according to how the tests they would run checked out—be the beginning of what might be a malignancy, or, more likely, an ovarian cyst.

The C.R. nodded. "Okay, so it's practical. I'm not so sure it's efficient." He pulled the curtain open part way. "Write it up," he said and walked away.

De Traunant got rid of the glove and began to reopen the curtain completely.

"Hey, no, wait," Stella said. "Like let's talk a minute. Hey?"

"Yeah?" de Traunant said, turning back.

She sat up and smiled at him and demonstrated her breasts through the hospital-issue, cotton nightshirt. "Like you're pretty cute," she said. "I mean like we could make it together sometime—dig?"

"Crazy," de Traunant said, and started to turn away.

"No, hey. Listen. This is for real, like maximum. You and that crazy white suit, I flip, I really do . . . Now, hey, like you've inspected the merchandise—anyway," she said, pointing her breasts at him even more dramatically, "the *business* end—you could maybe inspect the rest of it at your leisure? I mean like because we could make it to outer space and back. No re-entry problem."

De Traunant smiled and shook his head.

"No, hey. Really, I'm great . . ."

De Traunant laughed. "I'm sure you are."

"Sure I am, I wouldn't lie about it. You don't think I'd lie about it, do you?" she said, almost horrified by the idea.

"Never entered my mind."

She hunched forward in the bed, though she was careful to

keep her arms away from hiding her breasts. "I mean, I could even teach a doctor a few tricks. Anyway, hey, like I wouldn't do it for money with you, because you really you do, but, hey, maybe you could bring me a present? You know, just once in a while—something that didn't cost you anything? Something you could just sort of pick up around here, maybe? Dig?"

"Yeah. But it's not cool like. Dig? Now you get some of that rest you were complaining about not getting."

"Aren't you even gonna *up stethoscope?*"

He pushed the curtain back.

"I hope your goddam nose cone falls off!" she yelled after him.

The C.R. laughed. "Was it gonna be for free or did she want a little present?"

"How the hell did you know?"

"I could've told you before we ever saw her. What the hell, were you *asleep* down on GYN? Or did you have halitosis that month?"

"That was always free stuff."

"Yeah. GYN gets all the breaks. Ever accept?"

"Hell, no." De Traunant got a kind of ethereal look on his face. "But it's always nice to just get the proposition, anyway. It's always *interesting.*"

"Yeah. Ah . . . sort of keeps your hand in." He looked at de Traunant's lack of appreciation. "Ah. Well. My wife doesn't think I have a sense of humor either."

"She's right."

"Yeah. Ah. Well. Anyway, where'd you pick up that nutty jazz talk?"

"Nurses," de Traunant said. "My environment is otherwise very limited."

90

Dr. Samstog, New North's Neurology chief, sat next to the bed of his many years' patient, Kronkauer. Across the room, and somewhat further away from the bed (out of, Samstog thought, respect for his professional presence), Emma Kronkauer sat on a straight-backed chair, her hands carefully folded on a lap incongruously flowered by the depressingly dark floral design of her dress. Her face, Samstog had discovered, which in the last few months had seemed to become immutable, was not, in fact, immutable at all. It had just *ceased responding*—quite as if, Samstog thought, there were nothing to respond *to*. He imagined a second-generation Calvinist—back when the movement was new—as looking the way Emma now looked.

He turned away from her. Kronkauer had said something. "Sorry," Samstog said, *"what?"*

"Are you a religious man, Doctor?"

"I believe in God . . ."

"A particular kind of God?"

"No, no . . ." Being with Kronkauer was always somewhat unnerving, he'd found. Something challenging about the man. He would not leave the doctor-patient relationship alone. He was always worrying it He somehow seemed to expect and to demand that his doctor be responsible to him as a human being without professional status or duty. "I've seen too many of the ills of the world, I suspect, to be able to hold to any single set of religious beliefs." He looked at Kronkauer, wondering whether this was just one of those questions Kronkauer asked occasionally with no further point than to note the answer for himself, or whether he had best prepare for a lengthy personal challenge of some sort. He could not tell from Kronkauer's face. But because he was looking at the face so carefully, he again became conscious of one of Kronkauer's symptoms—nystagmus, an involuntary and rapid movement, or better, "flutter," of the eyeball. It was symptomatic of the disease in its final phase. Definitely terminal. And, in this case, now pursuing an extremely rapid course. A matter of weeks.

Samstog decided to be patient even if Kronkauer wanted a long conversation. If he survived his disease for two or three more weeks, he would not be able to talk at all. Or *move* at all. He would be as close to thorough vegetable existence as consciousness could get. Even the eyeball would cease to flutter. And even now and even in that very eyeball which was so madly active, Samstog believed he could see Horner's syndrome beginning to exhibit itself—a sinking in of the eyeball; ptosis, a sort of drooping or dragging of the upper lid, and a slight elevation of the lower lid, and a constriction of the pupil itself. He had long ago noted anhidrosis asserting itself. The man seemed now to sweat as little as a body in the morgue.

Kronkauer seemed to be considering something. Samstog waited and continued to be suddenly and acutely conscious of the symptoms in Kronkauer's face. He had noted long ago a condition of corneal areflexia. Now he saw it again, much as if he had not seen it before. An almost complete lack of reflexes in the cornea. When he had first determined corneal areflexia, he had waited. After all, no need to jump to conclusions. But then other bulbar symptoms had exhibited themselves so rapidly, the disease had been working so fast and upon such a furious, determined course, that it was obvious that Kronkauer had ineluctably entered the last phase of the disease. Incurable, unavoidably terminal.

Had it been syringomyelia alone, Samstog might very well have insisted that Kronkauer remain in his home. After all, the hospital was jealous of its statistics, of the incidence of fatalities that occurred on its premises. And, after all, Kronkauer could, up until the very last, be adequately attended by Emma. There was so little *to* do. But with the onset of the bulbar symptoms—indicating that the disease had extended itself from the spinal column up into the medulla, the brain itself—Samstog had had to accept how late it already was. For it was no longer syringomyelia moving persistently but slowly, it was also syringobulbia moving swiftly and rapidly establishing bulbous inflammations in the brain itself. Swiftly, rapidly, *and* lethally. Terminally. So Samstog had moved Kronkauer to the hospital, and damn the statistics. No one had liked it. There was nothing to be done, so why not leave him at home, why add a fatality that was unavoidable anyway to the hospital's statistics? Samstog was not sure why. But at the very least, the intern and resident staff would have a chance to examine and become familiar with a disease they might not otherwise ever see until one out of possibly the whole group someday suddenly had to deal with it himself. And then, of course, the hospital *did* have facilities to make things a *little* more comfortable for the patient than he would have been at home. A simple thing like dealing with decubitus ulcers. The unavoidable bed sores of a patient in this condition, suffering continual pressure as he lay in bed hour after hour, day after day, week upon week. The hospital, at least, if it could not pursue its primary function of treating and curing the disease, could at least treat and at least relieve (to some extent) the patient's pain—which was the hospital's, *and the doctor's,* second immediate function. So, for the bed sores, to prevent or at least slow their development, and to soothe those already established, the hospital could provide (which the home could not), and had provided, a water bed—a rubber sheath inflated with water which was used as a mattress. A little thing; but it was something of an excuse to himself for having admitted Kronkauer when he might just as easily have left him home. The inter-resident exposure was the excuse he had used for the hospital—not for himself—for he had a difficult time assigning a patient, any patient, the singular and limited role of merely being a study case.

Kronkauer began talking again. One of his vocal cords had already become paralyzed, giving the curious impression, if one closed one's eyes, that the voice ·was that of a creature from outer space as presented in science-fiction movies. The paralysis was still another sign of the extent that syringo-*bulbia* had established itself. A week, two weeks—then the other cord would probably be similarly paralyzed.

Kronkauer said, "But you do believe in *a* God, yes, Doctor?"

Samstog nodded. Then he could not tell whether this intelligence pleased or displeased Kronkauer.

"You believe in *interpreting* God's law? What we know of it?"

"As best we can, yes."

"Ah." Again Samstog could not tell whether Kronkauer was pleased or displeased. Kronkauer went on. "St. Thomas More. You know his work perhaps?"

"*Utopia* only."

"Ahhh." Kronkauer was finding it more and more difficult to get his words out. Samstog had half a mind to stop him from trying and make him rest. But then he remembered that it would make no difference anyway. "Here. I wish you to read something, my friend. You have perhaps read it before . . ."

Kronkauer handed Samstog a book. But he did not *hand* it to him; he *managed* it from where it had been lying next to him.

"You will excuse me. Open it please where I have marked. Read where the pencil lines are, yes?"

Samstog took the book and continued to observe Kronkauer's symptoms. He stayed himself and looked down to the book now in his own lap. He opened it and read as he had been told to.

Kronkauer interrupted. "He was, at that time, *Sir* Thomas More."

Samstog looked up, but Kronkauer had shifted his attention to a window. He looked back at the underlined words. It was a fragment, a detail, of More's vision of the utopian society:

> . . . *But if the disease be not only incurable, but also full of continual pain and anguish, then the priests and magistrate exhort the man, seeing he is not able to do any duty of life and by overliving his own life is noisome and irksome to others and grievous to himself, that he will determine with himself no longer to cherish the pestilent and painful disease. And seeing that his life is to him but a torment, that he will not be unwilling to die, but rather take a good hope to him, and either dispatch himself out of that painful life, as out of a prison or rack of torment, or else suffer himself willingly to be rid out of it by others.*
>
> *And in so doing they (the priests and magistrates) tell him he shall do wisely, seeing by his death he shall lose no happiness, but end his torture . . . They that be thus convinced finish their lives willingly, either by fasting, or else they are released by an opiate in their sleep without any feeling of death . . .*

Samstog closed the book, but left it on his lap.

Kronkauer said, "You will remember, please, that More was a Catholic and that Catholics are very critical in this area."

"Yes," said Samstog, the weight of the book on his thighs like lead ballast. "But . . ."

"His recommendation was most specific, was it not? Excuse me, but he was most careful in his recommendation."

"*Torment and torture . . .*" Samstog said. "I believe you followed some such line of reasoning with one of our interns. I remember because the line of argument stays in one's mind. 'If you knew a man was being tortured to death and his torturers were keeping him alive just to torture him more, and there was no hope of relief, wouldn't you help him to escape his torturers with death?' Wasn't that it?"

"Yes."

"Allusions to Thomas More or not, do you realize you were asking a young man to sacrifice his *own* life in your behalf? The time and study he has given when he could have been otherwise spending his youth more according to its natural desires? You ask him to sacrifice his professional career—the time he has given to it, the time *others* have given to it, the assistance he could give others in the future. Not to mention the personal, individual risk of jail. Or, Kronkauer, even death. *Did* you realize that, *at the time?*"

"Excuse me. It was not necessary that anyone discover him. This happens."

Samstog stared at him, *his own* line of argument somehow inappropriately deprived of its applicability. He found himself in the inglorious position of not knowing what to say when something had to be said.

Kronkauer nodded at him.

Samstog found, if not an answer, a partial escape. He turned to Kronkauer's wife. "And what do you say, Emma?"

"I have thought. Yes. Thought very much. There is nothing to say."

Her face had offered no expression, had changed not at all, had offered him nothing of what she felt, if she was now feeling anything at all.

Kronkauer said, "In the Bible there are six or seven suicides. All without condemnation."

"I wouldn't know, precisely," Samstog said. "At any rate, even before the law, suicide is not considered murder, or dealt with as such. Nor in the Bible."

"Ah, *yes,*" Kronkauer said. It was the first eagerness Samstog had seen in Kronkauer since Kronkauer had launched the conversation. "Ah *yes.* The sixth commandment. You refer to that, yes?"

"I'm not familiar with the number."

"Excuse me please, but it is the sixth commandment."

"Thou shalt not kill," Samstog said.

"The sixth commandment, yes. But you must understand, Doctor, it is a *mis*translation. The Greek and the Hebrew agree with each other in reading, 'Thou shalt not *murder.*' Murder is the word, yes? And you see the point, Doctor? The Greek and the Hebrew give us our original Biblical text."

Samstog found it difficult to counter an argument which he found primarily difficult to admit, much less answer. And yet,

to himself, he could only agree that the social and religious
and professional ethic was largely based upon this very point.
And yet again, he could not admit to argument so tenuous
and amorphous and insubstantial a basis for decision or belief as he considered the Bible. He could believe. But not in
words. He could accept an ethic. But not upon such a basis.
His beliefs had always been held by faith, and merely *rein-
forced* by logic and reason. Yet here the faith was being
left intact while the interpretation of its ethical tradition was
being challenged; challenged by a logic and reason that
would embrace its own interpretation in a matter of life and
death.

Samstog did not wish to argue. He desired only to withdraw. Without having to accept or reject either alternative.

Kronkauer seemed to interpret his silence as attendance
upon further detail, for he further offered, "The mistransla-
tion of the Greek to *murder* to the Latin *to kill* is I think
attributed to St. Augustine in the fourth century A.D." He
looked questioningly at Samstog for a reply, and, receiving
none, offered further substantiation for his implication. "You
see, Doctor, I have read that the word *murder* implies malice
as a forethought. In fact, excuse me, but it is my understanding that our laws demand that condition, *malice aforethought,*
before . . . excuse me, the phrase? . . . before they '*allow*
of murder?' "

Samstog found himself troubled by his fascination with
what Kronkauer was saying—and did not know why, except
that others must surely have been equally impressed. *Or
would be.*

"What of *mercy* aforethought, Doctor? Yes? Not malice,
mercy aforethought. You see?"

Kronkauer looked at him so directly, in spite of the exhibi-
tion of symptoms, that Samstog, for lack of anything else he
could think of to do, nodded back.

"Fifth Matthew. Yes? You are familiar? '*Blessed are the
merciful, for they shall obtain mercy.*'"

Samstog looked quickly at Emma. Her face still refused
to, or *could* not, respond. Yet she *knew* what they were talking about. "*Mercy killing* is the phrase you want, isn't it?"
Samstog finally managed.

"You are able to give mercy, Doctor."

"And take away a life, I remind you."

"Only *murder* is prohibited. Malice, yes?" He had to allow

himself to breathe and rest. Samstog waited. Then, "Doctor, mercy is *blessed*."

Samstog went to the window. It was not to consider what Kronkauer said. It was because he could no longer bring himself to look at his patient. It was the patient he found himself suddenly having to avoid—not the symptoms.

A dull day. Gray and septic. January and warm enough to make you sweat in an overcoat and cold enough to freeze the sweat if you took it off. The river, two blocks away, black and listless under an overcast sky. The streets in between mired with slush, the tenement roofs dulled and blackened with tar and lack of light. He looked for something moving on the river. A tug or a scow. But nothing moved. One of the Sanitation Department's purification and disposal plants was three blocks north, its long gray concrete sluices projecting into the river. But nothing moved there either.

"Mercy is blessed."

It was Emma's voice. Samstog turned from the window. "Then I must apologize. I no longer know what constitutes mercy."

The queer, volumeless high pitch of Kronkauer's voice darted at him, "Excuse me, you are arrested for not killing an animal in pain, why then—yes?—for helping to assist a suffering human being from the—yes?—*torment* of his life is it prohibited—yes?—and punished by law?"

Kronkauer was speaking so desperately—desperate for both the proper words and the energy with which to speak them—that Samstog felt himself amazed. "I am not here to argue the justification or legality or logic of the law with you. I do not intend to debate euthanasia with you. Or its legal aspects."

"Excuse me. But you have been."

Samstog was not listening. He had thought of Kronkauer's voice as being *queer*. He was thinking about that. He had lost his clinical objectivity. At any rate, he seemed to himself to be losing it. A word like *queer*. Descriptive. But not objective. How had it crept into his consideration of a *patient*? How had he allowed it to? Or how had it suggested itself? and he accepted it?

"You must relieve pain. Yes, Doctor?"

He was tempted to say, *If I can*. And though he believed it, he saw the trap it sprung on him and said nothing.

"Yes, Doctor. Excuse me, but yes. If you can not cure a

disease, you treat it. I know this. And if you can not deal with this disease, you can at least, yes? deal with the pain it causes, yes? I know this too. I have been under medical care for fourteen years, and I have *not* misunderstood what I have seen and heard, what it is to be a doctor, what it is that a doctor attempts as his responsibility. *No!* This I understand! We do not play *games* with each other, my fine Dr. Samstog!" He rested himself. Slowly, and then with increasing speed and effort and volume, he said, "When you can *not* cure disease, you are o-*bliged* to treat the suffering it causes. You are o-*bliged*," he said, furiously, "to *attempt* to cure pain. We argue now only about the *extent*, Dr. Samstog!"

"I am obliged to attempt to keep you alive. You understand that?"

"Against my wish? *Hah!* but we will forget that for now. You are obliged to keep me alive? When you operate, you are obliged before you operate to keep the patient alive?"

"All right, Kronkauer. But that is a calculated risk."

"When the patient will die anyway soon?"

"The patient wants to live. I am attempting to help him to do so," Samstog said, beginning to become angry.

"*Ah!* the *patient's* wish. I may decide to live. But I may not decide to die."

"That," Samstog said, still angry, "is essentially it."

"It is vain of you."

Samstog had become so angry that he refused to allow himself to answer.

"You are *not* God."

Samstog stood up and went to the window again. The man had turned and reversed the entire argument full circle. *And* had defiled his professional . . . Samstog started. His professional *what?*

Why was he getting so angry. He did not, after all, deny the man's stand *prima facie*. Did he? Or *a priori?* Or *empirically?* Or *ad hominem;* or any goddam way.

"If my life is my own, Doctor, is not my death my own? It is a very personal thing."

Samstog turned back, tired and sorry. "Granted, granted." He looked at his patient. He now had to *stare* to hear, for, alone, his ears could no longer distinguish words or make them intelligible, so completely had the volume of Kronkauer's voice subsided.

The words were said with acute difficulty: "The good

Lord gave us death just like He gave us all the other good medicines, yes? Death is His pain killer. Did He withhold it from the physicians? Did He, Doctor? *Did He?*"

Samstog got up. He had no answer. No answer he could give without commitment. Instead, he said, "You said that to interns also, I believe?"

Kronkauer managed to say swiftly and with all the volume available to him, *"No!* that does *not* affect its validity."

"I'll look in tomorrow."

Silence. Then, with difficulty, "I am not a beggar, Doctor, please. I say what is in my heart . . . *and mind.*"

"Yes," said Samstog, and nodded to Emma, and left the single-bed room. Walking down the corridor away from the room to the nurses' station where he would complete his orders for the day, he had a thought which he classified as hysterical. Syringomyelia was, in medical parlance, a *silent disease*—that is, an insidious and progressive disease which did not disclose itself until it was unchallengeably established and which caused no acute distress; at least, not distress in the sense of severe physical pain. He felt it to be a hysterical thought because, if the disease was supposed to be so silent, how did one account for Kronkauer?

91

"I don't understand any of them," Lew said. "You should've heard the talk I had with Pete the other day."

"What about?" Gloria said, wooshing a pair of stockings around in a basin full of suds.

"That's just it," Lew said. "I don't know." He watched her rinse the stockings, ball them up and squeeze them dry, and hang them on the towel rack over the bathtub. Didi had lent them her apartment for the night. "I really don't understand *any* of them any more. Like with Kronkauer. He's not human to them. He's a threat, or something that upsets them or disgusts them or interests them . . . he's a case history, or an orator, or something they look at like it's on a slide . . . He's anything but a human being to them."

Gloria's head moved slightly to one side. "You don't feel that way, do you?"

"That's it too. I don't know. Kronkauer even scares me

. . . because I see what the others are like with him and I think maybe I'm getting that way too."

"He's a poor old man, darling. You should feel sorry for him."

"I don't *want* to feel *sorry for him*. I'm not a doctor so I can feel *sorry* for people. And you're not a nurse, either."

"Not yet," she said sarcastically.

"I meant, not a nurse *in order* to feel sorry for him."

"I can't help it. *Lew* . . ." she lowered her voice. "You don't have to be callous to me to prove to yourself you're callous to him."

"I'm *not* callous."

"All right. *Immune*. Is immune all right?"

"What?" She'd gone back to the bedroom. He followed her. "I'm sorry. But see? See what I mean?"

"I see."

"You can turn around when you talk to me."

She did. "I thought *I* was the one who was supposed to be so sensitive."

"You are," he said, and kissed her. "That's why you chose me."

She smiled. "Lew, darling, don't *you* be so serious; you have such a difficult time at it."

"I have another one for you. *Pass the gas*. That's what they tell you to do on anesthesia." She smiled. It was part of his campaign to get her to have a little sense of humor about her work—all the slang phrases, *heat sheet* for temperature report, *chart cart* . . .

"Good," she said. "You've gotten entirely too serious lately."

"Me," he said. It was not a question. "I thought you said the one real advantage we have over other intern-nurse couples is we have our feet on the ground."

"*On* the ground, darling, not *stuck* in it."

Since he'd been with her, Lew had found himself, every instant, *acutely aware*. It had made him more serious, more demanding of himself. And more fearful. Because, though he wanted to love, he was fearful—since hearing Otis' story—of what love might require. And receive. Require and receive justly in love's terms, but not in the world's.

He said, and could not wonder why, "Are you going to practice—as a nurse?"

She was surprised. "I am."

"Even when we're married?"

"Unless you don't want me to. But I *want* to, darling. At least until we start having children."

"When will that be?"

"Whenever you stop prescribing prophylaxis."

"Not funny," he said.

"Well then that makes two of us."

"*Gloria* . . ."

"Lew, you're not being sensible about anything."

"I never was."

"Well you aren't now."

That seemed to close the conversation. Except that, he felt, they had been discussing Kronkauer, and had not evaded any issue, but abjured the man himself. Yet Kronkauer refused to be abjured. He insisted on being killed or nothing. Lew laughed.

"What?" Gloria said.

"Nothing."

"It didn't sound like it."

"It wasn't."

"Are we going to start again?"

He shook his head. How could a man who existed really not at all have so much reality? Whenever Lew thought of him he could see the old man studying him. He saw that studying look whenever he wasn't purposely thinking of something else.

"Will you help me with that new antibiotics table now?" she said.

"You don't have to know that kind of stuff."

"I do for me."

"No you don't. It's not required of you. It's not even your province. It never will be. You don't have to do it."

"I do for me," she said angrily. "Will you help me or not?"

"All right."

She brought it over and began asking questions.

92

Otis kissed the girl and raised himself on one elbow and got his glass and drank some ginger ale. She sat up and sipped her Scotch and soda. "I don't understand why you don't take to drink," she said.

"In time, in time," he said. "Give me time."

"The inquiry's over. They couldn't *prove* anything." She sipped again and studied him. "If you were going to go in for real drinking at all, I'd've thought you'd've done it then."

"Because they couldn't find a fetus in the wastebasket?" She slapped him.

He held her hand that was not holding the drink. ". . . or bloodstained instruments or instruments at all or somebody to testify?" He had to struggle to hold with one hand even the single free arm. "Don't talk to me about drink, honey. We're both just *lucky* there're strong rules of evidence in this state's courts."

"I've heard it before," she said, going back to her drink and relaxing her arm and drawing it free. "I still don't know why you haven't started hitting the bottle like any normal human being."

"I told you, *in time*, my darling mistress. In time. Right now there are other things on my mind."

She put her glass down. "I do love you, darling," she said, turning back to him. She was still sitting up, unclothed, the sheet just touching her belly.

"Yes," he said. "So do we all." He had not yet been able to make love to her.

93

The weather remained gray, still, and muggy. The atmosphere of limbo. A chill hung threateningly in the air. Not enough to make an overcoat comfortable; but quite enough to engender every kind of uncomfortable cold among numerous outpatients who came for relief to Medicine's clinic, overloaded it, and worked the staff to the point where some of them became weakened and weary enough to contract colds themselves—thereby occasioning their mandatory suspension from duty, lest they infect others, either patients or staff. Given the weather, relief from duty, relief thus from activity, was unbearable; and in turn occasioned both depression and restlessness, leaving the victim unable to concentrate on anything, but desperate to be *at* something. De Traunant came down with mononucleosis—"the disease of doctors, nurses, and students"—and had to be removed to De Witt's Contagion ward to wait out at least six weeks' worth of rest and antibiotics. The atmosphere (day after day gray, still, and muggy) seemed to suspend time, and even *will*, and finally succeeded in dissipating even anticipation of some sort of change. The lack of will itself became an atmosphere. Limbo.

94

Donnecker thought he saw the Aptshult pattern repeating itself. He had made the mistake of telling Jim his worries about Mildred. It had been a mistake because Jim had told him in detail what had happened with *him* and *his* wife. And Donnecker now caught glimpses (*or thought* he caught glimpses and so worried about just being ready to think it) of the same details marking his relationship with Mildred.

When he had been on TB, there had been in the children's ward, a three-year-old female Mongolian idiot. As was symptomatic, her ligaments were entirely relaxed: they displayed no tension at all. Her foot could be bent—entirely painlessly —up and back so that the instep touched the shin. She remained staring hopelessly wherever her eyes were focused.

He felt that he was being bent thus—painlessly, and almost unaware of it. He felt that no matter how he tried to manage differently, his eyes remained staring hopelessly somewhere that had no relationship to where he was, and where Mildred was. Where they were together.

Was it the circumstances of internship? What the hell, Jay and Lois Fishbein had worked it out—with a far more difficult problem to meet. Was it him? Why could he do nothing? *That* seemed to be his problem *both* at home and at the hospital. No opportunity to *do* anything.

95

Parelli slammed the textbook closed. He knew for a fact that the chapter he was reading was completely out of date. He said, "The trouble with these God damn things is, by the time they can revise them, the *revisions* are out of date." He had been talking aloud to no one. He was used to commenting to his roommate. Not that his roommate had been around much. But when he had been there, Parelli had used him to absorb similar comments. His roommate had been John Paul Otis. The bed was now covered with a dust sheet, only a bare mattress under it. One closet was empty, several shelves, and half the medicine chest over the basin in the corner. A bureau and a chair had been taken out. Parelli thought, Too bad they couldn't get anything on the sonofabitch! Even if Otis had been his own roommate.

Disgustedly, he threw the book on the unused bed. The book made a difference. He studied it. Its presence on the otherwise untouched cot made the room seem less unoccupied. He tossed some more books on. The effect was stupendous. There no longer seemed to be a no-man's-land on one side of the room.

What the hell, *what difference?* It wasn't *Otis,* or *Otis'* absence. It was Cynthia James and *hers.* What had he told Alicia? "There has been a general disenchantment on Cynthia's part that closely approximates anesthesia." That just about described it. Even if Lee *had* said Cynthia had been badly depressed New Year's Eve. Well, *he* hadn't been in such a hot condition either. Especially since the whole point of the thing had gone bust when he hadn't been able to throw himself in with Flynn. So if Cynthia was unhappy enough to cry all New Year's Eve *and* neck with everyone around (it made him angry, of course, but he wasn't fool enough to mistake it for anything but what it was—the same thing as the crying), all she had to do was pick up a phone. After all, *she* was the one who had stopped talking to *him.*

And all this angry thinking about it was just an excuse not to let himself realize he loved her. *Jesus Christ,* he thought. Why the hell do I have to suffer from insight into myself?

96

They were drinking beer in Aptshult's room. Even Jane Petschek, Male Medicine A's head nurse, had been gathered into the impromptu staff conference.

Mercouris: "That type just takes up bed space."

Van Wyck: "You know what he said to me today. He said, 'God is Someone you have only when you do not need Him. That is the single circumstance in which He has meaning.'"

Walters: "The old boy's got a brain all right."

Rosconovitch: "I'd hate to have a brain like that when it gets locked up in the dark."

Van Wyck, nodding: "Yeah. *Oh holy Jesus,* yeah."

Petschek: "I try to see him as little as possible."

Worship: "I'll tell you one thing, I have to *force* myself *to.*"

Mead: "He certainly is an *amazing* old man. But I can't look at him when I think what's going to happen to him."

Sprague: "That wife of his. She gives me the willies. You know, she half propositioned me to knock him off last week? Not in so many words, of course. But it was all there."

Parelli: "Yeah. Me too. She can't face his being unable to face it."

Liu: "Could you? In her position?"

Parelli: "God knows."

Donnecker: "I *know* I couldn't. I think I damn near crack as it is. He's had so God damn many years to *think* about it, knowing *exactly* what was coming. And it's not something you can get used to by familiarity."

Liu: "The more familiar you got with *that,* the more terrifying it would get."

Aptshult: "It's unusual. Most medical suicides come pretty soon after the diagnosis. This one waited all these years. I guess he managed to wait because he figured he could let himself out before the vegetable business."

Rosconovitch: "Or *get* himself let out."

Aptshult: "You blame him?"

Rosconovitch: "I wish I had the guts to help him."

Van Wyck: "Amen to that."

Parelli: "It sure would be the end if you got caught."

Van Wyck: "I want him to get out of it, all right. I just don't know whether I have the moral right to complete the decision for him."

Donnecker: "Maybe you're confusing worrying about *moral right* with just not having the guts to follow your conviction. *I* sure wonder about that."

Liu: "Maybe everybody does."

Rosconovitch: "Agreed."

Sprague: "Did you ever see a monster delivered? I mean a *true* monster. I saw one once. With a single mongoloid kind of head and a single trunk and duplication of all the limbs. The head was about twice as big as normal. The guy who delivered just neglected to resuscitate."

Liu: "That's not the same thing. It wasn't alive yet. And it couldn't properly be called a human being with a life. He didn't take a life away, he failed to start one."

Sprague: "Well, as you say, it wasn't a real life, anyway. It was medically and legally a monster."

The telephone rang.

Aptshult: "Yeah, he's here. Hold on. Pete . . ."

Van Wyck: "Hello, van Wyck . . . Yeah . . . Yeah . . . *Jesuschrist,* is *that* all? . . . Well give him some pheno and write it up. I'll sign and cover you in the morning . . . Yeah. Thanks." He hung up. "Jesus Christ. Mr. Protopo can't get to sleep. *So she calls.*"

Petschek: "Your troubles'll be over next week. Gloria and I're taking the midnight tour. We'll let you get your sleep—or your beer."

Van Wyck: "Of course, we'd wanta get called *if there was any danger.*"

Petschek: *"No.* I thought your sleep was more important!"

Parelli: "Since ever when?"

Petschek: "Then why do you bitch so hard when we have to wake you up?"

Liu: "Men don't bitch. They bastard."

Aptshult: "For godsake."

Liu: "Sorry."

Walters: "You're a helluva one to talk. After chewing me out this morning for getting one of your girls up for a drink."

Petschek: "I'm a professional hypocrite. But more important, the girl can't hold her liquor. She was yelling all the way down in the elevator. Singing and dancing—you're both lucky Dr. Rosen ran into her and quieted her down and got her into a cab home."

Walters: *"He* did that? Well I'll be damned."

Petschek: "He's *supposed* to report both of you."

Walters: *"Don't I know."*

Mercouris: "About Kronkauer again. You know, funny thing, guys who've already served on the floor keep coming up to visit him. Everybody's turning into sentimental-type doctors."

Petschek: "They're just very interested in the case."

Mercouris: *"Interested?"*

Walters: "Maybe you're planning to knock Kronk off yourself and you're just trying to divert suspicion in advance."

Mercouris: "That'd be very clever of me, wouldn't it?"

Donnecker: *"Hey.* Aptshult's asleep."

Liu: "He's got sleeping sickness lately."

Parelli: "And *who,* pray tell, might be the cause of *that?"*

Liu: "Never you mind. I'm worried."

Sprague: "Hell, it's been a long year. Everyone gets tired now."

Liu: "Not twenty-four hours a day."

Van Wyck: "Really?"

Liu: "Yes."

Aptshult: "I *hear* y'all talkin' 'bout me."

Van Wyck: "Why don't you get yourself a checkup, Jim?"

Liu: "There. Maybe you'll listen to *Pete."*

Aptshult: "Okay, okay. As soon as I hear from this lawyer."

Liu: "There're witnesses to that promise . . ."

Aptshult: "Let's get back to the Kronk. *His* symptoms are more interesting."

97

At first she was angry at him. Enraged, in fact. He knew she was married. What right did he have, what kind of despicable values? She couldn't tell Fred, of course. But she *wanted* to; and she almost could. He'd take care of Terry. He'd make Terry *need* a doctor, a whole hospital. He'd take care of her, understand and comfort her, and make her feel *his* again, with everything all right, and take care of her, and . . . She'd never see Terry again. *If he tried to see her . . .* why, she'd tell Fred . . .

Then Terry *didn't* call and she was furious at him for that. It had been two weeks and he hadn't called. What kind of a girl did he think she was? What kind of a girl did he think she was that he could just sleep with her and not even call afterwards? Well that was okay, she couldn't even remember what it had been like when he'd slept with her, he must have been a real nothing . . .

Three weeks after New Year's Eve she called him.

"Jesus, sweetie," he said, "I wanted to call you, you know—but I just didn't know what to do. Your husband and all, I mean. I didn't know when I could get you that he'd be out. I just didn't know what to do."

She was silent.

"Well, look . . . uh . . . couldn't we get together for a drink or something? You know, just talk."

She had gotten him started saying what she wanted to hear and now she was just listening and not even letting him hear her breathing.

"Just talk," he said. "You know, see how things are."

When he said nothing more, she finally said, coldly, "All right."

"Well . . . uh . . . when can you make it? I mean, when'll you be free?"

She thought. "The night after tomorrow."

"Well, gee, sweetie, I uh . . ."

"You'd better . . ."

"Yeah, sure. Okay. That's fine. I mean, where'll we meet?"

"The *man* usually decides that, doesn't he?"

"Yeah, naturally, of course. How about . . . how about downtown? The Astor Bar?"

"All right. But wait for me in the lobby."

"Sure," he said. "Nine o'clock?"

"Eight."

"Eight? Yeah, sure, eight."

"Good-bye," she said; but she waited for him to say good-bye too before she hung up.

She was pleased. But dissatisfied. *She'd* had to call *him*. She was unable to escape realizing that. He'd sounded nervous enough, almost apologetic—but *she'd* had to call *him*. She'd see him this once more, make him want her, make him want her *terribly,* and then refuse him.

98

It was all so very simple. It was, indeed, so strangely simple that Jim refused to accept it for what it was. "I can't believe that the results are at all what they seem to be. It's so ludicrously simple I swear it must be a trap."

Mr. Dykes said, "It always *was* this simple. You just failed to take the necessary action."

"No reflection on you, Mr. Dykes, but I don't think it's true."

"Well, Doctor, I don't want to intrude in a medical area, but, if I may speak as a psychiatrist might—for just one moment, you understand—I'd say you just hadn't let yourself —for reasons best *known* to you—just hadn't *let* yourself realize how simple it was. Otherwise, you would have *had* to take action. For, if you'd allowed yourself to *realize* how simple it was, you'd have had no excuse for yourself for not taking action, now would you have?"

"The word you want is *analyst*—not psychiatrist."

"I'm sorry. I don't pretend to be trained in either area, Doctor."

"No. Sorry. My apologies to you. I'm a little unsettled by all of this. Nothing to do with you."

"I suppose something happened to make you change your mind suddenly and take action?"

Alicia. Alicia Liu happened. The night before she'd told him she'd *consider* marrying him. But even if she said yes, it wouldn't be until six months after his divorce was final. And not unless they could manage residencies within commuting distance of each other, she wasn't going to be a grass resident. And if they couldn't, well, the institution wasn't going to disintegrate just because they hadn't signed themselves to it on paper. "Something," he said.

The information had been brief, simple. The associate firm had hired a detective. The detective had gone to the town where Jim's wife was living and gathered various evidence. Including affidavits. Everything would hold up in court. Louise had been not at all secretive. She was currently having an open affair with her lawyer, a gentleman named Mr.

Emory Harrison. A maid and a neighbor (who shared the two-family house) had given evidence that Mr. Harrison often spent the night with Mrs. Aptshult. In Jim's state, the divorce would be granted as soon as the evidence was presented in court. Jim would not even have to appear; unless the divorce was contested and the court subpoenaed him. The only question Jim had to answer was whether he would be willing to sue on grounds other than adultery if Mrs. Aptshult would agree, and put in writing her agreement, not to contest.

"I hate the whole God damn thing," he said. "A *detective*. You didn't tell me *that* was the way you'd go about it."

"It's not unusual, Dr. Aptshult."

"It . . . it *changes* it. Like I played dirty with her."

"Dr. Aptshult, if you'll permit me: *don't be a fool.*"

"A fool?"

"To speak plainly, you're letting an overdeveloped sense of obligation ruin your life. Again to speak plainly, she's been screwing up your marriage since you put the ring on her finger—*no matter why you put the ring on her finger.* Feel guilty about *that* all you want. But don't warp your *entire* life around it."

"Yeah. You're an analyst all right. How come you didn't take the orders?"

"How come your wife didn't accompany you here?"

"She didn't want to."

"Did you want her to?"

He thought. Then he said, "Yeah. But for the wrong reasons. So I wouldn't go cheating on *her.*"

"But you tried to get her to come?"

"*That* I did."

"Then I suggest that you decide about the grounds so that we may proceed with the divorce. Or else stop wasting time for both of us, Doctor."

"*Boy.* I change my ever-lovin' diagnosis. You should've been a *surgeon,* you're blunt enough."

"Well?"

"Look. This detective business still bugs me. You know that money? That five thousand? Well, whatever's left of it after your expenses and fee . . . well, I'd like to give it to her as a sort of settlement."

"Buy her off your conscience?"

Jim started. Then he almost got up. But he kept himself

seated. He looked at the man across the desk from him and finally said, "Do I appear that weak to you?"

"You do. Now listen, young man. You either want this divorce or you don't. *Now you tell me which it is.*"

"I do."

"Good. You've been making *noises* that sounded like it anyway."

"No settlement, hunh."

"For one thing, you'd endanger your case. The court would want to know *why* you felt it necessary to make a settlement. And Mrs. Aptshult's counsel might be able to turn it into grounds for a countersuit. And if you lost that—as you very well might—you'd end up carrying an alimony load that'd break your back."

"What about afterwards. Couldn't we fix it up *after* I had the divorce?"

"Young man, if you can't confront this thing and deal with it as it deserves, I will not handle your case. If you don't believe in your own justification, you make it very difficult for me to be a party to obtaining the release you claim you want."

". . . Yes. All right. I see . . . Yeah. But if we have all the evidence, why let her off the adultery hook? Isn't *that* paying her off?"

"Certainly. But for something entirely different. Facilitating our procedure. Well, yes or no, young man."

"Yes."

"Good. I'll get right at it."

"How soon do you think I'll get the decree?"

"As soon as we can get it before a court down there. Say, *four weeks.*"

"Funny. I feel a whole lot better already."

"I'm sorry, but, with your permission—*healing thyself?*" Jim laughed. "That must be it."

But on the way back to New North, he felt a terrible letdown. There had been no subway nearby, and it had been raining, so he'd taken a bus. The ride was a long one and a slow one, with frequent stops in traffic snarls. He found himself becoming more and more depressed. And inside his wet overcoat, the collar of his shirt damp from rain running down his neck, he felt himself perspiring again, as muggy in his clothes as the day was outside the bus. Then the dampness in his clothes against his skin turned chill, and his entire one hundred and ninety pounds started with suspicion. He clenched his teeth against terror. Had to dominate his entire body by clenching everything to hold the terror, the suspicion, the recognition in abeyance.

99

When they sat at the table, she felt fully in control—cool, and not only *capable* of command, but *in* command.

Terry said, "Well, uh, what would you like to drink?"

"Nothing thanks," she said, carefully smiling at him. "You go ahead though."

She'd decided to wear the deep-V-cut black jersey again, even though it *was* a repeat; and had found herself a new wired bra that didn't meet in the middle, and so displayed her cleavage without exposing anything *too* immodestly.

"Well, you ought to have *something*."

"Nothing, really," she said, and carefully smiled at him again.

"Well, *God,* we're *in* a bar, have at least something."

"No, I honestly don't feel like it, Terry."

"It's a bar. You *ought* to."

Smiling, "*You* chose the place."

"All right, all right." He ordered himself a double Scotch on the rocks.

The waiter said, "Nothing for the lady?"

Terry started to shake his head, but Mildred said, smiling brightly at the waiter, "I think I'll have a *crème de menthe frappé.*" She turned to Terry. "I believe that's the way you pronounce it, isn't it?"

"Very good," the waiter said, writing the order, and turning away.

"I thought . . ."

"I changed my mind," she said.

"You sure are peculiar this evening. What's wrong with you?"

"Nothing's wrong with me. Do you truly think there's something wrong with me?" she said sweetly, remembering her jersey and sitting up straighter so that there would be more of her showing above the edge of the table.

"Well look," he said, readjusting his position in his chair (she could see he was looking down the V of the jersey and uncomfortably trying not to show it), "I mean, I'm sorry about not calling you. I mean, I told you, your husband and all of that. I thought it'd be better for you."

"Better for me? I run my own life. Don't be a liar."

"*Liar*. Look, *honey* . . ." he said, sarcastically; but then he had to stop as the drinks were set before them.

"Look, *what?*" she said.

"I don't need you. I broke a date to see you this evening. Just remember, you called me, I didn't call you."

She took a long, cool, sweet, hard swallow of her drink. She hadn't meant to drink at all. She hadn't meant to lose command. She made her voice more reasonable. "I didn't mean *that* . . ."

He said nothing.

She took another swallow of her drink. "I *wanted* to see you," she said. She felt horrible. He was still saying nothing, and she had to go to him to get him back to where she could be in command again. "I wore this jersey for you. You liked it so much." She smiled and raised the trunk of her body again to show him.

"It's a nice sweater," he said.

"Is that *all*," she said sweetly.

"What's in it is nice, too." He looked at her, and then seemed to force himself to relax.

She had to be careful. She wasn't sure she was yet in command again.

"You want another drink?"

She thought. There *was a way*. There was a way. She would *really* hurt him. "Not here," she said. She tilted her head and raised her eyebrows meaningfully. "Maybe somewhere else?"

"Well, gee, I'd ask you up to my place, but under the circumstances . . ."

"Circumstances?"

"I mean, well . . ."

"What's wrong, honey, leather goods business not so good; can't spare the drink?"

"No, not that . . ."

"We can *talk* there. This place makes me uncomfortable. It's too, I don't know, *public*."

"Okay," he said. "I'll get the check."

She stretched out upon the couch again. They had been there a long time and it didn't seem to be working. But then he brought her a drink and stood above her looking down at her and raised his own drink and sipped. She moved her shoulders as if to stretch them and sighed. He remained standing above her and looking at her and then went and sat across the room.

She managed to keep her slight smile; but the fingernails of the hand that was hidden from him dug into the cushion of the couch. She was completely cold inside, cold and full of hate and violence, and also, though she held it in check, a little fear.

She sat up, her legs tucked under her so that her skirt was pulled up above her knees and the line between her legs showed. Then, carefully, she stretched, hands over her head, and then back to touch her hair. "Give me a cigarette?"

He had to come over to her to offer her his pack. After he'd lit the cigarette and was about to turn away again, she took his hand and pressed it against the skin that the upper part of the V exposed.

He still remained standing. And then, as she pressed his hand harder and pushed it down, he slowly sat beside her and moved his hand to her breast and pulled her face to his.

His hand moved on her and she thought, Next time, next time, this is just to get him really needing me so next time I can hurt him, really hurt him, really badly . . .

No *next time* materialized. Two weeks went by and Terry never called. It hurt her pride, but it no longer worried her. She was too afraid. One time was one thing; two times were many things—each of which were too terrifying to face. She was too afraid of Fred finding out to even be outraged at not hearing from Terry.

100

Dr. Samstog sat in front of a semicircular bank of some forty-five seats and watched the lecture theatre suddenly begin to fill with interns and residents. There were also a few students from the medical school at De Witt. Because they would be going on the floor and seeing the patient later, the students wore white jackets, which had the red De Witt emblem on the sleeve. They were surrounded by a variety of young male and female M.D.'s in whites and shoulder-button tunics, scrub suits and scrub smocks of either pale blue or pale green, dangling masks, forgotten caps—stethoscopes, ophthalmoscopes, pens, and other professional accessories protruding negligently and gleamingly from all manner of pockets and body sizes.

It was five to ten. He had scheduled himself to begin at ten. He was pleased to see present not only the immediate staff of Medicine and Neurology interns from Male A, but also a number of interns he did not recognize, but who, under the rotating internship system, would eventually be working on, or with, his service. There were also a number of interns who had already rotated off the service, but apparently, were interested enough in Neurology or the particular patient, to come to hear a lecture on a *specific* neurological disease that most of them would probably never have to see again, no matter how long they practiced.

101

At the door to the lecture theatre, Parelli and Worship were handed a mimeographed synopsis of Kronkauer's history. Then they found seats and began reading.

"*Jesus,*" Parelli said. "This is his *twenty-third* NNH admission. In just fourteen years."

"It's sure one helluva history."

Van Wyck saw them and hurried over and bent down to them—"What *the hell's* this business about Jim Apt—"

Parelli signaled him quiet and nodded toward the platfrom. "*Is it true?*"

Worship nodded. "Yes. Tell you later, he's starting."

"Preparatory to seeing the patient, I thought it best to describe the disease, and, in particular, the specific symptoms of it which he exhibits—so that you will know not only what you are looking *at,* but precisely what to look *for.*

"Syringomyelia is a neurological disorder which is believed to be embryologic in origin. That is, the disease would seem to establish itself in the form of a congenital malformation of a neural character. There is, as yet, no sign at birth which we have learned to recognize, and the disease, usually, does not assert or openly exhibit itself until rather toward the middle of life—the thirties or forties, though I have seen cases . . . Thus, the disease is developmental in nature. It may pursue a course in which it openly displays symptoms for a period of from ten to even forty years. There may be occasional remissions, even of long duration, or an apparent complete checking of all further progress. However, its manifestations almost always recur and become more complex and insidious; and the condition is almost always fatal. Thus, the disease itself is sub-clinical until rather late in its course; and the prognosis admits at best of little hope.

"Syringomyelia is primarily the existence of a cavity or lesion in the spinal cord. The cavity is usually found in the vicinity of the cervical enlargement—that is, I wish you to bear in mind, within brief and direct distance of the medulla . . .

"As you will note from what has been said, syringomyelia is, truly, a *silent* disease—lying hidden and unknown for years, but by no means lying dormant. When the cavity has expanded itself sufficiently, the disease sets about destroying those sensory fibers in the anterior commisure which conduct sensations of pain and temperature across the cord . . .

"Thus, as in the case of the patient you will be seeing, the physician's first indication of a neural disorder is when the patient comes to him for treatment of burns—which, of course, he was not even aware of receiving (since he was and is unable to feel them) and which he has only *come* to be aware of as a result of recognizing inflammation or blistering.

"Our patient, Mr. Kronkauer, first became aware of a neural disorder fourteen years ago . . .

"The burns are thus directly due to the sensory impairment caused by the destruction of the temperature fibers by the encroaching spinal cavity. Kronkauer was aware only of numbness and . . . These are all subjective symptoms of the effect of the disorder and of the next step in its course, atrophy. . . . the atrophy slowly claiming the entire arm.

". . . developed blebs, the blebs developing into ulcers. . . . became subject to spontaneous fractures and dislocations of bones and joints.

". . . sideways curving of the vertebral column—that is,

scoliosis. Eventually the curvature not only became more pronounced laterally, but began developing a backwards curve as well, a rather extraordinary demonstration of the development of *kypho*scoliosis—also as seen in syringomyelia. Coincidentally, *amyotrophy*—that is, *muscular* atrophy—began making inroads throughout the *entire* right side. As affected, segments weakened and wasted soon after the skin had become anesthetic . . .

". . . right shoulder blade raised and displaced. . . . difficulty moving his head more than a few degrees in any direction . . .

"The final note on syringomyelia *per se* is that in a case as far advanced as this, the cord has become a mere empty shell rather enlarged with cerebrospinal fluid. I shall discuss this aspect of the condition in more detail in a few moments when I take up the question of treatment.

"With the onset of bulbar symptoms the disease is working quite rapidly and fatally and has become syringobulbia as well. With syringobulbia, syringomyelia has extended itself into the medulla by therein establishing bulbars. The condition is, of course, terminal. . . . partial atrophy in the tongue—which will soon be complete and lead to . . . one vocal cord entirely paralyzed, with every indication that the other one is being similarly attacked . . . already has difficulty in swallowing . . . has been prey to a number of intercurrent diseases. . . . as well as inflammation of the bladder —*cystitis.*

"If Mr. Kronkauer manages to continue to survive the progress of the disease and its attendant complications, the prognosis is limited to a simple vegetable existence with successive physical degeneracy. . . . have to be fed intravenously, relieved by a catheter . . . and in all ways tended for as if he were, actually, a plant. The only difference being that he will still be able to think his own thoughts.

"Treatment in both syringomyelia and syringobulbia is largely limited to mere treatment of symptoms. That is, treatment of injuries sustained as a result of sensory impairment. Naturally, as best we can, we try to practice a complete prophylaxis against every sort of conceivable injury. We protect him, simply because there is very little else we can do for him.

"Electricity and massage have been tried, but with no appreciable therapeutic results. However, we have, until recently, continued it—for psychological reasons; that is, to make the patient feel that there is, at least, a course of treatment (though, of course, *there is not* as yet). For, if he feels there is a course of treatment, believes it, we at least do not leave him hopeless. Of course, again, it's almost as practical as doing nothing.

"Occasionally—though it is actually rare—deep x-ray therapy directed to the spine and the vicinity of the cavity has produced beneficial results, at least upon the pains which accompany the disease, by lessening them. There were no such results in Mr. Kronkauer's case. However, as the only course of treatment that had ever had any appreciably impeding effect on the disease, we decided to try a laminectomy and drainage to facilitate the application of deep x-ray therapy. The syrinx was duly cut out and the cord drained and decompressed. With no noticeable effect, upon the resumption of x-ray treatment.

"Thus, we continue treating symptoms. And are, at that, reduced to treating garden-variety symptoms. That is, bed sores. With the usual cleansing and antisepsis, bland dressing and water mattress. However, even these rather modest measures for rather modest symptoms have long since failed to have any effect.

"The course of the patient's disease has been of at least fourteen years' duration and without remission at any point, becoming recently unexpectedly vicious and rapid. That the condition is terminal is no longer even a significant observation. The single question is, At what point will the patient succumb and to what extent, previous to succumbing, can he survive a vegetable existence without literally going mad? To this last question it is unlikely that we shall ever have an answer—in that his condition will be such that we will have no way of observing his psychological orientation."

Jim Aptshult was not at the lecture. X-ray, sputum smear and culture, gastric smear and culture, an elevated sedimentation rate accompanied by fever of indefinite duration, the presence of albumin in the urine, and a positive tuberculin test had resulted in his being removed (as was the exchange practice of the two hospitals) to a private room in De Witt General's TB ward pending his placement, at the expense of New North's insurance company, in a private institution for the treatment of tuberculosis.

102

During the third night of the following week (the first week in February) John Kronkauer died in his sleep in Ward A of New North Hospital's Male Medicine service. The examining resident wrote a preliminary report attributing death to (1) respiratory paralysis as the result of (2) terminal chronic degenerative disease identified as syringomyelia and syringobulbia with the presence of syrinxes established and diagnosed in the medulla. The body was removed to the morgue by two night-duty orderlies accompanied by the resident.

Dr. Wohl glanced over the name on his fatality report the following morning. Mrs. Lawrence, as was routine, filed a standard request for permission to perform an autopsy to the next of kin, the wife Emma. Emma did not refuse immediately, but asked why, and Mrs. Lawrence explained that it was really the only way in which the interns and residents could learn with precision exactly what they had been treating; and that the measure of the autopsy's importance was to be judged by the fact that the American Medical Association rated and certified hospitals by, among other things, their incidence of autopsies per fatality, and set minimum standards below which a hospital would not be certified for internships and residencies; and that often enough to make it worth while, something previously unrecognized or unknown was learned about the nature of a given disease; and that . . . Mrs. Kronkauer granted permission for the autopsy, signed the required documents, and accepted Dr. Wohl's condolences and appreciation for the advantage she was rendering the hospital and its staff.

The body was put at the disposal of a staff pathologist.

103

Parelli received notification of a Century Veterans residency appointment in Psychiatry under Dr. Harvey Bonny.

It was the usual gray, listless day that it had been for over a month. But during the night there had been several telephone calls. And in the boxes, unexpectedly, there were a few ambiguously worded letters—which yet carefully stated what they wanted to state. A significant, but not large, number of hospitals had made up their staff or collective mind and, in addition, were not, for various reasons, taking any chances but were notifying their choices immediately.

Theoretically, appointments and acceptances were not supposed to be made until March. But appointments of residents that the given hospital wanted especially or just plain *needed*, were offered *sub rosa* early enough so that, in cases of refusal, the given hospital could re-offer the given residency within the dates specified by the various codes they had drawn up and agreed to but rarely abided by except officially. Offers and queries before the specified date were usually made over the telephone—and, when a hospital held to the code, it put in its calls at midnight of the morning of the date specified. The most reputable physicians and institutions followed both courses.

Alicia Liu received a letter which read:

My dear Dr. Liu,

As you may very well have known, our psychiatric staff at Century has always been, because of the nature of our patient problems, entirely masculine. Unfortunately, I have been unable to convince myself that this arrangement should be changed. Therefore, I must, with certain regrets, refuse your application for residency here.

However, your professional plans and intentions so impressed me that I have taken the liberty of writing my good friend Dr. Machbi Weil, Medical Superintendent and Chief of Psychiatry at the Clinic for Psychiatric Therapy and Research in Massachusetts, to inquire of him his possible interest in you. As you know, the Clinic has not in the past retained anyone in the capacity of resident— though several years ago it was certified for training on a residency level by the National Board of Psychiatry and Neurology. Dr. Weil was also so impressed by your qualifications (and, again, especially your plans) that he has instructed me to inquire of you your interest in such an appointment.

I must warn you that you will be involved in a severe test, in that, according to your success, or lack of it, Dr.

*Weil will decide whether or not to implement the Clinic
with a yearly, open schedule of residencies.*

*I should also like to suggest to you that the Clinic of-
fers you an opportunity for training every bit as thorough
as Century might—and certainly a good deal more vig-
orous. If you don't mind being a guinea pig (though in
your case it is probably somewhat more accurate to say
guinea hen—forgive me) I believe you will enjoy and
benefit from an extraordinary opportunity.*

*Please inform me of your decision so that I may thus
instruct Dr. Weil and he may in turn send you an official
invitation to apply. (Needless to say, such an application
will be accepted.)*

> *Sincerely,*
> *Harvey Bonny*

Alicia's first thought was, What fools these mortals be. Her
second thought was a reaction of shock that the letter had apparently (two sets of initials) been *dictated:* he'd managed
all that out loud, *off the top,* so to speak. Her third reaction,
was, What a sweet thing to do. And her fourth—she knew
the Clinic's reputation, all right, all right—was to write Dr.
Harvey Bonny a letter of thanks and acceptance.

Yet in a few minutes she was depressed because this *certain* knowledge of the future seemed to make her future with
Jim even less certain than it had become. And too, it depressed her that she was able to go on to her residency while
Jim could not—at least not for a year. It seemed that *she* had
been granted all the certainty in their life—and he none.

Amos Sprague had had a letter of written acceptance for
practice from his county hospital in his wallet for months.
Since he had graduated from med school and received his
M.D., in fact.

Jim Aptshult, bitterly, had to write two letters of explanation and refusal.

A carbon copy of a letter addressed to Dr. John Paul Otis
inexplicably arrived at Dr. Wohl's desk. A hospital Otis had
applied to wished him to commit himself officially, but *sub
rosa,* to a Medicine residency for the following year. Wohl
replied to it with a strong, but cautious explanation. Nothing
had been legally *proven* before the law.

A letter of inquiry from Tom Elwood's home hospital also

came to Wohl. Why had Dr. Elwood, Jr., not answered any letters? why had he not returned their application? Wohl dictated another cautious reply.

Conny Mercouris replied affirmatively to his first offer of a Radiology residency. He did not even wait to see what else the mail or the phone might turn up.

Walters, Donnecker, van Wyck, Eckland, de Traunant, Rosconovitch, and Fishbein received no answers or inquiries of any sort.

In light of acceptances that *had* been received, they could not explain it to themselves. (*Mercouris,* for God's sakes!) They could only remind themselves that the *official* date of reply—the twentieth of March—was yet over a month away. It was neither consolation nor comfort. Theirs was a mixture of anger, desperation, and anguished anticipation.

Parelli lay on his bed smoking cigarette after cigarette and staring up at the ceiling long after he had been offered and accepted the residency he wanted. He could not understand it. It was not just anticlimactic, it was empty.

After all his worries and arrangements, after all his planning and politics, after all his care and hope—after all that, *it was nothing* dramatic *after all.*

He did not feel cheated, he felt nonexistent. It was not a letdown, it was nothing at all.

It was just a mark along the way of his progress. High-school graduation. College graduation. Med school. Internship acceptance. Med-school graduation. Residency acceptance...

Yet, he knew, without it, his professional life would be over. And with a different one, his professional life might be strictly limited.

Yet having gotten it, he felt nothing—except sickness that it made him feel nothing.

104

It was a clean, bright morning for a change. The atmosphere no longer seemed like a culture for pneumonia inverted over the city. If it held—the weather, that was—for just three or four days, Wohl fully expected the pressure on Contagion and Medicine to lessen appreciably by the beginning of the

following week. It was the same every year. There was a
break; and then even with a recurrence, spring was only a
few weeks away. And spring would relax the in-patient quota
to something more like what New North could handle.

Spring reminded him of summer. Specifically, *July 1.*
When he'd have a load of new interns and residents on his
hands. Among other minor and irritating details it was his
duty to manage, he had not yet completed getting the necessary statistics for the new group. He sighed and dialed a number: "Hello, Gower? Good morning, you're in bright and
early, I didn't really expect to get you till later . . . *Yeah.*
That it is. Beautiful . . . Tell me, Gower, I'm just tabulating
bed space for the new staff— How many anesthetist residencies are you handing out? . . . Seventeen? Unofficially,
of course, have you gotten any commitments yet? . . . *Ah.*
Well, that was fast, we must have an impressive reputation.
Or you. Congratulations . . . Well certainly we wash the
walls, doesn't everybody? . . . Ah, I see . . . Tell me, Gower,
can you break it down male-female for me? . . . Yes, yes—I
see. Eleven men and six women. Now wait a second, let me
look at my calculations . . . Yes, I have beds for all of
them . . . I tell you, Gower, we're crowded for beds for men,
Surgery and OB both have a larger number of residencies
this year and they almost all went to men . . . Yes, of
course. And we *need* more anesthetists. Let me look at this
a second again . . . Gower? I have beds for two more women
. . . Fine . . . Yes, and if any of the men drop out I'll give
you a call . . . You think those two women will be definite?
. . . All right, Gower, I'll put them down, thanks, I'll . . .
Riccio *might*—he's as aware of the anesthetist shortage as
any of us . . . All right, Gower . . ."

His intercom buzzed as soon as he'd hung up. He clicked
on his speaker. "Yes?"

"Dr. Killian to see you, Dr. Wohl," Mrs. Lawrence said.
"He's all ready to push down your door."

"Tell him to open it, instead," Wohl said, flipped the
intercom off, and looked up to see his Pathology chief already standing inside the door.

Killian came directly to the desk. "You received a report
on a Medicine fatality the night before last, a patient named
John Kronkauer?"

Wohl nodded. "Yes. Got it yesterday morning." He shook
his head. "I can't say I remember anything more than the

name—I didn't look into the chart or the history . . . *Should I have, Ernie?*"

"Not the way it was written up. Mind you, the resident had every reason to diagnose it as he did. But he was wrong. Your man died of barbiturate poisoning."

Wohl nodded. And drew himself up in his chair. "Pheno?"

"Quite a bit of it."

"So here we go digging into a family again."

"Like Little Jack Horner."

"Except all we ever get is some poor soul wasted away by grief and sacrifice and indecision and . . . They never think we knew what the patient was suffering."

"It always unnerves me to give testimony in a case like this. Afterwards I have to wash my brain out with a fifth of Jack Daniels. And aside from everything else, I can't afford Jack Daniels and I don't like to drink."

Wohl crushed an unlit cigarette in an ashtray on his desk. "I'll get the Medical Examiner on the phone right away."

THE FINDINGS

105

When cause of death . . . is . . . in doubt . . . the Medical Examiner or his deputy shall so report . . . to the Office of the Medical Examiner . . . and/or the Office of the District Attorney . . . or shall be empowered to perform such autopsy and investigation as shall lead to . . . the completion of such report . . . to the satisfaction of . . . both offices . . .

"Essentially, Dr. Killian, myself, and your resident concur," the M.E. said. "Death was of the nature of a functional respiratory paralysis."

"But," said Wohl.

"Exactly. But." Dr. Hempner's fingertips ran two tattoo-like trills on the arm of his chair. "The cause of *this* particular paralysis was *not* functional. Respiratory paralysis was present—and it is a neat *descriptive* phrase—but, as Dr. Killian discovered, it does not suffice to *explain* the death." The tattoo began again, and then ceased. "Death was caused by the action of a chemical depressant upon the central nervous system: specifically, the respiratory control center of the brain. Chemical action simply prevented the mind from stimulating the body to breathe." The tattoo again. Two trills, the room otherwise silent. Then: "Thus, death was chemically *induced*. Or rather, respiratory paralysis was induced and death followed. The cerebral cortex was rendered inactive; that is to say, depressed by a chemical agent into inactivity, the rest of the bodily mechanisms subsequently rendered also inert and inactive."

"Then you've substantiated Dr. Killian's findings to your own satisfaction—I mean, to the satisfaction of the M.E. Office?"

"Luminal—or phenobarbital—is usually received into the blood through the small intestine. We ground up a portion of it, and, separately, the remaining contents of the stomach which Dr. Killian had preserved. The process of the toxicological examination is to place these grindings in solution —one which extracts chemical agents of the Luminal type." Dr. Hempner seemed to lose some of the tension in his body. "We sure as hell found a lot of barbital. It was barbiturate poisoning: beyond medical doubt."

"I see."

"It needn't disturb you that much. It's not at all unusual. We merely have to determine the responsible party and the nature of their responsibility."

"I understand," Wohl said. "However, it's not a happy quest."

"It is not. But until we know *precisely* how the deceased came into possession of so lethal a dosage; or by whom it was administered; or in what way made available to the deceased—until we know all that, we have no more right to assume that death was accidental than we do a right to assume that death was homicidal. The M.E. Office's investigation is really just exploratory—to determine whether or not there is a medical basis for further investigation by the D.A."

Wohl nodded. "I've worked with M.E.'s before. But never on something that might be the hospital's responsibility. Usually criminal abortions that resulted in fatalities. Or an outpatient dying at home without a physician in attendance . . . Well, go on, Hempner, I'd like to hear all you can tell me."

As the result of many years' service to two masters—medicine and law—Dr. Hempner had become jealous of the clarity of his statements and position. He was exceedingly jealous that he should not be misunderstood. Better too many words than too few, he had decided. It was a rare lawyer who could discover grounds in testimony by Dr. Hempner to question the man's authority or accuracy. Dr. Hempner was quite capable of saying absolutely nothing; but it would be accurate.

"It would seem that our chemical agent, our depressant—in this case phenobarbital—was ingested orally. Now, phenobarbital is a barbiturate and its toxic effects and depressant action are essentially the same as those of barbital—at least the clinical pictures are almost identical, except that phenobarbital is very much more powerful; both in its ability to sedate and in its ability to depress. Whereas it takes approximately four-point-five grams of barbital to insure a fatal effect, as little as one-point-five grams of *pheno*-barbital may be lethal. We found an enormous quantity in the deceased's stomach; and, completing our substantiation of barbiturate poisoning quite beyond any doubt, we found twenty-eight milligrams in one thousand grams of the brain."

Dr. Hempner played his tattoo twice again while looking quickly off to the ceiling as if to find his preliminary report notes there. He then looked immediately back at Wohl. "I mentioned that phenobarbital presents the same picture, essentially, as pure barbital; and that barbital is a barbiturate. Well, the barbiturates are *graded,* so to speak, according to the speeds with which they get to work and produce their effects. Toxicologically, phenobarbital is considered one of the 'long acting' barbiturates. Its effects may last several days, and, usually, its effect is to produce a coma which after several days ends in death. That is, of course, in quantities exceeding the therapeutic dosage—which is point one grams."

Tattoo on chair arm; eyes on ceiling; eyes back to Wohl. "However, its clinical course may be telescoped into a matter of hours, and, rarely, even minutes—depending as the amount ingested is increased, and, or, the patient's physical condition is accordingly weak and without resistance. Here we have a case of a patient so considerably weakened and wasted by his disease that the maximum dose allowed him by order of his attending physician was only point zero three grams. Or only one-third of the normal medicinal dose. And *that* allowed only rarely. On occasions when the patient's need for rest was clinically a more imperative problem than was his relative lack of resistance to the drug and its effects.

Dr. Samstog's orders, which he had renewed daily for the week preceding the patient's death, were framed loosely enough to enable the night charge nurse to administer the prescribed dose at her own discretion: *specifically,* whenever the patient had not found sleep by one A.M. . . . It was, and is, Dr. Samstog's belief that the patient was becoming psychologically *incapable* of sleep. Dr. Samstog had evidence to the effect that the patient very nearly induced in himself psychological trauma in his nightly speculations about the course of his disease. It was, according to Dr. Samstog, either induce sleep or the patient would induce insanity, or, at the very least, considerable physical damage as the result of lack of sleep.

"Now remember, Doctor—even though we are discussing a *'long acting'* barbiturate, the patient was in a condition that was already weakened and without resistance. *And,* he ingested an *enormous* quantity even by lethal standards. So, you see, the coma may have been produced almost immediately. And death may have supervened within the hour."

Dr. Wohl was making notes. But he noticed that as Hempner moved further from toxicological background into clinical and pathological theory, his remarks became—*for him,* anyway—more urbane and less pedagogic. It was at this point that Wohl decided that for his own comfort he had best pursue a somewhat independent and personal inquiry in addition to Hempner's official one. Hempner was becoming—for him—quite uniquely excited.

Hempner went on. "Barbiturate poisoning is a relatively painless death. Almost entirely painless, one might hazard. And, as I've said, we extracted *enormous* quantities of phenobarbital from both the brain and the stomach contents. The toxicologic examination is unassailable. Since the dose was so enormous and its result so swift that we were able to recover so significant an amount of the drug, it is likely that the dose was administered, and, or, ingested *deliberately.*

"We have only to determine, then, whether we are dealing with a case of homicide, suicide, or accident."

"I *see,*" Wohl said, almost angrily.

"Yes. And then, of course, we either make a report to the District Attorney's Office or we don't. Our status, legally, is really only advisory. We merely recommend action—when, of course, there is a medical basis for it."

"Yes. Of course."

The M.E. sat up straighter in his chair. His explanation over, he seemed to have become brighter. "You recall that I said we have every reason to believe that the poisoning was deliberate."

"Yes. I'm not likely to forget *that*."

"Of course you aren't. Now, as you must be aware, this may directly involve a member or members of your staff—the attendings, the nurses, the interns and residents, any one or several of them may be directly implicated."

"You mean administered a fatal dose themselves."

"If it was homicide or accident. The responsibility could also be *indirect*—if the case proves to be of a *suicidal* nature. By indirect responsibility, I mean that were it suicide, the patient must have gotten the drug from *somewhere*. Or *someone*. In the normal course of events, the drugs were simply not available to him. Someone must have at least assisted him to the extent of making the drug available to him. Either by bringing it to him directly or by leaving it where it would be available to him. *I* beg your pardon: if it were just left within his reach, the case might then be construed as accidental rather than suicidal. In this kind of 'accident' the responsibility would be indirect, as in suicide. Were it the *administration* —albeit unwitting—of the dose, then, of course, the responsibility would be direct."

"I understand," Wohl said, beginning to wish the M.E. would go about his business and stop talking.

But Hempner continued. "Essentially, if *intent* could be proven, or if the D.A. *thought* it could be, the person responsible would face a charge of first degree murder—since the case, of course, would be a simple matter of homicide." Hempner carefully lit a pipe, got it going, and, shaking out the match, exhaled with pleasure. "There is also the possibility of criminal malpractice. That is, a violation of a law. If, say, a doctor caused death out of sheer recklessness. But that's damnably hard to prove. He might be gotten on a charge of *civil* malpractice for it, though—the rules of evidence are a lot more lenient in a civil court."

Wohl began being unable to keep the distaste off his face.

Hempner did not seem to notice. He gestured pleasantly with his pipe. "Of course," Hempner said, "there are a few other ways to get him on *criminal* malpractice. For instance, if, say, he was drunk when he administered this lethal dose. There'd be a mandatory charge of manslaughter for him then."

"*Him?*" Wohl said with annoyance.

"Speaking nongenerically, of course. *Nonspecifically.*"

"Thank you," Wohl grunted, this time with sarcasm.

"Oh, you're right, of course, Doctor. It's never advisable to make a statement that might mislead in cases of this sort," Hempner said pleasantly.

"I *understood* you."

"Good, good," he said pleasantly. "Now then. We also have the category of *civil* malpractice. *Mistreatment,* essentially, is what *it* is. It becomes a civil case when the state has no legal grounds for prosecution—when a *criminal* law hasn't been violated. You know, like leaving a sponge or some instrument in a patient and sewing him up. The family of the deceased just sues hell out of him in a civil court. And the hospital, too. Or a nurse. Anyway, the hospital's always sued too—parallel responsibility. Had him on the staff, let him practice—or *her;* all that makes the hospital equally responsible. Family takes 'em all to court. For financial compensation, you know."

"I *know,*" Wohl said as drily as he could. Hempner did not seem to notice. Wohl wanted his midmorning coffee. But he was damned if he was going to offer any to Hempner. And that meant he couldn't get any for himself.

"Have to prove all kinds of things though. Have to establish that the doctor—*or* nurse, *or* hospital—owed the patient what they call 'duty.' You know, had obliged himself to treat him. Then you have to prove a dereliction of the duty. And then that the dereliction was the immediate cause of whatever damage the patient claims to have suffered. Not too hard to get a jury to find for the plaintiff, though. All they want to know, really, is just whether the doctor's insured. Or the hospital. Then they figure, let the insurance company pay, hell it's no skin off *anyone's* back and the poor bastard can get some money."

"I *know,* Hempner. This is a hospital and we have patients."

"Of course you do," Hempner said pleasantly.

Wohl wasn't going to let him off that easily. Let the M.E. suffer some explaining for a while. "We have almost as many cases of quickmoney suits like that as we do cases where I have to legally remove a patient because he's all fixed up but refuses to go home."

"Of course you do," Hempner said pleasantly.

Good God, Wohl thought. Don't let Mrs. Lawrence come in and *suggest* coffee.

"You wouldn't have any coffee around, would you?" the M.E. said. "I thought I spotted an electric percolator outside when I came in."

Wohl sighed. He flicked on the intercom. "Mrs. Lawrence, have we any coffee available?"

"Hot and waiting," Mrs. Lawrence's voice announced cheerily.

"Two cups, if you will, please. For Dr. Hempner and myself." He flicked the intercom off. *He* took *his* coffee black and he'd be damned if he was going to offer cream and sugar to this insufferably . . .

Mrs. Lawrence came in with two steaming cups. "Cream or sugar, Dr. Hempner?" she asked cheerily.

"Both," said Hempner, beaming.

"Naturally," Hempner said, nodding thanks to Mrs. Lawrence for his cream and sugar, "—naturally, the person responsible would, in almost any event, even the mildest, have his license revoked. Or at least be forced to resign from practice and the profession."

"Naturally."

Hempner looked surprised for once. Wohl was pleased. Hempner said, *"Why, Doctor*—don't you believe that such action would be *justified?"*

"I damn well believe it would be too little action!"

Hempner nodded. "I agree with you."

"Was there anything else, Dr. Hempner?"

"Well . . . no . . . no, there wasn't."

Surprised him again, Wohl was pleased to see. Hempner seemed quite uncertain about the tone in which Wohl had directed the remark. He looked quite uncertain about even finishing his coffee. Pleasantly, Wohl said, "Well then, if you'll excuse me, I have a good deal of paper work to get at."

"Certainly, certainly. I didn't mean to . . ."

Wohl grandly waved the apology aside. "Not at all. I appreciate your having been so . . . ah . . . *thorough* with me. It's just that a number of things are pressing at the moment."

Hempner put his cup and saucer down on Wohl's desk and

rose from his chair. "I quite understand. Please don't feel that you must excuse yourself."

The damned . . .

"Shall I keep you immediately posted, or . . . ?"

"Please do," Wohl said. "I'd appreciate it."

Hempner paused at the door. "Would you like to hear my immediate theory?"

"Yes. As a matter of fact, I would."

"Well, as you know, I don't usually indulge in this sort of thing . . . But . . . just for your ears, you understand . . . I rather thought you might be interested . . . From everything we've turned up so far, it seems to me pretty certain that some one, or some *ones,* on your staff is going to face criminal malpractice charges."

Wohl waited to make certain that Hempner had cleared the outer office. Then he flicked on the intercom.

"Yes, Doctor?"

"Get this damned china the hell out of here!"

106

The Office of the Medical Examiner was, Wohl knew, a highly responsible organization. It consisted of men who, without exception, discharged their complex public, legal, and medical duties admirably and with great integrity, responsibility, and accuracy. But Dr. Hempner possessed other qualities as well, which . . .

At about four in the afternoon, Wohl received a telephone call from Hempner. "I've just finished my second interview with Mrs. Kronkauer," Hempner said.

"Yes?"

"It's unusual, I admit—but in this particular case it seems more than ever unlikely that a member of the deceased's family might have assisted him in suicide . . . As you know, his family consists entirely of Mrs. Kronkauer."

"I know."

"Unusual. So often it's a member of the family—trying to release the patient from what the family can no longer bear to see continue—that is, when the prognosis is of a terminal nature anyway . . ."

"Yes, Dr. Hempner."

"At any rate, I've just concluded my second interview with Mrs. Kronkauer. As there is no conceivable motive for murder on her part except to avoid incurring further financial obligations as the result of her husband's continued illness, it seems all but impossible that Mrs. Kronkauer might have been responsible for a homicide . . . Are you there?"

"Yes. Listening."

"Well. She could not be placed on the floor or even near the hospital for eleven hours preceding her husband's demise. So that effectively rules out direct administration of the drug on her part. Don't you think?"

"Yes, Doctor."

"Yes. Now the only other thing would have been if she'd *brought* him the drug at some time previous to his actually having ingested it. We're checking to see whether she had purchased or otherwise come into possession of the drug . . . She admitted that there had been a supply in the house, but that she thought the capsules had all been used up by the time her husband was removed to New North."

"Any way you can check that?"

"Negative. Unless she herself changes her story—and then, of course, we still can't check it, we just have a different story."

"Quite so."

"Yes. She stated that her husband *had*, on numerous occasions, asked her to assist his suicide. As he did many members of your staff, Dr. Wohl."

"I'm aware of that."

"Yes. Well. She says she thought about it a great deal. I judge that she *wanted* to see his suffering terminated—particularly in view of the horrifying prospect he faced—but that she was unable to resolve her emotional inclinations, if you will, with her sense of the immorality of such an act."

That had been precisely Wohl's impression from having spoken to Mrs. Kronkauer after her husband's death; and from having interviewed Dr. Samstog on *his* impressions (based on many years of professional acquaintance) of the woman's attitude toward her husband's requests. At any rate, Wohl considered, he had already arrived at this conclusion before his interview with Hempner that morning. That meant he might still be one or two or more steps ahead of the M.E.'s own investigation.

"My feeling is that she had no motive, either emotional or

material, strong enough to override her moral objections. That, in fact, she was unable to even countenance the conflict within herself, and so began emotionally shutting herself off from empathy, so to speak, with her husband. That way the conflict was rarely subject to stimulation; and thus she was less subject to the torment of thinking about it. She has become somewhat dead herself, don't you think?"

"For several months, I gather." It annoyed him that Hempner was so quickly managing rather incisive psychological insights. It annoyed Wohl that, along with his dismaying personality, Hempner was capable of such swift and acute observations.

"Yes. Well. I believe that perhaps I'm rushing things. Our primary concern, you know, is to determine, as I told you this morning, the *nature* of the casualty. That is, homicide, suicide, or accident. I think I'd best frame my questions and investigation within that boundary for the time being . . . I'll be letting you know my progress from time to time."

"Thank you, Doctor. I'm naturally most interested."

"Of course you are, my dear fellow. Well, I'll be in touch. Good-bye."

"Good-bye." Wohl hung up, but remained hunched forward in his chair. Working from *that* angle, Hempner had given him, he hoped, extra time. For Wohl had long since directed his own investigation at *who,* not *what.* Under the circumstances, the *what* was likely only one thing. Was *certainly* only one thing. Could be nothing else. Suicide with the direct assistance of one or more of his staff members. Either by providing and making available the lethal dose, or by providing it and actually assisting with its administration.

Wohl had already conducted several personal interviews of his own with attendings, residents, interns, and nurses. He was trying to evaluate them according to their potential willingness to involve themselves in such a ministration—by their professional attitudes toward patients and disease, by their respect for their chosen profession, by their respect for the patient, by their concept of what they thought their duty to the patient consisted of, by their susceptibility to identification with the patient as the result of outside and nonprofessional personal problems, by their ability to act upon conviction, by their ability to test and formulate and accept philosophical argument, and by the extent of their moral conviction or lack of moral conviction regarding either belief in or opposition to euthanasia.

He was also beginning to examine the personal records of his staff members. And to draw up a time sheet indicating the presence of each on or off the floor through the evening preceding the fatality.

As he read each folder and interviewed each staff member, he wondered if he was dealing with *the* responsible party, *the* accomplice (—or *one* of them). There was in each case, he found, something—a personal doubt, a personal problem, a lack of professional adjustment, a lack of professional commitment, too much professional commitment, an inability to restrain emotional indulgence, a too intellectualized view of life, a less than objective sense of responsibility or status, a depressed view of life, an inexperienced or susceptible outlook, a penchant for strongminded action based on sudden impulse, an overdeveloped professional ego, a recent disheartening experience—in each case *something* that could have served as the basis for criminal malpractice.

107

Mildred thought she had slept, but she felt no surety. It seemed to her that she had been awake for a long time and only just realized it, had been in a half sleep wanting something and the want had finally awoken her completely. She couldn't tell what the want was, but she was aware that she was uncomfortable.

Her bedside clock showed a few minutes after four. She was suddenly jealous of Fred. It would not be night at the *hospital*. There would be people there, lights, sounds, for company. *He* would not be feeling the aloneness of night— not the way she did. He would have people to talk to; he would be doing things. She could see him walking smugly through the wards in his whites, receiving the adulation of his patients, people too helpless or too unthinking to see him as the insignificant, smug person he was. Lying there in the dark, in the night that felt to her like a trap, she discovered that she actively despised Fred; and wondered how she could have escaped so long from realizing how despicable he was.

She clenched her fists and sat up feeling a hostility so intense that she began to cry—almost tearlessly—for lack of an object to hurt. After a while she quieted and lay down again and composed her body for sleep.

As she lay there, her mind once again receptive—*sensitive* —to herself, she felt again the vague discomfort she had felt upon realizing that she was fully awake.

She realized that she wanted to urinate, and then realized that she was having the familiar nighttime experience of being too comfortable in bed to even let herself know she wanted to, much less get up. Then she experienced a sensation of throbbing that was so severe and so protracted that she found the energy to get up.

She was almost unable to relieve herself. It was far less painful to remain the way she was. But she waited, and continued to try. And each time quickly withdrew from the pain.

Maybe it was just what her mother had called "the night fear." But her panic was severe enough to be terrifying in itself. She realized that she was plainly unable to do what she wanted to because it caused such severe pain. Burning and clawing as if what was inside her there would tear itself or be torn.

She clutched herself. She had no control over her horror. She had had a friend once who had had a cyst there that had infected and the friend had had to let them cut everything out. *Maybe she had developed cancer there . . .*

She wanted Fred. She loved him. He'd know about it, what to do . . .

She remained there for over an hour and managed to relieve herself enough not to force further urination. She was still very uncomfortable, but it was better than that burning, tearing feeling . . . She went back to the bedroom and lay down, more composed than before, but still clutching herself as if guarding herself against the night.

She lay there and thought about what she was there and what it might be and what might be wrong, and thinking about herself there reminded her of Terry and she thought Oh God no she could never tell Fred, he might examine her and know she had been with someone else, a doctor could probably tell that, it would show there somehow . . .

108

Wohl got the call at his home, at ten of eight in the morning. "Hello, Sidney?" It was Hempner; and Hempner had never called him by his first name before and Wohl doubted whether professional courtesy extended *that* far. "I tried Samstog, but he was already out."

"Yes, Dr. Hempner?"

"Matter of preparing for my day's inquiries? Needed some information Samstog had. *Has*, that is—early morning and all that. Can't speak properly."

"Yes?"

"Thought you might be able to help me?"

"Be glad to if I can. Can't try till know what it is?"

"Ye . . . *what?*"

"What's your problem, Dr. Hempner?"

"Oh. Yes. Of course. Well. I wonder if you might be familiar enough with the case by now to have certain clinical information about the deceased?"

"*What is it*, Dr. Hempner?" Wohl pitied any attorney who had to examine *this* M.E.

"I know that Mr. Kronkauer was entirely paralyzed on his right side. But I wondered if, as recently as the evening of his demise, he yet retained sufficient articulation in his *left* arm to enable him to manage the drug to his mouth himself if someone else first put it within his reach."

"I believe he did, Dr. Hempner."

"Thank you, Sidney. I'll be in touch." Wohl almost hung up, but Hempner said, "In other words, someone need only have *supplied* him."

"That," said Dr. Wohl, "is my impression."

"Thank you, Sidney."

109

"What you've been experiencing, Mrs. Aptshult, is acute urethritis. That, together with your vaginal discharge, seems to indicate a gonococcal infection. Both are primary symptoms, you see . . ."

"But . . ."

"As you consulted me without reference, Mrs. Aptshult, I'll take the liberty of interrupting you long enough to make one or two other points. I don't wish you to leave uninformed or with the wrong impression . . . I'll be pleased if I haven't offended you, my only object is to give *you* some objectivity."

"Oh, please, I'm sorry."

"Thank you. So many girls won't *listen* . . . Ah, good. You have no idea the willingness with which most unreferred patients remain uninformed. They just get up and *go*." He looked at her. "God knows to where. Or for what."

"It's just that I have a very important engagement."

"Ah. I see. I'll try to be brief. I want to impress on you the necessity for pathological investigation. Laboratory tests? You understand?"

"Yes."

"Good. It might be a number of other things. But, informed of the possibility, I like to feel that the patient will not . . . *hazard* someone else's infection?"

She nodded. "Oh, of course not."

"I'm glad you understand . . . Now, please do not go away with an exaggerated notion of your condition. It is likely that you have a gonococcal infection. In effect, gonorrhea. Very scary words, yes? . . . That is only because the general public's lack of information is matched only by its propensity for picking up the disease. No, no, *no!* Do *not* interrupt. You must *listen* now. It is half the treatment . . . Good. Now listen to me. A gonococcal infection is no different from any other infection. It means only that something has *infected* you. You understand? . . . Good. Therefore we treat an infection. Fifteen years ago, yes, you might have had cause for worry. Now, *no!* Now it is a sore throat. We have made enormous strides in chemical therapy. *Penicillin!* Two days, only—and then a patient is cured sometimes. You must not *expect* such immediate results—but you must not forget them either. In a week, two weeks, all fixed up like new." He smiled.

"I'm going away."

He looked at her. "Ah . . . I see. You will arrange for treatment where you go?"

"Oh, yes."

"Yes, of course, you must. You will need my records?"

"No. I don't think so, I'll just *tell* the doctor." She smiled.

"But tests. I could run the tests and send the results to . . ."

She stood up. "No. Thank you, Doctor. I'm not sure exactly where . . ."

"You could write me. Save time for . . ."

"I don't think so. You see, we might be somewhere where it'd be just as fast to . . ."

"Yes, of course, Mrs. Aptshult. I understand."

"Doctor . . . I must have gotten it from sitting on some john."

"Certainly. It only depends who you were on the john with."

"Good day," Mildred said. She left.

The doctor buzzed his secretary-nurse-receptionist on the phone. He sighed. "Do not bother to send a bill . . ."

"But, *Doctor* . . ."

"How long have you been a nurse?"

"Four *months.*"

"Yes. And how long have you been a woman?"

"But, Doctor . . ."

"Yes. Twenty-two, twenty-three years. And I have no experience at all in that direction and yet I tell you that woman was not Mrs. Aptshult, whoever Mrs. Aptshult may be; and does not live at whatever address she gave you and does not want to hear from either of us again."

"But I could *try.*"

"It would make me feel worse. I would be depressed when the letter came back."

"Yes, Doctor."

110

Jim was being sullen. "Well, at least I complete the statistics for the year. One breakdown and one TB case per hundred interns."

"Do you?"

"Do I what?"

"Complete the statistics for the year."

He looked at her for a moment. "Alicia . . . Lee, *honey.* Don't *you* be sullen. It's *my* prerogative. *I'm* the one that's missing out on . . ."

"On what? The investigation?"

"Hey. Lee . . ."

"I'm sorry, darling. But I want it plain that I'm not marrying an invalid. TB or no TB. As long as you're physically able, you hold your head up and stop moping around or . . ."

"Jesus." He looked at her for a long time again and she stared back at him. "They've really got you going back there, don't they?"

"Oh, *Jim.* Darling." She almost let herself clutch him.

"They really do. *Hunh."* He nodded.

"They really do. Every hour. Even on rounds. *Dr. Hempner just called and wants you to come down."*

"That's the first time I ever heard you be bitchy."

She smiled. "Do you like it on me?"

"It's *exciting* . . ." he said, half making a question of it.

"If it gets bad enough you've always got Olga downstairs."

"I'm not up to her."

"I gather no one is."

"Lee?"

"Mmmm?"

"I love you."

She smiled and looked down at her hands. "I love you, too." She looked back up. "As long as you act like *you.* And not like a patient."

"I *am* one, for chrisake. Whaddya want? *Joy?"*

She took his hand. "No. Just you."

He reoriented himself and nodded. "You'll have me. As soon as I'm not *fucked up* any more," he said angrily.

"Unavoidably screwed or not, I'll take you. I've seen worse cases in my time."

He grinned. "You sure look silly in a mask with a street dress."

"It's a suit."

"Have they run your tests yet?"

"Yes. All negative, darling. Your germs aren't half as virile as you'd like them to be."

"All negative. Really?"

"All negative except the tuberculin and ten out of almost ten run positive on that. Everybody has the bug *sometime.* It just shows I did too."

"Thanks. I'm familiar with the statistics." He looked at her. "I'm sorry, honey. Really, nothing even on the x-ray?"

"A very small lesion I must have had before puberty."

"Ancient history, hunh?"

"You be quiet. Being your age doesn't make me a hag yet."

"It *sure* doesn't."

She feigned fright. "You want me to send for Olga?"

"Leave Olga alone."

"That seems to be the poor girl's fate."

"Yeah."

"Don't you *like* the bitch in me?"

He considered her. "It makes you more interesting . . . but I'm not sure I *like* it."

"Neither does that horse's ass Hempner."

"Oh for chrisake, *have you been giving him a hard time?*"

"He's been giving everyone else a *rotten* time. To *him* we're all criminals."

"Well? Aren't you?"

"Only occasionally. With provocation."

"I'd like to give you some provocation now."

"It'd give you a chill."

"True, true," he said with resignation.

She took his hand again.

"How long is this investigation going to go on?" he said.

"Forever, I think."

"No, really . . ."

"Till they find who they're looking for."

"*Who* they're looking for?"

"Who . . . But enough shop talk, my love. I have a letter for you." She reached in her handbag.

"*Yeah?* Who from?"

"Your lawyer. Apparently you haven't apprised him of his client's new address. Here."

Jim looked at the envelope. It was stamped *March 3.* He opened it and read the letter. Then he handed it to Alicia. "Read it."

She read, *That's some wife. It took ten minutes for her to capitulate. In writing. And only one day to gather the information that led her to capitulate.* Her eyes moved to the next paragraph. *That's some wife you* had. *See enclosure. Yours truly . . .* The enclosure was a photostat of a divorce decree.

Alicia began to cry.

"Hey. I thought you were only supposed to do that on your wedding day."

She took out some tissue and dabbed at her eyes. Then she said, "If you let me do that on our wedding day . . . *I'll* divorce *you!*"

Parelli signaled the waiter for another drink.

"You can't afford it," Cynthia said quietly.

"I'll do as I damn well please."

"You always do," Cynthia said quietly.

"Look who's talking. *I* didn't stop talking to me."

Cynthia laughed. Then Joe was unable to keep a furious look on his face any longer and laughed too. She put his hand on hers. "I'm glad we're not mad at each other any more."

He nodded. "Me too." He nodded. And then, as a gift he had a hard time giving, "I wish I wasn't built that way."

She put her hand on top of his and held it tightly. But quietly, she said, "So do I . . . you're just too impetuous, my darling boy."

"I thought I was right. I still do, even though it *didn't* come off. Even though it *didn't* get me what I wanted. It *might* have been the difference."

"You mean you're unrepentant?" She looked shocked and withdrew her hand from his. "You mean I'm going to have to *keep* putting up with this?"

"Short of analysis, I have no immediate plans for changing."

She sighed. "I read somewhere that the essence of love is compromise. *Not* defeat."

"Love and learn," Joe said, smiling happily.

"I'll love—if you'll make an effort to learn."

"We'll both learn," he said, "if we get a chance."

"I love you."

"*Nobody* loves an intern."

"You're drunk," Gloria said.

"Nobody, but nobody," Lew said.

"I do."

"Don't," he said suddenly.

"*Lew.*"

"Well then, don't say I didn't warn you."

"About *what*, darling?"

"About both of us."

"Are we off and running again?"

"We're off. I'm not sure who's running."

"Just what does *that* mean?"

"Nothing."

"*Nothing*," she mimicked. "Will you either stop talking in riddles or stop talking? *Please?*"

"Do you remember the case of an intern? One John Paul Otis?"

"Lew, what . . . ?"

"I'm telling you."

"*What* are you telling me?" she said.

"That I don't know who's running. Or from what."

"Are you *that* tired?" Joan said.

"It's just that I'd *rather* stay around the hospital to-night."

"You said that last time, too . . ." She studied him. He didn't look at her. "You know, you don't *have* to ask me out on dates. Especially since you don't bother to keep them."

Pete said, "Joan, please, understand a little. I just can't leave the hospital now. I can't *get* myself to."

"Well maybe you ought to get yourself to. Getting outside a little bit might get you out of this lousy mood you've been in."

"I'm sorry. Really I am. I've just gotten low lately. And a little nervous, I guess."

She laughed. "Maybe you ought to see a doctor."

"Maybe."

"Though a nurse might be better."

He didn't say anything.

111

Lew Worship sat down opposite Dr. Wohl in Wohl's office. This was not one of Wohl's investigatory interviews; Worship had requested the appointment himself.

"Yes, Dr. Worship?"

Wohl's machine-gun delivery had slowed recently. It was plain that he was both tired and easily annoyed by irrele-vancies—*anything* irrelevant to Kronkauer's death.

"*Yes*, Dr. Worship?"

Worship found the words were not there. He stared at Wohl.

"I assume you wanted to see me about *something*. I am not a work of art. The general public is not invited to come and just look at me."

Worship started. His face filled with flame—whether anger or shame or annoyance of his own, he could not tell.

"Dr. Worship, I'll have to ask you to leave. I have no time for personal difficulties in relating just now."

"I took twenty capsules of phenobarbital from the nurses' station . . ." He had difficulty. It was easy enough to commit himself to the idea and to the procedure. Hardly so to actually *tell* Wohl. "It was late, I was able to take them to Kronkauer. I saw him swallow them."

Wohl's face showed no sign of expression. No *change*. It seemed only to petrify.

Worship held on to the arms of his chair.

"Why, Worship?"

Worship didn't answer.

"Do you believe that strongly in euthanasia?"

"I do."

Wohl said nothing.

"Don't *you*, Dr. Wohl?"

"Whatever my beliefs in that regard, I wouldn't throw away my career and risk jail for it."

Worship said nothing. He faced Wohl with as little expression as Wohl offered him.

"You say, then, that you are responsible for the patient's death."

"I do."

"Formally?"

"Yes."

Wohl nodded. "I don't believe you."

"Dr. Wo . . ."

"Assuming that you were responsible, why admit it?"

Worship didn't even have to consider. "Because this investigation is doing a lot of harm to people I respect. They're being made to feel like . . . like they were *nothing*. Irresponsible. Incapable . . . And because I have no faith in Dr. Hempner's managing an accurate inquiry."

"Not managing an accurate inquiry? *Worship*, I think you think his inquiry is *too* accurate."

"Dr. Wohl, it wasn't easy . . ."

Wohl interrupted him. "I'm sure it wasn't. But in any event, I think you'll need some disciplinary action. You may consider yourself unofficially suspended. I'll arrange for you to be relieved of your duties." He stood up. "You will so remain until this thing is cleared up. I'll review my decision at that time. *And* my personal inclinations as to whether or not you should be allowed to remain in the profession."

Worship stood up. "You're a fool."

"No, Worship. You are." He nodded to impress on Worship his conviction. "But thank you, Worship. I think the person who did it will have to come forward now."

Worship started to leave.

Then he heard Wohl, "Young man, you disgust me."

"I only . . ."

"You've only succeeded in the ten minutes you've been here in disgracing every tenet of the profession." Wohl went on, thoughtfully, emotionlessly, as if reading a history to some students, "You've lied, insulted, betrayed, *dishonored*. Yes, and disgusted me. And I am not a man easily disgusted, Worship. It takes something offensive to disgust me."

Lew started to leave again, but again Wohl's voice stopped him. "What interests me," Wohl was saying, "is what sort of egocentricity enables someone to take the action you have. Do you think being called *Doctor* gives you privileges not accorded the lay person?"

Worship stared at him.

"I think that must be it," Wohl said. "That's what makes you offensive, disgusting." He regarded Worship. "You remind me of Otis, Worship . . . but even Otis did not dissemble."

"You're a fool," Worship said, almost pleading. "Knowing and understanding, Dr. Wohl . . . they're two different things."

"Worship, don't tell me you're upset?"

When there was no reply, Wohl went on. "I understand— or rather, I *know* you have tentatively received an appointment as resident in the OB-GYN service of this hospital . . . Well, Worship? *have* you? or must I merely take Dr. Tyssen's word for it?"

Worship remained silent.

"You *stupid* child!"

Worship continued to be silent. He could not talk. He was engulfed by a great lassitude, an uncompromising numbness.

"No, Worship, *you're* the fool."

Worship heard each word distinctly. But he did not allow any word to relate to another. Each word framed itself in his mind in its own separate abyss.

Wohl sat down behind his desk. He was still calm. "Oh no, Worship. Your story has less integrity than if you'd fabricated it to protect yourself. Less than if you'd come in here to tell me a fantasy . . . But why? I wonder . . . Let me see," he said. "Perhaps it's that you're trying to be very clever. Is that it? Perhaps you *are* responsible. Perhaps you thought you might cover yourself by telling me a story even Dr. Hempner would have contempt for, eager as he is to settle this. Perhaps you thought if you told me a story I could see through, I wouldn't bother looking in your direction any more . . . Is that what you thought? . . . You're wrong, you know."

Wohl's face relaxed, became as calm as his voice. "Do you think that residency will be offered to you *formally* now?"

The words came together, related to each other, in Worship's mind in spite of his desire for them not to, and his attempt to keep them from doing so. "I don't know," he said.

"No," Wohl said. "You wouldn't. That's probably one of the reasons you came in here. Now get out."

Lew had figured it out, had understood it so simply. It *was* very simple. The only person who had had immediate access to both the patient and the drug without being witnessed at the time the patient had received the drug, or was administered the drug, was Gloria Mead.

112

At a meeting of Male Medicine A's residents, interns, and nurses, Dr. Wohl announced Worship's unofficial suspension and the reasons for it.

Dr. Wohl had regained his machine-gun-like rapidity of speech.

"You will not talk about this. Not to anyone. You will not even imply that anything unusual has happened here. You do not know that Worship has been suspended. You will not know that until such time as it may become official. At that time, whatever reasons are given, *those* will be the reasons. Only those reasons publicly given. Anything you have any private knowledge of from our discussions today, you will please keep to yourself and not conjecture upon.

"I say these things not out of any desire to protect anyone who is not innocent. I say, and ask, these things in order to protect this hospital and its name. *And,* particularly, its ability to be of service to this community. Irreparable damage would be done to the ability of this institution to help the community it serves were there any reason for the community to suspect the capabilities of this institution. If you think about that, I believe you will agree with me. Loss of trust in this institution by the community it serves would do more harm to that community than the total dissolution of the institution would do to us who comprise the institution. And that *loss of trust* would be the least harmful result in an area which is already understaffed and underequipped by even urban standards.

"I have only one more thing to say to you. It is conceivable that one or more of you may have further information on this matter which—for reasons which I guarantee may remain your own—you have not wished to make known to me before now. I ask you to bring that information to me now. It is not beyond possibility that, unknown to you, such information might be of benefit to the case of that party or parties upon whose future in this profession I shall ultimately have to decide.

"Thank you and good day. You may return to your duties."

113

"Sure I knew," Terry said. "When I found out, that's why I didn't call you. Hell, that's why I didn't want you to come up to my place that night we met at the bar. Just remember, *sweetie,* you were the one who insisted on going up to my place that night at the bar. *You* were the one who insisted on—hell, you practically *raped* me, putting my hand on your boobs and . . ."

She hung up.

But two hours later she called him again. "Terry, *I love you* . . ."

He hung up on her.

She called again immediately. He didn't answer. She hung up and dialed again and let the telephone ring. She counted ninety-four rings before he answered. She said, *"Terry,* I *want* you . . . Even with . . . what's happened. I love you. I love you, Terry. I'll leave Fred. I'll get a divorce. We . . ."

"Listen, Mildred. Listen, *Milly*. You're a bitch and I wouldn't have you if your husband wrapped you up and gave you to me for a present. I feel *sorry* for the sonofabitch, stuck with you—" She sat listening, fascinated, unable to move the receiver away from her ear. "You're not even fun to be with, you're just a lay with a big pair of tits; if I didn't know different, I wouldn't be surprised if I got *my* dose from you . . . You still there? . . . Listen, *Milly,* one thing I wanna advise you, for your own good, you know? A cheap bitch like you could make a fortune, do it *wholesale,* you know? No reason why you shouldn't have fun and get paid too—since you like variety so much. I mean, after all, you could . . ."

She didn't hang up, really. She *managed* to get the receiver back in its cradle, her arm so weak she almost was unable to even hold the receiver till it was in its place. For a long while she was unable to get up.

114

After all the noise Donnecker had made, a neighbor had come out to see what was wrong and followed him in and helped him get the windows open and had gone off at Fred's direction to call the pulmotor squad.

As if reciting a prayer by rote, Fred checked the vital signs. Then he checked the signs of death. Judging by all evidence she had used both phenobarbital (a bottle he'd brought home from the hospital stood empty on top of the stove) and gas. She was dead and he didn't want to stay with her any more. He picked up the envelope that lay next to her at an askew angle on the floor. In the living room he stopped himself and opened it and read the note inside. *I do love you. I couldn't have been that way with you if I didn't.*

Don't hate me that way—I loved you. Maybe you can't love and that's why you wouldn't let it be us and let it work. You were the one who didn't. I tried so hard. You were the one who just let it go. You just wasted it like it counted for nothing. But I love you . . . Mildred.

He remembered his responsibilities and instead of taking it with him, refolded the note and put it back in its envelope and wrote on the envelope, *Sorry, I opened it . . . F.D.*, and put it back where he'd found it and, leaving the apartment, thought, I *did* love you, Mildred, I *did* try, we could have made it work if you'd given me a chance to work harder at it, the year was almost over, we could have had a vacation together, gone away together and worked it out and next year I would've had more time, I know how it was, how I kept doing it wrong, but I tried even if I was wrong, I *did* try, Mildred, I tried so hard even if I kept making it worse . . .

He was in whites and they didn't stop him, thinking he was from an ambulance or else part of the pulmotor squad. He was able to just walk out of the building and away.

It was too easy to accept the responsibility for Mildred. He had already subverted the guilt he was too willing, too able to accept. No, Mildred could not be faced, nor was there any reason to when responsibility was anyway now meaningless . . .

He did not even know that the note had not been for him. Had he, he might never have left the apartment.

115

The telephones began ringing at midnight (minus two or three minutes in some cases) on the evening of the nineteenth; that is, the morning of the twentieth. The calls were sometimes direct from the electing parties, sometimes indirect via telegram. All requested, quite firmly, response by return telephone or telegraph—not to comply would be to risk forfeiting precedence on a given hospital's acceptance and preference list. The risk was of being bypassed completely for failure to get a reply in soon enough, and thereby forcing the hospital—according to the hospital—to move on and offer the particular residency to a second choice. In effect, each institution filled its openings as soon as possible, accepting in order of affirmative reply the first five or ten or however many were needed.

A number of interns found themselves in the position of being unable to afford to wait for the next two days' mail. In fact, many had difficulty trying to stall till one A.M. in order to give themselves the opportunity to wait for their preferred choices to call when the first calls they had gotten had been from "insurance" applications, *not* preferred choices. The less sure each intern was of receiving the particular offer he wanted, the sooner he formally accepted a residency he found less desirable.

Alicia Liu, Conny Mercouris, Amos Sprague, and Joe Parelli had already committed themselves either formally or informally.

Working on the theory that there were eleven thousand residencies open and only six thousand American M.D.'s per year to fill them, Ted Eckland waited until three o'clock in the morning before he received an offer which he felt would place him in an institution which he could respect and which would also teach him something over the course of the three years minimum residency required for an internal medicine certification. He realized he had been far down on the hospital's list. But it was an excellent hospital—its lack of immediate recognition of his medical genius did not bother him at all.

Because of having contracted mononucleosis, De Traunant was going to lose too much time in De Witt's Contagion ward to be able to go on to his residency until he had completed the required twelve months of internship. Therefore, he had to begin making application all over again.

By one o'clock, Art Rosconovitch had turned down two Pediatrics residencies he had previously determined that he would accept if offered. He didn't feel that he was fit or ready yet to be a resident. He didn't feel that he was capable of discharging his duties as he felt he ought to. Then he began wondering, *Suppose I was able to later on? Then what? With no residency to go to.* The possibility panicked him. He put through return calls to both hospitals he'd already turned down. When he got through to them, each, respectively, had already filled its vacancies. The idea that maybe he *would* be all right in a while—by the time the year of internship was up—had become, if not quite believable, obsessively real. He *would* make it, he had been a fool to think he wouldn't. When a prime choice called him shortly after two, he accepted immediately. *I'm going to make it,* he told himself as he got ready for bed. *I'm going to.* He could already feel his residency like a physical office that was privately his.

Fred Donnecker, pending further investigation of his wife's suicide, was not allowed to accept the ENT residency he had wanted and been offered. Nor any other.

Jay Fishbein accepted an ophthalmological residency at a hospital he'd wanted. Jay said, "Now *all* we have to do is get through the rest of the year." Eckland said, "It's beginning to seem like it'd just be easier to switch to nuclear physics." Jay: "Don't laugh." Eckland: "I'm not."

Courtney Walters had also applied for ophthalmology residencies, but then received such an advantageous offer of a straight surgery residency that, rather than turn it down on the spot, he asked for, and got, twenty-four hours in which to consider this complete change of specialties. By the time he went to bed, he realized he wanted the surgical residency very much. By breakfast he had decided that by God he'd take it.

Van Wyck received several substantial offers and rejected them all. He was still waiting to hear from the Public Health authorities to whom he had applied for an internal medicine residency at one of the hospitals they maintained to serve U.S. government Indian reservations. Van Wyck wanted the appointment because he hoped and expected to work there under conditions similar to those he would eventually find in one of the underdeveloped countries he wanted as an assignment from the World Health Organization. Riccio had offered him a New North Surgery residency. He had rejected this absolutely.

The following morning Dr. Wohl summarily called a meeting of all the interns from Male Medicine A and its associate Neurology and Contagion divisions. His machine-gun delivery lasted for less than fifteen seconds: "I will be brief. Those of you who have committed yourselves by telephone, telegraph, letter, or in any other way, will write a letter stating that you have been, along with the other interns currently doing duty on your present service, at this hospital, forbidden to accept any position as resident until your medical superintendent instructs you that you may. You may use my name and refer your correspondents to my office. Until this is cleared up, I will not put this institution's approval on any acceptance."

Later, at lunch, after she had been told, Gloria was quiet and did not notice when Lew offered her a cigarette. Not even when he held the pack out directly in the line of her gaze. He was startled. "What is it?" he said. "Something wrong?"

"I don't know," she said. "Something. Nothing."

They walked toward the elevator to go back up to the ward. When she remained silent, he said, "Well, if it's nothing, why are you so . . ."

"So *what?*" she said angrily, and stopped walking.

"Abstracted, I guess," Lew said, knowing it was the wrong word.

A down elevator came. She got on it and the door closed behind her before he could follow.

All those boys—and Alicia too, she thought. Why won't he let them accept? If someone did it on purpose, he'd have to resign later anyway. Why does he have to ruin them all? And she thought, It couldn't be—the thought having just come to her while she was listening to what Wohl had said. It *couldn't* be me.

After letting his mind examine its own impressions for a while, Wohl once again reached for his personal record folders, time charts, and interview transcripts. But he only glanced at one or two, and then pushed the whole bunch aside. His recognition of each page was too perfect. He knew each page too well to read it. He already had, as it were, photostats in his mind.

No. He was not going to get the answer that way . . .

116

Gloria Mead said, "I don't know. I don't *know* if I did it consciously." She looked at Wohl to see if he understood. "I know I'd *thought* about doing it on purpose, but I don't know if I *did* do it on purpose . . . You see, I didn't plan it, I didn't go into his room with that intention in mind. Except maybe unconsciously . . ."

Wohl said, "There's plenty of time, Miss Mead. I'll hear you out for as long as you want—for as many times as it takes you to get it all out to your own satisfaction . . . I realize it's difficult to be as precise as Dr. Hempner wishes. But we both appreciate your effort to *be* precise about . . . about *elements* as amorphous as these." He turned to Hempner. "Isn't that true, Dr. Hempner?"

"Yes. Yes, of course it is," Hempner said abruptly and statically.

Wohl turned back to Gloria. "We also appreciate your straining to be as honest and accurate as you are. But please, Miss Mead, don't strain yourself into collapse. As I say, we'll listen for as long as it takes you to explain it to your own satisfaction."

Gloria nodded as if she had hardly heard. "I don't understand it exactly myself. I'm not even sure if I *recall* it. Not in any way that I'm *positive* about . . ." She looked at Wohl helplessly.

Wohl nodded. "We understand that, Miss Mead. Just give us as complete a statement as you can. We can always ask *you* questions."

"I'm not . . . Well . . . You see, just then, we had a *number* of patients with orders that said we were to give them sedation of various sorts and in various amounts . . . under specified circumstances . . . at our own discretion. That meant . . . Well, you see, usually the sedative was phenobarbital. And we had to go and see that the patient was awake before we gave it to him. Just after we came on duty at midnight. After we'd read the report cards from the last tour, we'd go around and check everyone . . . But you see, since it was at our own discretion, we had no *specific* order to fill. So we couldn't make up a tray. Do you see what I mean? We couldn't fix up a tray with little paper cups and precise medication in each cup for a specific patient . . . We just took a bottle of pheno capsules . . ."

"Do you have the bottle?" Hempner said immediately.

"*Later*, Dr. Hempner," Wohl said. "Let her . . ."

"No, Doctor. It was probably used up afterwards. There were some capsules still left in it afterwards. I remember because there was another patient after Mr. Kronkauer. I mean, another one I gave a capsule to . . ."

"And then?" Hempner said.

"Then?"

"After the patient after Kronkauer. What did you do with the bottle?"

"Oh. I put it back in the cabinet . . . But it's probably been used up. And replaced. There were only a few capsules left . . . and it was so long ago, I wouldn't even know how to be sure it was the same bottle, they're all exactly alike; the one that replaced it would look the same . . ."

"Yes," Hempner said. "But you mentioned it being so long ago. Perhaps you'd care to explain why it took you so long to come to Dr. Wohl and myself?"

Wohl was furious. The girl had been trying so hard. Had made a good start at being precise about things it was very difficult to be precise about. Attitudes of mind, indecisions, responses . . . And then this fool Hempner had interrupted her to be daintily specific. They had to know *what* before they could get to *which exactly* and *specifically*. But, fortunately, in spite of Hempner's determined irresponsibility, in spite of his determined lack of suitable conduct, the girl was *still* trying. Even though she had already satisfactorily answered the question about why she had taken so long before coming to them.

She was saying, "At first I didn't even know what had happened. I didn't realize *anything* had happened. I mean, anything *I* might have been responsible for . . . And then I gradually realized what I thought *might* have happened—what I've been telling you . . . I realized how it *could* have happened. And then, the more I thought about the way it *could* have happened, the more I thought it must have happened that way . . . that it *did* happen that way . . . But you see, I don't *know*." She looked at both of them helplessly. "I just don't *know*." One hand tightened on the other.

"All right," Wohl said quietly. "We understand that. Just go on as you were before . . . about what you think may have happened."

Mrs. Lawrence said, ready to put her shorthand pad down, "Excuse me, Dr. Wohl, Dr. Hempner. Perhaps we might all be a little less tense after some coffee?"

"No," Gloria said. "*No.* I want to keep going till . . . until . . ."

"Yes. Certainly," Hempner said. "No, thank you, Mrs. Lawrence."

Mrs. Lawrence went back to recording the interview in shorthand.

"All right, Miss Mead. As I say, take your time."

"What I think happened was . . . I mean, I *know* this part happened, it's just that I don't know whether what happened afterwards happened the way I think it did . . . or whether I *intended* for it to happen that way . . ." She looked at Hempner and Wohl. They said nothing. She shook her head again slightly, and then got herself to go on. "I brought the bottle in. And I saw that Mr. Kronkauer was awake. At least, I *thought* he was. He seemed to open his eyes just as I came in."

"It was then about quarter of one?" Hempner said.

God *damn* him, Wohl thought.

"Yes. I think so. Jane and I . . . I mean, Miss Petschek and I had just left the station . . ."

"And she—Miss Petschek—had gone to awaken another patient for some medication?"

Damn, damn, *damn* him, Wohl thought. Why couldn't he just let the girl go on and get it all out?

"Yes. An injection. I think it was . . ."

"That's all right," Hempner said grandly. "Go on, Miss Mead."

"Well . . . I came in alone. Miss Petschek was down the corridor. I had the bottle of pheno with . . ."

"Pheno*barbital*," Hempner said.

"Yes. That's what I meant, Dr. Hempner. I . . ."

"Unfortunately, I must press for accuracy." He smiled at the girl.

"Dr. Hempner," Wohl said. "Under the circumstances, I believe Miss Mead is being *uncompromisingly* accurate. I think we should appreciate that."

"Ah, I do, I *do* appreciate that fact, Dr. Wohl. However, in *my* somewhat more *legally* involved position? I cannot risk any sort of discrepancy in what I am led to understand about this case."

"Yes, yes, Dr. Hempner. My apologies. I *appreciate* your position." He turned to Gloria. "Now go on, Miss Mead."

"I . . . I had the bottle of phenobarbital . . . phenobarbital *capsules* with me . . . I thought Mr. Kronkauer's eyes opened for, for just the slightest instant. I'm not sure, though . . ."

"Did you speak to him?" Hempner said.

"No. I was *about* to. I was standing by his bed. But then . . . then a patient down the hall screamed . . . and then . . .

almost at the same instant . . . Jane called for me to come immediately . . ."

"Did you?" Hempner said.

"Yes."

"And the bottle?"

"That was when I was standing by the bed. Next to the bed table. My . . . my arm was hanging down . . . like this . . . I guess my hand was resting the bottle on the table . . ."

"And?"

"And . . . well, when the patient screamed and Jane called me, I just left the bottle there and ran."

"You were gone how long?" Hempner said.

"Well, the patient who screamed . . . He was a postoperative gastroenterotomy. We didn't think he belonged on the floor anyway. We thought he still should have been up in Surgery . . . Anyway, he was hemorrhaging externally. I went and called Dr. Rosen. He came up immediately and then had me get a Surgery resident down right away. Well, a Surgery intern showed up in just about a minute, and he said the Surgery resident was on his way too, and then Dr. Rosen said for Jane to stay with them, but for me to get back to whatever I'd been doing and then quiet the patients who had awakened . . ."

"You then went back to Mr. Kronkauer?"

"Yes."

"And how long do you estimate you'd left him alone with the bottle of phenobarbital capsules?"

Gloria thought. "As closely as I can approximate it—fifteen minutes."

"I see. Then what did you do?"

"Well, I saw that Mr. Kronkauer was definitely asleep. I took his pulse, though. It was always a little weak and below normal . . . so I didn't feel that there was anything unusual. I picked up . . ."

"Was the bottle of phenobarbital capsules open or closed?"

"Closed."

"Are you *positive*, Miss Mead?"

"Yes. That's one thing I'm positive of."

"Then what is it you're *not* positive of?"

Gloria was silent for a moment. "I'm not positive that I did it on purpose. I'm not positive I actually *intended* for

him to . . . to take the capsules . . . the phenobarbital capsules . . ."

Wohl said, "Miss Mead, I want you to concentrate on this
before you answer. Can you remember *consciously* considering the possibility that Mr. Kronkauer *might* avail himself of
the capsules if you left them within his reach? Can you remember *consciously* considering that possibility before you
went in to him?"

After a moment, Gloria shook her head. "It must have
been unconscious. If I thought it at all just then."

Hempner said, "But you *did* believe the patient should be
afforded the surcease, the acquittal from pain, of death?"

"Yes. I believed that. I still do. When a case is terminal
and painful or that horrifying to the patient so that it's worse
than physical pain, and the patient himself wants . . . Yes.
I believe everyone should have the right to terminate his pain
or horror—if a physician agrees that the case is terminal
anyway and can't be relieved in any other way."

"I see," Hempner said.

"But I don't think I *consciously* acted on that belief. I
don't think I'd *ever* be able to."

"I see," Hempner said. "I shall have to discuss this with
Dr. Wohl and make my report. And, of course, indicate
whether the District Attorney's Office should interest itself
in this case. You may go now." He turned to Wohl abruptly.
"*Unless,* of course, Dr. *Wohl* has any further questions?"

"*Thank* you, Dr. Hempner. No, Miss Mead. You may go.
Please remain in your room in the students' quarters except
for meals until you hear from us."

117

Hempner spoke for an hour and fifteen minutes.

Wohl tried to rebut for another half an hour. Then he
said, "Let's at least establish what we *do* agree on. Now, the
sequence of events *seems* to have been . . ." After another
half an hour, Hempner said he wanted some coffee. Wohl
got it for him. While Hempner sipped, Wohl pressed him
further. "I want to point out to you that nothing has been or
could be *proven* satisfactorily before a court. The case very
likely might be thrown out for lack of evidence. And too,

there's just too much conjecture involved here. Even on the girl's part. Defense would merely cite everyone else's equal opportunity to make the stuff available to the patient at almost *any* time previous to the patient's having *actually* administered it to himself. And again, there *is* no evidence that the lethal dosage was provided by or taken from *that particular* bottle at that particular time—or any other time."

Hempner was reflectively studying the top of Wohl's desk from over and behind a cup raised to his lips. He put the cup down. Dreamily, he said, "Previous intent of suicide would be easy to prove." He looked at Wohl. "It's very important here. It *would* of course mitigate the student's responsibility to a certain extent. She would have *assisted*, so to speak. Her responsibility would thus be, perhaps, less direct."

"Hear, hear," Wohl said.

"Your points are well taken, Dr. Wohl. However, it would still be up to the District Attorney's Office to evaluate the case on the basis of my report and decide whether or not to proceed further with an investigation or perhaps even an indictment for criminal malpractice." He nodded. "Even if I recommended that no such investigation be pursued as being unnecessary. But they might not be able to avoid prosecution. The girl *did* admit . . ."

"The girl admitted no such thing, Dr. Hempner. She only admitted *the possibility*. And, too, unless she is directly charged with manslaughter, I do *not* believe she can be brought to trial. At least, not for criminal malpractice. She is, as yet, unlicensed, you realize."

Hempner looked embarrassed. "I had forgotten that. In the heat of these other considerations. Please excuse me."

"Oh, Dr. Hempner . . . Well, anyway . . ."

Hempner smiled. "Anyway, Dr. Wohl, I should think that a trial for manslaughter would be entirely unlikely. The prosecution's case, as you've pointed out, would be untenable for lack of admissible evidence. Even if the judge *allowed* the trial, which would seem just as unlikely on the basis of what the prosecution could offer as admissible evidence, all defense would have to do would be to remain quiet. That way, nothing inadmissible, nothing *conjectural* would get in. And the judge would either *then* dismiss the case, or else be forced to instruct the jury to bring in a verdict of *not guilty* for lack of evidence."

"Well then?" Wohl asked.

"Well then, this. The girl must not be permitted to continue her studies, to graduate, or to be licensed."

"That would seem justifiable. But on what grounds?"

"Negligence. She herself admits *leaving* the bottle within reach of the patient."

"She could fight it, if she chose. And if she did accept the dismissal, she would, on those grounds, also leave herself—and, of course, the hospital—open to a suit of *civil* malpractice on negligence grounds."

"A suit by Mrs. Kronkauer, you mean?" Hempner said.

"Yes."

"I think that extremely unlikely, don't you?"

"Yes, in point of fact, I do," Wohl said.

"Then perhaps you'd better speak to Miss Mead and see if we can settle this thing."

Wohl explained to her, "You could, if you so chose, fight the dismissal by retracting your admission of leaving the bottle." He nodded. "You might very well win such a fight, you know."

She slowly shook her head. "No . . . I don't think I'm . . . *properly adjusted* . . . to be a nurse . . ."

Wohl looked at her and allowed himself to almost smile at her, "I think that's an admirably objective insight on your part, Miss Mead."

"What . . . now what happens?"

"We see what the District Attorney has to say."

The District Attorney's Office withheld comment, but proceeded with an investigation of its own which consisted of several lengthy interviews with Gloria Mead, Dr. Wohl, Jane Petschek, Dr. Samstog, Mrs. Kronkauer, and several other members of New North's staff.

Jane Petschek was reprimanded for lack of adequate supervision of a student nurse. But she was allowed to retain her status and duties. In effect, it was actually a mere perfunctory reprimand on Wohl's part. No nurse was expected to supervise a student *every* instant in *every* procedure or situation.

Mrs. Kronkauer formally declined to begin a civil suit of malpractice against Gloria Mead, Jane Petschek, Dr. Samstog, and the hospital for negligence. At this point, the District

Attorney's Office formally closed the case by refusing to formally open it. They would not even grace the information they had with the designation conjecture. It was merely completely refutable information.

Within twenty-four hours, Gloria had accepted her dismissal formally and moved out of the hospital's student-nurse quarters. She didn't know what she was going to do or what she *wanted* to do. She didn't want to go home, especially, though; and so Didi Loomis persuaded her to move in with *her* for a time.

A few days later, she refused to accept an engagement ring from Lew Worship.

Donnecker and Worship were formally reinstated. The entire Male Medicine A complement of interns was allowed to accept the residencies they had chosen. Fortunately, each found the residency he had accepted to be still kept open for him.

118

Otis knew that it was easier to pass himself out than to go to sleep. He knew this medically and he knew it empirically. In college, he had learned to pass himself out with liquor when he had been working so hard that his body would probably break before it allowed itself to sleep.

But passing himself out when he couldn't get to sleep was an escape, a weakness he would not allow himself. It seemed very nearly to be the last hold on himself that he could look to with any degree of acknowledgment. The constant temptation was to call it *completely* quits with responsibility (what little he still managed to nurture) and subside completely into amoral existence. This one breach with society he would not allow himself. Tenuous as it was, he would not let go of what scraps of a personal moral fabric he still possessed.

Undoubtedly, his life—in any way in which he had ever previously imagined it—was over. He could no longer even summon prospects into fantasy. The context was gone.

It was as if he had suddenly been removed from an oxygen environment and placed in a hydrogen environment. And he could not forgive himself for being able to adapt to the new environment or survive the transference. That he *had* survived and adapted, depressed him more than any single other factor. He would far rather *not* have found himself able to adapt to this half-world existence. His very ability to do so left him no grounds on which to respect himself at all.

The girl was still with him. Refused, in fact, to leave him. Nor did he really want her to. Yet it was no longer that he loved her. Rather, it was that he suffered his own love for her and hers for him.

They had moved to another city. And, through former clients (he still could not bring himself to call them, even to himself, *patients*, though he *considered* them to be exactly that) in the first city, he was introduced to a new clientele—a clientele which expanded almost geometrically as he applied all his time to it. He would not continue the practice, though. With ten thousand dollars (he had raised his fee and now included surgical procedures when the client so demanded and was willing to pay accordingly)—which would only take a few more weeks—he and the girl would move themselves to one of the South American countries that needed doctors so desperately that they were not too particular about certification or previous background, but only demanded that the would-be practitioner pass an examination and not practice conspicuously in the more international metropolitan areas or in any situation which would infringe upon the practice of a more substantially accredited physician. That was the plan. He had found himself lately less and less able to believe in his commitment to it.

Again he realized he need not pursue this particular vocation. But his commitment to the practice of medicine *was* complete, whether that practice was legal or illegal.

The trouble wasn't money. The real trouble was not being able to communicate with the profession he loved. He could even forgo the girl. Just so he had professionals to talk medicine with. If he had foreseen *that*, he would still be an intern at New North. That would have dominated his commitment to the girl. Just foreseeing that one so seemingly insignificant detail.

Even loving the profession, he was able to resolve the discrepancy between his love and what he was doing. He *did* believe in abortion. Not criminal abortion, but abortion available to the patient by choice. It would, he believed, repudiate, *prevent* a great deal of subsequent human disaster. It was, he believed (and now *had* to believe, though before he had believed out of theory only), a technique of prophylaxis, preventive medicine adapted to emotional malignancy. Therefore, he did not believe he dishonored the profession. Only that he dishonored himself by accepting the codes the profession had set up to police its own conduct, but, while accepting the code (*because* it was the profession's), acted reprehensibly and contrary to it and his own acceptance. *That* was what made his practice immoral to him. He believed, thus, in what he was doing, but not in what he was doing it for.

It was true he had capitulated himself into it. But now he found himself also drawn into it and pushed into it by the profession having (*rightfully*, he believed) denied its society to him.

He hoped they would get him before too long. He half knew that was why he was staying in the States. He wanted his life to be finished *for* him. But he knew, too, it was unlikely they *would* manage to get him. The girl was too adept at caring for them both and for that possibility. Eventually, she would probably save him from losing so much of himself that he was unable to love her—by managing him to South America. But that would not be for some time yet. Not until she fully realized what was happening to him, and therefore, to her. He wondered if he really expected to be caught whether he would stay. Maybe not, maybe not . . . The realization produced an indomitable fatigue in him.

119

Wohl watched Dr. Riccio take a new group of interns through a surgery ward. They had just come in a few days before. And Wohl thought: *My God, they're so young, are we really going to put patients in their hands? Thank God it's not my responsibility alone, I wouldn't have the courage, would we ever have new doctors?*

Joe Parelli discovered that he had undergone a completely unexpected, but in no way insignificant psychological change. He could at last regard himself as a doctor. No. As a *physi-*

cian. Med school hadn't done it. Nor receiving his M.D. But those two things *plus* the year of internship *plus* getting a residency with Dr. Harvey Bonny—all that had finally convinced him he was indeed a physician and not only entitled to, but also prepared *for* responsible practice.

He looked down and tried to see himself in the surface of liquid he held in a glass in his hand. He knew, of course, he couldn't. Martinis weren't *that* reflective. *But I am,* he thought, blissfully high. *I must reflect on other things.*

"What *are* you grinning about?" Didi Loomis said.

"Because I'm reflective and martinis aren't."

"No reflection allowed. You're supposed to be enjoying the party."

"I *am.* It's the first chance I've had to reflect in five years." He put his hand on her bottom. "Or would you prefer me to enjoy it this way?"

"Go back to your reflection, *please.*"

"Yes m'am," he said happily. He could see Cynthia looking at him furiously from the other side of the room. He grinned back at her foolishly and shrugged. Her eyes rolled upwards. Indicating hopelessness, Joe decided, convinced it was a real insight on his part.

Grand opportunity to reflect. Lots of fuel to keep the reflection intact, too, so it didn't shatter. *Hoopla!* he thought, enjoying his own company immensely, *Got another one off.* Come to think of it, he hadn't *had* an opportunity to enjoy his own company for God damn five years. Of course, even if he had had the opportunity, he probably wouldn't have enjoyed the opportunity very much. He wouldn't have enjoyed the company he would have been able to give himself. *Too goddam serious,* Joe thought.

Yes. He certainly *had* loosened up lately. So much so he was afraid Cynthia was *really* getting serious about him. Was *really* deciding she liked him and enjoyed being with him, as well as loved him. Well, he thought, *nothing* wrong with that. Unless, of course, I start *reciprocating.* Oh well, nothing wrong with that either. Unless I reciprocate myself right into marriage. And God knows what might be wrong with *that.* He wasn't sure it was worth finding out.

He sure had loosened up lately. And enjoyed doing it. He thought about the way in which he had helped break in the new group of interns. There was one *real* jerk. In making an examination the guy had been so nervous Joe had even had to remind him to check the vital signs. Temperature, heartbeat, for godsake. Even how to take a history . . .

"Listen, Cooper, for chrisake. A history's more important than a diagnosis. A good history is ninety percent of a correct diagnosis. So pay attention . . ."

"Yeah, but . . ."

"No buts," Parelli had screamed, exasperated.

Placidly, Cooper had gone on. "But this here. *Children by other women.* What . . ."

"Cooper, a history is *complete.* The *milkman,* Cooper, *also* asks 'How're you feeling today?' *That,* however, Cooper, does not result in a medically valuable history."

"Jeez, I wish I were taking off to be a resident."

"Don't wish, Cooper. You'll probably be too disappointed next year this time." *Boy,* Parelli had thought, I *am* a resident. Just look at my form. "Now, Cooper, look how this is done. Here you abbreviate ARD for acute respiratory disease. And here you put what is essentially the intern's diagnosis. You write R.O. That's for Rule Out. Understand, Cooper? Or have you never before had any experience with abbreviation by initials?"

Loosened up? Hell, he'd damn near relaxed to the point of collapse. Later, Cooper had said to him, "Do you think that could be a case of latent diabetes?"

With no further thought, Parelli, grinning, remembered himself saying, "Better latent than ever, old boy," and walking out.

With another new intern, he had gone through an entire examination, by way of demonstration, and had then said to the patient, "Now the doctor will examine you, I'm just the dentist." And had walked out, leaving the intern with the job of straightening the situation out.

Loosened up? He had even fixed up his room to resemble something occupied by something human. And *enjoyed* it.

Worship was telling how he had even had to explain to one of the new interns that, "For godsake, you *don't* argue with a resident. You're *responsible* to him, for chrisake, Munson. He has the right to *report* you. And if you get fired from a hospital, Munson, it is very hard to re-establish yourself in the profession. Especially if you do not propose urinal sterilization as your specialty."

And I'm the boy who knows, Lew thought. If it hadn't been for Granchard going to Tyssen and Wohl afterwards . . . And he thought, I would probably have spent the rest of my life specializing in writing descriptive brochures for a pharmaceutical company.

He had been closer to it than he'd realized until it had been over and he could safely admit to himself how close.

And now he had the next year, when almost he'd had nothing. But he could not think about it, he had never been able to think into the future, give it a face, and he had not learned how to even yet. Instead, he thought about the year past. Thought not about a week before or two months before, but of the beginning of the year, the first day on duty, the Surgery ward, July and hot . . . And before that: the procession. The black academic gowns and the green Doctor of Medicine cowls hanging down in back, walking two and two in a procession on a green campus, the trees overhead, dark gold and green over them, the cool spring morning as they walked along to receive . . . And then the hot July day, the ward . . .

He felt the same, and wondered at how he had not changed.

The light in the room was the same hot July sun he had sweltered in in the ward that first day almost exactly a year ago. He wondered at it, and looked at the light around the room, the faces, these people that he thought he could *see* were professional, had a look he did not have or feel . . . that he was not *of,* he thought, but merely among, and wondered if he ever would be and if it made a difference and if that difference was important.

And looked at Lois and Jay Fishbein standing in this second July light, holding drinks in their hands, and wanted to go over and kiss them both. It was the drinking that made him feel that way, he thought. But no, he knew equally, it wasn't. It was just that they were there, that it could be done. *That a couple like that exists makes me love you* . . . he began, and thought, No, it's the drinking, I won't say it to you, Gloria, looking at her standing next to him and taking her hand.

Parelli regarded Worship with affection. He realized he was regarding *everyone* with affection. Well, why not? The year was over and this was their celebration party. And maybe even the last time he'd ever see some of these people.

He looked at Gloria Mead standing next to Worship, her hand held in his. Her *other* hand, the left one, now displayed an engagement ring. This gave Parelli great satisfaction and he decided to drink to it with another martini, maybe several. Probably several. It was so nice and warm and sunny outside and in the room, he thought maybe he didn't even need another drink to stay looped, but he wasn't going to take any chances.

Courtney Walters was leaving to catch a plane out to the hospital and residency he had to report to the next day. Parelli shook his hand. "Don't do anything I wouldn't do, out there," Parelli said.

Slowly, Walters' singularly serious face slowly surprised itself with a smile and then a long, clearly unaccustomed laugh.

"What the hell are you laughing at so hard, you bastard?"

" 'Cause that gives me so damn much room."

He watched Walters shake hands with his roommate, van Wyck. *There* was a guy, Parelli soberly realized, he was really going to miss. He *liked* just about all the people he'd interned with. But he *respected* van Wyck. Pete was certainly the finest intern he'd seen. *Huh vonduhful doctuh,* Parelli thought. Yes. Really. A physician.

Parelli had loosened up enough after the residency results and the Kronkauer thing to suffer through, with van Wyck, the failure of the Public Health people to reply to van Wyck's application for residency. He had finally talked van Wyck into calling them direct. They said, after many dollars of long distance time, and several different calls and return collect calls, that they *had* sent him a notice of acceptance and had him down as having accepted. They couldn't find a copy of their letter though, or the copy of his reply. Did he wish to change his status? *Good God, no!* van Wyck had roared, and hung up, and immediately written the letter of formal acceptance he was already supposed to have written, and eventually received an acknowledgment and instructions. "There's one explanation," van Wyck had told him. "That's what you get for working for the government."

Van Wyck looked around him.

So. He was finished now. Two weeks before he had to be out at the reservation. He would have liked to have gone home, seen his parents for a while, rested for a while. But

they were in Europe. And here he was with two weeks. He'd
forgotten about having these two weeks . . . All of a sudden
he wasn't sure that he had ever known that he *would* have
them. That was his trouble, he remembered (thinking about
the satisfaction he'd had—satisfaction almost to the point of
complacency—of just fulfilling his duties and doing a good
job of it day to day), that was his trouble, never planning
ahead. Well, man, he said to himself, don't just stand there
with your highly trained face hanging out. There're no rounds
to make today, and in two weeks you'll be at the reservation.
Do something.

In between, he decided he'd have himself one helluva ball.
He went over to his date, Joan Feldman, and kissed her
tentatively on the cheek.

Parelli smiled. He wondered if van Wyck would survive not
having Joan. Probably. But he'd also probably discover himself having a difficult time of it. Joan was the only non-
practical, *affectionate* thing in van Wyck's life. And Parelli
doubted that she would replace very easily.

Joe turned his attention to Art Rosconovitch. Very drunk,
that Rosconovitch. Sitting alone in a big, overstuffed chair,
nodding and grinning to himself.

After accepting his residency and orienting himself to the
future rather than the past, Art had discovered himself once
more *willingly* alive. He had never even known, up till the
rediscovery, that he'd *been* unwillingly alive. But he had
been. And, realizing it and being frightened and disappointed
by his ever having been that way, he had begun not only to
live his life again, but to seek it. And, at the same time, he
had discovered that Phyllis was no longer a distasteful image
(he had not realized that that had been the case, either), but
a tender, compassionate memory. An image, or memory, that
in itself offered him tenderness and compassion. And thereby
stimulated him to live as entirely as possible the life *he*
had available to him . . .

So, he sat (drunk and pleased with his own drunkenness)
in the great, overstuffed chair in Didi Loomis' living room,
and thought jealously of the new interns and their occasional
opportunities for really raucous living. He had been as rough
on them as any resident in the hospital. As rough on them as
any other about-to-be-resident intern. But still, Residency

was a *really* responsible position. Very little opportunity for raucous living. Not like the raucous living you managed every so often when you were an intern . . .

He remembered, jealously, drinking beer on the roof with a nurse. Just a little bit more than a year ago. Up on the roof with a nurse, the night hot, lights in tall buildings downtown like regularly ordered stars, the beer drunk ice-cold from a can, occasional other intern-and-nurse couples scattered around the roof out of sight or hearing. Practically planned roof, that, for hanging and airing horribly infected mattresses. (He laughed out loud at this, laughing at the ribaldry of the situation.) All those mattresses hanging around. Like immense tired tongues hung out to rest. And the young nurses. Possibly the less well educated of the lot, but still, very female . . .

And he was going to be a *Pediatrics* resident, he thought, with disgust. Everyone knew that the nurses who were socially wildest were the nurses in the emergency situations. Like Surgery or Obstetrics. My God, he remembered jealously —what a fantastic social life on Obstetrics . . .

Parelli grinned at the expression on Rosconovitch's face. Then he looked around to continue his survey. And saw Amos Sprague. Sprague was, he had told Parelli, "Really living it up, man—before I'm off and back to the sticks." Good old Sprague who had wanted nothing more all year except to get back to his home and to work at his county hospital. Parelli smiled again.

He began walking around the room. He was beginning to find it difficult to actually *see faces* as distinguished from home movies being run off in front of him, several at a time.

He missed Alicia Liu. He had had great affection for her even *before* this party. He had always thought he might have managed a little pursuit there himself if he hadn't been saving his energy for more professional things. But Alicia wasn't at the party. She had gone to visit Jim at the upstate TB place he'd been sent to. She had felt *dis-happy,* she'd said, about missing the party, but she only had so much time before she was to report for her residency and she'd wanted to spend all of it with Jim. And Jim had written that he was thinking of changing *his* specialty and eventual residency to TB.

And Elwood and Otis. How did you account for them? Did

they just *happen,* or should they be remembered? Was there something not in what each had done, but in their having been, and that alone? In their still being. Not why, but what. Yes, Joe thought, because they haven't been dismissed from *being* and so they *are* and they happened to all of us, they didn't just not be from the beginning because they're not standing here now and don't forget it and boy, you better lay off the booze till the fog lifts . . .

What surprised Parelli was not so much the faces that weren't there, but the faces that *were.* Mercouris. Who had made it. In spite of the fact that he couldn't stand patients. And could stand medicine itself very little better.

Or Donnecker. Who seemed to have made peace with whatever it was he had been trying so long to make peace with. He was back to some reality that he had been becoming less and less a citizen of. Peace, was it? No. Maybe truce. Or amnesty. But he was back. Had gotten to be as serious-faced as Walters, but was back. And why the hell *shouldn't* he be serious-faced? Looking at him, Joe thought of Rosconovitch. Art had also managed a return to the land of the living . . .

De Traunant. Another face that surprised him by just being there. Over in a corner, sipping ginger ale, having a determined conversation with Didi. De Traunant, who, in effect, very nearly had to go through an entire year of internship again.

The thought of that prospect actually excited his adrenal glands. He shook his head. It was a fascinating stimulus.

He remembered the question he had asked himself during the Kronkauer investigation. *Why are we doctors?* And he had decided, *Not because there are those who need to be cured, but because there are those who* can *be cured.*

. . . But to go through very nearly the whole year again, he didn't know how anyone could psychologically gear himself to accept it . . .

Joe went over to Cynthia, and, removing her from a conversation group, took her in his arms and kissed her.

"What was *that* for?" she said.

"Because I feel like a human being."

HOSPITAL STAFF

Medical Superintendent: Sidney Wohl

*Service Chiefs and
Attending Physicians*

Gower Bloomberg
Luke Killian
D. L. Riccio
Aaron Samstog
John Tyssen
George Wexler

Residents

Robert Baker
Dick Chester
Eugene Duane
Dennis Ford
Hugo Granchard
Leo Grenatti
Norman Kalik
Jack MacDonaugh
Brian Mason
Yukio Sato
Chuck Stein
Dave Rosen

Interns

Jim Aptshult
Mike de Traunant
Fred Donnecker
Ted Eckland
Tom Elwood

Jay Fishbein
Claude Langley
Alicia Liu
Constantine Mercouris
John Paul Otis
Joseph Parelli
Austin Peterson
Art Rosconovitch
Amos Sprague
Peter van Wyck
Courtney Walters
Lewis Worship

Nurses

Bobbie Gwynn
Joan Feldman
Flo Richards
Victoria Flynn
Helen Ingles
Cynthia James
Didi Loomis
Gloria Mead (student)
Jane Petschek
Phyllis
Ann Wafford

*Secretary to
Medical Superintendent*

Mrs. Lawrence

I should like to thank a number of people who were both gracious and generous to me with their time, advice, knowledge, experience, and assistance while I was doing research for this book:

Dr. Samuel Averbuck, Dr. Georald de Catlogne, Miss Diane Daly, Miss Arlene Daly, Dr. Alan F. Guttmacher, Dr. Leslie Libow, Dr. Robert J. Lifton, Dr. Jack Lipman, Dr. Robert Martin, Dr. Benjamin Natovitz, Miss Florie Proctor, Dr. Edward E. Reisman, Jr., Dr. Steven Rouse, Dr. John J. Stapleton, Jr., Dr. Paul A. Stavrolakes, Mr. James L. Smith, Dr. John P. Thomas, Dr. Walter E. Uhlman, and Dr. Harold Wachen.

I should particularly like to thank Dr. Wichard A. J. van Heuven, though it is impossible for me to do so properly in less than a several-page tribute.

And for editorial labors before, during, and after the preparation of the manuscript, I am equally grateful to Miss Diana Chang, Mr. Robert Loomis, and Mr. Richard Roberts.

R.F.

ABOUT THE AUTHOR

RICHARD FREDE was born in Albany, New York in 1934 and attended the Birth-Wathen School and Yale University. Upon graduation he worked with *Sports Illustrated* magazine until he was awarded a fellowship at the MacDowell Colony in Peterborough, New Hampshire, where he wrote *The Interns* and *Entry E.*